WICKED

RUSH

RUSH

KYM GROSSO

WICKED RUSH

Club Altura, Book 2

Kym Grosso

MT Carvin Publishing
West Chester, Pennsylvania

Editor: Julie Roberts
Cover Design: Alivia Anders
Cover Models: Jase Dean and Angelica Kotliar
Photographer: Golden Czermak
Formatting: Polgarus Studio

DISCLAIMER
This book is a work of fiction. The names, characters, locations and events portrayed in this book are a work of fiction or are used fictitiously. Any similarity to actual events, locales, or real persons, living or dead, is coincidental and not intended by the author.

NOTICE
This is an adult erotic romance book with love scenes and mature situations. It is only intended for adult readers over the age of 18.

ACKNOWLEDGMENTS

~My husband and kids, for supporting my writing and books. Keith, thank you for being patient with me while I work long hours, for making dinner when I can't, for standing by me every single day and never ever giving up on me. I seriously would not get to one single signing or be able to finish writing books if it weren't for you. There are no words to express how grateful I am for everything you do. You guys are my world and I love you so much!

~To my readers, who encourage me every day to write. Thank you so much for being supportive and patient with me while I wrote Wicked Rush, allowing me to stretch my wings and write contemporary. You are the reason I continue to write! I can't wait to dive back into Immortals of New Orleans, with my wolves and vamps. I promise you all that Jake's book is coming next. ☺ You all are the best readers ever!

~Julie Roberts, editor, who spent hours reading, editing and proofreading Wicked Rush. You've done so much to help, teach and encourage me over the years. You are a great editor and friend. I was so happy to meet you in person this year, visit with you in the UK. Thank you for teaching me how to drink a proper British tea and for taking me to see that incredible castle in Wales. I loved visiting with you! I realized as I'm writing this that once again the sparkly unicorn you suggested did not make it onto the cover, so I will try to do so in Jake's book. I have to give a special shout out to Constantine, your cuddly kitty, who puts up with listening to all the love scenes in my books. Lastly, keep the faith writing, as your books are amazing! I can't wait to do a signing with you! ☺

~Shannon Hunt, Once Upon An Alpha, for promotion and assisting. I'm not sure where to begin, because you do so much for me and are an incredible person. You are unbelievably amazing! Let's start there. ☺ Dedicated. Caring. Creative. You've helped me with so much over this past year, from book releases to signings, just too many things to name. You're a cheerleader, making me laugh every day and keeping me going when I sometimes feel like quitting. You are a great friend to me, and I'm so glad we've been able to work together. It was awesome hanging out with you at RT & then again in San Francisco…which definitely influenced my thoughts for Jake's book. Hour-long phone calls, hand-holding and keeping me on track…you just are the best ever! Hopefully I'll live closer soon, in sunny California, and can visit with you. You are irreplaceable, and I'm so grateful for your help and incredibly lucky to have you. #BTCW

~To Jase, Thank you for helping me with the Wicked Rush photoshoot, from ideas for poses to location selection to implementation. You're an incredibly talented model and it's been a pleasure watching you work. You have been an inspiration, someone who has had faith in me even when I don't have it in myself. You've pushed me outside of my comfort zone on more than one occasion, helping me face my fear of heights, from holding my hand the first time we hiked Torrey Pines to getting me across the Golden Gate Bridge. By the time we reached Big Sur, I was able to hike at Pfeiffer Falls and enjoy the view. Pacific Coast Highway was spectacular but terrifying, but hey, I did it. 'Good Enough'. ☺ And yes, what we did at Big Sur totally counts as camping…just sayin'. ☺ Kayaking in La Jolla was an incredible experience. Even though I was scared, we had so much fun…it still cracks me up that, for at least one hour, I thought I was good at it. Always remember, that under no circumstances are you allowed to bring your phone near the water. ☺ You are one of the most adventurous people I've ever met in my life, and even though you scare the shit out of me some days, I'm in awe of your bravery and fearlessness, and continually impressed with your creativity. #dumbanddumber #luckiestwomanintheworld

~My Alpha readers, Maria DeSouza and Rochelle McGrath. I really appreciate your insightful critique of the storyline and unique perspectives, caring about my characters and books. You both are dedicated readers and my cheerleaders. I'm sorry it took me so long to get a book out this year, but I promise you both, my wolves are coming. You have both been great friends to me and I appreciate everything you've done to help me along the way. You both are awesome!

~My dedicated beta readers, Denise Vance Fluhr, Janet Rodman, Jessica Leonard, Jerri Mooring, Karen Mikhael, Kelley Langlois, Lacy Almon, Laurie Johnson, Margie Hager, Stephanie Worne, and Rose Holub for beta reading.

You guys are the best beta readers and so supportive! Thank you so much for your dedication to beta reading my books and for all the valuable feedback you provided.

~Alivia Anders, for cover design. You are incredibly talented and thank you so much for designing such a unique and gorgeous cover. I appreciate all the work you did helping me to create the stepback cover as well. I love it!

~Golden Czermak, FuriousFotog, for images and photography. Thank you so much for custom shooting all the images for my Wicked Rush release. You take spectacular photos. I love the cover and teaser images you shot for my book, they are amazing!

~To Angie, cover model, you look unbelievably gorgeous in all the images, and it was awesome having you on one of my covers and teasers. I really appreciate your support of the release!

~Jason Anderson, Polgarus Studio, for formatting my books in both e-book and print. Thank you for doing such great work on another one of my books.

~Rose Holub, Read by Rose, Maria DeSouza, and Janet Rodman, for proofreading. Thank you so much!

~Denise Shelmerdine, subject matter expert, for giving me input on what is and isn't possible in medical situations. Thank you for sharing your extensive knowledge and helping me run through scenarios that would make my scenes more realistic. I'm lucky to have you as my friend and so grateful for your help!

~My awesome street team, for helping spread the word about the Immortals of New Orleans and Club Altura series. It has been a great experience getting to know all of you and meeting some of you in person at signings. I appreciate your suppormore than you could know! You guys are the best! You rock!

Chapter One

Lars' heart pounded in his chest as he swam through the icy Pacific. His palms stretched into the seawater, propelling him forward, a sweet burn radiating through his thighs. The sting of rising swells wasn't enough to thwart the memory from playing through his mind. Nearly two months ago he'd been surfing with his colleague, Seth Termaine. A hail of gunfire had erupted from a cliff precipice, spraying across the beach and into the ocean. While he and Seth had avoided the bullets, they'd caught sight of a terrified brunette taking a direct hit to her shoulder.

Without hesitation, Lars had swum to shore. Running toward her, he'd fallen to his knees in the bloodstained sand. As another shot sounded, he'd scooped her up in his arms and sped toward an alcove in the cliff. Cradling her to his chest, he hid within the darkened cave. Laying her on the ground, he'd removed her jacket and located the puncture wound. Her fierce emerald eyes had blinked up at him. With his name on her trembling lips, she'd pleaded, 'Lars, help me.'

Broken and beautiful, she'd succumbed to the impending loss of consciousness. As sirens blared in the breeze, he'd held onto her; minutes stretched like hours. When the medics had finally arrived, Lars had insisted on going in the ambulance, remaining by her side until they'd whisked her into surgery.

Lars had sat in the waiting room staring at his hands, the dried blood caked on his skin. He'd reluctantly accepted a warm washcloth from a nurse, who'd repeatedly encouraged him to get examined. Shaking her off, he'd stubbornly remained, steadfastly waiting on news of her condition. By the time the police had arrived, he'd composed himself, hiding his frustration that neither he nor Seth could provide a detailed description of the assailant.

While she'd survived the procedure to repair the tear in her artery, she'd contracted a hospital acquired sepsis infection, which had left her unresponsive for a few days. Never leaving her bedside, he'd willed the mysterious Jane Doe to heal. When she'd regained consciousness, a flicker of recognition registered in her eyes. The nurses immediately sprang into action, assessing her condition. Lars hadn't been able to speak to her as the medical team hastily ushered him out of her room.

After calling into the office and catching up with his secretary, he'd returned to see her, but a hospital administrator had greeted him at her door. In a matter-of-fact tone, the perky businesswoman had explained he was no longer welcome. He couldn't believe that after everything he'd done for her, she'd lie, not even as much as say thank you. The news sent him reeling. Although he'd explained that he'd donated millions to the facility, as the victim had claimed she didn't know him, he had to leave.

Angry that she'd refused to talk to him, Lars had exited the building pissed as hell. He'd told himself the entire fucking mess was none of his business anyway. Whatever fleeting feelings he'd developed for the injured woman were nothing more than a false sense of responsibility. He told himself that despite saving her, he had no obligation to watch over her recovery. *She has the finest doctors in the country. Not my fucking problem.* Tomorrow he'd wake up, purge the memories of the attack from his mind and go back to business as usual.

As the weeks passed, anger turned to curiosity. With no answers from detectives, he'd sought help from his friend Dean, who was an assistant District Attorney. The victim had been identified as Dr. Braelynn Rollins, a prominent marine biologist. Dean explained the police investigation had been stalled. There was nothing more they could do to find the suspect. Neither Seth nor Lars could describe the shooter, and Dr. Rollins had been unable to name her attacker, claiming that it had been a random act of violence. Her car had been located a mile down Pacific Coast Highway, carefully parked and locked. No purse or keys had been found. Along the top of the cliff and on the beach, no evidence had been left by her attackers except for the tire marks left from the shooter's car.

"There's nothing else we can do," Dean had told Lars, imploring him to move on and forget what had happened on the beach. He'd promised him he'd follow up with Dr. Rollins in another month to see if she remembered any other details.

Another frigid wall smacked over Lars' head, breaking his rumination. *Get your fucking shit together.* Having swum the same San Diego shoreline for the past five years, he knew the dangers of swimming in the open ocean. He should have been paying attention to his surroundings instead of daydreaming. Lars tread water, assessing his location. Relieved to see the familiar beach from where he'd started his swim, he rode a wave toward the shore.

As his toes sank into the sand, he gave a wave to his friend Seth, who was chatting it up with a couple of blondes. Lars smiled but made no move to approach the trio as he unzipped his wetsuit and peeled it from his limbs. The taste of the saltwater fresh on his lips, he reveled in the warmth of the sun. He closed his eyes, breathing in the ocean mist.

Lars picked up the neoprene skin and set out to return to his car. He paused as his eyes caught sight of the cave that he'd deliberately avoided. The police had already searched the beach, he knew. But none of it made sense. Although he was obsessed with the truth, the cave reminded him of Braelynn. After she'd booted him from her hospital room, he preferred not to dwell on the beautiful face that had spurned his kindness. Yet as he put one foot in front of the other, he decided enough was enough. He needed to search for the missing clue to what had happened the day of the shooting. Braelynn Rollins had nearly died that day, and the perpetrator could have killed all of them.

As Lars entered the darkened crevice, the chill from the shaded tunnel caused gooseflesh to break across his skin. The bone-dry sand told him that the surf only reached up into the cave during high tide. He scanned the area for evidence, catching sight of a tiny crab scurrying off into obscurity. Falling onto his knees, he palmed the cliff, tracing his finger pads over the earth.

Lars spied a cracked sand dollar jutting up from the sand. His mom had always loved them when he was a kid, and he still couldn't resist the temptation to collect the little treasures. Lifting it out of its gritty tomb, he inspected it. The brittle shell crumbled in his grip, and he opened his palm, letting the pieces float back to the ground. As he brushed off the remaining sand, a silver fleck caught his attention, and he reached for what he initially thought was broken oyster shell.

He rolled the grainy bit in his fingers and tugged on it, its weight resisting his grip. Excitement set in as the thinly braided string rose from its sandy tomb. A tiny metal object dangled from the end, and Lars pressed to his feet, surging toward the entrance so he could get a better look. It was only an inch long, but Lars was able to make out the shape of a tiny brass key. Its intricate pattern was easily discernable in the glaring sun. After running his fingers over the green corroded metal, he slid them along the cord. What he'd thought to be a shell was a small silver charm. Although the initials had been worn, he easily recognized the monogrammed inscription: *BR.*

Lars' close friend and colleague, Garrett Emerson, CEO of Emerson Industries had insisted on seeing him. He sensed the impending lecture, but it wouldn't deter him from his decision to investigate the shooting on his own.

"I know I should, but I can't let it go." Lars swirled the cognac and glared into the snifter.

"I'm not telling you what to do. I'm merely suggesting that you need to get your shit together. You're letting this eat you up," Garrett told him. He gave a quick glance up to the stage, where a band was beginning to set up their equipment.

"I know this. But at the same time...I was shot at. I've got to know what happened."

"Jesus Christ, already. It's been a couple of months since you found the girl on the beach. I know you think she said your name, but did you ever think you might have heard her wrong? She told the police she didn't know you. Nothing has gone down since the accident. Yeah, what happened sucks. You all were shot at, but it could easily be just what it looks like, a random act of violence."

"She's got a name."

"You haven't been on a dive for two months," Garrett pressed.

"Dr. Braelynn Rollins." Lars knew damn well he hadn't been skydiving since the shooting. He'd been closing several million dollar contracts, and blamed business for interfering.

"What's the fucking difference what her name is?"

"She is a person, that's why."

"Yeah, and so are you. Selby tells me you haven't been going to work every day."

"That's bullshit. I've been offsite. She doesn't even work for me full time anymore. She's transferring over to Emerson. And no offense, G, but it's none of her goddamned business what I do. Besides, DLar-Tech is thriving."

"Seth told me you've been swimming every day."

"Yeah, I have."

"Said you got crushed by a wave. You know what that tells me?"

"What?" Lars sipped his drink, letting the mellow liquid roll over his tongue.

"You don't have your head in the game."

"Had a lot on my mind that day. Don't say you don't do it too sometimes. I'm a big boy. I can handle it."

"This story is a short one, Lars. Girl got shot on the beach," Garrett said.

"The police left the case wide open. Exactly how does that happen?" Lars asked, shaking his head.

"It's unsolved. Happens all the time," Garrett argued. "The key witness can't provide a description of the shooter. Can't say why she was shot at. Can't say how it started. Can't help with a motive."

"Can't or won't?"

"Maybe she's got no freakin' idea why she was shot at. No matter what her reasons, she still didn't want you there in the hospital. Even after you pretty much saved her ass, she didn't even say thank you. Come on, man. This isn't like you. Take the hint and move the fuck on. It's time to get on with things."

Lars leaned back into his chair and reached into his pocket. Slamming the key onto the glass table, he blew out a breath.

"What's that?" Garrett's eyes widened but then he quickly glanced away.

"It's a key." Lars fingered the metal object.

"No shit. And?" He picked up his beer and held it to the air before taking a long draw of the amber ale.

"I found it buried underneath the sand. It was in the same cavern where I took her after she was shot on the beach."

"You're serious?" Garrett asked, his voice laden with sarcasm. "How do you even know that belongs to her?"

"It's got the initials B.R. Braelynn Rollins. I don't know if it's really hers, but I'm going to find out." Believing the key had something to do with the shooting was a long stretch but Lars had already decided he was going to launch his own investigation, and it gave him an excuse to see Dr. Rollins. He locked his eyes on his old friend, and continued. "I don't know if this is a clue or not, but I'm going to pursue it."

"Even if it belongs to her, it could be nothing. You need to give this up."

"When Evan died you wouldn't have given up..." Lars knew he'd hit a nerve by the twitch in Garrett's jaw. Their mutual friend had been murdered. "Saving her life on the beach that day," Lars sighed and shook his head, "it was intense. That shooter was trying to kill her. They shot at us too. I didn't hear her wrong. She knew my name. Now she might want to conveniently forget what she said, tell the police she doesn't know me, but I can't forget it."

"I know what you think you heard," Garrett countered.

"I heard her. Doesn't really matter, because the situation isn't resolved. Why would she lie about knowing my name? Why not at least take two minutes to thank the guy who saved her? Why is she saying she can't remember anything? Why did the police give up trying to solve the case so quickly? Dean has been dodging my calls for weeks, refusing to answer my questions. No. This ends now."

"I'm just sayin' you might want to just let all this go. The club is almost restored. We're going to have a party soon. You should ask one of the girls from the hangar to come with you. Anne-Marie. The redhead you've been seeing. She's kinda hot. That's what you need to take your mind off all of this."

"Anne-Marie's just a fling." Lars blew out a breath. It wasn't as if he didn't enjoy fucking her every now and then but she was a release and nothing more.

"All the better."

"Look, I know my head hasn't been in the game." Lars set his attention back on Garrett, pinning him with a hard stare. "It's why I haven't been going out. There's something about this situation. It's nagging me. I've let it eat me up for weeks. I need to know what the hell happened out there even if no one else seems to care."

"You need to be careful. Setting out for long swims…"

"G, you know I appreciate you worrying about me, but there's nothing more to say. I was shot at on that beach. Seth too. Dr. Rollins is going to talk to me. Now maybe she doesn't think she owes me jack shit, but I've got news for her; this isn't over. And she may have been able to throw me out of a hospital, but we're going to have a long sit down."

Lars slammed back his liquor and set the glass onto the bar, ignoring Garrett's eye roll. As the band started playing, relief set in that the loud music made it nearly impossible to hear anyone. He loved Garrett like a brother. They'd been friends for over ten years, their businesses intimately tied. As much as Lars respected his opinion, the lovely little doctor would be seeing him soon. He'd discover her secrets, and the asshole who had tried to kill him would regret the day he ever stepped into San Diego.

$\sim$❦· *Chapter Two* ·❦$\sim$

Braelynn's once steady hands trembled as she stood in front of the floor length mirror. Her thoughts churned as she recalled the day she'd been shot. Although her physical wounds had healed, she remained very much in danger. Closing her eyes, she called to mind the piercing blue eyes that had stared down at her. Lars' calming presence had soothed her even as she'd lost consciousness on the beach.

When she awoke in the hospital, she'd been shocked to find him still at her side. Cognizant of her situation, the need to protect him had superseded her desire to tell Lars the truth. She'd lied, telling everyone she didn't know him. It had nearly killed her in the hospital to refuse Lars permission to visit her, but she'd known that initiating a relationship with him would put him at risk.

For months, she'd been working undercover for Garrett Emerson, seeking to expose her corrupt uncle, Armand Giordano, and recover stolen research. When her uncle repeatedly questioned her about her attack on the beach, why she'd followed his shady business associates from the office, she'd played dumb, insisting she'd merely left the building at the same time. Braelynn had explained that she'd planned to visit a friend in Imperial Beach and had coincidentally traveled the same route. She downplayed Lars' involvement in her rescue, saying that he'd been nothing more than a stranger on the beach that day, one who she'd thanked briefly but had no desire to know.

Trained as a marine biologist, Braelynn had dedicated her life to studying and exploring the ocean, searching for new species. Her love of animals had kept her from taking more lucrative assignments. Observing large fish and mammals in their natural environments, she couldn't stomach the thought of keeping the great beasts in tiny aquariums for circus tricks.

After obtaining her doctorate she'd accepted an internship in the Caribbean, working with Chase Ellsworth. Together they'd made a key discovery, and he'd convinced her to leave the field to go work for Emerson Industries. He'd explained they could use a specialist of her caliber to assist in the development of top secret technologies that would help the nation's armed forces. It was in the hallways at Emerson where she'd first seen Lars, watching him from afar.

Having her credibility called into question by the CEO of Emerson Industries had been devastating. Nearly nine months ago their data and samples had gone missing. She'd vehemently denied the accusation, but Garrett claimed they'd had video of her stealing. He'd had a longstanding feud with Giordano, and had initially suspected his involvement. Once they'd discovered Braelynn's relationship to her unscrupulous uncle, she had no choice but to accept her fate, agreeing to infiltrate his company and recover the research.

Estranged from her uncle, it had been difficult for Braelynn to reestablish a connection. But after several attempts, feigning complaints about Emerson Industries, she'd been able to convince him to hire her, securing a position within Giordano's private company, Bart-Aqua. Due to their strained relationship, the one condition of her employment was that no one but her bodyguard and her uncle's mistress knew of their familial relationship. Within the walls of Bart-Aqua, Braelynn was simply a researcher, nothing more, nothing less. Initially working in a lower level position, she slowly gained his trust. With each promotion, she gained access to secure rooms within the building and was closer to accomplishing her mission.

The day she'd been shot, it had been an impulsive decision that had proved far more dangerous than she'd initially thought. Outside her uncle's office, she'd overheard the strangers discussing an exchange of data. Suspecting they were talking about the stolen data she was trying to retrieve, she'd foolishly followed them as they left Bart-Aqua. As they drew closer to the border, they'd spotted her tailing them. Panic set in as they'd swerved their car and began following her.

Exiting the main highway had done little to deter them. By the time she reached the coast, she'd mistakenly thought she'd lost them. She'd pulled her car along the side of the cliff, hoping to hide inside one of the sea caves on the rocky beach. But before she was able to make it down the stairs, they'd begun shooting at her.

Who have I become? Braelynn blinked, her thoughts drifting back to this evening's event. Tonight was her first public appearance since the shooting. Barely recognizing her reflection, she attempted to shake off the stress. The black silky dress, slit up the side, clung to the curves of her body. The scar from her injury could be seen underneath the delicate shoulder straps. While only a small reddened lesion remained, she'd be forever reminded of her attack.

Braelynn ran her fingers over her long brunette hair, her nerves on edge. She'd carefully straightened her naturally curly hair, slicking it back on the sides, and had applied a light lip gloss. She considered her beauty both a weapon and weakness, hating that her uncle viewed it as a commodity to be used as he wished. She was expected to charm clients at his expensive charity gala, to wine and dine with a smile on her face.

Braelynn shuddered as the doorbell rang. Shane Whitman, her uncle's private security guard, had come to escort her to the party. After the shooting incident, he'd been assigned to protect her at events. At Bart-Aqua, he kept watch over her activities. She'd attempted to flirt to gain his favor. Feigning interest, she'd successfully rebuked his advances, all the while gaining special treatment, which had allowed her more time to look for the data she sought.

Braelynn took a deep breath, the loud knocking reminding her that she needed to go. Wrapping her fingers around the cold brass knob, she painted on the friendly smile she wore every day to work and opened the door. Shane greeted her with a hard stare, annoyed she'd taken too long to answer.

"Your uncle expects us there on time, princess." As Braelynn brushed past him, he touched the small of her back and she swiftly stepped out of reach, avoiding further contact.

"Pet names are for children and lovers." She turned to meet his gaze, giving him a coquettish smile, concealing her irritation. "And last I checked, neither applies."

"While you do intrigue me with your fiery responses, I prefer princess."

"Don't break our deal, Shane. You're one of the few people at the office who calls me Braelynn." Within the sterile corporate environment, staff had been directed to call her Dr. Rollins. While she hadn't been comfortable with the formality, the rules were strictly enforced. Braelynn glanced around Shane, taking in the sight of the stretch limo.

"We can't be late. Your uncle is a stickler for punctuality."

"I know my uncle better than anyone, and I also know traffic on the I-5. This time of night, it should be clear. We have plenty of time." Reining back her anger, she allowed Shane to shut the front door, and approached the waiting car, hoping she didn't topple over in her three-inch heels. She gave the driver a brief smile as he ushered her into the limo.

"Why are you so contrary this evening?" Shane slid

inside, sidling up next to Braelynn.

"I'm sorry. I had trouble sleeping last night."

"You work too much."

"So does everyone else. I don't want to be treated any differently." Braelynn's stomach clenched as he ran his hand along the side of her thigh. Ignoring his advance, she reached for the console and moved to the seat across from him. She'd rather ride backwards and stare at his face for the next twenty minutes than allow him to touch her again.

"You were injured."

"I'm fine now."

"I'm just sayin'. Maybe you shouldn't have jumped back into work this week."

"I need this." Braelynn didn't have time to wait until she healed emotionally. Critical research was on the line to be sold, and Garrett never ceased the pressure, expecting her to retrieve it in a timely fashion.

Braelynn clutched her champagne flute, scanning the room, taking in the sight of the elegant affair. Violet orchid arrangements sat atop white table linens. Sparkling white lights danced throughout the potted palm trees that lined the seaside patio. The roar of the ocean was offset by music streaming from the live band playing on the stage.

As she made her way across the deck, smiling at guests, Braelynn sensed the eyes watching her every movement. Shane had assured her that none of her coworkers knew of her shooting but she couldn't be certain the rumor mill hadn't carried the news. Shrinking into the darkness, Braelynn leaned against the railing and turned to the beach, captivated by the flickering lights of a passing ship.

"We meet again, Dr. Rollins." The sound of his smooth voice sent shivers over her skin.

Lars Elliott. CEO of DLar-Tech. Extreme sports enthusiast. Never without a date, but not committed to any one woman, the charismatic leader was well known for his altruistic contributions to environmental programs that supported sustainability of aquatic communities.

As her eyes met his, she struggled to remain calm. Her heart pounded against her ribs. She hadn't seen him since the hospital. Dressed in his black tuxedo, he was far more handsome than she remembered. His striking blue eyes penetrated her. Tanned, his skin glowed in the light of the gas heaters that warmed the night air. Resisting the urge to reach for him, she dug her fingernails into the wooden railing.

"Cat got your tongue? No 'hello' for the man who saved you? No 'thank you'?"

"I'm sorry?"

"Lars Elliott." Lars raised a questioning eyebrow at her.

"Mr. Elliott," she began. "I'm sorry, I didn't recognize you."

"Lars. It's what you called me that day on the beach. You do recall it?" he asked. A small smile formed on his lips, yet his dark eyes warned he was serious.

Braelynn forced her gaze toward the shore, afraid that

he'd read her expression. She'd come too far to let her crush on the adventurer keep her from attaining her goal. She glanced over her shoulder, hoping neither her uncle nor Shane could see her speaking to him. His voice snapped her attention back to the conversation.

"You know, this type of behavior could be construed as rude." He gave a small laugh and reached for a glass of champagne off a passing waiter's tray.

"I didn't mean…" Braelynn's gut twisted at his words.

"But you see," his voice never wavered as he paused to take a sip of his drink, "I've learned that people aren't always who they appear to be."

"I'm sorry but I'm not sure what you mean. I'm exactly who I am." Braelynn nervously tucked a strand of hair behind her ear.

"And who is that, Doctor?" He cocked his head and smiled. "Are you the marine biologist who worked in the Caribbean? The one, who as a grad assistant, did a stint in South Africa researching sharks off Cape Town? Or the researcher who now works at a biotech company?"

"Seal Island. I was only there for a month," Braelynn corrected him. It had been the most amazing four weeks of her life, documenting great white behavior. "My current occupation is far safer."

"Interesting you should say that, because as I recall you were shot on a beach recently. Seems much more dangerous. How's the shoulder?" Lars edged next to Braelynn, his attention moving to the waves crashing loudly onto the rocks.

A quiver ran through her as his jacket brushed her dress. She took a deep breath, inhaling the aroma of his masculine aftershave. Jesus, she thought she'd learned to command her emotions.

"My shoulder…my shoulder," she stammered, slowly lifting her lids. There were days the residual pain haunted her, but the doctors assured her it would fade with time. "It's fine."

"You look gorgeous tonight."

"Mr. Elliott, I…" The compliment took her off guard. How could he possibly be interested in her after the way she'd treated him, ignored him?

"Lars." He set his glass down on the railing and swiveled to face her.

"Lars?" Braelynn repeated. Her cheeks heated, causing her to briefly avert her gaze. Summoning courage, she turned back and locked her eyes on his. "I'm sorry I didn't thank you in the hospital. You have to understand. Sometimes we do things…things that don't make sense. I needed my privacy. I couldn't meet with strangers." She exhaled, knowing the lie was laced with the truth.

"I found you on the beach, stayed with you." His voice softened. "I waited during your surgery. Then you had the infection. When you woke up…"

"Thank you." She gave him a small smile, wishing she could tell him how much she appreciated all he'd done for her. If he hadn't been there that day, the killer may have finished the job.

"We need to talk, doctor."

"I think we've said all we should say." The band resumed playing and she looked to the stage. *Fly Me to the Moon* echoed in the night.

"Dance with me." Lars extended his hand. While his gesture implied asking for consent, the tone of his voice told her it wasn't a request.

"I can't. This is a company function. What if they…" *They see us? They suspect I know you?* It was a stupid risk, she knew, yet she lost the words to refuse.

"Sinatra," he commented, pulling her closer. He took her glass and set it aside.

"Um, yes." Braelynn gave in to her secret craving, allowing him to lead her to the dance floor.

"Ol' blue eyes." He smiled.

"Like yours." The words fell off her lips before she had a chance to stop them. Her nipples strained against the silk, and even though she knew he'd see the physical evidence of her desire, she made no move to leave. She closed her eyes, the heat rushing to her cheeks. *Holy hell, Brae, you sound like a schoolgirl. You need to walk away now. You're going to fuck this up.* "Mr. Elliott…"

"We're back to that again, are we?" Lars laughed and spun them in a gentle circle. "Here's the thing, doctor. I have questions."

"I already talked to the police."

"Yeah, I heard."

"Did you go to them?" *He knows all about me.* Her pulse raced in fear as her arousal faded.

"You sound surprised."

"I can't tell you anything." Braelynn tried to pull out of his embrace but he held her tight.

"Listen to me very carefully, Doctor." The music continued to blare as he stopped dancing, his eyes locked on hers. "With or without you, I will get answers. You may have been the one who ended up in the hospital, but the party you brought to the beach that day could have killed Seth or me."

"This isn't my fault." Her eyes darted over to Shane, who glared.

"I didn't say it was, but your behavior isn't what I'd call consistent. There're too many holes in the story." Lars slowly started moving again, brushing his cheek to her ear. "You almost died. You told me, 'help me, Lars'. Now why is that?"

"I…I don't remember." Goddammit, she didn't recall calling him by his name.

"That may very well be true but I think I at least deserve a few minutes of your time to talk."

"We are talking."

"Alone."

"Lars…" His warm breath on her neck sent tingles over her skin, and she sucked a small breath.

"That's it. I knew you'd say my name again." He retreated and gave her a wink. "Dinner. Alone. Tomorrow night."

"I can't possibly do that." Braelynn spied Shane struggling to leave a conversation with a chatty client.

"Why not?"

"You don't know what you're asking me to do. You're going to put us in danger." Braelynn's eyes darted to her uncle, who made a beeline toward them.

"Tomorrow night. We can do this in secret or in the open but you owe me at least an hour of your time."

"I said I can't. Please." Braelynn yanked her hand out of his, her eyes widening in terror. She didn't want him to get hurt.

"Tell me. Did you happen to lose a key that day on the beach?" he asked, a lilt of mischief in his tone.

"What did you just say?" Braelynn's stomach clenched at the mention of the object she'd lost. Although she'd wanted nothing more than to go search the beach, she'd decided it wasn't worth the trouble. They were watching her, and if she'd managed by some grace of God to actually find it, they might catch her.

"A key." He gave a sly smile, cocking an eyebrow at her. "Lose one, did you?"

"Keep your voice down," she whispered. Taking his hand, she pulled him close. "Keep dancing."

"Braelynn, if you need…"

"I'm going to walk away in exactly five seconds, so let me finish. I'm meeting a friend tomorrow for dinner in Mission Beach. I'll meet you at the roller coaster at eight. Don't be late. If I don't see you, I'm gone." Braelynn allowed her lips to brush his ear, and she closed her eyes, wishing she could stay in his arms all night. But it was much too dangerous to speak to Lars even one second longer. She held his gaze for a moment, then releasing him, she turned on her heels and spun away, striding across the dance floor.

"Darling," her uncle cooed as he approached Braelynn.

"Mr. Giordano. The party is a success. Have you raised a lot of money this evening?" Nausea rose in her throat at the trill of his voice, yet she forced a bright smile.

"I see you were entertaining the guests," he observed.

"Mr. Elliott. Apparently he's as fond of wildlife conservation as you are."

"Did you have much to discuss?" Shane's baritone voice sent shivers over her arms.

"Apparently, he was the one who rescued me on the beach."

"You don't recall what he looked like?" Shane pressed.

"I told you before that I didn't remember who brought me to the hospital. I, uh, I thought he looked familiar but as you both know, as soon as I regained consciousness, I refused to see anyone. You know as well as I do that I was nothing more than a Jane Doe. If I hadn't woken up, it's likely I'd have gone missing forever." The truth rolled off her tongue easily. She had been unconscious with no belongings; they hadn't been able to identify her.

"Frankly I'm surprised he didn't contact you sooner," her uncle observed.

"I certainly appreciate that he helped me, but Mr. Elliott is a stranger. I'm a private person. Besides, the last thing I needed during my recovery was having to deal with some guy trying to play Florence Nightingale. I'm surprised he stayed."

"He's probably some kind of creeper." Shane scrunched his face in disgust.

"Exactly," she agreed, cringing at the lie.

"Don't you think you're being a bit harsh?" her uncle said, smiling at a passing client.

"Perhaps." Braelynn took a deep breath of sea air. Relief washed over her, having successfully redirected the conversation. Concealing her feelings and intent was paramount to bolstering the ruse. "I prefer to think of it as realistic. Besides, you told me he's in bed with our competitors."

"He probably stalked you down here," Shane added. "It's a public function."

"I think you're both getting a little paranoid," her uncle chided. "Mr. Elliott, along with many other industry professionals in the southern California region, is simply attending tonight as a guest. And it's a delicious coup. All are welcome. Our allies. Our competitors as well. Tonight is about making a presence. Let them take in a taste of my success and where we're going."

"You most certainly did. It's a spectacular event," Braelynn told him, stroking his ego.

"Top notch." Shane nodded, the veins in his temple pulsing with tension.

"All right, then. Let's get on with things. Come join me on stage, Braelynn. I want you by my side," he declared, offering her his arm.

"Of course." Giving a brief glance to Shane, she placed her hand on her uncle's jacket. Sickened by both of them, the best she could do was obey and get through the next two hours. The lethal game she'd agreed to play was very near to its end.

❦ Chapter Three ❦

Lars watched from afar as Braelynn walked off with the older gentleman. Mogul Armand Giordano, well known for his ruthless business tactics, had recently relocated from the east coast after a congressional hearing on the environmental impacts of a new plastic technology he'd pioneered. Its use had resulted in higher levels of cancer in a rural town of Pennsylvania, and his ethics had been called into question. While he was never indicted, his company's stock had plummeted.

Lars focused in on the powerhouse bodyguard, who towered above Braelynn. His burly hand brushed over her shoulder blade, and she glared at her unwanted suitor. Holding Giordano's arm, Braelynn appeared to be close with him as he led her up to the podium. Lars' gut clenched, his mind rolling through the possibilities of the nature of their relationship. *Lovers? His mistress?*

His fleeting concern dissipated after watching their interaction. As she released his arm, a flicker of relief shone in her eyes. It lasted but for a second, quickly replaced by irritation as she glanced to Shane. Giordano tapped the microphone, and she recovered, a too-perfect smile frozen on her face.

When they'd danced earlier, Lars had sensed her fear, and wondered about the source of it. He suspected her trepidation arose from fraternizing in front of her boss, Giordano, but she never once faltered as she played the role of the appreciative employee. An actress, he suspected, giving applause on cue as the greedy bastard bestowed accolades on donors in the crowd.

A familiar face caught his attention, and he made a beeline for Garrett, who glared at the stage. Both he and their friend and fellow skydiver, Chase, stood attentively watching Giordano's speech.

"What the hell are you doing here?" Lars hadn't meant to sound so aggressive, but failed to hide his surprise. Garrett had testified against Giordano, and he knew there was no way Emerson Industries was doing business with him.

"Enjoying the sea air at this fine San Diego fundraiser. You?" Garrett raised his glass and nodded. With a cold smile, he focused on Giordano.

"Looking for answers," Lars replied, aware Garrett wouldn't support his decision to go after Braelynn.

"I take it you didn't find what you were looking for." Garrett's eyes flashed to Chase and back to Lars.

"Why are you here?" Lars pressed.

"Friends close. Ememies closer." Garrett gestured to the path that led out to the parking lot. "Shall we?"

"Yeah." Lars nodded in agreement.

"This isn't the place for this discussion." Garrett's lips pursed and he raised an eyebrow at Lars.

"The car." Lars gave the stage a parting glance as he exited the lavish event. On his way down the stairs, his eyes caught Braelynn's, and he swore he detected a faint shade of pink in her cheeks. He gave her a small smile, and continued until he reached the landing.

A black stretch limo pulled up in front of the valet stand, and a bellman reached for the door. "Sir?" He gestured to the interior.

"Let's talk," Garrett stated, his voice serious as he and Chase slid into the car.

"Just a minute." Lars reached for his cell phone and texted his driver, then quickly followed his friends' lead. As the door slammed behind him, he blew out a breath.

"Okay, would either of the two of you like to tell me what the hell is going on?"

"How well do you know Armand Giordano?" Garrett asked, reaching for a bottle of cognac. Accepting a snifter from Chase, he poured two fingers, and offered it to Lars.

"Plastic magnate. Got in deep with the feds a few years ago. Has been doing penance out here on the west coast." Lars accepted the drink, but didn't move to bring it to his lips. "You testified against him. He got off."

"Emerson Industries had a conflict with Armand." Garrett's eyes darted to Chase who shook his head, his eyebrows narrowing in anger.

"We incorporated his supposedly safe ultra-plastics in

our scuba gear. We had plans to expand their use into other products as well." Chase wrapped his fingers around the glass Garrett had poured, and took a long draw of the mellow liquid. With a loud exhale, he continued. "Cancer."

"He's an asshole." Lars' eyes darted to each of his friends.

"Employees working with the polymer were the first casualties. People living near the production site started showing signs as well. Whatever they'd used got into the water supply. You know how it is with rural towns. People are still using well water." Garrett paused and sighed. "He'd skimped on testing. Fudged a few studies."

"He's an asshole," Chase commented with disdain.

"Doesn't surprise me he got off, though. These douchebags get in with a few members of congress, the truth is bent," Lars commented.

"A strong reprimand." Garrett shrugged. "That's it."

"A slap on the wrist," Chase said.

"They couldn't definitively prove it. It was a new technology. He rushed it through approval channels. They don't really know what other long term effects exist as of yet." Garrett set the bottle back into its cabinet and took care to make sure it was secure.

"He greased a few palms," Lars surmised. He plowed his fingers through his hair, tousling his neatly combed locks.

"Let's just say he knows how to play the game in Washington. Is said to be involved with a well-known super PAC."

"Tears down any candidates that oppose his environmental atrocities," Chase commented.

"Alleged," Garrett corrected.

"Whatever. You know how it's done. Candidates who support his causes, they get the money."

"He reached out and touched a few someones. That coupled with a lack of airtight evidence…"

"But clearly he wasn't untouched? His stock took a nosedive," Lars said.

"But as you saw tonight, he's recovering well. Thriving in sunny San Diego."

"So what…you're making sure he knows he's still being watched?" Lars shifted in his seat.

"I don't want him getting too comfortable in our town." Garrett brought the rim to his lips, and paused. "But what I'd like to know is what you were doing there."

"You know why." Lars set the glass into a cup holder, and tugged his bow tie loose. "And before you say anything, I already made a decision about this. You know I respect you, G, but I need resolution."

"She works for that bastard," Chase spat at him.

"Yes, it appears she does. But that doesn't mean she has anything to do with his unethical business practices," Lars countered.

"You talked to her tonight." Garrett glanced at Chase, his expression somber.

"What the hell difference does it make if I choose to see her?" Lars knew Garrett well enough to know that his friend wasn't interfering without purpose. A mastermind of secrets, he was probably planning a corporate takeover and didn't want Lars involved. "There's no direct conflict. I don't work for you."

"This isn't about Emerson Industries," Chase interrupted. "You can't tell me you haven't done a cursory investigation on her. There's rumors…some of her research was called into question last year. It wasn't reported in the papers but if you ask around, it's easy enough to find out."

"Of course I did." Lars rolled his eyes, and sighed. "Have I uncovered some information about her? Yes. And yeah, I heard a few things mentioned about her research but seriously, none of it was substantiated. I pulled up the journal articles myself. It's not like they've been pulled from the online registries. And you know what that tells me?"

"What, Sherlock?' Chase asked.

"It tells me that it's not true. It tells me that someone out there maliciously attacked her reputation through online groups. It could be anyone. Now why they did it is yet another question in this mystery." Lars noted Garrett's silence and continued. "And before you say another word, this is a mystery. No one found the shooters. I'm convinced she lied to the police. She says she can't remember anything. Come on, man. I am not buying any of this."

"Maybe it's because the woman is a liar. Maybe she got in with some bad people. Did you ever think that she's tied up with Giordano's next scheme? Did you see her out there? He's using her like a goddamned spokesmodel." Garrett held up his hand and hit the intercom, quickly confirming the driver was returning to Lars' home.

"I can't say one way or another yet. But I do know this. I've been investigating, and so far, I'm noticing there are some big gaps in her job history, where she's lived, family history, stuff like that. Places where there should be information, there isn't any. And you know that means someone has been scrubbing her data. Who? I don't know."

"Again, maybe that's on purpose. Maybe Giordano did that. He has connections. You saw her with him," Garrett said.

"I saw, but maybe she's just good with the clients. He's a businessman. Look, don't get me wrong, I'm not defending that asshole." Lars sighed. "I've just started uncovering the pieces of the puzzle. Take Dean for example. He put me off for weeks after she claimed she didn't know anything. There was an attempted murder on a beach in broad daylight. There have to be other witnesses. Clues. Why did the police give up so easily? This makes no fucking sense and you goddamn know it."

"Maybe all this is as simple as her being as shady as Giordano," Chase stated.

"Maybe they're sleeping together," Garrett added.

"I don't know why you all are changing the subject but shit, G, we're friends. If you can't tell me why you're warning me off her, I get that, but don't try to bullshit me." Lars suspected both Chase and Garrett were concealing information, and while he was sometimes part of whatever top secret project they were working on, clearly he was out of the loop on this one. "I get business is business, and you've got certain reasons for keeping your cards close to the chest. Clearances and all that shit. But I'm telling you right fucking now, I don't care what project you have going on, and from the sounds of it, if I had to guess, you're getting ready to take Giordano down with an anchor around his neck. But before you go hanging Braelynn out to dry, give me a chance to find out what is going on."

"You know I can't tell you what we…" Garrett began.

"No." Lars held up a silencing hand. "Something is going on with Dr. Rollins. I don't know what yet, but I'm finding out what it is."

He'd had enough with the diatribe. There was a reason he was the head of his own IT company. He'd graduated top of his class and had been a well-known white hat. Hacking came as easy as breathing and given he already had access to all of Emerson Industries' files via their freshly inked outsourcing agreement, he had data at his fingertips. He knew it. Garrett knew it. Both of them also knew he'd break a thousand rules if he needed to, the same ones he'd killed to preserve. DLar-Tech represented the pinnacle of integrity and ethics, which was why he hadn't gone through their system already. What he hadn't told Garrett was that he'd already bent some rules, gone digging for information on Braelynn in places where he shouldn't, and could tell someone had deliberately erased sections of her history.

"Obviously there was another reason why you guys were there tonight. Don't know why. Don't care. All I know is that a couple months ago, I got shot at while I was riding some waves. And the next thing I knew I was covered in someone else's blood. You don't just have that kind of thing happen and settle for no resolution. I tried, I really did. But I can't let it go. I can't say what's going on with the doctor, but I'll tell you this. She seems scared. And frankly, my gut tells me…now, I've got no proof, but I think she could still be in danger."

"She's not your responsibility," Garrett pointed out.

"See, that's where you're wrong. I tried to tell myself that, but I just can't do it anymore. Look, I know damn well I could wash my hands of this thing. I could…no, I probably should walk away and pretend like it all never happened. But you both know that's not me. You can judge me if you want but you know that if the shoe were on the other foot, you'd be doing the same thing as me. I'm not looking for your help with this, but don't get in my way. I don't know what the hell you both are planning with Giordano and that shit company of his. You guys know that if you need me, I'm here. But leave Braelynn out of this for now."

"If she's involved…" Garrett began.

"If she's involved in any of the things he was working on with the plastics, I'll find out. I'd be the first one to hand you over evidence. But right now, I need to find out what happened that day on the beach. Something is off with this whole thing. Dean won't tell me…"

"There are people who might not want you snooping into this," Chase warned.

"Their problem, not mine."

"All right. Well, just be careful," Garrett warned, and changed the subject. "Hey, do you mind if I stop by the office before dropping you off? I know it's pretty far out of the way, but Selby forgot her sneakers. Something about needing them for a class tomorrow morning."

"You're kidding me, right?" Lars asked with a smile.

"You know I love her but she has me running around for her favorite pair of shoes."

"Why doesn't she go get them?"

"She's planning something special." He gave Chase and Lars a sly smile. "So who am I to say no?"

"Yeah, okay." Lars laughed.

"Hey, you know what they say, 'happy wife, happy life'." Garrett shrugged.

"You guys aren't married yet." Chase smiled at Lars.

"Whatever. Gotta keep my woman happy."

"No worries. I'm not going anywhere," Lars said. "Get her kicks and then drop me off."

On the long car ride to the office and back to his home, Lars mulled over his interaction with Braelynn at the party. She couldn't quite look him in the eye as she denied knowing him. She'd insisted on a clandestine meeting, but had agreed nonetheless, supporting his theory that not only did the key belong to her, but it held significance. He'd caught the flash of desire in her eyes, but it was the fear that tore up his gut. He suspected whatever secret she was hiding was dangerous, and her life might still be at risk.

Lars approached his front door, and slid his finger over the cool glass of the biometric lock. As he pressed through the entryway, a cold wet tongue brushed over his hand, breaking his contemplation. *Sasha.* A streak of moonlight reflected off her midnight black coat and he fell to one knee, embracing the furry beast that had stolen his heart.

Three years ago, he'd adopted her on a rock climbing trip in the Black Hills of South Dakota. On his way to the cliffs, he'd run into a group of local rescuers at a diner, learned of their mission and assisted as they'd picked up a pack of stray dogs. Although nearly a dozen puppies had been taken into safety, Lars had connected with their mama. She was shaking in his arms on the ride back to the shelter, and he'd refused to leave without her. Knowing that her odds of adoption were low, he'd given her a forever home.

Lars pressed to his feet, and threw off his jacket. Stalking toward the kitchen, he went in search of a drink. Not bothering to turn on the light, he reached for the refrigerator door. He considered a beer to break his tension, but snatched a bottle of water instead. He twisted off the cap, fingering its ridged edges and glanced to Sasha, who whimpered, her eyes darting from him to a glass jar full of bones. She barked in response as he unclipped the top, retrieving a treat.

"Sorry, girl." His gentle giant bit down onto the large biscuit, and scampered down the hallway with it.

"You're welcome." He smiled.

Thoughts of Braelynn spun through his mind. She'd been even more beautiful than he recalled. Embracing her in his arms had stirred an erotic fantasy he couldn't shake. As she'd brushed up against his chest, her pert breasts had revealed her arousal. He looked forward to seeing her again tomorrow night and hoped like hell she was innocent. Lars cursed to himself as his cock rushed with blood. *Jesus, Lars. Just stop. Fuck, I need sex.*

He retrieved his phone from his pocket and scrolled through his text messages, his finger hovering above one name. *Anne-Marie. Sexy as fuck, Anne-Marie.* He'd slept with her a few times, all the while aware the redhead was more interested in his bank account than his bedroom. He was used to women wanting him for his lifestyle. He'd fuck them, go on a few dates and move on. But he made it a rule to never date anyone who worked at his company.

As he clicked her text, a picture of her smooth round ass filled his screen. He smiled, giving a small shake of his head. *Fuck.* His dick went limp at the sight of the perfect cleft beckoning him to tap her number.

"Goddammit," he muttered under his breath. It irritated him that he couldn't shove Braelynn out of his mind long enough to get a hard on.

With a flick of his finger, Lars switched to check his email. After responding to several urgent issues and letting Sasha out for a run, his eyes flashed to the time, noting that an hour had passed. He yawned and made his way up to the second floor, slowly ascending the open-planked stairs. Illuminated by moonlight, the cherry hardwood steps contrasted with the surrounding stark white walls. As Lars reached the landing, he went still and glanced up at the stars through the floor-to-ceiling window that lined the hallway. Pausing to appreciate the celestial reflections glimmering in the peaceful ocean, he caught a shadow emerging from the path that led up from the beach. It faded into the darkness, and he swore his eyes had played a trick on him. Like a sleight of hand, the movement was gone, stillness blanketing the night.

Lars blinked, and continued to his bedroom. Exhausted, he threw his tux jacket on the back of a chair and unbuttoned his shirt. He flipped on the light, and was heading toward the bathroom when he heard it through the silence. A rush of adrenaline flooded him as the outdoor motion lights activated, the distinctive sound of Sasha's barking coming from downstairs. *Intruder.*

-⊛· *Chapter Four* ·⊛-

Braelynn closed her eyes and counted to ten, attempting to calm her nerves. *How the hell did I get myself into this situation?* There was a time when a darkened beach under moonlight would have conjured romantic thoughts. But as the wind whipped over her shoulder she shivered, and she couldn't decide if it was from fear or the cold sea air. She shone the flashlight onto the small strip of beach, and trod toward the steep wooden staircase that was nearly fifty feet away.

Braelynn considered the evening's events. She'd been shocked to learn that Lars had her key. She'd lost it the night of the accident. How the hell Dean and Garrett had known he had it, she wasn't certain. Garrett had texted her, convincing her to leave the party to search for and retrieve it. Easy entry, easy job, he'd told her. They'd keep him occupied. No one would be home. She'd been given Lars' address, the code to his back door and alarm, and instructed how to bypass the security system. Braelynn had been warned as to the dog, assured that the animal was friendly and would accept a treat in exchange for entrance. Lars' office was located adjacent to the kitchen entrance.

Corporate espionage. It wasn't as if she had any training. She'd been a biologist, for fuck's sake. Instead of rescuing seals or helping to protect the ecological sanctuaries of marine life, she'd been forced to learn hard and quick the intricacies of clandestine operations. But unlike Garrett, she was the only one who worked for Bart-Aqua and had access to the stolen research.

HWB614. Her joint discovery with Chase had resulted in the identification of a unique protein. Braelynn had theorized that it could be developed to allow soldiers to retain oxygen in their bloodstream for longer periods of time. The practicalities on land existed as well, enabling humans to survive at higher elevations without needing oxygen tanks.

Within the walls of Bart-Aqua, she'd attempted to steal the research, but her first mission had failed. Concerned that partial files had downloaded, she locked the chip away in a location only known to her. Although it was possible that the key could be replicated, she sought to collect the evidence of her covert activity.

Braelynn had parked her car at a local hotel up the street from Lars' home, and crossed the street onto the beach. She'd decided against entering the front entrance, concerned someone would see her. After venturing down the long stretch of open sand, her path had narrowed. Up against the cliffs, she prayed that the incoming high tide would remain at bay long enough to let her pass through to the staircase. She shone the flashlight onto the sand. Only ten more feet, and she'd safely reach the stairs.

Braelynn screamed as the sleeper wave rolled onshore, taking her by surprise. She lost her footing and collapsed into the gushing swell, unable to fight it. The mighty current dragged her out into the breakers. Sucked underneath the crest, she held her breath and struggled to find her way out of the churning sea. Although she was a strong swimmer, panic registered within the turbulent dark abyss. Her energy drained as she kicked her way upward. Piercing the surface, she sucked a deep breath. She lost track of time as she tread water, bobbing helplessly.

Attempting to orient herself to her surroundings, she searched for the lights that twinkled from the shore. As another large wave rumbled toward her, she ducked into the tube. Icy whitewater swirled around her but she swam with the flow, praying to God she'd reach shore. As she smashed into the hard sand, she fought the returning tide. Clutching onto the edge of the rock, she cried as the water finally retreated. She heaved for breath and shoved to her feet, stumbling against the muddy bluff.

Braelynn had never been afraid of the ocean, but without a wetsuit she knew she was vulnerable. Coughing salt water, she pressed her forehead against the cliff. Gooseflesh broke over her skin as the wind roared. Exposed, she reasoned that she had minutes before she'd succumb to the elements. Tears streaked down her cheeks as she managed to find her way to the stairs. She wrapped her trembling fingers around its railing and began the long ascent.

By the time she reached the top, numbness had set in, and she shuddered. A forceful gust whistled past her head, but she forced herself to continue. Setting one heavy foot in front of the other, Braelynn trudged toward the door, her cold soggy clothes clinging to her skin. She blinked, her vision blurring as her body temperature dropped. Even though her mind understood the physiology of what was happening, she was unable to stop the inevitable. If she didn't get to shelter and warm her body, she could lose consciousness.

"You can do this," she mumbled, her words slurring.

As the back door came into sight, a surge of adrenaline propelled her toward the home. Her hand found the security panel and she braced her back against the stone exterior. She wiped a frozen hand across her eyes, straining to read the numbers. They danced, doubling as she fumbled to enter the code. A tiny voice in the back of her head urged her to hurry but she could not process the command.

One. Eight. Five. "No, no, no," she repeated. Her heartbeat raced as she attempted to tame her thoughts. *Eight. One. Five. Three. Zero.* Her fingertips fluttered over the keypad, searching for the pound sign. Depressing the button, she grunted, her body shaking uncontrollably. The red flickering light above flashed to yellow and back.

"No!" The back of her head slammed against the wall as she lost her balance. As her legs gave out, she released a jagged breath. A bright light temporarily roused her. Like a deer in the headlights, she froze as the door swung open.

The same piercing ice-blue eyes that had gazed upon her

in the hospital stared back at her. Hardened, his lips tensed in anger. Defiantly, she locked her eyes on his, yet her tears revealed her vulnerability. His contempt evolved to concern as he addressed her.

"Dr. Rollins," she heard him call, her thoughts confused. *I'm sorry.* She opened her mouth to speak, but no words came.

"Dr. Rollins, can you hear me? What's going on?" he asked. His hands reached for her, and she attempted to jerk away. As if he'd been touched by electricity, shock washed across his face. "Jesus Christ. What the hell happened to you?"

"No…" she began. Unable to finish her thought, she closed her eyes, humiliated, a sense of dread rushing through her. Garrett and Dean would prosecute her for certain if she didn't recover the research. If her uncle found out about her duplicity, it'd be likely his associates would finish the job they'd attempted on the beach. Dread lodged in her chest and a large lump formed in her throat, knowing Lars would expect answers.

"Let's go, Doc." Lars slid his arms around Braelynn, cradling her wet form against his body.

"No…" *Yes. Oh God, please.*

"Yeah, that's not a request."

Braelynn inhaled warm air into her lungs and coughed. The clean scent of his skin brought back the memory of dancing with him earlier in the evening. She wanted to fight, to escape, but energy eluded her. He'd demand she tell him what she was doing at his back door. She'd lie. He'd probably call the police. Garrett would deny he'd sanctioned anything. She'd go to prison. With a myriad of disastrous possibilities swirling through her mind, she fought the nausea that rose from her belly.

"Hey there, Doc. You're going to be okay, now." His voice softened, a loving hand touched her cheek.

No longer able to meet his gaze, she gave in to the comfort his strong arms provided. She wondered where he was taking her, his footsteps pressing up the stairs. Despite her curiosity, her body fell limp. So tired, her mind wandered, drifting into slumber.

"Hey, no sleeping yet. I don't know what's going on with you but we've got to get you warm."

"Hmm, no," she responded with a yawn. She didn't protest as he laid her onto the soft bedding. "Yes."

"No, sweetheart. For a smart lady, you don't seem to listen very well, you know that?"

"I've just...a little nap...please." The drugging exhaustion consumed her, she was no longer able to fight it. A jerk to her arm alerted Braelynn that her clothing was being removed. Her eyes flew open, locking onto his in panic. "No!"

"Yes." He sighed, his eyebrows narrowed in irritation. "Dr. Rollins. You're wet. Cold. Moderate hypothermia from what I can tell."

"No," she protested, tugging at the sopping fabric. Confusion rolled through her. *Where am I? How did I get here?*

"Yes. We've got to warm you up," he argued.

Braelynn's heart caught as he leaned toward her, his lips within inches of hers. *Lars.* Mesmerized by his striking eyes, she went still.

"Braelynn…"

"Yes." Her breathy response emerged in acceptance of her current reality. The long pause that followed stirred thoughts of arousal. *This man. Lars Elliott.* She'd fantasized about him long before he'd rescued her. And although logic screamed to her that she'd fucked up any chance of ever being with him, it also told her she was in his bed.

·❦· *Chapter Five* ·❦·

Braelynn Rollins. What the hell was she doing at his house? Soaked to the bone, the damn stubborn woman fought him despite the fact she'd succumbed to hypothermia. *How the hell did she get so fucking wet? The ocean?* He'd seen the movement at the top of the bluff. *Jesus Christ, yes.* Lars glanced at the clock out of habit but already knew it was high tide. He shook his head in frustration. What the fuck was she thinking? She could have been killed. One good wave could have crushed her against the rocks or simply washed her out to sea. Even the strongest swimmer could become disoriented at night. Between rough currents and low water temperatures, she'd struggle to get back to shore.

As he cradled her in his arms, Lars forced himself to take a deep breath, to evaluate the situation. He'd caught her trying to break into his house, and couldn't figure out for the life of him how the hell she'd thought she'd be able to get away with it. On the off chance she got lucky and entered the correct code, there was a secondary security pad inside the kitchen that had to be disabled or else the alarm would sound.

He glanced to Braelynn, her green eyes blinking up at him. The flicker of defiance attempted to conceal her deception. Dark brunette hair clung to her cheeks, and although she'd stopped shaking, her soft lips still trembled.

"You know, there's nothing wrong with my front door," he quipped. Snatching a throw blanket off the end of the bed, he laid it over her.

"I'm sorry, what?" she whispered. Her eyes fell to his hands which lingered over her belly.

"You've got to get these off. Can you...uh...do you need help?" Lars hesitated. To treat hypothermia, he knew he needed to get her core body temp warmed up slowly. Her sodden clothes had to be removed so he could wrap her in blankets. Undressing a girlfriend would not have been an issue, but Braelynn wasn't his lover. Nor was she a friend.

"I can do it. I just..." she began. Her hands fumbled with the button on her jeans. After several minutes passed, she threw her arms to the side in frustration. "Shit."

"Look Doctor, as much as I'd like to be chivalrous, you need to get out of these clothes now. So I'm just going to help you off with them." Lars shook his head, aware of his attraction to her. *How the fuck did I get myself into this situation? Do not think about sex. This is so wrong.* "I think maybe...let's start with your top."

"I can't. My fingers, they feel...I'm so cold." She coughed and rubbed the back of her hand across her eyes. "Get them off. Do it."

At her request, Lars didn't waste a minute. Like ripping off a Band-Aid, he tore her shirt over her head as fast as possible. Stealing a glance, he sucked an inaudible breath; her dusky pink nipples pressed through the transparent fabric of her sodden bra. Focusing on his task, his eyes met hers as his palms slid underneath her back, deftly unhooking her bra.

"I can..." she began but went silent as he dragged the straps over her shoulders. Revealing her bareness, he tossed the undergarment aside, and covered her with a blanket.

"Now, your jeans. We'll get you warmed up. You'll be okay."

"I'll be okay," she repeated.

Lars hesitated for a moment before his hands went to her jeans. With his eyes locked on hers, he slipped a digit underneath her waistband, fingering open the button with his thumb. She shivered under his touch but didn't move to stop him.

His face remained impassive as he pulled the zipper down and tugged the waistband over her hips. But as he attempted to remove the drenched denim, her hands moved to his wrist. Lars lifted his head in question and glanced below her navel. Slowly and deliberately, she released him. Sliding her fingers over her bared mound and down into her jeans, she covered herself.

Lars sucked a breath, and tore his eyes from her soft belly. With a swift yank, he stripped off her jeans. Feigning indifference, he casually covered her thighs with the blanket. He quickly shoved off the bed and headed to his closet, plowing his fingers through his hair. *Holy hell. No fucking underwear?* She might as well have hit him with a baseball bat.

The whole situation was fucked six ways till Sunday. He cupped his half-hard dick and threw his head back in frustration. He knew full well she was colder than shit, but at the present moment he couldn't return until he calmed down. *No, Lars. Fucking quit this shit. She just tried to break into your house*, he told himself. He took a deep breath and counted to ten, willing his cock into submission.

A small moan echoed from his bedroom and he returned to the bedside. Praying she hadn't noticed his reaction, he spread a fluffy comforter over her small body and sat on the edge of the bed. The haze in her eyes told him she might still be in shock. She'd need sleep to recover.

Taking in the sight of her in his bed, Lars wondered why she'd ever risk walking down near the cliffs at night. A scientist, she'd know to respect the ocean. None of what had just happened made any sense. He suspected she wanted the key, but at what cost? Instead of waiting to meet him, she'd come to his house directly? No, not to meet him, she'd come to break into his home. She had to have known it wasn't safe.

"Lars," she whispered, her lids closed.

"Yeah, sweetheart." Although he couldn't bring himself to smile, the tone in his voice softened at the raw vulnerability that resonated through her strength.

"I'm sorry." She turned on her side to him, bringing the edge of the white cotton blanket to her chin.

"Why are you here?" he asked.

"I just…I need…" her words faded as she drifted into sleep.

Lars sighed and reached to cup her cheek. Warmth radiated in his palm, and a small smile crossed his face, relieved her temperature was rising. His other hand reached for hers, and although logic told him to release her, he gave in to indulgence, his fingers brushing over her soft skin. He stroked her delicate wrist, discovering the tiny black dots lining her inner arm. *What the hell? Who did this?*

Anger burned swift inside his chest, aware that the bruise on her arm had to have been caused by force. The distinct five-fingered handprint appeared fresh, its bluish edges telling him it had probably happened within hours. Lars blew out a ragged breath and gently placed her limb underneath the covers.

He pushed to his feet, glanced to the clock and then to the pile of soaking clothes on his hardwood floors. *Fuck me.* Nearly two in the morning, and he was set on an early rise. It could wait. If he didn't get some sleep, he wouldn't be able to function.

Exhausted, he considered his options. Torn between calling the authorities to arrest her ass and interrogating her himself, he chose the latter. The last time he'd left things to the police, they'd done nothing, refused to investigate further. Braelynn wasn't going anywhere anyway. Four hours of shuteye, and he'd get answers. No more excuses, Dr. Rollins was in for a rude awakening. He suspected the extent of duplicity was far more elaborate than her plea of innocence. Despite his attraction for the lovely doctor, he'd show no mercy.

The shift of the bed roused him but it was the sound of her metal zipper scraping over the wooden planks that caused Lars to focus. He fought a smile as the sight of her bared bottom came into view. Bent over, she'd clutched at the blanket, sorting through her clothes. The throw draped down her back, the nape of her perfectly rounded ass peeking up at him.

A small part of him knew that it was wrong to indulge in the delicious sight of her. *I earned it though*, he inwardly argued. All the hassle she had already brought into his life coupled with whatever secrets remained, seemed a decent exchange for the morning delight. But as she moved to exit, he sprang from the bed, wrapping a strong arm around her waist.

Her movement thwarted, she yelped. With the heat of his chest against her back, he made no effort to release her.

"Let me go," she insisted.

"Settle…" She wiggled her bottom against his morning erection, and he cursed. *Jesus Christ she feels good. Down, boy.*

"You need to let me go. This is kidnapping," Braelynn stated.

"Sorry sweetheart. I'd consider this a citizen's arrest."

"I didn't steal anything," she insisted.

"Breaking and entering," he countered.

"I didn't even get inside. I didn't break anything. I didn't enter. Now let me go."

"You need to check the law in California. You were

attempting to break in with the intent to steal."

"Steal what? I just said I didn't take anything," she spat at him.

"Intent is the key word here." Lars smiled as her eyes sparked with defiance. As she relaxed into his arms, he sensed her capitulation. Naked, she couldn't get very far.

"I'm sorry," she whispered. "Please."

"Maybe you'd prefer I call the cops?"

"No. Please. You don't understand," she pleaded.

"No I don't. None of this makes any sense. I want answers." The blood drained from his cock, the conversation turning serious.

She quivered in his arms, and he slowly spun her so she faced him. Clinging to the wrap, she appeared fragile and broken, and he wondered what the hell could have driven one of the world's promising scientists to do something so stupid. Tears brimmed in her eyes, and Lars resisted releasing her completely.

He considered his next steps as the room filled with silence. They both needed showers. The image of their wet flesh entwined together flashed through his mind, but the fantasy was as fleeting. No matter his attraction to her, he wasn't pursuing it. If and when he made love to Dr. Rollins, she'd be wet with desire, begging him to fuck her.

"Look Doc. I have a proposition for you."

"What?" She shrugged her arms from his grip, and stepped back.

Lars gave a small smile, knowing that Dean would fucking kill him if it got back to the police. But desperate times called for desperate measures, and if this woman had the balls to walk the stretch of beach at the bottom of the cliffs at night, she'd tear out of his house the first chance she got. He reached for her hand, without giving her a chance to escape.

"What are you doing? I told you…I'll talk to you, okay?" she asked.

There were no words that would make what he was about to do any easier. While she resisted slightly, her feet shuffled alongside him until he stopped, reaching to his nightstand. Opening a drawer with one hand, he retrieved a shiny pair of handcuffs. As he dangled them in the air, he watched the color drain from her face.

"No." Her lips trembled as her anger rose.

"I usually use these for pleasure," he said, amusement in his voice. "Not that I'm ruling that out for the two of us sometime, but I'm afraid that's not happening this morning. So I'm settling for peace of mind."

"Are you insane?" she exclaimed.

"I'd like to say this'll hurt me more than you, but all I can guarantee at this point is that I'll be as gentle as possible."

"You have no right…" She attempted to back away but he held tight to her hand, preventing her from leaving. "I'm not agreeing to this. No way."

"Consent. Good point." Lars snapped open a cuff and smiled. "I'm all for it."

"Good. I didn't give you my permission." Her eyes focused on his.

"So you do know how this works?" He laughed, guessing she'd never been restrained in her life. The fear in her eyes spoke volumes.

"I never said I've ever…"

"Here's the deal. I want answers. You have them. Now while this can all be very sensual, that's not exactly what this is about today." Lars hovered the shiny metal over her wrist.

"No."

"The police? They book you for burglary. It's a felony, you know. Granted, you might get away with a misdemeanor, but I do have video surveillance. I'm sure that will provide all the necessary evidence." He paused and took a breath, his voice trailing off as he suggested the alternative. Lars knew he shouldn't be making sexual innuendos given the situation, but fuck if his cock didn't stir as his mind wandered with the possibilities of restraining her.

"I can't go to the police. You know…you know…what happened on the beach," she recalled, her eyes pleading.

"Or, the alternative is you let me cuff you. I'll take a shower and then we'll talk."

"That's not fair," she accused.

"On the contrary, it's more than fair. I risked my life that day at the beach to save your ass." His voice grew louder as he recalled the incident. "This is not up for discussion, Dr. Rollins."

"There's nothing to tell."

"Very well. Do you know the assistant district attorney? His name's Dean. He's a good friend of mine." Without releasing her hand, he reached for his cell phone. "I'll call him right now."

"No," she cried. With a loud sigh, she snapped her head toward him, briefly met his gaze and then rolled her eyes in anger.

"So do you give your consent?" he asked. Drawing her closer, his chest brushed against hers and he slowly dragged his finger along her jawline, tilting her head toward him. "Doctor."

"What?"

"Look at me," he demanded. Her fiery eyes bored through him as she locked them on his. "It's your choice. Police or cuffs? As soon as I'm finished getting dressed, I'll release you. Yes or no?"

Lars watched her face soften as she accepted her fate. What she didn't know was that he had no desire to call Dean. He couldn't get the answers he sought without her.

"Yes," she whispered.

"What's that? Louder, Dr. Rollins," he insisted.

"Yes, Goddammit." She rolled her eyes.

As she relaxed her arm, Lars grew confident that for the first time in weeks, he was a step closer to discovering the truth. He gave a sly smile as he clicked the cool metal around her wrist, taking care to double lock it.

"Easy," she muttered under her breath.

"Bed? Or bathroom? I'm not generally a fan of an audience when I shower, but for you I'd make an exception." He winked as he gave a small laugh. Lars knew it was wrong to get a thrill out of restraining her, yet she'd given him enough trouble over the past couple of months. Compared to a jail cell, a few minutes in cuffs in his bed was nothing. Hell, most women would pay to be in her shoes.

"How about neither? God, you're an asshole."

"Now, sweetheart. That's not a very nice way to talk to the person who has the keys." He glanced at the handcuffs and back to her. "The *other* key too. Although I'm dying to find out why it is so important that you'd try breaking in my house to get it."

"I didn't break into your..." She stumbled over her words as the blanket slipped from her hands, revealing the swell of her breasts. Quickly recovering, she yanked the fabric upward, covering her bared flesh. "I hate you."

"Someday, Dr. Rollins...not only are you going to beg me restrain you, but you are going to get a nice spanking for that mouth of yours. It is a beautiful one." Lars couldn't resist baiting her. The sight of her hardened nipples sent a jolt straight to his dick, and he shifted as his cock rushed with blood.

"You are seriously not flirting with me," she replied, her eyes widening.

"When I'm trying to arouse you, you'll know it. Right now, this is far from foreplay." *Bed, definitely bed*, he decided. The last thing he needed to do was to have her watch him shower. "Bed it is."

"What? I'm not getting in bed with you again. Last night you took ad..."

"Last night, we danced. Last night, you tried breaking into my house. Last night, I saved your pretty ass. Correct that...frozen ass. Now why would someone who knows the ocean as well as you do risk going down alone by the cliffs at night like that? Let's just put it this way…you need to sit here and think of some really good answers while I'm taking a shower. I'd prefer the truth, because honestly, I don't have a lot of time for lies."

"I wasn't…" she began and went silent.

"Hmm? What's that? Got nothing? Yeah, how about you think on things." Lars reached over the back of the sleigh bed and pulled on a cord that he'd had designed to secure to a hook on the wall.

"What is that?"

"Don't you worry your pretty little head, Doc. This is a special little attachment." He snapped the cuffs through a brass ring and tugged, testing it. Once it was secured, he backed away from the bed and took in the sight of her.

"Do you routinely tie women to your bed?" she asked, a hint of a smile threatening to break her fury. "Who the hell has this kind of thing in their house?"

Something in Lars snapped. A lack of sleep coupled with sexual energy that teetered on explosion jolted him forward. She startled as he knelt one knee on the edge of the bed, and leaned over to her, his lips inches from her ear.

"Someday, Braelynn, you will find out exactly how I use these." As her first name rolled off his tongue, he imagined she'd be difficult to tame, a challenge he'd enjoy for certain. In truth, he wasn't looking for blind compliance. The banter was more conversation than he'd had in months from his bubble-headed dates. Intelligence coupled with beauty was sexier than any perfect ten he'd picked up in clubs. Perhaps her sexual naivety was the only truth she'd exposed. Yet that didn't deter him from hoping that eventually she'd trust him enough to share whatever dark secret haunted her.

With his lips so close to her skin, he resisted the temptation. Whatever drove her to try to steal the key back must've been some serious shit, he knew. His intuition told him not only was she in deep trouble, but the danger surrounding her would be brought to his doorstep by his mere association with her. Innocent or not, the truth would be exposed.

⤛⤜· *Chapter Six* ·⤛⤜

Braelynn watched Lars stroll into the bathroom. She tugged her arm and tested the restraint, frustrated with her predicament. She should never have attempted to steal from Lars. No matter what Garrett and Dean had told her, she'd known it had been a long shot. Approaching from the rear, she doubted she'd be seen from the front of the house. She'd predicted her trek on the beach would be dangerous, but having walked a similar stretch of sand many times during daylight, she'd been willing to take the risk. The sleeper wave, however, had taken her by surprise.

She glanced to the handcuff and sighed, realizing she had bigger problems. Braelynn had fantasized about Lars Elliott for well over a year. She pretended to look away as he stripped off his shirt and revealed his tanned corded back. As she caught sight of his rippled abs, she'd bitten her lip, her breath hitching slightly. Arousal bloomed, an ache throbbing between her legs. She hated her desire, aware she'd never have a chance to be with him. As he closed the bathroom door, she caught his knowing smile, and her stomach clenched. Despite being angry, she failed to hide her reaction to him. Caught in her indiscretion, her cheeks heated.

As she lay in bed, her mind spun with excuses in anticipation of Lars' interrogation. *What the hell am I going to say to him? Think, Brae.* Within seconds, she'd decided her strategy. She'd admit to wanting the key back, which was true. Although it would be difficult to lie, she'd have no other choice. She'd insist that after the party, she'd changed her mind and decided to go to him directly. She'd claim she'd chosen a moonlit walk. After falling into the ocean, she became disoriented and attempted to use the security keypad. If he pressed for more information about the shooting on the beach, she'd stick to the cover story she'd originally told the police.

With no choice but to wait for him, Braelynn closed her eyes, willing herself to relax. She brought the blanket to her face and inhaled the aroma of his cologne that lingered on the fabric. As she listened to the cadence of the water droplets spilling onto the shower floor, she pictured Lars showering, and her nipples ached in response. She recalled how he'd undressed her the previous night. As he'd peeled her clothing away, revealing her bareness, her heart had pounded in both embarrassment and desire. She'd never given a care to going without undies until he'd slid his fingers against the soft skin of her mound.

Aroused, Braelynn reached for the comforter, cloaking her body. She slipped a hand underneath the covers, brushing her fingers over her breast. A tingle of arousal spiked between her legs and a small moan passed through her lips. *Oh God, I shouldn't do this*, she thought. *More like the devil. This is so wrong but....* Her core tightened as she imagined the touch of his fingers on her skin. She silently cursed the erotic images and sensations threading through her thoughts, ones that she knew she'd never experience.

Braelynn never noticed the sound of the shower ceasing. But as his freshly cleaned scent filled the room, her eyes flashed open and her heart caught. Lars gave her a broad grin, and she wished she could disappear. Mortified she'd been watched, she blinked her eyes shut.

"Someone looks like they are having a nice dream," he commented, reaching to unlock her binding.

"I'm not dreaming. I'm just...I'm just..."

"You really do have a problem with telling the truth, don't you, Doc?" he accused as he removed the metal cuff.

"I don't trust you." Although it hadn't been tight, she rubbed at her arm and then shoved up to sit.

"Now that's a good one. You break in my house. Refuse to let me see you after I saved you. But you," he laughed, "you don't trust me?"

"I don't trust many people." At one time, she had. She'd been innocent, willing to let people in, but no longer.

"You'll learn how to trust me." Lars lost his smile, his voice firm but gentle. "Dr. Rollins. Between the bullets on the beach and the bruises there on your arm, I can see you've been hurt plenty. But I can promise you one thing. I'm not going to ever hurt you."

Braelynn grew silent, thinking on his words. Her fingers

ran over the bruises on her arm. She wanted desperately to trust Lars, to have an ally. She'd been alone for so long. Lars stood strong and confident, promising her what she desired most. She couldn't remember the last time she'd felt safe.

"Brae," she whispered. A small crack in her impenetrable exterior became exposed as she granted him a sliver of trust. Her eyes darted from her clasped hands to Lars.

"I'm sorry, what?" Lars moved to the edge of the bed, sitting next to her.

"My name. You can call me Brae."

"Brae." With an easy confidence, he repeated her name and rose off the bed.

"Yes." She wasn't sure why but her name on his lips caused her emotions to ease. He'd kept her at a distance like a quarantined animal. With the formality broken, she hoped he'd be more willing to let her go.

"I know your name," he commented. Lars never looked at her as he rummaged through his drawers. "I talked to you in the hospital."

"I'm sorry I didn't thank you." Braelynn's stomach flipped. When she woke up after the accident, she had a scant recollection of his soft voice.

"I don't know what's going on with you, and I'm not sure that you're planning to tell me today, but you should know that I'm done with the game." Lars threw a t-shirt and sweatpants onto the edge of the bed and reached into the drawer once again. "I already told you I found the key. I don't know why it is so important to you. Nor do I understand why you'd send the police down a rabbit hole.

Your story doesn't hold water with me. I'm lucky I wasn't shot that day."

"I'm sorry. I didn't see you…"

"I'm not sure what that even means. My friend was there too. The bullets made their way out into the waves. All I'm lookin' for is a little bit of the truth."

Braelynn watched in fascination as Lars shoved his feet into a pair of loose cotton shorts and pulled them up under his towel, never revealing his skin. As he tore it away, she glanced to his well-defined chest. There wasn't a day she hadn't wanted to see Lars in the flesh, yet this was all wrong. With her fantasy tainted by her lies, she dialed down her lust. The reality of the situation blanketed any hope she'd had of a future with him. She hadn't earned the right to feel anything for this man, let alone have him care about her in return.

"There's a robe on the door inside the bathroom. I'll take your clothes downstairs and throw them in the dryer. You're welcome to use the shower." He nodded to the bathroom and shrugged. "I'm gonna go downstairs and make us something to eat. I have an appointment this morning so we've got to be quick."

"Thank you." Braelynn swung her feet over the edge and watched in silence as Lars left the room.

She hated what she'd become. Her emotions rose in her chest as he turned back to address her. It occurred to her that after he'd left her alone, he'd changed his mind, worried she'd steal something. Wishing she could crawl into a hole, she rummaged for the last bit of dignity she possessed and lifted her gaze to meet his.

"And Brae," he called down the hallway, "I'm not sure what's going on in that pretty little head of yours, but I meant what I said. You will learn to trust me. I don't know what happened to you, but if you let me in just a little, I'll help you."

Braelynn opened her mouth but no words came as he disappeared down the stairs. She didn't deserve a second chance, nor would she get one. As she put one foot in front of the other, she reconciled herself to her destiny. She'd have to continue the lie, somehow convince him to give her the key and forget him. In too deep, she had little choice. Accused of stealing by Garrett and Dean, she'd become what they'd suspected she was; a liar. She resolved that although she might never have Lars in her life, she still could fulfil her mission, and perhaps she'd have freedom.

Braelynn stared at herself in the mirror. When she'd gone into the bathroom, she found he'd stacked fresh towels on the counter along with an unopened toothbrush and a comb. Despite her indiscretion, he'd put forth an effort to be kind. In the short time she'd known Lars, she'd learned he was so much more than his playboy reputation. Loyal, he'd never left her side at the hospital and appeared determined to help her. Courageous, he'd saved her life, putting his own on the line as he did so. Rescuing her again last night, he'd quickly taken command of the situation in the morning, cuffing her to the bed. Strong and confident, the fire in his eyes told her he wasn't to be trifled with. He offered her refuge, yet she knew the steep price was the truth.

A chill ran through her, and she reached for his robe. She slipped her arms into it, and lifted the lapels to her nose, gingerly indulging in his scent. The soft fabric curled around her face and for but a moment, she wished she could stay, confessing all her sins. She dreamed that one day he'd forgive her, give her a chance. And while she told herself she was not worthy of a relationship with him, a tiny voice in her head whispered, encouraging her to open up to him.

Braelynn glanced around his bedroom, which was sparsely decorated. He only had one small picture on his dark mahogany dresser, of his dog. The simplicity of the décor perhaps reflected Lars. She'd heard he'd come from humble beginnings. The technology capitalist had started his company straight out of college. Unlike so many of his colleagues, he wasn't born rich. Self-made, Lars was well known in business circles for both his integrity and his assertive nature.

The sound of metal clanking disrupted her rumination. Her stomach clenched from nerves, but the sweet smell of bacon wafting into the bedroom tempted her. She tightened her belt and shivered, recalling it had been over eighteen hours since she'd last eaten. As she heard her name called from below, she made the decision to face the music.

Braelynn padded down the hallway toward the grand spiral staircase. As she descended, she held tight to the silver railing, careful not to stumble, distracted by the breathtaking sight of the bright blue Pacific Ocean. She could see clear up the curved coast, majestic cliffs welcoming the rolling waves. No matter how long she'd lived in California, she never stopped appreciating its beauty.

"I love it, too."

Braelynn stopped mid-step at Lars' deep voice. Butterflies danced in her belly and her heart sped at the sight of him smiling up at her.

"Watch your step. The staircase is cool but you don't want to take a spill."

"It's beautiful." *You are too.* She forced her gaze away from his, attempting to shove her feelings back deep inside where they belonged. Braelynn sucked a breath and scanned the spacious living room below; its vaulted ceiling angling upward appeared to have no end.

"The ocean?" Lars offered her a mug.

Carefully, she continued until she reached the very bottom. As she stood before him and reached for it, she gave a small smile. He towered above her and the split second thought of him inside her sent a jolt of desire to her core. *No, no, no. Stop thinking about sex. The man just handcuffed you.*

"Did you hear me?" He laughed.

"Um…sorry…what?" she responded. *Jesus Christ, I am totally losing my mind. Concentrate.*

"The ocean? It's beautiful." He smiled, tilting his head. "You feeling okay? You did get pretty cold last night. Come with me."

As he reached for her hand, the sparks immediately returned and she quietly answered him. "I...yeah, I think I'm feeling maybe dizzy." *Liar. Horny? Yes. Dizzy? No. Please let me leave soon. I can't do this.*

"When did you last eat?" His voice grew concerned.

"I don't know. Maybe the party? No. I think lunch maybe." Braelynn fingered her bony wrist, aware she'd lost weight since the shooting.

"I'm almost done cooking," he commented, leading her through the spacious living room. A majestic white stacked stone mantle stretched up to the apex of the ceiling, its classically designed glass-encased fireplace resting at the bottom. Cream-colored area rugs topped the reddish-brown Patagonian rosewood planks. An octagon pattern etched into the carpet gave a stylish accent to the expensive home.

As they passed through a set of double paneled doors, she took in the sight of a huge kitchen. Its black granite countertops drew her attention, giving a balance to its light interior. She caught the sight of her unruly hair in the shiny aluminum refrigerator, and quickly tucked a strand behind her ear.

He gestured to a large oval ceramic plate stacked with bacon resting on the kitchen island. "Do you like eggs? I've made a ham and cheese casserole."

"Um, yes." Braelynn gave a small smile, warmed by his hospitality. She inwardly laughed, wondering if he did this for all the women in his life. "You cook?"

"Sure do. My mama taught me well, you know. I wasn't always into technology." Lars reached for a piece of bacon and approached her. "Open."

She gave a broad smile at his gentle demand. At no point in her life had she ever let a man feed her nor had she trusted one to do so.

"You need to stop being so stubborn, Brae," he challenged. "I think we're going to have some lessons in trust. And truth be told, I don't trust easily either. But you've got no choice this morning. You need to eat. And I'm going to make sure you do."

"Lars..." she began, setting her coffee cup on the counter.

"Open."

Braelynn's pulse raced as he stepped closer. The heat of his body radiated to hers, yet the inches between them stretched like miles. Desire urged her to close the distance. Reason warned her that she couldn't trust anyone, let alone someone she barely knew.

"Open," he said a third time, his thumb tracing her bottom lip. His heated stare pinned her in place.

She reached for his wrist as he guided it into her mouth. As she bit down, he released the food, gently brushing the back of his hand against her cheek.

"Trust, Brae." His voice went soft. "Not always easy, but it feels good."

Braelynn's gaze fell to his lips and returned once again to his eyes. *How in the hell did eating bacon become so damn sexy?* Her cheeks heated as he smiled at her as if he'd read her thoughts.

"I rearranged a few business meetings so we'd have more time," he said, changing the subject.

"Meetings," she repeated. *Holy shit. I have officially become inarticulate around this man. Help me.* She shook her head and continued. "I could come back another time."

"Sorry, sweetheart. Nice try, though." He laughed and reached for a towel, wiping the grease from his hand.

"A girl's gotta try." She almost asked if she could lick his fingers but thought better of it.

"It's a gorgeous morning. If you promise not to go scaling down the cliff, we can eat out back."

"Ha, ha," she said, rolling her eyes.

"Come," he said, walking toward the sliding glass door.

He flicked a switch and the glass wall slid open, exposing an immaculate patio. Braelynn followed him in awe, taking in the sight of the enormous rectangular swimming pool. Surrounded by herringbone brick pavers, the water sparkled in the morning sunlight. She looked to the lawn. What had seemed like miles in the dark was only fifty feet to the cliff's edge.

"Have a seat." Lars pointed to a lounger.

"But what about you?" she asked, ignoring his demand.

"I'll be right back. We'll eat out here in a few minutes."

A bark sounded from behind her and she turned to see a tumbling ball of fur spiraling toward her. She laughed, and instinctively went to her knees. As the dog ran into her, she embraced the sweet animal.

"Who are you?" she asked, her voice high as if she were talking to a baby. "Oh I know…you are such a good dog, aren't you?"

"Sasha," he half-heartedly scolded.

Braelynn glanced up to see him smiling, shaking his head.

"Sasha. What a beautiful name. Oh yes." She giggled as a wet tongue brushed her cheek.

"Okay, girl, come on now." Lars clapped his hands and the pup obediently ran to him. "Sorry about that. She, uh, she gets excited pretty easily."

"She's adorable." Braelynn shoved to her feet.

"Thanks. She's a rescue." He rubbed his hands over the dog's ears, who enthusiastically wagged her tail in return.

"I love dogs. I used to have…" Braelynn reconsidered sharing the tragedy of what had happened to her beloved family pet. It was found dead along with her mother's body in the car crash. The painful memory gutted her and the discussion would only lead to more questions she couldn't answer. She turned to the chair and sat, hoping he'd drop the topic.

"You have pets, huh? Where do you live?"

"San Diego." She ran her palm over the ultra-soft covering, avoiding eye contact. "I've got a cat."

"San Diego, huh? Never would've guessed." Lars tilted his head and blew out a breath. "Bacon. Trust."

"What's that supposed to mean?" she asked, aware she hadn't answered him. As she had no intention of providing her address, the vague reply suited her.

"That means we are going to be here a lot longer than I anticipated." A beeper sounded in the kitchen, and he pointed to Braelynn. "You. Stay here. No running down to the beach."

"I like the beach," she countered.

"Did you know that San Diego has over seventy miles of coastline?" he asked as he turned to walk away.

"I study organisms in the ocean, not geography, but that sounds about right." She blinked as the sunshine blinded her.

"Big place," he replied with a sigh. "It's going to be a helluva long morning, Doc."

Sasha happily trotted beside Lars as he disappeared into the kitchen, and Braelynn threw her head back against the chaise. She hated lying to Lars. She glanced to her bitten fingernails and wondered if she could survive another day. She was so close to getting the data back. Soon, she'd be free.

She took a deep breath and wrapped her arms around her waist. As the healing sun penetrated her skin, warming her entire body, she dreamt of a life where she no longer lived in fear. What if Lars could forgive her? Let her into his life? Wanting to tell the truth, yearning to trust, it seemed so easy to roll the dice and let the chips fall where they may.

·❦· *Chapter Seven* ·❦·

Frustrated, Lars swiped his hand across his mouth. He couldn't fathom what had Braelynn so scared she couldn't even tell him where she lived. Although her data had been scrubbed, he'd still been able to find out her coast side address in La Jolla.

The sound of the doorbell ringing interrupted his racing thoughts, and he glanced at the monitor. *Seth. Fuck.* He'd forgotten they were supposed to go surfing before he headed out to his appointments. Lars tapped a code into the security system's control pad and spoke into the intercom. "Hey, come on in."

Worried he'd burn the meal, he quickly removed the dish from the oven and set it onto a stone trivet. The sound of the door closing echoed throughout the house, and he gave a small wave to his friend.

"Niiiice," Seth greeted him, running his hand through his shaggy blonde hair. Making himself comfortable, he slid onto one of the leather-bound stools, and reached for a piece of bacon.

"Sorry," Lars said, referring to the plans they'd made.

He'd already called his secretary, rescheduling meetings. Lars considered asking Seth to leave but as he glanced out to the pool, he thought that perhaps he could use a second opinion. His attraction to the lovely woman on his deck had clouded his judgement. He'd already gone as far as telling her she wasn't leaving his house. At the time it had seemed the best course of action, but now, with her in his robe, making his cock stir with the simple sound of her voice, he wasn't so sure.

"No worries. Smells awesome. What is that? Looks kind of heavy before going out for a ride but what the hell?" He reached for the pitcher of orange juice and an empty glass. "You didn't need to go to all this trouble for me."

"I didn't." Lars glanced outside and back to Seth.

"I wish I could cook like you. I just don't have it in me. Now my ma, she could make any…" Seth went quiet, scanning the kitchen. He craned his neck to see around Lars, then stilled. "Wait. Is there a…" Seth pushed off the seat far enough to view Braelynn's brightly colored painted toes. "Yes…ah, ha, there is a woman. A beautiful woman, I bet." He gave a laugh. "Dude, you could have told me. I'll just leave."

"No, don't." Lars held up his palm. "Stay."

"You sure? I don't want to interrupt anything." Attempting to get a better look, he stood, straining to see.

"Sit down," Lars commanded, keeping his voice low.

"What's the big secret? You've got a girl." He shrugged.

"Not just any girl," Lars replied with a small grin. He

shook his head and opened a drawer, rummaging through it looking for a pie server.

"Ah, I love intrigue." Seth laughed and sipped his juice. "I mean who could make Lars Elliott whisper in his own house? Can't be bubble-headed red?" Seth leaned over and peeked once again. "No, a brunette. Can't see her face. Hmm...Sloane from the club. I can't believe you'd sleep with her. I mean I know she's been after you for months but you told me you weren't interested. I don't get why you'd..."

"Not Sloane." Lars lifted his eyes for a second to address the accusation then continued his task. "Where the fuck is the damn server?"

"Use a butter knife."

Lars stopped cold, glancing to him. "Dude, it's a casserole. Homemade. I'm not butchering it with a damn butter knife."

"Homemade, huh? She must be pretty special."

"Oh, she's special all right." Lars rolled his eyes, continuing his task.

"What's that supposed to mean? I can't see much of her. Tan calves. Blue toes," he noted. "What the hell is she doing in that damn robe?"

"She's probably just a little hungover from her spill into the ocean last night." Lars held up the shiny triangular instrument in triumph. "Found it!"

"Congratulations," Seth responded, his voice laced with sarcasm. "Jesus, you'd think you were a woman."

"I'm a cook, asshole. Cooking is an art. Neither

masculine nor feminine." He pointed the utensil at Seth with a smirk.

"Yeah, yeah. Whatev. Stop stalling. Who's the girl?"

"She's…she's someone who I've wanted to get with for a long time." Lars plunged the server into the pastry and began to slice it.

"A girl from the club? Does she skydive? Surf?"

"Not that I'm aware of."

"So…she hasn't been to Altura? Interesting."

"Nope. In fact, I get the feeling the only adventurous thing she's done lately isn't exactly legal."

"Hey, I'm not sure what that is even supposed to mean, but if she isn't into diving or anything else, I can only assume she's a one nighter."

"She's not a one nighter," he said decisively. "I'm not sure what she is."

"Wait. So you slept with her, right?"

"Slept?" Lars paused and gave a chuckle. "I suppose you could say that. We did *sleep* together."

"So you had sex then?" Seth raised a questioning eyebrow at Lars.

"Sex? Ah, now that's a different question." Lars eased the breakfast treat onto a plate.

"You slept with her but didn't have sex? What kind of a sleepover is that?" Seth laughed.

"The kind where the girl tries to break into my house, gets caught, that's what kind." Lars shook his head, continuing to plate breakfast.

"Who is she?" Seth's tone grew serious.

Lars glanced over his shoulder, and turned back to Seth. "Chill on this, 'K?"

"Yeah."

"You cannot go to Garrett. He and Chase already had a shit fit over this last night."

"What happened last night?" He paused and gave a small smile. "Lars. What did you do?"

"You know I haven't been able to put what happened aside…"

"Me either," Seth interrupted. "We almost got killed that day. I get that Dean wants to bury this for some reason but I'm with you. I don't buy that chick's story that it was some random attack."

"That chick," he sighed, arranging the last slice onto a dish. "She works for Bart-Aqua."

"They got in some trouble a while back, right? Didn't Garrett testify against them?"

"'Bout two years ago. They got off. Moved to the west coast."

"You think she's into something dirty?"

"Not sure," he replied.

"What's this got to do with the girl out there?" Seth glanced to the pool.

"My girl." Lars set the knife down in the sink and rested his palms on the edge of the counter. "She's Dr. Braelynn Rollins."

"You're shittin' me? You mean she's here?" Seth raked his fingers through his long hair, and scrubbed his hand over his scruffy cheek. "No, wait. Didn't you just say the chick out there tried to break into your house?"

"Yes, yes I did. Look, Seth. You're welcome to come out and have breakfast with us, but this morning, I'm getting some answers."

"But I thought the chick from the beach was some kind of scientist. How the hell did she think she'd break into your house?"

"That's the thing. I'm not sure on the why. But she didn't succeed. Not even close. I found her outside my back door fumbling with the key pad. By the time I got her upstairs she was frozen."

"So let me get this straight. A person tries to break into your house, and instead of calling the police, you take her up to your bedroom?"

"Yeah, that's about it." Lars smiled, amused by how funny it sounded. But no matter how irrational it seemed to others, he'd been confident it was the right decision. "Don't give me that look. I didn't fuck her. I just, you know, warmed her up a little."

Seth gave a loud laugh. "I bet you did. Holy shit, bro. You can't just keep women in your house like that."

"I kind of can. I did. How the hell else am I supposed to get answers? I told you I found that key down at the beach. Well guess what? The doc would like it back. Apparently that's what she was after last night. When I went to the gala, I had a little chat with her. We were supposed to meet tonight, but she tried to lift it. Still don't know why she thought she'd be able to break into my house. She's not exactly telling me the whole truth, that's for sure."

"So she just voluntarily decides to spend the night with you?" Seth glanced outside and back to Lars with a suspicious smile.

"She was tired. Hypothermia does that to a person. Now this morning…that was another story. Come on," Lars told him, setting forks and napkins onto the counter. "Breakfast is getting cold. We'll eat outside."

"Hold up there. How'd you get her to stay?"

"Let's just say I struck a deal."

"What kind of a deal?"

"I, uh, you know…I may have cuffed her to the bed." Lars shrugged.

"What the hell? So you're telling me she sleeps in your bed and then allows you to tie her up? No way."

"I wouldn't exactly say she was a fan…"

"Holy shit, Lars. You handcuffed her? To your bed?" Seth shook his head in disbelief. "Hey, it's not that we don't do this kind of shit, but if I'm understanding you correctly, you aren't having a relationship with her. Restraining someone in your house without consent…you're treading a slippery slope."

"What was my choice? If I called the police, hell even if I'd called Dean, there's a good chance she would have been arrested. She would've ended up in cuffs one way or another. No matter what she was *trying* to do last night, and believe me I've been thinking about this, it wouldn't have worked. I think she was coerced into it. That woman out there isn't a criminal." Lars sighed and blew out a breath. "Let me rephrase. She isn't the kind of person who makes a living out of breaking into houses. I don't think she knew what the hell she was even doing. She could have been killed down at the surf. Her actions scream desperation. Now why she's doing these things? Who's making her do it? Who shot at her? Shot at us? I don't know."

"Let's say all this is true. Someone is making her do these things. Silencing her. Why handcuff her?"

"I didn't want her leaving when I was in the shower. She hasn't opened up yet. I need answers and I need her to trust me."

Seth gave a hearty laugh. "And handcuffing her to a bed is gonna do that? Seriously, man. I've been around a lot of women in my lifetime, and tying them up if they don't want to be tied up, that's, uh, that's a new approach."

"I just told you. She would have taken off. So the choice was cuffed by me or cuffed by the cops. If Dean came to the house, she'd be in serious trouble with the law. Probably have a record. So you tell me, which would you choose?"

"I get what you're saying, but I'm just a little worried that maybe she's not as innocent as you're thinking she is. Maybe, Lars, just maybe, she should be locked up."

"Too soon to tell. But I just have a feeling she's innocent. Something isn't right. I can't let it go." Lars turned to Seth, a sober expression crossing his face. He couldn't be certain he should confide in him, but since he'd been shot at too, he deserved the truth. "Garrett and Chase. I can't ask you to keep this from them if they press you on it. But last night I saw them at the Bart-Aqua event. They wouldn't say why they were there but I know he's keeping a watch for

Giordano. You know how Garrett is. He's a tight lipped son-of-a-bitch. It's why I trust him when we're thirty thousand feet in the air. But last night." He paused. "I don't know. They don't want me investigating what happened on the beach. Frankly, it doesn't make any sense to me. What difference does it make to them?"

"It shouldn't affect Emerson Industries," Seth commented.

"Exactly. It doesn't directly affect Garrett or Chase or Emerson Industries. Now Dean? He's another story. He was A-Okay with buying Dr. Rollin's story, and leaving the case open. If he thinks I'm questioning his integrity or the competence of the police force, he would have every right to be pissed that I'm questioning Brae behind his back. But Garrett? It's not like him to warn me off of this."

"Not unless he's got a stake," Seth responded.

"Exactly." Lars went silent as their eyes met in a moment of understanding.

"You know I can't divulge what's going on at Emerson. I've got my own division I run, and my hands are full with that."

"I'm not asking you to breach confidentiality." Lars knew full well that any divulgence would be a serious offense. They each had top secret clearances, and it would jeopardize their businesses if he even asked. "I want to be clear. We both have loyalties to our respective companies. But if you know whether Garrett and Chase are involved in this, I'd appreciate a heads up."

"I swear to you, I don't know. I've never even heard

Garrett discuss Dr. Rollins. I knew about the congressional hearing, but that's it."

"I'm going to ask him again and see if I can get him to bend. This thing with Braelynn...none of it is adding up." Lars stretched his neck left to right, attempting to ease the stress that had crept into him. He hoped like hell that his instinct on this was wrong, but he suspected Garrett had withheld critical information about the shooting.

"I'll keep my eyes and ears open. If this business with Dr. Rollins has to do with Emerson, you know I won't be able to tell you details, but I'll sure as hell confront Garrett. Chase too. We could've been killed that day."

"Absolutely. To be fair, both of us do shit every week that could get us killed, but bullets whizzing by our heads while we're out catching waves is an entirely different scenario." Lars glanced down to breakfast and began to slide the plates into his hands. "Hey, can you grab the forks and napkins?"

"You got it."

"And Seth," Lars said, giving him a look of warning.

"Yeah."

"When you meet her...go easy, all right? I don't know what's going on with Brae but she had a rough go of it last night."

"Brae, is it?" Seth asked with a grin and a nod. He stood and reached for the utensils.

"What about it?"

"Nothing." He rolled his eyes and laughed.

"What?"

"Just sayin'. You've gone from Doctor to Brae. Already got a nickname."

"So what? Just because I shortened her name, that doesn't mean…" Seeing the smile on his friend's face, Lars stopped his thought. "You're an asshole."

Seth laughed harder, pleased he'd found a weak spot. "You'd better watch yourself, friend. You aren't usually this, how should I say, taken with a woman."

"What the hell is that supposed to mean?"

"It means you seem kinda obsessed. And before you get all riled up, you know I mean that in the nicest way. It's just you know…" Seth shrugged.

"I know what?"

"You, uh, you've got a lot of ladies in your bed, out of your bed. At the club. At the office."

"I don't date at the office."

"Come on, Lars. Get real. You know you don't even have to try to get women. You just show up and they flock to you. Blue eyes. Good looks. Charm. Throw in the money and the girls get wet just standin' next to you."

"Yeah," was all Lars could manage. He knew it was true. He could have a different woman every day of the week, and on a good month he did. Selby had been the only woman he'd ever cared about, the only one he'd ever thought to date seriously. When she'd moved in with Garrett, the flavor of the week no longer sated him. He'd always known he'd never marry Selby, but a part of his heart belonged to her.

"All I'm sayin' is that you aren't usually this preoccupied with a woman. Granted, we both almost bought it because of her little incident. But still. You've been talking about her ever since you left the hospital. You just stalked her at that charity event. And to top it all off, she was in your bed all last night and you didn't even touch her."

"I did touch her."

Seth tilted his head, giving his friend a pointed stare.

"What?" Lars exclaimed with a small laugh. "I did touch her. But not like you mean. Come on...stop looking at me like that. She just broke into my house. She was freezing cold. I only touched her to take off her clothes."

"Jesus." Seth shook his head. "Do you even hear yourself? You took off her clothes and you didn't make a move on her? Ah...my hero is falling. Taking a sword."

"I'm not falling for anyone. I don't even fucking know her."

"Whatever. Call it an irrational crush. You're like a damn woman."

"Fuck you." Lars gave a smirk, aware his friend was calling him out on his shit. He knew he'd gone over the edge finding a way to meet her, to tell her about the key and find out what the hell had happened. But ever since she'd tried to break into his house, he felt vindicated, convinced more than ever he'd been right to do so. "As if I would try to make it with a half-conscious woman. Not happening in any universe. That's not how I roll."

"I bet if I ask her right now, she'll tell me she was awake a good part of the time." He raised an eyebrow at Lars. "Oh yeah, I'm right."

"Fuck you again."

"This is going to be fun, you know. Bustin' your ass. Almost makes me feel not so bad for missing some killer waves this morning…almost."

"I'm serious. Be nice to her," he warned.

"I have manners," Seth countered.

Lars ignored Seth's comment as he walked out to the patio and set the plates onto the table. Braelynn glanced at him, giving him a small smile that he swore would kill him on the spot. *Jesus, she's beautiful.* Her curly brown locks spilled down her shoulders, her green eyes piercing through him. It was the first time she'd appeared relaxed, her face softened with the morning sun. Pleased she hadn't tried to run away while he was in the kitchen, he hoped he'd earned her trust enough to tell him the truth. But as her focus flashed to Seth, her expression went cold, and he rushed to ease her mind.

"It's okay, Brae. This is a friend of mine. Seth."

"You said you wouldn't call the police," she immediately replied, her voice distressed.

"Ho, ho, hold the presses there, darlin'. Not even close to being a cop. You got me all wrong, Doc." Seth set the forks onto the table and slowly approached her, holding both hands up in the air. "I'm just a friend. One," he paused as his eyes darted to Lars and back to Braelynn, "who, uh, likes to surf."

"Your appointment?" she asked quietly.

"Yes, well, one of them. I forgot I was meeting Seth, and as always happens, he stopped by to look for me." Lars knelt down to Braelynn, taking her hand in his. His eyes met hers, a warm smile on his lips. "I promised you I wouldn't call the police and I meant it. You can trust me."

Braelynn's gaze went to Seth who gave a small smile, and back to Lars. He sensed her fear but the gentle squeeze to his hand told him that no matter her hesitation, she clung to him. She may have been unable to articulate their developing connection but her touch didn't lie.

"Seth is just going to have some breakfast with us. Then he's got to…"

"Yeah, I, uh, should probably get going. I can still get a few sets in," Seth told her. "I promised a friend we'd go hike Torrey Pines later this afternoon."

Lars gave him a nod, appreciating his tact. "Let's just have some breakfast and then we can talk. I'll take you back to your car."

"Thanks. Sorry." The color returned to Braelynn's face.

"No need to be sorry. I didn't mean to interrupt," Seth offered.

"You okay?" The empathy in his voice surprised Lars. His protective streak had never been a secret but until now it had been reserved for those close to him. He prayed his attraction was skin deep, but as she blinked up at him, he suspected otherwise.

"Yes, thanks," she replied, her eyes locked on his. "I'm sorry. You won't hurt me."

Lars couldn't be sure if she meant it or if she'd said the phrase to convince herself. The words rolled through him and he wished he hadn't invited Seth. He needed time to talk with her privately, to reveal her secrets, to touch her…body and soul. Desire coiled in his chest and he deliberately sucked a breath, swallowing the emotion. Seth would read it as easily as fear, and he wasn't ready to reveal his cards to anyone.

She stood and released his hand, and he watched in fascination as her courage returned. Approaching Seth, she extended her hand, briefly shaking his. Her intrepid greeting ended quickly and before she sat at the table, her eyes darted to Lars, an easy smile forming on her lips. He brushed his palm over her shoulder, but catching the look of interest on Seth's face, he broke the contact.

Lars turned to his friend, meeting his gaze directly. "Are you going to Altura tonight?"

"Yeah, Garrett wanted to have a get together before the big charity event next weekend. The building's almost ready," Seth responded, concern in his eyes.

"I'll be there." Lars mentioned Club Altura, aware he'd enjoy taking Braelynn.

Its purpose or membership wasn't discussed openly with others. Admittance by invitation only, the members were a select group of friends engaged in extreme sports, reveling in risk. While it had been Garrett's baby, the team contributed, selecting monthly adventures. When not jumping out of planes or rock climbing, they enjoyed the social aspect. They held private parties with few rules. Push limits as far as you want, be safe, have fun. Not all members indulged in the open sexuality, yet no one judged.

"This is really good." Seth changed the subject.

"You need to learn how to cook."

"This is, hmm." Braelynn briefly closed her eyes, savoring her bite. "Sorry, it's just I don't get homemade food like this often."

"It's a recipe from my mom, but I prefer it with avocados." As she dragged the tip of her tongue over her lip, blood rushed to Lars' cock.

"I eat out a lot. I love to cook too, but…" her words drifted off and she averted her gaze from Lars. Stabbing a piece of the delicious creation, she lifted it to her mouth. "I used to cook before I moved here."

"How long have you been in California?" Lars asked.

"Less than two years." Braelynn slid the fork into her mouth and shrugged.

"You did work in the Caribbean, right?"

Braelynn chewed her food and nodded, not answering.

"What kind of work do you do here in San Diego?" Seth asked. He glanced to Lars, who gave him a pointed stare.

"I, uh, I have a degree in marine biology," she responded, not divulging the information he sought.

"Do you surf?"

"No, I, um, I used to spend a lot of time in the water, though. I scuba dive." Braelynn glanced to Lars, her eyes pleading for the questioning to stop.

"She's in research," Lars commented, a hint of irritation in his voice.

"You're in an office all day? No way." Ignoring the anger emanating from his friend, Seth continued. "You go in the ocean, right? Anyone who lives down here has got to like the beach?"

"Yes, I love the beach." Braelynn set down her fork and laid her palms calmly on the table. "Marine biologists. We don't all work in the field, I'm afraid. Of course, that's what I love but sometimes…well, we can't have what we want. We grow up. Settle. Do what's best."

"Best for who?" Seth asked, his voice gentle.

Sadness washed across her face, and she wiped her mouth as if she were trying to erase the pain inside. "Sometimes…we do what we think is right. Not just for us but for everyone."

"Hey man, you mind if I talk to you for a few minutes on the way out? I know you're in a rush to get in a few waves." Lars stood, waiting on Seth.

"Yeah, sure." Seth gave him a guilty grin, and Lars shook his head in response. "He's right. I'd love to eat more, but not great before a ride. I'd better get going."

As Seth shoved to his feet, Lars noted Braelynn's solemn demeanor. No matter how hard she attempted to conceal her torment, she wore it like shackles. He'd lost patience with the conversation as it did little to expose the catalyst for her pain or what had happened on the beach.

"It was nice meeting you, Doc. Hope to see you soon." Seth waved and nodded as he slowly backed away from the table.

"Can you give me a minute?" Lars asked Braelynn.

"Yes. But Lars." She paused.

"Yeah."

"I need to go home soon."

"Talk first," Lars said, her words cutting through him.

No matter the kindness he'd shown her, she doubted him. "Don't move."

They exchanged a heated stare as he went to follow Seth. Braelynn turned her gaze to focus on the rolling waves, and Lars grew more determined to expose her secret before letting her go.

"Hey, what we talked about," Lars began as he reached for the door knob. "Brae. Don't mention this to Garrett."

"Dude, I'm not going to tell him that she's here. But if he asks me flat out, you know I can't lie to him." He sighed, plowing his fingers through his unruly hair. "You know I want answers too. But thinking on this...if Garrett was trying to warn you off last night, well, then, he's in this deep. I don't know how far or why."

"Chase. He doesn't want me pursuing this either." As he spoke out loud, a realization slammed him. "Interestingly he is also a marine biologist. Does a lot of deep sea diving."

"Yeah, but he's hardly ever in the office. What would he have to do with Braelynn? I've never seen her at Emerson."

"True, but maybe Chase is the one driving the bus?"

"It's all speculation."

"You're hardly ever in the office. You're out testing products, and let's get real, it's not like you have to work."

"Pot meet kettle." Seth shook his head with a sideways grin.

"All I'm saying is that neither you nor Chase are married

to the office. Maybe he knows her from one of his assignments. She's worked in the Caribbean. Chase has been there."

"He's been lots of places, though. Not that you're going to see his name on the projects because you know how he is. And the doc has been here in San Diego for almost two years. You ran a background check on her, yeah?"

"I did. Interestingly, she's only been at Bart-Aqua for about nine months."

"Before that?"

"Looks like her data has been scrubbed. Some jobs are there. In college, she's worked some of the ecotours. Kayaking. Hiking trips. Stuff like that. She had a one month job she did in South Africa. Then her work in the Caribbean. Post-doctoral work or something. Then there's a big gap."

"But I thought she had been doing research prior to her move here?"

"Exactly. Why does a brilliant scientist jump from major league field research to no job at all and then back into research again? Not to mention that Bart-Aqua isn't exactly known to be environmentally friendly."

"I don't know. Something is off with this whole situation."

Lars opened the front door. A cool sea breeze tunneled through the foyer.

Seth passed through the threshold and paused. "Lars."

"Yeah?"

"Braelynn."

"What?"

"She's an attractive woman." He smiled at Lars, unfolding the Ray Bans that hung on the front of his shirt. Pushing them onto his face, he gave his friend a cool smile. "You, uh, mentioned Altura in front of her."

"I did," Lars admitted.

"Do you really think that she's innocent? That you can trust what she tells you?"

"That remains to be seen."

"But you said something about Altura in front of her," he pressed.

"There's something about her. You and I were both there that day. The beach." Lars scrubbed his hand over his chin. "But it's more than that. I was with her in the hospital. Last night, the party. Here at the house. I need to know what happened."

"Do you need to know what happened or do you need to know her? Because Lars, and you know I love ya, boy, but you are…" Seth bobbed his head while he searched for the perfect word, "a bit of a player."

"Last I checked, you have no room to talk."

"True, my friend. But you're courting trouble where you don't need to,' he advised.

"It's not that simple. It's not like I fucking met her in a bar."

"She's attractive."

"Yeah, you mentioned that."

"Maybe you're thinking a little too much with your dick?" Seth laughed.

"I can't say that I don't want her." He shrugged.

"Well, maybe you need to be careful not to get that precious dick of yours shot at again."

"Maybe you need to mind your fucking business."

"Club Altura is my business. You don't even know how open she is."

"She agreed to let me restrain her today. She's staying in my house. She just had breakfast with two men and knows she's going to face off with me."

"So?"

"All those things tell me she's brave. She isn't begging to leave, or crying her eyes out. No, she's calm. She might be afraid to trust me or to ask for my help but she's strong."

"That may be true but you'd better be willing to test her if you're planning on bringing her into Altura. And I'd suggest you run that by Garrett."

"Oh I know he wouldn't like it, but we all get to use our own judgement about who we want to bring to the club. And besides, I didn't even say I was going to bring her." Lars knew he'd need to be fairly confident in her ability to handle the situation if and when he ever brought her into his world. For the longest time, he'd warned Selby away, not believing she belonged.

"You sure 'bout this?" Seth reached into his pocket, retrieving the keys to his Jeep.

"I can promise you this. If I ever bring her to Altura, she'll be ready for it," Lars assured him.

"As long as you know what you're doing." Seth began to walk to his car then turned to his friend. "I'd be happy to help if you're interested."

"Yeah, I bet you would."

"Hey, now. Just think on it." He waved before opening his door and sliding into the front seat.

Lars and Seth had shared women on occasion, and Braelynn should be no different than the rest. If they had sex, and she wanted the pleasure of another man, he'd consider it. As Lars' mind began to wander, rolling the idea around in his mind, he heard Sasha barking. A scream echoed and he tore through the house, toward the back yard. *Braelynn.*

·❦· *Chapter Eight* ·❦·

Braelynn took a deep breath. With every second that passed, the more she contemplated telling Lars everything. Despite her paranoia, he'd been true to his word, hadn't called the police. But doubts persisted about his motives. He was friends with Garrett and Chase. For all she knew, he'd already contacted them.

Her eyes darted to the cliff where she'd trekked the previous night. It was nearly fifty feet to the edge. If she sprinted, she reasoned she could possibly make it back to her car. But as she ran her palms over the soft robe, she remembered that she'd left her keys in her jeans pocket. Lars had told her he'd thrown her clothes in the dryer and retrieved them.

Her mind wandered to the handcuff he'd used to fasten her to the bed. She'd consented, but not willingly. He didn't trust her. She'd been treated like a criminal. Yet his touch was that of a lover, his hands gentle on her skin. She rubbed her wrist, recalling how he'd caught her daydreaming, lost in her fantasy. The man made her hotter than hell, and she hated the loss of control over her emotions. A relationship with Lars was impossible. The best she could hope for was a life free from bars.

A bark in the distance drew her attention and she caught sight of Sasha barreling toward her. Braelynn knelt to greet her, steadying herself with one hand to the ground. As the rambunctious pup ran toward the patio, she glanced at the pool. Braelynn struggled to maintain her balance, reaching for the ball of fur. Unsuccessful in regaining her equilibrium, she toppled into the water, giving a loud scream. Her laughter carried in the wind as she broke the surface. But as the sodden thick cotton robe began to drag her under, she started to panic, fighting to keep her head above the water.

Fumbling to untie the belt, she cursed. Her legs burned, treading water. *Calm down. Breathe. You've got this,* she told herself. Although she'd always loved the water, she'd already nearly drowned once in the past twenty-four hours. She shoved down the fears of the memory, relief tearing through her as the sash loosened, allowing her to shed the fabric.

Braelynn swam to the side of the pool and reached for its edge. Clasping at the stone, her breasts brushed its smooth inner surface. Coolness passed between her legs, and the realization that she was stark naked hit her. *Lars.* Any second he'd be back. She scanned the patio for a towel, but the only covering of any kind she could spot was a stack of chaise longue cushions sitting five feet away.

Beggars can't be choosers. It wasn't the first time in her life she'd improvised. Without giving thought to the ladder to her right, she flattened her palms onto the patio. As she pressed upward, she caught sight of Lars staring at her. Blood rushed to her cheeks in embarrassment, and she dipped back out of his line of vision. *This isn't happening.* A nervous smile broke across her face, and she buried her forehead on her crossed arms. *Of all the stupid things I've ever done...no, no, no.*

"You okay?" she heard him ask. Braelynn lifted her gaze, settling on his.

"I'm wet." *Sweet baby Jesus, I did not just say that.*

He laughed and approached slowly. "Yeah, I can see that."

"I fell," she managed.

"You know, when I heard you scream, I assumed you were in danger. And here you are," Lars never took his eyes off her as he walked the length of the pool, "taking a morning swim."

"I just said I fell," she responded, irritated that he was playing with her.

"Fell in the pool. Swim. Whatever." He nodded in approval. "Naked, though. You know, I can say I was not expecting that."

"Neither was I." She rolled her eyes and pursed her lips, watching as he turned back toward the house. "Where are you going?"

"Relax, Doc. I'll be right back." He gave a half salute, disappearing into the house.

"Get me a towel," Braelynn yelled. *What the hell is he doing?*

She considered shoving out of the pool and running up the stairs, but her short-lived plan was thwarted as Lars returned. Braelynn squinted, the sun in her eyes. She held tight to the edge with one hand while she brushed the water from her face. As he drew closer and she caught sight of the string wrapped in his masculine fist, her pulse raced.

"Something wrong?" he asked, raising his eyebrows.

"You have it." Braelynn's eyes went wide as he held up the brass key she'd hidden in the sand.

"I told you I had it. You see, that's the thing about me, Brae. I mean what I say." Lars crossed to meet her and settled into a large contemporary sofa. Its red and white stripes stood out against the grey stones. Dangling the key in the air, he locked his eyes on hers. "You're going to learn you can trust me."

"Why should I trust you?" Her voice grew louder; she was frustrated more with herself for everything she'd done. "You didn't call the police, I'll give you that. But you don't owe me anything. I don't know why you are even bothering."

"Do you know who I am?"

"I know exactly who you are. Lars Elliott. CEO." She gave him a sideways glance and continued, "Playboy."

"Seriously?" he interrupted. "You're gonna go there?"

"Playboy," Braelynn gritted out, not giving a fuck about hurting his feelings after he'd toyed with her. He wanted the truth, after all. Everyone at Emerson knew the score. She was wet and naked in a pool, and her limit of patience had been reached. "You do something athletic. Besides the surfing. I don't know what but I can tell…" she stuttered, her eyes washing over him. "Smart. Brave. You saved me. The hospital. Nice voice."

"You remember?" His voice softened.

"It's hazy."

"I want answers, Brae."

"I want a towel." She shot him a wicked smile, cocking her head.

"How about we help each other?" he suggested, standing.

"I can't…" Braelynn stopped short of begging and considered climbing out of the pool nude.

"Towels," he continued, approaching a large teak armoire. The doors opened, revealing neatly stacked rolls of brightly colored beach towels. Lars tucked a couple under his arm and returned to the edge of the pool, twirling the key.

"Can I please have one?"

"I'm thinking we should do an exchange. A towel for the truth. Fair is fair." He shrugged and tossed them onto a chaise. "But this key here. It's what I'm most interested in."

"You weren't lying."

"There's something I don't get." Lars fingered the inscription. "What could this open that is so valuable you'd be willing to break into my house?"

"I'm not doing this," she challenged. "I'm not answering another question while you're out there and I'm here like…" Braelynn glanced down at her breasts, and quickly peered back up to him, pressing her body against the side of the pool, concealing her nudity.

"Ah, is that all?" he replied.

"What the hell do you mean 'is that all'? I'm not dressed."

"I told you you can trust me."

"I don't," she fired back.

"If it was just a matter of clothes, you should have said so." Lars gave a laugh and strolled to the set of stairs that stretched the entire width of the far end of the pool. With a tug, he peeled off his white t-shirt.

"What do you think you're doing?" Braelynn's pulse raced at the sight of his hard broad chest. She noted the flirtatious flicker in his eyes, his sexy smile leaving her tingling in desire. As he slid his thumbs into his shorts, tugging downward and revealing a deep v, she covered her eyes with her hands. *Oh no…he doesn't think he's going to…* "You can't do that!"

"Do what? Just leveling the playing field."

Every traitorous cell in her body lit in awareness as she heard the splash of him entering the water. Braelynn tried not to stare at him but couldn't resist the temptation. Like Neptune himself, he broke the surface, shaking the moisture from his hair. Droplets rolled down his chiseled abs, the edge of the liquid teasing his pelvis. Her breath caught as he brushed a hand over his hair, continuing to grin. He lifted his right hand out of the water, and the key came into view.

"Do you like games, Brae?"

"Um, what? Games?" she stuttered, unable to look away as he grazed a palm over his chest.

"You want a towel so you can go home. I want answers about what's going on here."

"But…"

"Ah, ah, ah…my turn to talk," he shushed her. "You see I'm a patient man. But last night, well that changed everything."

"I told you I…" she began but he held up a silencing hand.

"This is how this game is going to work."

"I don't want to play…" she tried to interrupt.

"You don't have a choice." Lars dangled the key in the air. "Here's how this is going to work. For every question you answer, I move a foot toward you. I figure I have about ten questions max. Truth for the key."

"You're serious?" She let go of the edge and tread water.

"Completely. Once I reach you, it's yours."

"I'm free to go?"

"Yes."

"And a towel?"

"Yes. Your clothes are inside the kitchen bathroom. Dry."

"My car keys?"

"With your clothes."

"What's the catch?"

"No catch. But I don't move forward until I get the truth. If you're lying to me, it's a no go."

Braelynn's conscience warred with her sense of self-preservation. With little choice, she agreed to play.

"Done."

"Very well then. First question. Why did you make me leave at the hospital?"

"I didn't know you."

"No lying. Truth only. That's how this game works."

"It's the truth. I'd heard of you in circles." Before she could stop it, the half-truth spilled from her lips. "You give lectures to companies. I have a friend. She's heard your speech."

"Ah, but how do you know me?"

"That's a different question from the first," she challenged with a small smile.

"A two-fer. Answer it," he replied, not moving.

"My friend. She, uh, she's showed me your picture. She heard your motivation speech. Everest?"

"Yeah."

"She has a bit of a crush on you. That's how I knew it was you."

"Why make me leave?"

"Because…" Braelynn began, "there are some people in my life right now."

"What kinds of people?"

She averted her gaze as he pressed her but summoned the courage to bring her eyes back to his. "They're very bad people, Lars. The kind you don't want to know, okay? These people…they are protective of me. No, no, not protective," she corrected. "They're possessive. There's a difference, you know. You helped me, and I didn't want you involved with them. I didn't want them to even see you there."

She knew she'd said too much but as she'd confessed, the weight of her burden lifted. That much was true. Secrets seeped into the open like smoke through cracked wood. She no longer felt alone, and her desire to tell him more bloomed. As he moved closer toward her, Braelynn's heartbeat soared.

"Who shot at you on the beach?" he asked, his head cocked to the side.

"Lars." Braelynn kicked her feet to the side, her fingertips brushing the edge. "I already told you. There are dangerous people in this world."

"Why didn't you identify them?" he pressed.

"I can't…" Braelynn stuttered, her eyes drawn to his chest as it disappeared underwater. *Closer.*

"You won't…" Lars interrupted.

"I can't."

"Goddammit, Brae. Can't is not an answer."

"I don't even know who they are. I only know they work for my…" Braelynn sucked a breath, almost divulging her relationship to her uncle. They were his associates, and she didn't know their names or where they lived. "It doesn't matter. I can't…I don't know who they are. That night is a blur."

"Why the key? This." Lars held it up into the sun, the light flickering off its exterior. "Why was this so important? You must have had it in your jacket. When I took it off you, I'm thinking it somehow fell into the sand. Must have gotten covered with sand in the tide. But you had it on you that night? In a pocket?"

Silence blanketed the air as she contemplated her answer. His penetrating stare held her in place, and she chose truth. "Yes."

"Yes," he repeated.

The subtle grin that emerged on his lips told her he was pleased with his small victory. She briefly closed her eyes in response, aware that her own desire to make him happy could jeopardize her mission.

"What does it open?"

She blinked her eyes, noting he was closer still. Within four feet; she could almost touch him.

"Brae?" His smile faded when she failed to reply to his questions. "What does it open? What is so important that these people are willing to kill for it?"

"I need it…" Braelynn took a deep breath and blew it out. The pressure inside her chest tempered the lust. "There's something I need. Something important."

"But you work at Bart-Aqua. Did you take this key from someone? Did you steal it?"

"Lars…I…things aren't always black and white. Sometimes people get themselves into situations. Tough situations. Things get complicated."

"Did. You. Steal. It?" He emphasized each word, inching toward her.

"It opens something I borrowed," she lied.

Braelynn licked her lips as Lars stared at her as if deciding whether she was a criminal or not. He towered above her, standing in the same section where she'd been forced to tread water.

"Borrowed? Is it safe to assume that whoever this key belongs to doesn't know you have it?"

Braelynn shook her head no, her heart pounding as he held it in front of her face. It wasn't the key that was the issue, it was the data it kept safe.

As he closed the distance, she resisted the urge to reach for him. Her body pricked with sexual awareness. She shivered, not bothering to hide her nudity.

"Whatever is locked up with this key must be pretty important. I don't suppose you'd like to tell me what you are going to do with it?"

"It might not work anymore. It's been compromised." Braelynn startled as his palm settled next to her fingers. "Corroded by the sea water."

"Possibly." He smiled. "But what does it unlock, my little fox?"

"Fox?"

"Ah, yes, beautiful animals…shy, but resourceful. You're running scared, Brae. With good reason, after being shot. Something, someone made you desperate. These bad people you speak of still surround you." Lars tossed the key onto the patio, and Braelynn jumped. "But here's the thing about foxes; they're very intelligent. Even though they are afraid, or harmed by predators, humans, they, too, can learn to trust."

Braelynn went silent as he caged her with his arms, her back against the edge of the pool.

"You can trust me." Lars leaned toward her, his lips brushing her ear. "I promised you. I will not hurt you."

"Lars." Her breathy voice carried into the breeze. As his rock-hard cock grazed her inner thigh, she sighed. The cool water did little to assuage the heat between her legs.

"I can see." He paused, retreating slightly. Raising her left arm, he inspected the bruises. "Someone else hurt you. I want to know who."

Shane. When she'd insisted on leaving the event early, they'd argued. As she'd spun to leave, he'd grabbed her arm, yanking her against him. She'd long suspected his violent nature, but it'd been the first time he'd laid a hand on her. Braelynn had struggled and tore away.

"I, uh, I got in an argument with someone. It was nothing."

"A real man doesn't leave bruises on a woman."

"Please, Lars. I'm okay."

"Let me help you, Brae. Whatever you're into, it's far more dangerous than the shit I do."

"I don't want you to get hurt. I can't…" Emotion rushed through her, moisture brimming from her eyelashes. For so long she'd been alone and for the first time, someone was offering her a lifeline. Yet she knew if she took it, it'd be likely she'd put him in danger as well.

"You see, there's that word again…can't. Life is about choices." Lars released her arm, cupping her cheek. He brushed a tear across her face with his thumb, leaning toward her.

"Some choices can't be undone," she whispered.

"Let me help you."

"I want to…" Braelynn lost her words, desperately

yearning to open up to him. She flattened her fingers on his chest, the heat of his skin searing her palms.

Her eyes fell to his lips and darted back up to meet his gaze. Lars commanded her attention, and she thought of the empty nights she had touched herself, fantasizing about him, yet never ever relieving the craving that had escalated inside her. The man she'd dreamed of now held her in his arms, his thumb gently brushing over her lower lip. She gasped as his arm slipped around her waist, the slippery skin of her stomach grazing his muscular abdomen.

The long pregnant pause morphed to passion as his lips took hers. Braelynn lifted her fingers from the edge, reaching her arms around his neck. She abandoned what she'd held onto as reality, allowing herself a moment of pleasure as her body came alive under his touch. She wound her legs around his waist as his palms slid under her bottom, yanking her to him. Braelynn shoved the errant logic away that screamed why she didn't deserve Lars. His tongue danced with hers, and she lost herself in the kiss she'd always imagined. Sweeter than honey, spicy and hot, his mouth wove a spell, binding her to him.

His grip teased the cleft of her ass escalating her hunger. Fingers traced over her delicate skin, edging between her legs, yet never entering her.

"Lars," she cried into his lips.

"You want me in you, my little fox? Right here?" he asked, his pinky brushing over her mound.

"No," she breathed, ignoring his question. As he removed a hand from her bottom, she moaned in protest.

His fist wrapped into her hair, the tight grip taking her by surprise. The sweet sting on her scalp reminded her he was in control. Her lips parted, a gasp escaping from them.

"You can lie to me about your past, Brae. But not the present."

"I…I…" she stuttered, unable to complete her thoughts as his fingers grazed through her labia and over her clitoris.

"Do you want this?" he demanded.

Her hips tilted toward him, seeking contact to relieve the growing ache. Her smooth pussy slipped against his wet abs, increasing her frustration.

"Lars, please," she begged, but her plea resulted in him tightening his grip on her locks.

"Say it," he growled.

"Oh God…I…fuck…Lars, please just…"

"Do you want my fingers inside you, sweetheart?"

Braelynn's eyes flared as he demanded an answer. Her breasts jutted out of the water as he leaned her backward. She watched helplessly as his mouth dipped to her breast. His tongue darted out, its tip lashing her stiff nipple.

Unable to take a second more of his delicious torture, she caved. "Yes, yes I want it."

"Say it." He gave a sly smile as he wrapped his lips around her peak.

"I said it," she panted. Braelynn's pussy contracted, her pelvis rocking up against his torso. A firm stroke over her swollen pearl caused her to cry aloud.

Releasing her tip, he teased it with his lips, locking his

eyes on hers. "No, no, no. This is an exercise in the truth. Say it."

Jesus, he's testing me. Anger flared in conjunction with the heat piling through her whole body.

"I want you inside me. Now. Oh God, yes," she screamed as he rewarded her candor. Her pussy tightened as he drove two thick fingers into her core.

"That's a girl," Lars praised her.

Braelynn saw stars as he rocked in and out of her tight length, his thumb flicking over her sensitive nub. Threading her fingers through his hair, she clasped the back of his head. She splintered apart at his touch and embraced the sweet ecstasy that rippled throughout her whole body. Releasing his head, her hand searched, reaching between their bodies. Her fingers brushed over the head of his cock, but a firm grip to her wrist prevented her from taking him in her hand.

"I need you inside me," she heard herself beg. As her pleading eyes caught the rejection in his, her stomach dropped.

"Not now, sweetheart. Not like this."

"What?" she asked with a confused sigh. Although she'd come, another orgasm lingered as he withdrew his fingers. "Please. Lars."

"Not like this," Lars repeated. He pressed his closed lips to hers and pulled away.

She startled as both his hands went to her waist, lifting her clear out of the water onto the ledge. With her legs spread open to him, she shivered as his fingertips trailed down through her crease to her inner thighs.

"You're going to learn that you can trust me. But Dr. Rollins, there will be no secrets between us when I fuck you." Lars backed away into the water, his hands falling to his sides. "And be assured, that beautiful pussy of yours is going to be mine."

"Lars," she said breathlessly, watching him swim across the pool to the stairs.

"No secrets," he said, climbing the steps.

Braelynn's heart pounded in her chest as he rose from the water, his firm buttocks coming into view. *Holy hell. Breathe, Braelynn, breathe.* She'd expected him to turn, to reveal himself to her but instead he reached for a towel, quickly wrapping it around his waist. Rendered paralyzed by his touch, his words, she sat still, waiting for him to come to her.

"Your clothes. I'll leave them in the guest bedroom. It's on the left. Change," he told her with a devious smile. "I'll be down in a few minutes and I'll drop you off at your car."

"How can you just leave?" Shock rolled through Braelynn as she realized he wasn't returning. "Why?"

"One way or another, you're going to tell me the truth. And until then, you'll have to wait." He gave a wink, turned and walked toward the house.

"Who the hell do you think you are?" Frustration speared through her. Fucking asshole teased her on purpose. He'd made her come, leaving her desperate for more. She tightened her legs, the ache between them still lingering.

"No secrets," he yelled, continuing through the glass doors. "Get dressed."

Chapter Nine

Braelynn stared at her reddened eyes in the mirror. Holding her arms around her waist, she fought the tears that threatened to fall. Lars Elliott shouldn't matter to her. Before yesterday, he'd been nothing more than a crush. Yet the past twenty-four hours had changed everything. He'd toyed with her, making her want him even more.

After he'd left her stark naked on the patio, she attempted to reconcile what had happened. She recalled his fingers in her pussy, and a shiver ran through her. She brushed her hand through her hair, remembering the sting to her scalp as he'd pulled on it. Yet, he hadn't come, wouldn't even let her touch him. He'd sought to demonstrate control, dominance, and she'd given in to what he'd sought. After it was all said and done, he'd kept his word, had given her the key.

Braelynn glanced to the clock, shaking her head. It was nearly noon. She slid her feet into her damp sneakers, and cringed, thinking she had little choice but to set forth on her original mission. Yet as she reached for the door handle, she remained determined to get the research, and destroy the remaining files. Once she delivered it all on a silver platter to Garrett and Dean and left San Diego, she'd be free of her uncle forever.

Gathering her strength, she intrepidly stepped out of the guest room. Her nerves danced, as she was aware she'd have to face Lars. She wanted to hate him for leaving her at the pool, put him out of her thoughts forever. But as she stepped into the kitchen and he came into view, Braelynn's heart skipped a beat. Her anger dissolved into arousal with one flash of his sexy smile, and she knew the struggle to resist him would be difficult.

His gaze painted over her body, and she averted her eyes, warmth churning inside her. *Desire. Temptation. Deception.* The touch of his lips on hers fresh in her mind, Braelynn struggled with reality, knowing she was leaving. Eventually Garrett would tell him everything and she'd disappear. She'd have to find a way to cleanse him from her mind, before he ripped her heart to shreds.

Braelynn parked her car in the garage, noting that there were no other cars parked on the street. Although the upscale neighborhood was generally safe, she'd become obsessive about her surroundings. From the black van that occasionally drove down her street, to her neighbor, who seemed all too interested in her recent activities, she'd become paranoid.

She'd been unable to prove it, but suspected that what she'd thought was luck in acquiring a low rent oceanfront condo had actually been arranged by her uncle. Playing along and acquiescing to her uncle's demands had become the easiest way to infiltrate his business. Though she'd been careful to ensure neither Shane nor her uncle knew her whereabouts, she was concerned they'd grow suspicious.

Braelynn turned off the engine and yawned, leaning on the steering wheel. It was nearly one in the afternoon, and she considered that she should nap before trying to go back to the lab. But as she ran through her plan in her mind, she decided it would be best to get to the office as soon as possible. If she played her cards right, today would be the last time she walked the halls of Bart-Aqua. She'd retrieve the data, and after the deed was done, she'd drive directly to Emerson Industries. She'd already packed most of her personal belongings in the trunk. Her cat, Benny, would have to wait in the car. A childhood pet, the elderly feline was the only tie she still had with her parents.

"Benny?" she called as she exited the car and walked into the kitchen entryway.

Greeted with silence, Braelynn repeated his name and slid open the slider, revealing a spectacular view of the ocean. She breathed in the rush of fresh air, and placed her purse on the counter. As she opened the refrigerator to reach for a bottle of water, the hair stood up on the back of her neck at the sound of mewling. Benny's muffled cry soon followed, spearing panic straight through her.

Braelynn sprinted down the hallway, and gasped as

Shane and her uncle came into view. Both men were sitting in her living room. Shane propped his feet on her coffee table, his expression grim. Her uncle held her cat tightly yet it made no movement.

"What the hell are you doing in my house?" she screamed. Braelynn had never lost her temper with them. Always the actress, she'd pasted a smile across her face. A demure and obedient employee, she'd tried to give them no reason to question her actions.

"Did you forget something?" Shane glared, crossing his arms.

"Last night," her uncle began.

"What's wrong with Benny?" Braelynn's heart pounded at the sight of the lifeless animal.

"Don't interrupt."

"What's wrong with Benny?" she repeated, louder. She caught Shane glancing at the cream-colored couch, a scarlet stain smeared across its fibers.

"This." Her uncle gave a cruel grin, holding the limp black mass in the air. "It scratched me."

"You didn't!" Braelynn brought her hands to her mouth.

"When I call you, I expect an answer." He threw the animal at her feet.

"How could you?" Falling to her knees, she scooped up the cat, its broken neck flopping to the side. She shook her head, burying her face in its still warm body. Pressing her lips to its head, she sobbed uncontrollably. "No, no, no."

In her grief, she didn't notice them approach her. A thick fist seized Braelynn by her hair, dragging her onto her feet.

Her arms fell open, and the dead feline rolled onto the floor. She sucked a hard breath, the excruciating grief slicing through her chest. Without warning her uncle slapped his open hand across her face. Shock rolled through her as the pain registered; iron-tanged blood dripped into her mouth. As he lifted his arm again, Shane intervened, throwing her onto the sofa.

"Hold her for me," her uncle demanded.

"We are in a sensitive situation, Mr. Giordano. She can't go to the office with a bruise on her face."

"Listen to me, you little slut," her uncle continued. "The next time you decide to whore your body around at a company function, you'd better think twice. Lars Elliott fucks anything that has legs. Is that who you spread open for last night? Tell me!"

"What are you talking about? Last night, you weren't upset. You said he was there as a guest. I was entertaining him." Braelynn crept backward on the sofa, scanning the room for an object she could use as a weapon. She wiped the blood from her mouth. "Besides, where I go when I'm not at work is none of your business."

As her uncle attempted to go after her, Shane blocked him. "Sir. Please. We don't know if she's even done anything. We still need her."

"We'll hire another scientist."

"But how would you explain her absence? She's well known. Brings respectability to the west coast operation."

"I wasn't with anyone," she lied. "I…I went to the beach. I always go to the beach."

"You're lying," he accused her, kicking the dead cat across the room. "You've got a goddamned beach in front of your house."

Her reddened eyes looked at Benny's lifeless body in horror. She shuddered inwardly, but resisted the urge to react.

"It was high tide. You know I do research at night. I went to the strand. Pleuroncodes planipes."

"What the fuck? Stop with the mumbo jumbo. Speak English," he demanded.

"Red tuna crabs. They've been washing in recently. I miss it. The field work." Braelynn summoned her courage, straightening her spine and defiantly challenging her uncle. "How can you expect me to stay in the office all day? I must maintain my connection with nature if I'm to continue in this field. Ever since I arrived at Bart-Aqua, I haven't been permitted to leave."

"Who gives a shit about the damn crabs?" Shane interjected.

"El Niño. They've been washing up the past couple of years. I wanted to observe the latest wave." Braelynn knew full well she could have seen them in the daylight, but it was the first excuse that popped into her mind. "There is a whole nocturnal ecosystem that occurs on the beaches."

"Clean yourself up and get to the office." Her uncle brushed the sleeves of his fine Italian suit and avoided eye contact with her. "I need you to review the Mead report that's going out on Monday. It's a big contract. Jeannette said you weren't in today. You can imagine my concern when we couldn't locate you."

"I...I fell asleep." Braelynn's eyes went to Benny, who lay lifeless on her white tiled floor. Fresh tears emerged and she choked back a sob. "On the beach. When I woke up, I ate breakfast in Coronado and checked out a few shops."

"If I find out you're lying to me..." He paused, wrapping his fingers around the brass door handle. The threat lingered, his cold eyes drilling into her. "If I find out you're fucking Elliott, you're done, little Braelynn Sadie."

"Don't say her name!" Braelynn cried at the mention of her mother.

"My sister was a bitch. You're living under my control now, niece. You do what I say when I say it. I don't tolerate lies."

"I didn't lie," she protested.

"You work for me now. Your mother's dead. Your father...is missing. You wouldn't want to go missing too, now would you?" Her uncle approached her slowly. Shane sidled next to her but didn't move to stop him when he grabbed her chin. "You will not disgrace me. My work here is important. Confidential. If you go blabbing those little lips of yours," he smudged his stubby fingers over her mouth, smearing blood over her swollen cheeks. With a firm push, he shoved her onto her side, "you could go missing too. Do we understand each other?"

Braelynn nodded, shocked at the sight of him tasting her blood. *A monster.* He glared at her as he opened and walked out the front door.

As Shane went to leave, he turned to address her. "Don't

forget to lock your doors." The tone in his voice sounded sincere but anger burned in his chestnut eyes.

Braelynn shuddered as a loud slam echoed throughout the house. Her uncle's threats were nothing new, but it was the first time he'd hit her. A devastating cry tore from her throat.

"Benny." His name trembled off her lips as she crept slowly towards his body. She brushed a bloody hand across her cheek, sobbing, before crumpling onto the floor next to him.

❧ *Chapter Ten* ❧

Lars cursed as Braelynn took off down the street in her midnight-blue Prius. He was ten minutes down I-5 on his way to meet a client when he decided there was no way he could leave her by herself. Even though she'd given him partial answers, his instinct told him she was still in danger. She'd carefully avoided telling him where she lived, but Lars already knew her address, one of the few things he'd learned during his investigation. He tapped at his phone, quickly entering her location and got off at the next exit.

Thoughts of his encounter with Braelynn in the pool threaded through his mind. Chemistry had sizzled between them. Her response to his kiss had been explosive, her lips accepting and sweet; she'd come apart at his touch. It had taken every ounce of his discipline to walk away from her. At the time, he'd told her that he wanted the truth, but the irony wasn't lost on him. He was no angel. He'd fucked many a woman, never asking or caring about their lives. But Braelynn wasn't just any woman.

As he drove through her affluent neighborhood, he

wondered how a scientist could afford to live in one of the recently renovated beachfront properties. He couldn't imagine Bart-Aqua paid her anywhere near what she would need to live in one of the trendy homes abutting the spectacular cliffs.

Lars pulled his convertible alongside the curb, turned off the engine, and tapped the steering wheel, deliberating his next steps. He caught sight of a black limo rolling from the far end of the street, and slid down into his leather seat, concealing his face with his baseball hat. From his peripheral vision, he watched as Armand Giordano emerged from her home. A second man, who he'd recognized from the gala followed. *Why the hell is her boss at her house on a Saturday afternoon?*

Lars glanced back to the stretch, watching as Giordano removed his suit jacket that revealed a bright red streak across his shirt. Lars' heartbeat sped up at the sight, but before he had a chance to call out to the departing limo, the old man disappeared into the car and slammed the door shut. As it screeched down the street, Lars took off running toward her home.

He reached the door within seconds, but logic warned him not to break it down. He pounded on the whitewashed wood, telling himself that he'd give her five seconds to open up, or he'd smash through it. He figured if he was wrong, he'd apologize later. *One. Two.*

"Get out!" Braelynn screamed.

Lars immediately shoved through the door and ran into the foyer. Guilt stabbed through him as he took in the sight of Braelynn sitting on the floor. With her head resting against the wall, she cradled a black ball of fur, her eyes staring blankly at him. A trickle of blood was smeared down her chin.

"Don't," she whispered, shaking her head back and forth.

"Brae." Lars approached slowly. "What did they do to you?"

"My cat." Her voice cracked as tears rolled down her face. "He killed him."

"Jesus Christ. We have to call the police." Lars reached for his cell phone but went still at the sound of her voice.

"No." Panic laced her words, her hands trembling as she petted her cat's fur.

"Okay. Just…" Lars took a deep breath and knelt. Adrenaline pumped through his veins. Not only had they hurt her, they'd killed an innocent animal. He struggled to contain his rage, but he forced himself to remain calm. He'd been in life and death situations, but nothing compared to seeing her hurt again. He lowered his voice, careful not to scare her. "Listen sweetheart. I'm a witness. I just saw Giordano leave here. I don't know if it was him or the thug who was with him, but I have a friend. He can help."

"No, no, no," she repeated.

"I promise he won't hurt you."

"You don't understand. I'll never be safe. I'll never escape." She closed her eyes, her head drooping forward.

"You can't let him get away with this." Lars began to peck at his phone's screen.

"No!" Her eyes flew open. "I'll deny it."

"Jesus, Brae. Would you please open up and tell me…" Lars blew out a breath, realizing she was traumatized. Without her testimony, it'd be hard to make charges stick. He stuffed the phone in his pocket, and crept toward her.

"I'm sorry. I'm so sorry. This isn't your problem. My fault. My fault," she repeated.

"Please. Just, here…let me take the cat." His eyes locked on hers as he reached forward.

"It's going to be okay. I promise. You don't have to talk right now. Let's just get…it's Benny, right?" When she nodded, he placed his hands over hers, giving a stroke to its fur. "Let me take him. I promise I'll take care of him, okay?"

"You promise?" Fresh tears emerged.

"Promise." Lars gave her a comforting smile, trying his best to subdue the anger boiling in his gut. Armand Giordano was a dead man.

"I'm sorry. I shouldn't have gotten you into this." She closed her eyes, releasing a sob.

"I promise this is going to be all right." Lars scanned the room and stretched his arm out to snatch a throw blanket off the back of a chair. Unfolding it onto the floor, he focused his attention back on Braelynn. "I'm going to wrap him up now. You ready?"

"Yes," she cried. Lifting the cat, she kissed its head.

"That's it, Brae. I'm just going to…" Lars took the animal and carefully placed it onto the fabric. Wrapping it up gently, he folded the material until it was covered.

"I don't know what to do…I…" she gulped back the

tears. Wiping her face, she shook her head. "I have to get out of here. I have to go to the office. I have to…"

"Brae, please. I've got you." Lars sighed as she fell into his outstretched arms. He embraced her small form, cursing the bastards who'd this done to her.

"I'm leaving San Diego," she confessed.

"What?" Lars asked, his hands stroking her hair.

"I'm leaving. I can't stay here." Braelynn clung to him, her palms pressed to his chest.

Hot tears burned through his shirt as the vibration of her shivering broke his heart. Whatever was happening in her life scared the hell out of her. He glanced over to a wall full of photographs of different locations across the world. He recognized the waters of Bali, Mexico as well as several from southern California and Florida. Braelynn's bright smile made him wonder what evil could have crushed her spirit.

"I don't know what happened here. I don't even need you to tell me right now. But Braelynn…look at me," he told her, cupping her chin with his hand. She blinked up at him, and he wiped away a tear with his thumb. "I meant what I said. I know we don't know each other very well. But you can trust me. Whatever we just shared back in the pool, that was real. And even if there wasn't anything between us, you could still trust me. That day on the beach…we both could have died. Things like that have a tendency to bring people together. I know you're hiding something. Something bad. And I have no reason to trust you either…especially after you tried to get in my house. But none of this makes any sense to me. You can't tell me that someone who goes through all you've been through to earn your spot in this industry as a leading biologist throws it all away for nothing."

"I told you I can't tell…"

"You can tell me. But you won't. Because you're scared."

"Lars…you don't know these people. I can't ask you to get involved," she began.

"You didn't ask. The asshole who shot a hole through you that day on the beach? That guy asked me to get involved. I tried to let it go after the hospital. I really did. But I kept seeing you lying there in the sand. Hearing the bullets. Whoever did this is still out there. He can do it to someone else."

"You can't catch them. They…" Her lips tightened as she went silent.

"See, that's where you're wrong, sweetheart. The bad guys are going to end up in jail or dead. And when this ends, I prefer the latter." Lars had long considered that perhaps Dean had bought into her act of denial all too easily and that was why he hadn't pursued her attackers. But whatever trouble she was in ran far deeper than the incident on the beach. And he suspected that whatever she planned with the key could get her killed.

"I have to go to work," she protested, attempting to pull out of his arms.

"You're in shock," Lars told her.

"I have to get it over with. You don't understand. He expects me."

"Who expects you?"

"My un…Mr. Giordano," she corrected.

"You seriously think you're going back to work for him? Sorry, sweetheart but I've got news for you. You're quitting."

"No, I've got…there's something I need."

"You're not leaving San Diego either," he told her.

"But I can't live here. I can't work here. I just told you…"

"I know what you told me, but I'm putting an end to this circus."

"I have things…things in the office I need," she persisted.

"We'll have your things sent for."

"No, I need to get them myself. I'm not safe."

"Braelynn. I know you don't know me very well but I have a feeling whoever was involved with the shooting has something to do with Giordano. Your lip." He brushed his finger over it and she winced. "Look what he did here."

"I don't want to leave, but I have no choice. I have to get my things," she pressed.

Disgusted with the situation, Lars shook his head as he glanced to the entombed bundle, and back to the broken woman before him. Braelynn was in some serious shit. He wished he could turn her over to the police. Whatever answers he thought she'd give him were far from forthcoming. He reasoned he could go back to enjoying his life, riding waves at dawn and women riding him at night. But both the strength and vulnerability inside Braelynn drew him to her. Saving her twice wasn't enough, and he wondered if he'd ever be able to let her go.

"Lars," Braelynn said, breaking his contemplation. "Please, you have to know that I don't want to lie to you. But some things...I can't talk about them. You know this is true. You are in the business. We can't say everything."

"Please don't tell me that you're trying to protect Giordano."

"God, no," she sighed. "I'm talking about...you know...clearances. I have them. You have them, right?"

"Of course, but if there is something illegal going on, you can report it."

"It's complicated."

Lars gave a small laugh, irritated that she'd even try to explain it away.

"No, please, you've got to listen to me. You keep telling me to trust you. And God, you have no idea how much I want to. But this thing, it's dangerous. There's something I need in the office."

"Something that doesn't belong to you."

"Technically, no." Braelynn speared her fingers up into her thick locks, twirling it into a ponytail. "And I can't tell you who I'm giving it to either. Just me telling you this much could put you in danger."

"I'm going to make you another deal."

"Does this involve handcuffs?" She raised an eyebrow at him.

"Only if you want it to." He gave a small grin, hoping that she was starting to feel well enough to leave.

"I refuse to answer that." The corner of her mouth ticked

upward but she couldn't manage a smile.

"Let's pack up some of your things. Come stay with me for a while. I'll take you to Bart-Aqua."

"You can't come in with me."

"I didn't say I'm coming in with you. I said, I'd take you. They might not let me in but I'm sure as hell not letting you go by yourself. You go in and get whatever you need and then get out. After what happened here today, there's no way I'm leaving you alone." *Corporate espionage.* Lars suspected she was stealing information. Why and for who were two questions he had no answers to. Whoever wanted the information was either threatening her or possibly willing to kill her as well. "I get you don't want the police involved, but I need to think on this. I know about classified information, I really do. That's my business. But whatever you're involved in…"

"Please," she begged, concern in her voice.

"Hold on. Let me finish." He held up his hand. "For now, I won't. But I'm not going to lie. If I need to call them I will. I have a friend in the department…I reserve the right to call him if anything else happens. Killing an animal? Someone who does that kind of thing? There's something seriously wrong with them."

"Lars." She took a deep breath, her eyes flashing to his. "When this is over…you need to know, I won't be able to stay in San Diego."

"We'll cross that bridge when we come to it."

"Why are you helping me? I didn't even thank you for what you did for me at the beach…at your house…" She flattened her palms on the floor, preparing to stand.

Lars struggled to answer the question, aware he should probably call Dean and leave the situation in his hands. Whatever she'd gotten herself into wasn't his business. While Lars had initially told himself he'd needed resolution to the shooting, holding her in his arms at the charity event and later touching her in the pool had sealed his fate. He couldn't stop thinking about her slick skin against his. With the spark of desire ignited, he considered that he wouldn't be satisfied until he was buried deep inside her.

"Why?" she pressed.

"It doesn't matter why," Lars lied. He'd told Braelynn that he needed the truth from her before they had sex. But the more time he spent with her the less he thought he'd get it. He considered that if he just fucked her, he'd get over his obsession, and could let it all go.

Braelynn went silent at his response, and Lars suspected she knew he was having second thoughts about helping her. She reached for the blanket and he blocked her hand.

"Go pack your things. I'll take care of this."

"But I should…"

"Leave him. You should pack." More irritated with himself than anything else, Lars ignored the desire to comfort her. The small connection between them broke as she turned cold in response to his demeanor.

Braelynn shook her head as silence filled the room. She stared down into her hands, stained with fur and blood. "I need to take a shower."

Lars watched as she ascended the steps, aware she hadn't

agreed to do what he'd suggested. She was stubborn, involved in something way more dangerous than she was capable of handling. He resisted going to her, taking her in his arms and telling her it was going to be all right. He'd told her that he wasn't going to call the police but the more he considered what had just occurred, the more the idea appealed to him.

Lars called up the steps to Braelynn. Nearly twenty minutes had passed, and she hadn't said a word. He'd already pulled his car into her driveway, placing the remains of her pet inside the trunk. Lars retrieved his cell phone from his pocket and scrolled through his phone numbers, his finger hovering over Dean's. If he called him, he'd take over the situation, keep Braelynn safe, but he'd also arrest her. He clicked it off, deciding that although they'd only been together for less than twenty-four hours, losing her wasn't an option.

Lars double checked the locks on her doors before venturing up the steps. As he ascended, he noted several lone nails on the tan-colored walls, where he assumed pictures had once hung. As he passed a guest room, he noted the vacant space, dust scattered across the dark cherry hardwood floor. It was as if she'd never fully moved into the house.

As he glanced down the darkened hallway, he detected movement in the distance. The scent of lilacs filled his senses, and he didn't try to keep quiet as his knuckles tapped on the smooth white wood of the door. Its salt-air rusted hinge creaked as it opened, and he caught sight of Braelynn staring at herself in front of a floor length mirror. Her wide reddened eyes caught his in the reflection.

"Whatcha doing, sweetheart?" he asked, coming up behind her.

"I love California," she replied.

"I do too. You don't have to go," he told her, his voice soft. He glanced to the emptied dresser drawers and back to her. She brought her hand to her face, wincing as she touched it. "Let me get you some ice."

"No. This is a reminder of what I deserve," she sighed, running her fingers through her wet hair. "This is my fault. I'm a mess. My life is a mess. I'm leaving."

"Stay. I'll keep you safe," Lars answered. "I'll hire a security team to protect you twenty-four seven. We'll get whatever you need. I have friends."

"I'll never be safe."

"You need to let go, Brae. Let me in. I can't help you if you don't."

"Today at the pool," Braelynn turned to Lars, her towel wrapped tightly around her chest, "I didn't want you to stop. I just wanted to feel. I know it's all going to end, but I don't want it to. Did you ever feel that way? Like at the end of a vacation. You know it's coming but you can't stop it."

"There's certain things in life you can't stop."

"I want to trust you. I want to think that maybe there's a one percent chance something is going to fucking change. That I can fix this."

"You don't need to fix it alone."

"I can't ask you to get involved in this. Even if I did, I'm not allowed to tell you." Braelynn scanned the room and shrugged. "When I first came here, I was so happy. I loved watching the ocean from my balcony. Everything I'd worked so hard for? It's all packed away now. My clothes. My things. My life."

"You need to let me in. Forget whatever shit someone told you. Because whoever they are…let me tell you, they aren't helping." Lars took a step forward, closing the distance, his palm brushed her cheek. His heart melted, looking into her eyes. Someone had hurt her, and it wasn't just Giordano.

"Oh God," she breathed, her eyes slowly blinking. "Please don't…"

"Brae." Lars' chest tightened as she leaned into his touch. Her smooth skin on his palm spiked his lust for the mysterious brunette. *Don't be a fucking asshole,* he told himself. *This isn't right.* She was vulnerable, not willing to share her secrets. But if they had sex, he might be able to get her out of his system. He'd call Dean and he'd help her. Lars might never see her again, but she'd be safe and he could move on with his own life.

"Let me in." *Just a taste…make her feel good.* It was all he could manage. She drove him mad. He needed her capitulation.

"I want this…" she began, but didn't say the words he needed to hear. "But today at the pool…I don't want to play games."

"Lessons, my sweet fox. Perhaps we begin there." Her heavy eyelids fluttered up to his as he trailed his fingers over her collarbone. They flittered down her chest, edging the fabric. She went to reach for his wrist and he quickly corrected her. "Don't touch. If you can't trust me. If you can't let me in, I'm going to show you how to do it."

"But Lars, I already told you…"

"I heard you. Now I'm telling you. We're at a crossroads." Braelynn dropped her hands to her sides, allowing him to glide his fingers over the swell of her breast. *A beginning.* "Sometimes we have to learn lessons to build trust. It appears that is the direction you and I are going. Because I'm going to tell you this." He flicked his finger over the tucked flap, enjoying the gasp that escaped from her lips as the material fell away to the floor. "You and I are going to learn how to trust each other. I'm not letting you go off on your own. I told you that I wouldn't call the police. So as long as you're with me…" His energy surged at the sight of her gorgeous form. She released a breathy sigh and closed her eyes as he brushed the back of his hand over her taut tip.

"Look at me," he demanded. Her eyes snapped to his, and he delighted in the fire dancing in her expression. "You want to control what you tell me? This big secret you've got going? I'll give you that for now but here," he looked to the bed, and back to her, "when you're with me, this is mine."

"Lars," she sighed as he caressed her breast.

He rounded behind her, warning her not to move. "Stay where you are, little one." His cock hardened to concrete, and he rocked his erection into her ass. "You want this?"

"You said no games." Braelynn tilted her head to the side as his lips grazed her neck. She startled as he dug his fingertips into a fleshy globe, his other hand caressing her breast.

"This is a lesson, not a game," Lars growled. The taste of the skin on her neck tempted him further. Jesus, he could lose control with her. He knew she was leaving, but couldn't resist the temptation. At least they could have tonight. He'd push her as far as she was willing to go.

"Ah…" Braelynn cried as he teased his fingers through her slick folds.

"That's right, baby. You're wet. But you know what I want to see."

"I don't…" her words faded as he drove another digit inside her.

"I want you spread wide open for me." Lars withdrew his hand and she groaned in protest. As she attempted to turn around, he slid his hand over her stomach, holding her firmly against him.

"Lars, what are you doing?" Her hips tilted backwards seeking friction. "I want…"

"Oh I know you want it, sweetheart. But sometimes," he ran his fingers along her bottom lip, teasing them open. His cock thickened as she sucked them into her mouth, "you have to work for it."

Fucking hell, this woman would drive him mad. As he spun her around, his fingers withdrew with a pop, and he tossed her on the bed. She went to lie back but he crooked his finger. In silent understanding, she inched forward and sat on the edge. Opening to him, she parted her knees and trailed her fingertips slowly down her stomach.

He sucked a breath at the spectacular sight of her hand hovering above her pelvis. Although he sensed her desire to go further, her hesitation told him she sought permission. How far would she go? he wondered. Taking her to Altura, he'd be free to experiment, to push her further publicly.

"Show me. Touch yourself." Braelynn's head fell back as her fingers grazed through her labia. Lars dropped to his knees, drinking in the sight of her doing as he asked. "That's it. You're so beautiful, sweetheart."

She relaxed into a rhythm, and he crouched to the floor, settling between her knees. Lars unzipped his jeans, freeing his steel-hard dick, stroking it as he watched her. A wild beautiful creature lurked beneath the scared woman he'd met; one who appeared desperate to escape her bindings. As he knelt before her, he promised to discover her secrets, hoping she'd learn to trust him.

❧ *Chapter Eleven* ❧

Every cell in Braelynn's body awakened as she let go of her inhibitions. For so long, she'd denied herself a connection to another human being. The lies and secrets had overcome her life. But with Lars, for the first time in a very long time, someone cared about her, giving her hope to go on one more day.

When he'd come to her upstairs, she'd stood lost, staring at the shell of the person she used to be. She wore the bruises as reminders of her failure. She assumed that no one could love someone who'd made so many mistakes. Lars promised her a refuge she didn't deserve, but he was becoming impossible to resist.

Starving for affection, she'd collapsed into the delicious temptation he offered. Lars had denied her in the pool earlier but something had changed. She didn't know or care why. This man, he breathed life into her soul.

Abandoning the anchors of her guilt, she obeyed him, and sighed as she touched her pussy. The brush of his shoulders to her inner thighs brought her focus to the blue eyes that pinned her in place. Braelynn glanced down to his thick cock, and drove her finger deep inside her heat, wishing it was him. She didn't know if he was testing her like he'd done earlier, but it didn't matter. His words encouraged her to let go, to embrace what she'd been afraid to do with anyone.

"My turn," she heard him growl.

Her palm slid upward and he caught her wrist. As he sucked her fingers into his mouth, her core tightened, her thighs gripping his shoulders.

"Lars, please don't tease me," she cried. The devious flicker in his eyes told her she'd never be the same after the night was through.

"Do you like to watch?" he asked, releasing her hand. His head dipped to her stomach but he never took his eyes off of hers. She sucked a breath as he kissed her hip. "Or do you like to be watched?"

Braelynn knew her answer. To admit it would leave her more exposed that she'd ever been. There'd been no one in her life she'd ever been able to be herself with, no one who'd understand her forbidden desires. *Be a good girl*, her parents had told her. *Don't be a slut*, her friends had warned. The only serious boyfriend she'd ever had never approved of her fantasies, shut down her thoughts as perverted.

"Pay attention, my sweet little fox." A slap to her mound snapped her out of her reverie. She gave a ragged breath, the sting drenching her with desire. As he slid a firm finger inside her, she clenched around him, tilting her hips upward. "Hmm...you know what I think?"

"I don't know...yes," was all she could manage in response.

"I think you like being watched." He smiled as his lips brushed over her aching slit.

"Please," she begged, arching her back. The warmth of his breath on her drove her mad.

"Maybe you do like to watch but, oh yes," he said, with a kiss to her inner thigh. "I think I'd love to fuck you in front of an audience. Is that what you'd like, Doctor? Would you like to scream while I fuck you? Have people watch you come?"

Braelynn closed her eyes, her nipples hardening in response to his dark suggestion. No man had ever spoken to her the way he did, and while she knew she'd have to leave, the seduction of his offer was too great to resist.

"Oh, no, no. Eyes on me, baby. Today, you watch. Tonight, you will be watched," he promised.

Braelynn's gaze went to his, unable to imagine what he planned. She spread her legs further, offering herself as a feast. Captivated, her eyes widened as he dragged his tongue deep through her pussy.

"Ah," she cried as he lapped over her clitoris. His hungry eyes stayed on hers, and she swore he could see into her soul.

"You do like watching, don't you?" he spoke into her lips.

"Yes," she admitted, her voice soft.

He gave a small laugh, lashing her clit with his tongue. As he sucked her swollen nub into his mouth, she raked her fingers into his hair. His fingers clutched tight to her ass,

KYM GROSSO

and she craved his imprint on her skin.

"Oh God, yes. Lars, that feels so…" Braelynn struggled to keep upright, bracing all her weight on her palms. Her breast ached, full with need. The intensity in his eyes never wavered as he relentlessly licked her.

He drove two fingers into her tight heat, and she arched her back, screaming his name. "Lars! Fuck, yes." Braelynn shook at the intrusion, her body writhing in pleasure. As if struck by lightning, her body sizzled as she convulsed around him. Gasping for breath, she fell backwards onto the bed, her body quivering.

"Hmm…did I tell you that we were finished?" she heard him ask, his tone firm.

Her eyes blinked open, catching his fiery stare. He tore his shirt off over his head, revealing his muscular chest, and kicked off his jeans. Her eyes darted to his stiffened cock and back up to his face. She squeaked as he grabbed her legs, swiftly flipping her over onto her stomach.

"What are you doing? Ow," she cried as he administered a firm slap to her bottom. His fingers brushed over her cheeks, tugging her upward.

"I told you to watch. You don't listen well," he reprimanded.

"It felt so good. I couldn't…" Braelynn sighed as his fingers slid under her belly and over her breasts. Her ripe tips ached for his touch and she moaned as he took them between his fingers, gently tugging. "Yes."

"I will take care of you. But you must trust me, you understand?"

"But we just met," she answered breathlessly.

"True but sometimes the strength of a relationship isn't measured in time." Lars lifted her upward. "Hands and knees, sweetheart."

"But I want…"

"This isn't about what you want, Brae. This is about what you need. You want to close your eyes? Keep them closed now. You can't see me but you're going to feel every last bit of me," he promised.

"Lars," she breathed as the tip of his cock probed her entrance. Braelynn pressed backwards, attempting to force his hand. A slap to her other cheek rewarded her efforts and she cried out in pleasure, the pain only causing her to ache even more.

"Braelynn…something about you," he grunted, "ah fuck, don't move."

She moaned as he released her, the loss of his touch unbearable. The sound of the crinkling foil reminded her how reckless she'd been. She would have fucked him without regard to protection and not given a shit. No, she wanted him deep inside her, and with death and danger looming over her, nothing mattered but Lars.

"Good girl," he praised, his warm hands returning to her skin.

Her head lolled forward as she presented her ass to him. She shivered as his hand ran over her cheek, teasing the cleft.

"Please, I need you. I need this," Braelynn begged in anticipation.

"Rewards for trust," Lars grunted as he plunged inside her tight channel.

"Ah, yes, yes…oh wait." A delightful twinge rocked through her. She took a deep breath, releasing it as her core adjusted to his size.

"Jesus, you're so tight," he told her, withdrawing and sliding deep inside again without waiting.

Braelynn relaxed into him as he began a slow rhythm in and out of her. While she desperately wanted to look into his beautiful eyes, her body seized with pleasure, his fingers grazing through her folds. As they circled her swollen nub, she cried out, her orgasm building.

"You feel so damn good," he praised her.

"Fuck. Ah. Me." She responded to each strong thrust, his flesh pounding against hers. His relentless touch to her clit became more than she could bear. She lost control. A scream tore from her lips as her release slammed into her. With tendrils of ecstasy threading through her body, her quivering pussy milked his cock.

"Yeah, ah, you're killin' me." Lars stilled his movement. "Don't…just…"

"So good, so good," she repeated, her hips tilting into his hand. In the haze of her release, she slowly became aware of his thumb trailing down the crease of her ass. As it dipped further, she sucked a deep breath, as his finger circled her rosebud.

"That's right, sweetheart." His seductive voice danced in her ears. She relaxed as he entered a tip inside her tight hole. "Have you ever been fucked here?"

Braelynn had craved for a man to touch her the way he did, but the embarrassment of admitting her secrets kept her in silence. Her bottom wiggled into his touch, and she gave a soft moan of approval.

"You do enjoy this. Ah, how did I know that?" Lars slowly withdrew and pressed inside her again.

His finger teased deep inside her back hole. With each deepening thrust from his cock, his thumb worked in tandem. Braelynn clutched at the sheets accepting every brutal stroke. Overwhelmed with sensation, she panted for breath. She'd never allowed another man to take her from behind, had never trusted anyone, but losing herself to Lars came easily. As his other hand moved to her breast, giving a pinch to her stiff nipple, the delicious sting sent her over the edge. Braelynn buried her face into the pillow, coming hard. Trembling, she repeated his name, barely cognizant of him stiffening against her.

As his climax tore through him, his loud cry of satisfaction echoed through the room. Braelynn tumbled forward, and his protective muscular form covered hers completely. Their slick heated bodies melded into one as they fell into a dizzying blissful haze.

Lars shifted slightly. With his chest against her back, he slung his leg and arm around her. Braelynn closed her eyes, and a rush of emotion surged through her chest. Never in her life had she let a man take her the way he'd done. Wild and rough, he'd possessed her body. But as his lips pressed to her shoulder, it reminded her that he hadn't kissed her.

She attempted to shake the loss of intimacy. As he removed himself from inside of her, she hugged the pillow, praying she wouldn't cry. She felt the bed move, and her stomach fell as she realized he was leaving. *Stupid Braelynn.* Slamming her eyelids tight, she gave a deep sigh. Just as she was about to spiral into sadness, his warmth returned, surrounding her like a blanket.

His fingers teased away the long hair, his lips peppering her neck with kisses. "Stay with me. Just this one weekend."

"Are you giving me a choice?" she replied, a small smile on her face.

"I want to hear you say it. I can help you, and we'll have more time."

"I need help," she admitted. "Lars?"

"Yes."

"I'm in a lot of trouble. I have things…things I have to do." The dam broke, the confession spilled from her lips. "I don't want to get you hurt, but I'm not ready to let go."

"It doesn't have to be over. Stay with me."

"Is it true what they say about you?"

"What's that?" He laughed, spooning her more tightly.

Braelynn hesitated, and reached for his hand, bringing it to her chest. His strength reinforced her own resolve, and she embraced the safety he gave her. "Do you really do crazy things?"

"I'm not sure what that's supposed to mean. Compared to your stunt on the beach last night?" Lars' lips lingered on her earlobe.

"Like how you climbed Everest."

"Now how do you know that?"

"My friend, remember," she lied.

"Yeah, I climb. I swim. I do all kinds of things."

"Dangerous things?"

"Sometimes." His hand caressed her soft flesh. "There're a lot of things about me you don't know, Brae. You're not the only one with secrets."

Braelynn went quiet at his statement, and she wondered if he had a girlfriend. She'd never even thought to ask. Although his sexual prowess was rumored to be great, she'd never heard he was taken. *Don't ask*, her conscience warned her, but she couldn't stop the question from leaving her lips. "Are you dating anyone?"

"You mean besides you?" He laughed.

"We're not dating. We're…I don't know what we're doing. Things I haven't done before." Braelynn paused, her thoughts drifting to their anal play.

"Things you want to do?"

"Maybe," she admitted. "But this isn't dating. This is…"

"Having sex? Yeah, maybe. But it was amazing." He kissed her shoulder. "And I have a feeling we're just getting started."

"Are you dating someone?" she persisted. *Fuck, I'm an idiot. Brae, you're going to sound more desperate than you did before you had sex. Stop it while you have a shred of your dignity left. Oh hell.*

"I've dated lots of someones." Lars let the silence fill the room. As if sensing that he'd hurt her feelings, he continued. "Brae. What happened here between us was great."

"Great, yeah," she replied, disappointment in her tone.

"I'm not saying I don't want to do it again. I just…hell, Brae, it's not like this is easy. I've wanted to make love to you ever since we danced. But I date other women. And you said you're leaving, remember?"

"No, it's okay. Just casual. No worries," Braelynn told him, her heart tightening with the lie.

"I'm attracted to you. But like you just said, you've got some serious shit going on. You aren't telling me everything. You told me you're leaving…"

"I'm sorry," she interrupted. *Selfish, selfish, selfish.* She wished she could get up and scrub the delightful memory of their lovemaking from her memory.

"One weekend. I'll keep you safe. You'll get whatever the fuck you need out of your office and then we'll take it from there. It's all I can promise right now."

Braelynn's pulse raced as he rolled her over to face him. Her fiery eyes met his, the connection growing more intense by the second. He took her hands in his, bringing them to his lips.

"I don't know what's going on between us. I just know that I don't want it to end."

"Yes," she responded.

"What?" a look of confusion washed across his face.

"Like you, I can't promise anything after I get what I need. But for tonight, I'll stay with you."

"One more thing, little fox. No holds barred, you understand?"

"How do you mean?"

"The things I do? Pushing limits. This isn't something I do for fun. It's how I live. Day in, day out, there's an adventure waiting." He sucked her finger into his mouth then released it, teasing his tongue over its tip. "When it comes to sex, I'm not looking for vanilla. This is only the beginning."

Braelynn took a deep breath, closing her eyes and opening them. As his fingers threaded into her hair, she lost herself in his mesmerizing gaze. She knew what he meant. Lars Elliott sought to splay her open, revealing her darkest desires. Eventually, he'd break her down, she knew, but the thrill of exploring her sexuality within the safety of his arms proved to be too great of a temptation.

"I know you don't want the police involved, and I told you I wouldn't, but if push comes to shove, they are always an option. I can tell you this. I'm sure as hell not going to leave you here in this condo by yourself. Not after what he did to you." Lars' demeanor turned serious as he spoke deliberately and slowly. "And Brae, if at the end of this weekend, you're still lying to me, if you can't open to me, maybe it's best that you leave."

"I don't want to leave," she replied, ignoring the heart of the issue. He still wanted answers, would not abandon discovering her clandestine activities.

"As for us. This pure sexual rush? Let's make some memories and see how far we can take it," he suggested, his lips closing in on hers.

Braelynn trembled as her mind spun with the possibilities. Demanding, he'd test her limits, and she suspected would bring her to the precipice of rapture.

"So what's it going to be, Doctor?" His mouth brushed over hers, and she sighed in arousal.

"Yes." Braelynn's heart pounded as she committed to his proposal. With danger and death looming in the distance, she no longer wished to fight alone. She might not be able to fully disclose her mission, but she sure as hell would accept his help.

Gravitation to the charismatic CEO was impossible to resist. She closed her eyes and submitted to his devastating kiss. Nothing would ever be the same again nor did she want it to be. Lars had already commanded her body, challenged her mind. He was transforming her life. Whether he became her savior or her greatest vice, she was helpless to stop his influence. The loss at the end of the weekend would bring her to her knees, she knew. Yet she hopelessly craved his touch. Giving in to her hunger, she hoped like hell she'd survive.

The masculine scent of Lars fresh in her mind, Braelynn smiled as she finished dressing for the party. Lars explained that he had a commitment that he wanted her to attend. She'd reluctantly agreed not to attempt to go back to Bart-Aqua until tomorrow. Then they'd made love one more time before leaving her house. Exhausted, she'd fallen asleep on the drive back to his home.

She glanced in the mirror. Her wild curls spilled over her tanned shoulders. The sexy fitted cami exposed a hint of cleavage, her mini-skirt flowing with the sway of her hips. She slipped into a pair of canvas wedge sandals, and took one last look at herself before leaving the bedroom.

Braelynn's heart bloomed as she walked down the hallway. It wasn't as if she'd completely dismissed the inordinate amount of danger she was in or the task that remained, but even if it were for just one night, she was determined to enjoy every second with Lars. She accepted the reality, that he'd never choose to stand by her if he found out what she'd been accused of doing. But leaving San Diego hadn't been an empty statement. By Sunday night, it was likely she'd be on a plane halfway across the country.

As she turned into the hallway, the sound of a woman's voice stopped her in her tracks. Arguing filtered throughout the contemporary home, and jealousy took root as she wondered who it was. Braelynn attempted to bury the ugly emotion, yet the nagging thought persisted. She considered spinning on her heels and retreating to the bedroom. But with her curiosity spiked, she padded quietly toward the staircase.

As she descended, the loud squabble evolved into whispers, and she took sight of a gorgeous red-haired woman standing in the foyer. Her long tresses were perfectly curled as if she'd come straight from the beauty salon. Impeccably manicured peach fingernails matched her skin-tight bandage dress. She tottered on ridiculously high fuck-me shoes that left scuff marks on the floor. With her hands planted on Lars' chest, she leaned forward, whispering into his ear.

"Lars, I'm ready," Braelynn announced. She delighted in the expression of surprise they both wore as she strode over to them. *Fuck her*, Braelynn thought to herself. *Lars may not be mine forever, but for this weekend, he is.*

"Brae, I…this is…this is…" Lars stuttered, backing away from the ginger beauty. A broad smile replaced shock as his eyes painted over Braelynn. "…Jesus, you look beautiful."

Braelynn didn't hesitate, asserting her dominance. Strong and confident, she never took her eyes off Lars as she wrapped her arms around his waist. Pressing up onto her toes, she kissed him, taking command in the way he'd done to her. As if they were the only two people in the room, he cupped his hands to her cheeks, gently sweeping his tongue against hers. Braelynn had almost forgotten about the woman, but as he slowly withdrew, she heard screeching. Never backing away, Braelynn remained at his side with her arm around him.

"Who the hell is this?" Red demanded.

"Sorry, this is…" Lars began.

"I'm Braelynn," she interrupted, giving her an icy smile. Braelynn glanced up to Lars, softening her expression. "Hey baby, would you like me to take Sasha outside while you finish things up with…" Braelynn glared at the seething girl, and grinned sweetly up at him, "her?"

"Um, yeah, that would be great," he responded with a small laugh.

Braelynn turned into his embrace and kissed him briefly on his lips. She reached downward, cupping his ass and he chuckled in response.

"Do hurry, baby. We don't want to be late." She winked,

and released him. Giving a brief, cold glare to the redheaded Barbie, Braelynn strode out of the room, calling Sasha's name. The sweet puppy rushed to her side, and she turned her head, catching Lars smiling as she walked into the kitchen.

By the time she reached the patio, a fine sheen broke across her forehead, her heart pounding like a drum in her chest. She couldn't see straight as the irrational green-eyed fervor coursed through her veins. *Get your shit together, Brae.* Reason told her to calm down. Screwing him a couple of times hardly qualified him as belonging to her. Yet, knowing they'd committed to the rest of the weekend, there was no fucking way she was letting that plastic bitch put her hands on him.

"Jesus Christ, Braelynn…deep breaths, deep breaths," she repeated, rolling her eyes at her own behavior. Lars would confront her, she knew. He'd already told her that he dated other women, and Red was most likely one out of a hundred bimbos waiting to sink their claws into him.

Momentarily distracted, Braelynn gave a small giggle, watching Sasha run circles in the yard, chasing a leaf dancing in the wind. But as her focus went back to her own behavior, she broke into laughter. Whether a nervous release or simply unable to come to terms with her feelings, she couldn't control it. Lars' voice sounded behind her and her amusement immediately waned. Anticipating his reaction to what she'd done, she cringed, yet was unable to wipe the grin from her face.

"Doctor," he called to her.

"That's me." Braelynn raised her hand without turning around. She jumped as strong arms coiled around hers. As he nuzzled his face into her hair, she melted into his embrace.

"You surprise me. Gentle but strong."

"I used to be strong," she responded.

"You still are."

"I'm a fighter." Lars had given her a newfound confidence. She'd almost died because of her uncle and the evil that surrounded him. She'd grown more determined than ever to take him down.

"You don't like to share, little fox?" Gooseflesh broke over her skin as Lars' lips hovered over her earlobe, his warm breath on her sensitive skin.

"Maybe I just didn't like your friend," she managed, arousal igniting as he placed a kiss to her neck.

"Ah, I'm seeing a new side of you. Hmm…no sharing me, but would you like to be shared?" he asked.

The thought of her making love to two men flashed in her mind, and she cursed the heat between her legs. Tempting and teasing her, the man was pure evil. He gave a small laugh when she didn't give a prompt answer.

"We're going to have fun tonight. Just remember to keep an open mind." His tone of voice promised a sexual tease.

"Where are we going?" Braelynn asked, afraid of his answer.

"A party. A barbecue of sorts. With friends."

"What kinds of friends?" Her pulse raced, aware of the company he kept.

"My friends." He paused. "They're fun, adventurous, like-minded individuals. We have a clubhouse, but it's under repair."

"Do your friends climb like you?"

"Yes, but that's one of many things. We're a private bunch." Lars released Braelynn, turning her so she faced him. His expression, while still soft, was entirely serious. "What you see tonight, what you do…it's meant to be seen and enjoyed but not repeated to others, do you understand? I need to be able to trust you on this."

"Of course," she found herself agreeing, without fully comprehending of what he was speaking. "But when you say, 'what you do'…I mean, what does that mean?"

"You'll see. Just remember this conversation. And Brae?" He smiled at her, pinning her with his gaze.

"Yes?"

"That little performance you just gave in there?"

Braelynn's cheeks heated in embarrassment and she closed her eyes, wishing she could disappear. She may not have known Lars for long, but she knew him well enough to predict he'd call her out on her action.

"I don't know what came over me," she began. Braelynn desperately wanted to take a breath, but like a dam bursting, the words spilled from her lips and her cheeks burned as if they were on fire. "I just saw you with her and I don't know. No, I take that back. I do know. We just had sex, and there was no fucking way I was giving up one second of the weekend I promised to that…that…oh God…I'm sorry. No, okay, I'm not really sorry. I'm not giving you up to someone else this weekend. I may never see you again after this is all over and I'm not sharing. Just no."

By the time she'd finished her rant, she heaved a breath, staring up into his amused eyes. *What the ever loving hell did I just do?* Convinced she lacked any restraint whatsoever, she buried her flaming face in her hands. Strong fingers threaded into her hair, lifting her gaze to his.

"You are a wild one, aren't you?" He laughed. She conceded a small giggle at his statement. "Brae, I really enjoyed your kiss tonight, but this thing between us..." He gave a sigh, averting his gaze, and then his eyes locked back onto hers. "Let's just enjoy it for this weekend. You're special to me but we both know the reality of the situation."

Braelynn's heart dropped with his reminder. *Friends. Lovers.* It was all they were, all they ever could be. In a matter of hours, she'd be gone forever from his life. As he continued with his warning, her senses went on alert.

"As for tonight, I'm serious. You need to keep an open mind. We're going to a special place, with very special individuals. So strap on your seatbelt, sweetheart. We're going to Altura."

~❧ *Chapter Twelve* ❧~

As they pulled up the long winding driveway in Lars' Aston Martin, Braelynn tugged nervously at the hem of her skirt. She ran her palm over the car's black leather seats, unable to conceive of how much it cost. She glanced to Lars, wondering how someone so affluent remained entirely down to earth. A living contradiction, he looked sexier than ever in his well-worn jeans. His white cotton polo with rolled-up sleeves accentuated his tanned skin. Unpretentious, he spoke directly, and she could tell from the short time they'd been together that he did most things himself. From cooking breakfast to drying her clothes, he didn't rely on staff for everyday chores. He'd even dug a hole in his yard, burying Benny with respect, holding her while she'd mourned.

He gave her a sexy smile, and quickly focused back on the road. Her thoughts turned to the barbeque. She wondered why he'd decided to bring her, knowing she'd be gone by Monday. He could have easily canceled his plans, keeping her out of sight. Despite her lack of transparency, he'd insisted on her meeting his closest friends. She'd been afraid to ask if Garrett was going to be at the party, praying she didn't have to see him. He'd texted her several times, and she'd reported briefly that she had the key, without making mention of being caught or her involvement with Lars.

She reflected on the redhead who clearly had dated Lars. Braelynn cringed at her jealousy. She told herself it hardly mattered, given that she was leaving. She had no right to claim Lars, yet at the time she'd done exactly that. While he hadn't stopped her from doing so, he'd been quick to point to the reality of the situation. They'd be lovers, but only for a weekend.

As the car slowed, Braelynn's attention was drawn to a large rectangular fountain. Streams of illuminated water shot high into the sky, their prismatic display of colors dancing to the beat of a bass pounding in the distance. She caught sight of an enormous building that appeared to be under construction. Staff dressed in reflective orange shirts directed cars down a narrow cobblestone road. Lars pulled into a large open field which gave unobstructed views of the Pacific. With the sun sinking into the horizon, the pinkish hues lit up the sky.

Braelynn steeled her nerves as they slowed to a stop. She took a deep breath, unaware of the valet opening her door.

"You're going to be okay," Lars told her.

"Are you sure this is a good idea, bringing me around your friends?" she asked, her hands clutching the edge of the seat.

"You're my friend." He reached for Braelynn, brushing his fingers along her inner wrist until his hand joined hers.

"So you've told me." Braelynn's stomach clenched at the 'f' word.

"Hey." He smiled, bringing her palm to his lips. "You're never going to forget tonight. I promise. Wait here." Lars released her, and gave a seductive wink before exiting the car.

Braelynn returned his smile, his kiss branded on her skin. Her stomach flipped as he rounded the car, shooing the attendant away. She reached to accept his hand, carefully stepping onto the uneven walkway. Despite the flurry of activity around her, she couldn't take her eyes off him. He commanded not just her attention but that of all those around him. She heard his name being called from afar but he ignored it as he pinned her with his gaze.

"Ready to have some fun?"

Yes, I'd do anything with you. The words lingered on her tongue but she'd already revealed too many feelings, ones he'd never return. Instead she smiled and nodded.

"Say yes," he whispered, his voice low and demanding.

"Yes." Braelynn gasped as he put his arm around her waist and drew her to him.

Arousal flooded between her legs as his lips took hers. His tongue swept into her mouth, stealing her breath, reminding her that he could have anything he wanted, whenever he wanted and she'd give it to him. He deepened the kiss and she moaned as his hand found her breast. Having lost touch with space and time, Braelynn gave herself to Lars.

Laughter resounded across the yard, reminding her that they weren't alone. What the hell had he done to her that she'd stop everything and make out with a man in public? Although the rational thought had merit, she still moaned in protest as he ended the kiss. Her knees weakened from emotion, she clutched at his shirt.

"I'm starting to reconsider bringing you here," he growled.

"Um…what?" Braelynn's eyes fluttered open, and she caught sight of his sly smile. He leaned into her, brushing his lips over her ear.

"Part of me wants to keep you all for myself. I want you so much."

"We could go home, get back in bed," Braelynn suggested.

"I won't make it very long, my little fox. I might take you tonight…here."

"Here?" Braelynn's heart sped at his words, the haze of their kiss clearing.

"That's right. You like to be watched?"

"I'm sorry…what?" she began. Was this a trick question? Did he really think he was going to have sex with her at a party? "I don't know if…"

"I'm so goddamned hard, I could bend you over the car and fuck you right now."

"Lars." She laughed off his proposition, yet the ache between her legs didn't lie. She couldn't be sure if he was serious but the thought of an audience made her wet.

"But good things come to those who wait. And

now…it's time for introductions." Lars kissed her cheek and took her by the hand.

Braelynn took in the sight of the enormous white tent that sat adjacent to the bluff. Intertwined branches arched into a magical entrance which greeted partygoers. Illuminated crystal garlands dangled from its ceiling, and dusk came alive with its sparkling lights. Streams of gleaming organza hung from the entryway, its lustrous fabric serving as the gatekeeper to festivities.

"Mr. Elliott." A tall gentleman dressed in a white suit pressed through the drapes. He didn't offer to shake Lars' hand but merely nodded. His focus went to Braelynn, who gave a small smile. Considering his attire, she hoped she wasn't underdressed for the event. A barbeque, he'd told her, but she suspected whatever lay beyond the curtain, it was far from a simple campfire on the beach.

"Willem," Lars acknowledged, while he brought his hand to the small of her back.

The gentle touch ignited an intimacy that she hadn't expected to experience in front of a stranger. Her gaze caught his, lingering for several seconds.

"This is Brae Rollins."

Willem ignored Braelynn, swiping his finger across the glass of a tablet. "She's not on the list, sir."

"Ah yes, I know. Last minute invite," Lars explained.

Braelynn startled as Lars traced a line down her back,

resting his palm on her bottom. Her eyes flew open in surprise, making brief eye contact with his, but he continued to speak to the staff member with a nonchalant easiness.

"He doesn't like surprises," Willem's line of vision went to the construction, "especially after the fire."

"None of us do, but this lovely lady here, is no surprise. She's my guest."

Braelynn attempted to ignore the instinct telling her something was about to go wrong. Paranoia swept through her; she strained to see through the waving fabric. Familiar laugher thundered behind the curtain, and her stomach tightened. *Garrett Emerson.* Her heart beat a staccato rhythm, anticipating his wrath.

"Brae," Lars stated, and her eyes snapped to his. "Everything okay?"

She nodded, concerned he'd sense her trepidation. Garrett would press her, wondering why she was with Lars. Braelynn took a deep breath, preparing for the inevitable. Keeping the lie burned a hole inside of her, and she wished Garrett would tell Lars everything. But they'd all be in jeopardy if any of them talked about the classified data.

"You're cold," Lars noted, rubbing her hands. "Willem, do you see what you've done, keeping us here talking? It's time to go."

"I take it you'll tell Mr. Emerson?"

"No worries," he said dismissively. Wrapping his arm around Braelynn, he brushed a kiss to her forehead. "Gets cool as soon as the sun goes down, doesn't it?"

"Yes," she whispered. Cuddling into his embrace, she

wished she could lose herself within the sexy sandalwood fragrance on his skin. Unable to stop the inevitable, she put one foot in front of the other as the soft wavy drape swept over her shoulder, and they pressed through it.

Braelynn's eyes blinked open, widening in amazement as she drank in the sight of the astonishing affair. Immediately drawn to the ceiling, she stared in wonder at the hundreds of illuminated balloons glowing a neon effervescence. An illusion of royal blue jellyfish danced within enormous standing lava lamps. A DJ gave a fist pump as the crowd danced enthusiastically to the music. Shimmering flesh sparkled underneath the prism of colors spearing through the darkness. Undulating bodies, adorned in luminescent jewelry, emanated a sensual aura.

Braelynn's pulse raced as she caught sight of a nude woman, pressed between two fully dressed men. Abandoned to the music, the feminine creature fell back into the arms of one male, while the other knelt before her. Her legs opened to him, allowing him access as he licked along the crease of her inner thigh. Braelynn sucked a breath as the man's eyes flashed to hers, giving her a devious smile. Caught staring, she should have looked away, but instead her eyes remained fixed on the man as he teased his tongue over the woman's hip. Braelynn shivered at the sight, heat blossoming between her legs.

The brush of Lars' palm on her arm caused her to startle, her eyes meeting his in wonder. "I...I...I'm sorry," she stammered, embarrassed and confused by what she'd witnessed and her reaction to it.

"This is Altura." He smiled. Cupping her cheek with his palm, he slid his thumb over her lower lip, giving a small laugh as her tongue darted over its tip. "What you see here tonight is for your eyes only. The events here," his focus perused the room, and he cocked his head, "let's call them unconventional, shall we? Our small group experiences life hard and fast. And while we do hold business events here at these facilities, this is our private time. I can trust you?"

"Yes." Her response came effortlessly, yet the lie tasted bitter on her lips.

Braelynn gasped as he took her by the waist, jerking her body to his. Her gaze briefly fell to the oblivious dancers, but quickly returned to his commanding voice which demanded her attention.

"Trust is essential, Brae." He gave her a sexy smile that brought her to her knees. "Altura is special. You can be free here...free to explore. To enjoy. To be or do whoever you want."

Her breath caught as his thumb hooked around the spaghetti strap that supported her cami. Her mind seized with the emotions. *Arousal. Fear.* Helpless to stop him, she locked her eyes on his as he tugged it down, exposing her breast, her taut tip snapping free of the elastic. As he dipped his head to her chest, she burned with desire. Aware of the strangers mingling among them, her pulse raced as his lips fell to her nipple. Delicious pain speared through her as he gently bit at the engorged flesh.

"Lars," she sighed. Her pussy ached as his fingers slid up the back of her thigh.

As he flicked his tongue over her stiff peak, her eyes followed his to his good-looking friend, Seth, who approached from the side. Her cheeks flushed, and she attempted to pull away, but he held her firmly in place.

"It's okay. You're safe here." Giving her a devious smile, he continued his task.

Releasing her inhibitions and giving Lars her trust, she relaxed into the cacophony around her. Braelynn's head lolled backward as Lars caressed her ass. Her gaze lingered on Seth, her unease melting under his heated stare. Lars' fingers teased the cleft of her ass as he made love to her breast. He released her swollen tip, and blew a teasing breath across it.

Holy hell, I could fuck him right here in the middle of this party. In front of everyone. The realization slammed into her that Lars was releasing her shackles without her ever knowing she needed to be freed. For so long she'd happily always done what good girls did. But Lars, he gave her permission to be the very bad, the naughty girl that wanted to learn, to indulge without judgement. Within the safety of his erotic world, she suspected she'd do anything and everything he asked.

"You enjoy being watched," he commented. This time it was a statement, not a question.

"God, yes," she managed, her breath ragged. Exposed, it was the first time in months she'd been so honest.

Braelynn trembled as he skimmed the pad of his thumb over her wet peak. A fine mist sprayed through the multicolored lights and she blinked. With her eyes on his, she fought the overwhelming sense of loss as Lars retreated.

He adjusted the strap onto her shoulder, tugging the stretchy fabric over her bared flesh. Lars leaned into her, his lips brushing hers. Braelynn tasted the man who she'd dreamed about for months. So sweet was his essence, she thought she'd been drugged by his kiss.

"Very good, my little fox," Lars praised, his lips on hers.

Braelynn's thoughts raced as he repeated the possessive pet name he'd given her at the pool. She'd give anything to be his. She knew it was all going to come crashing down around her eventually. But for the ticking seconds, she'd embrace the feral animal she'd become. As she drifted into the hypnotic haze, a firm voice slammed her back into reality.

"Hey, who's your friend?" Garrett asked.

"You remember Dr. Rollins," Lars said.

"Yes, yes I do," he stated flatly as his eyes landed on Braelynn's.

She cringed under his hard gaze but forced herself to stand upright. Her face heated, and she adjusted her top. *Please, for the love of all that is holy, he didn't see what I just did.*

"She's the one from the beach," Seth offered with a smile.

"I know who she is. I'm just surprised to see her here at Altura."

The cold tone in his voice softened but Braelynn didn't fall victim to the false sense of security. Underneath the niceties he simmered, and soon the questioning would begin.

"Hey, would you mind helping Chase over at the bar?" Garrett asked Lars. "He's been fucking up the latest round of signature martinis, and I've been having a hard time finding Penny."

"What's going on with the bartenders?" Lars scanned the room.

"Mattie is out on a trip and Shelley has been filling in."

"Shel's not a bartender." Lars gave a chuckle and raked his fingers through his hair.

"I know but she offered to do it. After the fire, you know how it is…hell, I'm not ready to let any new workers into Altura. Too soon," Garrett commented freely, but as if he'd said too much, his candid demeanor turned cool. "Please go give her a few pointers. I'd love to talk with your unexpected date."

"She's someone who is very important to me," Lars told him with a pointed stare. His tone of voice was serious, and Braelynn got the distinct feeling that they'd discussed her in private. She attempted to tame her paranoia. Lars hadn't called the police. She reasoned that perhaps they'd discussed her in regards to the shooting incident long before this weekend.

"Is she now?" Screaming emanated from the bar area, flames bursting into the air out of a metal shaker. "It's like she's trying to burn the damn tent down. Please, Lars. I need you to get this under control. There's not many of us here tonight but Shelley needs a hand."

Lars gave a sigh, his eyes narrowing on Garrett. "Fine. But only because I don't want anything else bad happening to Altura. But I'm telling you right now, G. Be nice to Braelynn. She's my guest."

Braelynn's heart melted as Lars brushed a kiss to her cheek and gave her a wink. "I promise I'll be back in just a few minutes. I'm going to be right over there." He pointed. "You going to be okay for a minute?"

She nodded, not wanting to draw attention to her relationship with Garrett. Her anxiety spiked as he disappeared through the smoke, making his way toward the bar. Her eyes went to Garrett's. He wasted no time addressing her, and she braced herself for the exchange.

⊷⊰ *Chapter Thirteen* ⊱⊶

"What the hell are you doing here?" Garrett asked, tugging her by the wrist.

"I…Lars, he brought me." She stumbled behind the large glass fixture, her attention momentarily drawn to the gleaming strands of neon lights that floated inside it.

"Yeah I can see that. You were supposed to get the key from him not fuck him. In and out. We gave you everything you needed. Jesus," he swore.

"Don't yell at me." Braelynn yanked her hand away, and crossed her arms over her chest. "I texted you that I have the damn key. And he knows that I need something…I didn't tell him what, but…."

"What the hell?" he began, but Braelynn continued, not giving him a chance to launch into a dissertation about how she'd fucked up her mission.

"Look Garrett. I've told you and Dean before. I had nothing to do with the missing research. You dragged me into this situation. I didn't ask for this."

"We've been over this a thousand times. There was no

one else who had access to the files except you. You didn't disclose your background when you came to work for my company. Your uncle. At this point it doesn't even matter, because you are so close to getting the data back. Then you'll be free to do whatever you want."

"Oh my God! Are you high?" Braelynn had spent months feigning respectful responses but she could no longer contain the indignant wave that crested inside her.

"What did you just say?"

"All this smoke must be messing up your brain," she spat.

"It's fog, not smoke. And you have exactly ten seconds before I drag your smart ass out of here. Talk now. Do not leave out details."

"I will never be free, Garrett." Braelynn didn't bother to use his title. Given that she was about to lose everything, formalities hardly seemed necessary. "I will never be able to live here in California again. Whoever shot me, they could come for me again. My uncle's not going to take this lying down. He's going to know exactly who took it. He's going to know it was me."

"What you are taking…it never belonged to him." He blew out a breath and scrubbed his hand over his chin. "They could have already sold the information."

"I'm telling you that there is no way they've made enough progress to have it worth anything. It won't make any sense." *What they need is in my head.* Given how they'd treated her like a criminal, she refused to divulge all her cards.

"Maybe you're right. But we still needed that key. I want the partial files too…just in case. You need to get in the office and get it all this weekend."

"Garrett, I get this situation is serious but I'm telling you that I did not fucking steal from you. This was my baby. My discovery. I would never have done that. I don't care if I don't have an alibi. Or about the stupid video you won't show me that supposedly shows I was there." Braelynn plowed her fingers through her hair. "The *only* reason I'm even helping you is because there is a small part of me that knows you're right. My uncle is an asshole of epic proportions. He'd sell his own flesh to get what he wanted. It's all about the money."

"All true, but why are you here? Lars wasn't supposed to see you."

"Well he did. And before you say anything, I told you from the very beginning that I didn't think I could do this. You and Dean…insisting that I could play super spy. Well, guess what? I suck. I almost died the other night."

"What?" Garrett's eyes widened at her statement.

Braelynn noted the empathy in his tone, and hope blossomed. Garrett had always been nice, a leader everyone admired. The ugliness of the situation had clouded her view of him, but she wondered if he would ever see the truth. She took a cleansing breath, and continued.

"Last night. I thought I could get it…it was stupid of me…"

"What did you do?"

"I parked my car and took the beach to his house. I was afraid."

"You walked on the beach alone in the dark? Along the rocks?" He shook his head, but quickly established pointed eye contact.

"I had to get to the back door. The front of the house was lit up. He could have seen me if I went up his driveway. You said go in the back."

"Goddammit, Braelynn, you could have died. Do you have a death wish?"

"No, I don't have a death wish. A sleeper wave rolled up...I didn't see it." Tears sprang through her lashes, but she resisted crying, recalling her mistake. "I'm tired. The stress. I told you I didn't do this. And working for my uncle? He's impossible. I'm worried that he follows me. They already were upset with me for leaving the party. If they saw me going to Lars' house....I couldn't put Lars in danger. I just thought if I parked up the road..." Her words fell into the din of the night as she attempted to compose her thoughts. "Garrett, please. I know when the data was first stolen, all the evidence pointed toward me. I mean, seriously, even I would have thought I'd done it, but I swear to God I had nothing to do with it. Someone else...I don't know who, but there has to be someone else who did it. And you know what? It doesn't even matter. If you'd just come to me, and asked for help, I would have helped you. I'd do anything to help my country, including going through all of this hell again."

"Tell me why you are here." His eyes narrowed in on her, but she didn't let his examination shake her.

"Lars found me at his house. He knew I was breaking in

although, hell…I couldn't do the lock. My fingers were frozen. I'd fallen in the ocean. I collapsed right there outside his house. Minor hypothermia. I'm fine." She held up both hands and glanced over to the bar. Through the sea of bodies, she caught a glimpse of him lifting a silver shaker into the air. "I know you can't possibly understand this. But Lars…I…" *I've wanted him forever.* She reconsidered her words. Garrett would never understand. "I like him…and, it's more than that, but I know," she averted her gaze, unable to look at him directly as she confessed her feelings, "I won't be able to ever see him again once I hand over the data. I'll never be free until I leave."

"How much have you told him?"

"Not much." Her eyes met his, and she forced the truth from her mouth. "He doesn't know about you, if that's what you're asking. He has no idea that you're involved. Or how I got myself into this situation."

"The data?"

"He knows there's something I'm trying to steal back from Bart-Aqua. He knows that Giordano came to see me at my house, but doesn't know he is my uncle."

"What are you talking about, he came to see you?" His voice was edged with concern.

"When I drove back to my house this morning, he and Shane…they were waiting for me."

"What happened?" Garrett's eyes softened.

"He…well, you probably can't see my bruise. It's dark in here. I tried covering it." She licked her bottom lip, recalling the pain as he'd hit her. "He killed my cat."

"Jesus Christ," Garrett growled. "I'm sorry, Braelynn. All I can tell you is that you've never been truly alone in this. I'd never put you in real danger. But you know the data…it could be given to our enemies. Our national security is at risk."

"No real danger? Are you kidding? I was shot!" she spat. "You can't protect me. The police can't protect me. No one can. And you know what? It doesn't matter. It will all be worth it once that piece of shit can't sell this information, even better when he rots in jail. But I'm right about this much; as long as he's alive and out of jail, I'll never be safe. Not here. Not on the east coast either." She sighed, resigned to her future. "I need to leave the country. I figure his reach will be limited to the States."

"We'll help you relocate," he assured her.

"Garrett, I'm here tonight because I couldn't take going in the office today. And Lars wants me here. He's, uh," she took a deep breath and gave a ragged exhale, "he's never going to forgive me."

"Lars is one of my best friends. If he trusts you enough to bring you here, that says something." Garrett gave a wave to a group of girls calling his name, but immediately refocused on Braelynn. "I'll admit. I'm starting to question your involvement in this whole thing."

"I didn't do anything wrong," she pleaded.

"Just know this. You may feel alone, but you aren't. Tomorrow, get the data and bring it to Emerson Industries." Garrett rubbed his hand over the back of his neck, and continued. "As for Lars, what happens after tomorrow? It's too soon to say."

"I'd love to fantasize about a happy ending but we both know that isn't happening." Braelynn sucked in the emotion overwhelming her ability to think. The loss of Lars and her home would crush her, yet she couldn't fathom any other outcome. "Just please…after I do this. Please let me be the one to tell him."

"We're in this together. He's going to be pissed at me too. But neither of us can tell him. Top secret information comes before friendships. It isn't even a consideration. But I've known Lars for a long time. He'd be in agreement. He'll forgive you."

"I think you underestimate his reaction." Braelynn smiled to Lars as he approached, noting that several women stopped to stare as he pressed through the crowd. The man was sex personified. A pang of jealousy was interrupted by the brush of Garrett's hand to her forearm.

"Braelynn. You've got this. And we've got your back." Garrett nodded to a group of men calling to him through the curtain. "But tomorrow, let's get this done. We'll have an exit strategy planned. Just get the data to Emerson. If for some reason you can't get to us, we'll come to you, but you have to be off your uncle's compound. That's the one place I can't go."

"Tomorrow," Braelynn repeated, nausea rising in her throat.

"Everything okay?" Lars asked, approaching from behind.

His smooth voice wrapped around Braelynn, comforting

her, and she instinctively reached for him. He embraced her small frame, brushing his hand over her head. Braelynn clutched at Lars, but quickly released her hold, afraid he'd suspect something was wrong.

"I'm fine," she answered, pressing her lips together tightly.

"You sure?" Lars pinned his attention on Garrett.

"Yes, of course. It's a beautiful party. I think maybe I just need to get some air." She coughed. "This fog...I can't breathe."

"We've got some food and blankets outside," Garrett offered, ushering them toward the exit. "It's set up for the show."

"Outside?" she asked. Confusion swept through Braelynn, and she glanced to the dance floor, noting the partygoers had cleared.

"A special treat," Lars promised, giving Garrett a broad grin.

"He's right. Go enjoy the evening."

Braelynn returned Garrett's smile, unable to tell if he was serious.

"Dr. Rollins."

"Braelynn," she corrected.

"It was nice talking with you." Garrett nodded.

"It's going to be time soon." Lars reached for Braelynn's hand. "Come, let's get some glow sticks."

"Against the wall." Garrett pointed to several bins lined along the edge of the tent. "See ya out there."

Lars ushered Braelynn away from the corner. As they

went to leave, she caught sight of the threesome she'd seen earlier on the dancefloor. Braelynn's eyes widened at their heated interaction. Bent over a white sofa, a woman was being fucked by one man while she sucked the cock of another. Braelynn's heart raced, heat flooding between her legs. As if on a seesaw, her emotions ran the gamut. From fear to anger to arousal, she didn't know which end was up, had lost her bearings.

"Enjoying the show?" Lars asked.

"I just never…I never…I'm sorry." She blushed, turning her head. "It's private. I shouldn't be looking."

"Watch them," he told her.

No, I can't do this. It's wrong. I'm so going to hell. Her inner thoughts were thwarted as strong hands wrapped around her waist, his hard cock pressing into her ass.

"Watch, Brae. Don't think. Just do it."

"It's not right," she protested, but did as he said. The woman screamed as the man slammed inside her. And while Braelynn couldn't hear their words through the music, she imagined the sound of his pelvis slapping her flesh.

"There's nothing wrong with pleasure, sweetheart. Sebastion and Ryder. They like to be watched."

"Who's the woman?"

"Sloane. She doesn't usually do open play like this."

Guttural moans from the threesome speared through the din. A fine sheen broke across Braelynn's skin, her body igniting in response.

"It's okay to be turned on. I think it's hot as fuck too. That is what's special about Altura. It's safe to explore."

"Everyone here has sex at parties?"

"No, as I said, this is merely an open place. You can have everything or nothing at all. What we have in common is our love for skating the edge. Bending the rules if you will. For some, that means scaling a rock face hundreds of feet up in the air. Others like to add a sexual element to their experiences. What they've done right here is about the safest thing they'll do all week. All three of them plan to make a trek to Everest next month."

"You do this?" she asked, accepting a long plastic tube from Lars. He broke and shook his, revealing its bright indigo glow.

"Lift your hair," he told her.

She did as he'd asked, noting he didn't answer, smiling as he placed the brightly colored coil around her neck.

"There, you're set." He winked.

Braelynn picked up a shorter segment, breaking and freeing its illumination. "Your arm, please." Taking care, she fastened it onto his wrist. "Do you do…what we just saw?"

"I heard you the first time. Let me ask you a question, little fox. Have you ever been with two men?"

Braelynn opened her mouth but Lars never gave her a chance to respond as he ushered her out of the tent. They settled onto a blanket overlooking the cliff. Their quaint picnic sanctuary was surrounded by intricately carved iron luminaries. Although it gave the illusion of privacy, rumbles of conversations drifted across the cool sea breeze, and Braelynn spied the reflection of eyes across the dimly lit lawn. Lars handed her a flute of champagne, and she reached for its stem, her fingertips sliding over the smooth glass. Although it was a cool night, there was a slippery condensation along its sides.

Braelynn sat silently, ruminating in her own thoughts. She glanced to Lars' seductive smile, and wondered how she'd ever get over him. An overwhelming sense of melancholy was tempered by the arousal she'd failed to shake after watching the threesome. Braelynn had avoided further conversation about what they'd seen inside the tent. She'd never been with two men, and wondered why Lars encouraged her to watch, pressing her to confess her own fantasies.

While she'd only been with him for a day, the intensity of the past twenty-four hours had brought them close, the intimacy between them increasing with each passing minute. However fragile their relationship, he'd promised to help her.

Guilt ran through her, and she considered telling Lars everything about her relationship with Garrett. But there was no way she could divulge top secret information. She'd told herself a million times that it didn't matter. After tomorrow, it'd be likely she'd never see him again. She reconciled that for one night, she'd be his. Tomorrow, however, the magic and her dreams would shatter, and she'd pick up the pieces in a country far away.

"Hey," he said, breaking her contemplation.

"Hey, yourself." She met his gaze, her voice leaving a trace of sadness she knew he'd detect.

"I know you're worried about...hell, there's a lot to worry about. What's happened, what's to be done, but Brae," Lars raised his glass into the air, "none of tomorrow's problems will be solved tonight. So let's focus on this moment. I want all of you."

"You have all of me," she stated without hesitation.

"How far do you want to go?"

"What's that supposed to mean?" She laughed, noting the lights of a boat anchored in the distance. Her eyes darted down into her cocktail, the golden effervescent mist teasing her lips. *Sex. Limits.* There was something about Lars; she couldn't say no, didn't want to deny herself the adventure of indulging in the forbidden.

His fingers brushed over her thigh, reaching for her hand. She went quiet, her skin burning with passion as he held it in his. The sensual gesture was that of a lover; his forefinger brushed the inside of her palm, sending tendrils of electricity through her body. A streaming firework shot high into the sky, a boom echoing over the ocean. Her gaze followed his to an enormous arch of red twinkling sparkles that lit up the heavens.

Ignoring the spectacular display, she closed her eyes, blocking everything but his touch. More intimate than a kiss, the caress of his calloused fingertips to her palm melted her heart. The energy intensified, her chest rising with every deep breath she took. Arousal flooded between her legs, and her hard tips painfully strained against the fabric.

The warmth of his lips grazed over her cheek. Blind to the night, she gingerly set her glass on the ground. Engrossed in Lars' presence, all her senses went on alert, and she took no notice as it spilled onto the grass. Her mouth parted, in anticipation of the kiss she couldn't see.

"Lars," she breathed, her voice drowned out by the cracking explosions. She swore she heard her name in return as his lips met hers.

"Brae." His kiss brushed her lower lip. "I'm going to make love to you right here."

"I…" Braelynn knew what he was asking. Like the couple in the tent, she'd be exposed. Nearby party guests could see them, watch them, hear them as they made love. Her pulse sped, the fantasy sending a spike of desire to her pussy.

She blinked, finding his eyes locked on hers. His penetrating gaze reached inside her soul, and her stomach twisted as she nervously waited for him to make a move.

"Are you ready for the rush?"

She gave a nod. "Yes."

"Yes," he repeated.

Braelynn gasped as his mouth crushed onto hers, and he shoved her onto her back, pinning her arms above her head. She shivered in relief as the pressure of his hard cock rocked up between her spread legs. Their lips frantically sucking and kissing, they melded into each other.

As he wrapped his hands around her wrists, she groaned in protest as his lips briefly left hers and moved to her neck.

He shoved up her skirt, exposing her, and she sucked a breath. With one hand he tugged at the sides of her panties, dragging the fabric down her hips. She grunted as his fingers slipped through her slick folds, a thick finger entering her tight core.

"Lars…" The heat of her body sizzled against the cool air.

"You're so fucking sexy."

"Please." Braelynn arched her back as he plunged inside her. So close to coming, she lifted her hips, meeting his penetration.

"Open your eyes," he demanded, his gaze locked on hers. "This, you, me. This is being alive."

"Lars, yes." Braelynn struggled to maintain friction to her clit, the heel of his hand applying pressure. Shivering, teetering on the precipice, she begged. "Please, I need you…this."

"Everyone can see you, Brae. Is this want you want?" His devious smile was amplified by the fire in his eyes.

Braelynn's eyes darted briefly to Seth who sat nearby on his blanket watching. *It's wrong. Dirty. No.* Yet, as his heated gaze lingered, her arousal flourished. Braelynn gasped as Lars peeled her cami upward, exposing her breasts. Seth never lost focus, and she moaned as Lars sucked a pink nipple into his mouth. Unable to reconcile her feelings, she closed her eyes, submitting to her dark desires.

"Ah," she cried out loud as he teased the sensitive strip inside her pussy. With her orgasm shattering around her, she clutched his shoulders. Her eyes flew open to Lars, who gazed at her, his devilish tongue circling her aching pink tip.

"That's it, sweetheart. Look at you. You're amazing. I know it. Seth knows it."

"Lars, I can't," she panted, unsure what she was saying. An enormous spray of purple fireworks fired into the sky. Embracing the surreal experience, she went silent, her heart pounding a rhythm as Lars tore her shirt over her head.

"Tonight is about you," he told her, his lips pressed between the hollow of her breasts.

"I want your cock now," Braelynn demanded. She could hardly believe the words she spoke, but she meant it. She'd never craved a man the way she had Lars. All the while, she knew he'd push further, harder, until she shed the conservative skin she'd worn for so many years.

"Do you now?" He gave a sexy low chuckle.

Her eyes widened as he rose to his knees above her. As he moved backward, she went to protest. "Lars, no...stay."

"I'm not going anywhere. Oh, no, no. You're coming to me."

"What?" she asked, as another loud burst splintered overhead. Her eyes went to the draping flickering lights for only a second, then his commanding voice drew her attention.

"Come to me." His demanding stare, telling her he meant business, was slightly tempered by his mischievous smile.

"I, but they'll...they'll see me." Braelynn looked to either side, noting that while some strangers watched the fireworks, many eyes were upon them. She glanced to Lars, who stroked his dick. The sight of his spectacular cock brought her focus back to the hunger that threatened to tear her apart.

"Now, Brae. Or would you like me to spank you instead?"

"What?" she asked, shocked he'd suggest punishing her publicly. Sure she'd enjoyed the occasional slap to her bottom but the serious expression on his face told her he wasn't kidding.

"It's pretty loud out here, but I think you heard me." He leaned back onto his heels. "You asked for it. Come take it."

Braelynn's courage surged as he challenged her. He'd push her, yet she'd take everything he'd give and then some. Her desires weren't as innocent as her past. Casting trepidation aside, Braelynn pushed up onto her knees. Crawling toward him like a dangerous animal, she stalked her prey.

With her peripheral vision, she noted the audience around them, her breath quickening. As she approached him on all fours, she detected eagerness in his eyes, the power shifting from her adventurer. His broad smile rewarded her efforts, and she paused to tease him.

Braelynn stretched her palms toward him, allowing her fingertips to brush his jeans. Her hair fell over her face, fanning over the ground. Sliding her hands slowly up his thighs, she flipped her mane away, revealing her face to him. Gone was his smile, the intensity in his stare devouring her as he let his cock spring free. He froze as her mouth grazed between his legs, warming the fabric. Her tongue darted upward onto the denim, and she bit through the thick material, gently teasing his balls.

"Fuck," he breathed.

She pressed her face into him, skimming her cheek against his velvety steel shaft, dipping her lips to his pelvis. Kissing along his hip, she inhaled his masculine scent, and dragged her fingernails up his thighs, finally rolling her palms over her prize. Gripping his hard erection, she wasted no time, laving her tongue over its broad head. A feast before her, she lapped at its slit, delighting in the shiver she elicited from him.

Pressing the broad crown through her lips, she glided him inside her warm mouth, taking his entire length down her throat. Withdrawing him out of her mouth slowly, Braelynn heard Lars grunt in frustration, his fingers raking into her hair. She gave a small smile of satisfaction, reveling in the salty taste of him on her tongue. Sucking and licking, she moaned as he pumped into her, fucking her mouth.

Although she'd briefly had control, the tables turned quickly, her pussy aching for his cock. His hand wound around her locks, the tight pull creating a sweet sting to her scalp.

"Open to me, sweetheart. Yeah, just like that," he said as she widened, swallowing him down to his root.

Lars yanked her skirt over her hips, allowing the cool air to blow over her heated core. His pace increased slightly, and Braelynn choked as his fingers trailed down the cleft of her ass. "Holy fuck, oh God."

Obsessed with pleasuring him, she'd only given but a

second to think about how she'd become exposed. *People are watching me.* Desperate, her hips rocked into his touch, yearning to have him buried inside her.

As he abruptly withdrew his dick from her mouth, she released a ragged breath, licking the saliva from her lips. Her head lolled forward, but she held her position, waiting as he tore off his jeans and donned a condom. She sensed him move behind her. Fingers brushed between her legs and she moaned, a firm slap to her ass focusing her attention.

"Ah, Lars. Jesus," she cried, immersed in the sensations around her.

His head breached her entrance without warning, and she screamed as he slammed into her readied pussy. Biting her lip, she braced herself as he pounded into her. Firm hands wrapped around her breasts, bringing her upward with her back against his chest.

"Open your eyes, little fox," he told her. "Here comes the grand finale."

His fingers tightened around her nipple, while his other hand delved between her legs. As he brushed over her clit, Braelynn called his name, the fantastic convulsions of her release rolling through her once again. Bared to the world, she let go as if the only thing that had ever mattered in her life was his touch. She splintered under it, the illumination of the fireworks dancing on the waves.

Falling, falling, falling down the rabbit hole, her perspective blurred. She heaved a breath as he withdrew and eased her onto her back. As rough as he'd been, he'd swiftly changed gears.

"My beautiful girl." Lars gently pressed his lips to hers.

She widened her legs as he settled between them. He rocked deep inside her heat, locking his eyes onto hers. Braelynn's emotions flared in her chest, aware that when she left San Diego, she'd be forever heartbroken. She breathed in relief as he kissed her, closing her eyes to the pain that lingered in her heart. His strong lips made love to hers, and she thought she'd been pushed off a cliff. There was no returning from this moment; no one would ever compare to Lars Elliott.

❧ *Chapter Fourteen* ❧

Braelynn cried his name, her pussy pulsating around his cock. As the explosive finale crashed around them, the flickering of sex in her eyes consumed him and the sweet moan from her lips was all he heard. She wrapped her legs around his waist, drawing him deeper, tilting her hips up into each thrust. The sting of her fingernails digging into his ass reminded him she was wild, far from being tamed.

Lars made love to Braelynn, capturing her mouth with his. Biting and sucking at her lips, he increased the pace. Giving a final glorious thrust into her quivering sheath, the crest of his orgasm slammed into him.

His eyes blinked open and her gaze burned through him, a swirl of lust in her eyes. The mist on her eyelashes gave away the emotion she tried so desperately to conceal, and it gutted him. Lars shoved away the urge to beg her to stay. Rolling onto his back he brought her with him. The warmth of her body formed to his, and his thoughts churned, as he realized what he'd done.

Lars had lost control, and it scared the fuck out of him.

He'd never pushed a lover the way he'd done Braelynn. Although she hadn't specifically said otherwise, he'd suspected she'd never had public sex. Lars had told her earlier he wanted to fuck at the party, but he'd simply wanted to test her, to see how far she'd go. Encouraging her to watch the ménage had been all he'd planned.

At Altura, he and his friends routinely pushed the boundaries life offered. Engaging in extreme sports, they pushed each other harder, faster, took calculated risks, having each other's backs at every turn. While he'd never been fully committed to any lifestyle, he'd dominated lovers, shared others. Like everything in his life, he sought to not just blur lines but break them altogether. Braelynn, however, was a temporary interloper, who he'd brought into his erotic, rush-fueled world for just one night. He'd told himself he'd let her go, that she was nothing more than a passing fancy. Yet making love to her again had done nothing to sate his hunger for the sexy doctor.

As he stared up into the dark sky, the broad universe appeared to close in on them. Her lips brushed his chest, the sound of her soft moan vibrated against his skin. Embracing her, his fingers tunneled into her hair. He told himself that it was his protective streak causing his angst. A relationship simply wasn't acceptable, not part of his plans.

"Braelynn," he said, deliberately breaking the intimate silence. She mewled in response and he gazed down into her tired eyes. "Are you hungry?"

"Hmm?" Braelynn cuddled closer.

"Would you like to get some dinner?" he asked.

"It's a barbeque?" She laughed, raising an eyebrow at him.

"Maybe we should go home." Lars paused, regretting his words.

"Home?"

"My home, not yours. But yeah." Lars reached for her cami with one hand and shook it out. Brushing it over her bared back, he set it into her hands. *Jesus, I sound like an asshole.* Logic warred with his emotions. *She's not your girlfriend. If you let her get too attached, she'll be hurt.*

Lars cursed himself for what he'd done. As it was, he was going to have a hard time shaking the growing feelings that he'd sworn he'd never develop. He couldn't commit to any woman, let alone one who wasn't part of his world. Flirting with death was a permanent hard-on, one he'd never stop trying to stroke. He was lucky to have survived some of his more dangerous stunts. Testing mortality often involved broken bones, and bruised egos weren't uncommon. Addicted to the chase, dancing with the devil to achieve the high, Lars wouldn't ever change.

He didn't know what drove him to risk his own life. He didn't care. The one thing he did know was that he wasn't going to stop for a woman. Braelynn knew nothing of his lifestyle. She'd never accept it. No sane person would.

His mind spiraled, and he grew irritated. *Stop thinking and let it go. You don't need this, Lars. Help her. Fuck her. But you can't keep her. She's not a stray dog. She's a woman who has serious fucking issues, one who doesn't rock climb or jump out of planes.*

"Lars?" she asked, breaking his rumination.

"Hey." Lars shifted away a few inches and reached for a towel, cleaning himself. He broke eye contact, adjusting his dick into his pants and zippering them.

"So, um, you want to go to your house?" she asked, smoothing down her clothing.

"Yeah, this." He glanced to the others, who'd begun to return to the tent. "I'd stay longer but this place, it's…" *My world. You don't belong.* Lars realized that he couldn't let her form friendships with people in an exclusive club she'd never join. This family was his, one she'd never be a part of. "They're going to party all night. I think maybe we'd do better getting some rest, given what we have to do tomorrow."

"Yeah, sure, okay."

Lars read the flash of disappointment in her eyes, noting she was quick to blink it away. A small smile replaced her dejection. He'd sought to create emotional distance and within minutes he'd achieved what he'd set out to do. Guilt speared through him, and he plowed his fingers into his hair, blowing out a breath. Pressing to his feet, he extended his hand to her.

"No, no. I'm fine, really." Braelynn refused his assistance.

She brushed her hair behind her ears, but the curly locks resisted, springing forth. She wrapped her arms protectively around her waist, and stepped ahead of him.

After what they'd shared, he knew he should go to her. Yearning for her touch, he refused to give into the craving.

His lips tensed, the crease of his forehead deepening. Trailing close behind her, he shoved his hands into his pockets.

Ahead in the lights, he caught sight of Garrett waving to him. He didn't want to argue, knew he'd warn him off Braelynn. Hell, maybe he deserved the shit he was about to receive.

"Willem," Lars called. Braelynn turned toward him, but the brief eye contact was severed as the good-looking servant crossed the lawn. "Can you please get my car? Take Braelynn with you?"

"Yes sir," he replied politely, yet didn't smile.

"Brae," Lars said. Her gaze snapped to his, her expression serious. It wasn't as if he didn't know why. He'd caused it, fucked up the entire night. *Don't do it. Don't go to her. It's too soon, too fast.* He continued to tell himself that it didn't matter, she'd be gone tomorrow. It would come to a bitter end. He'd feel bad for a few days then move on. It was for the best.

"Yes." She gave a terse reply, her lips pursed.

"I'm sorry. I've gotta talk to Garrett. Business," he lied. Braelynn avoided eye contact as she brushed past him and her cool demeanor stung. As he watched her disappear into the parking lot, he heard Garrett's voice.

"Lars."

"Yeah." He gave a small smile.

"You shouldn't have brought her here."

"I'm not looking for a fight." He blew out a breath. He knew Garrett was right.

"She's not ever going to be a member here."

"You're right. But I wanted to come tonight, and I wasn't going to leave her alone. It's the first time we've all gotten together here since the fire. And Braelynn," he looked to the passing car lights, "tomorrow she might not even be around. This is just a weekend thing for us, okay? No strings."

"You sure about that?" Garrett shook his head and raised an eyebrow at him.

"Yeah, I'm sure." As the words rolled off his tongue, doubt crept into the pit of his stomach.

"You seemed pretty serious out there on the lawn."

"Fuck you, G. You know we don't judge here."

"Who's judgin'? I'm just observing things. You brought her here for the first time. She doesn't know anyone and you fuck her in front of everyone?"

"Yeah, well, I recall you fucking Selby the first night you brought her here. So glass house. Just sayin'," Lars replied.

"True, but I used a little discretion."

"Hardly." Lars had been pissed the night Garrett had brought Selby to Altura. While it was true that they'd been hidden away from the party, he'd seen his friend leaning Selby over the balcony and slamming into her from behind.

"Don't tell me you're still pissed about Selby."

Lars shook his head, refusing to talk about the past. "I'm not going there today."

"Braelynn, then?" he pressed. "What is it about this chick? You can't just let go?"

"Like you let Selby go? Seriously?" Lars asked.

"She kicked you out of her hospital room. So what did you do? Follow her to the charity event? Hook up for the weekend? I don't get you."

"It's complicated, all right? She's in trouble."

"You can't save the world."

"I'm just trying to do the right thing, that's all." Lars contemplated telling Garrett everything. A best friend with connections, he could help. But he'd promised Braelynn not to tell anyone, or go to the police. If he told Garrett, it would be a matter of minutes before Dean knew. The situation was hardly black and white but they'd see it as breaking and entering. He'd be at a loss to argue. "All I can tell you is that there are extenuating circumstances, okay? You've got to just trust me on this one."

"You should stay away from her."

"Yeah, well, I told you this is just a fling. So you don't need to worry about me." *She's leaving.* The thought was like a punch to the gut. He pushed the caustic emotions to the back of his mind.

"So you're done with her?"

"Jesus, Garrett. I didn't say I was going to marry her. I fucked her, that's it. Nothing more, nothing less. You know how I get. I wanted answers, which I didn't get. She pushed me away, and I was intrigued. But like all the other women, she caved. I got what I wanted. Now it's over." He scrubbed his hand over his beard and sighed at the lie. He'd almost convinced himself but knew the deception couldn't be further from the truth. *Oh it's over all right*, he thought, but not because he wanted it to be. He'd had a taste of Braelynn and craved more. He wondered if it would ever be enough.

"Something tells me this isn't the end of the story, but fuck, Lars. If you aren't going to level with me, I can't make you. But I'm going to give you a bit of advice."

"I just told you. I couldn't stop myself from hooking up with her. And yeah, I went to the charity ball. We danced. We fucked. I brought her here, fucked her again. Probably a poor judgement call but whatever…she won't be back. I don't need the Spanish inquisition."

"You're getting it anyway, asshole."

"Please, G. Don't shower me with compliments. It's going to my head." Lars grew tired of Garrett's incessant questions about his relationship with Braelynn. Confusion as to his friend's motive swept through him. Garrett had never reacted strongly to anyone he'd dated.

"Leave her be. You had her, now be done. Move on. She works for the same company I testified against. I don't want her here again."

"So now you're telling me who I can and cannot bring to Altura?" Lars' face went impassive and he took a slow breath, restraining the anger that fired through him.

"I didn't say that…"

"I just told you. Let me repeat it slow and clear. You don't need to worry about Braelynn because after tomorrow, she's out of my life." Lars went to pass and Garrett blocked him. His eyes fell to his friend's arm and his lips tightened in a straight line. "Move out of the way, G. I've got limits and even though we're friends, you just crossed one."

"I just don't want to see you get hurt." Garrett backed away with his palms up.

"Won't happen. I'm cool." Lars brushed past him, irritated with Garrett for not trusting him. A knot formed in the pit of his stomach as he stomped away.

Pissed as fuck, Lars climbed the hill into the parking lot, remnant embers crunching underneath his feet. The distant pounding bass dwindled as he moved toward the line of cars. A halo of light morphed into two silhouettes, their laugher spilling into the night. A feminine giggle caught his attention. *Braelynn.* Seth's familiar voice followed hers.

A stab of envy pierced his chest, and Lars stopped short, stilling in the darkness. He took a deep breath, questioning not only the jealousy that stirred within but how Braelynn could enjoy another man's company so easily. He wiped his hand over his hair, disgusted at the existence of his feelings. Exhaling the negative thoughts, he coughed, deliberately drawing attention to his presence.

"Lars," he heard Braelynn whisper.

"Hey, dude. Nice tonight, yeah?" Seth asked, his reflection shifting in the path of twinkling lawn lights.

"What's going on?" Lars forced his casual tone.

"Seth," Braelynn laughed. "It's embarrassing."

"Hey, no worries. You're good to go."

"What happened? You okay?" Lars' attention went to Braelynn, whose wide eyes caught his.

"Nothing," she whispered. Her broad smile faded as her palms flattened down her skirt.

"She took a tumble," Seth explained. "Rolled down the

hill. But it's all good. I managed to snag her before she took off over the cliff."

"I was not rolling!" she insisted, a small grin forming on her lips.

"All a matter of perspective, girl. I say rolling. You say rolling." His laughter died quickly as the tension thickened between Lars and Braelynn. "Hey, you know I just remembered Chase needs some help before the games start."

"Games?" Braelynn softly repeated, not taking her eyes off of Lars.

"It's time to go," he stated.

"Lars…" she began, breaking eye contact.

"Home," he growled. Lars loathed the seeds of possession that threatened to take root.

"Yeah, okay." she agreed.

"Get in." Lars silently cursed.

The anger of the situation with Garrett was replaced with self-doubt, as he wondered how the hell he'd gotten himself in this situation. Emotion swirled like a hurricane vortex. Unable to thwart the storm, he took a deep breath. Soon, he'd help her steal whatever secret she'd refused to tell him about. Then like a feather in the wind, she'd be gone.

⋙ *Chapter Fifteen* ⋘

Tight as a spring wire, Lars leaned his forehead onto the granite tiles, letting the hot spray sluice down his hard body. He let the tension wash away as his mind raced with thoughts of the evening. They'd taken the short ride home in silence. When they'd returned, Braelynn insisted on taking a shower. Leaving her alone in the downstairs guest room, he'd locked up the house and immediately retired to his bedroom.

Lars brushed the lather through his hair, and her raw beauty flashed in his mind. His cock thickened and he stroked his palm over it, recalling how her tight pussy had pulsated around him. His little exhibitionist had blossomed in the heat of the night, trusting him to give her pleasure in front of others. Her soft moan as he'd slid into her a final time remained fixed in his mind.

Thoughts of Seth with Braelynn threaded through him, and he considered all the times they'd shared women. None of the girls had been particularly special yet, and perhaps that was why jealousy had never factored into the equation.

When he'd fucked Braelynn at Altura, Seth's interest hadn't gone unnoticed. Had it been another woman, he'd have invited him to play. But with Braelynn, her induction into his world belonged to him, and him alone.

After they'd had sex, he'd thought putting distance between them had been for the best, but knowing she was downstairs waiting for him, the only thing running through his mind was continuing what they'd started. Lars cursed in frustration and released his erection. He wasn't going to stroke off when he could be buried deep inside her again.

He switched off the water, and grabbed a towel. As he dried himself, a loud clank sounded from downstairs, and he wondered what the hell she could be doing. Although he'd brought a few women into his home, he'd never left one alone. Lars scrubbed his fingers through his wet hair, considering that he'd lost his fucking mind.

Pulling on a pair of shorts, he stopped short and sniffed. The spicy scent of Italian gravy drifted into the bedroom and his eyes widened. *Oh hell no. She's cooking.* He'd been so preoccupied, he'd forgotten about dinner.

He took off down the hallway. As he bounded down the stairs, he slowed his pace. He caught sight of a small figure huddled in front of the gas fireplace. The flickering light flashed onto the bleached brick wall. With her back leaning against the leather sofa, Braelynn sat on the area rug, holding a glass of wine, his oversized robe bunching around her wrists.

Lars glanced to his dining room table where the candlelight from the thick decorative white pillar candles danced over the classic meal she'd prepared. Pasta. Salad. Bread. A bottle of wine sat on the edge, a half-filled glass next to it. Lars brushed his hand over his chin, angry at himself that he hadn't taken better care of her.

"Hey, you didn't need to make dinner. I just needed a quick shower before I…" his words faded. As he came around the sofa, he observed the trails of tears down her cheek. "Brae."

"Lars." Her voice trembled as she stared at the blazing logs. She sucked a deep breath, her eyes darting to meet his gaze and then quickly focusing back onto the fire.

"Sweetheart." His voice softened as he knelt down to her. "What's going on?"

"I can't do this."

"Do what?" He couldn't be sure if she was referring to what they'd done at Altura or tomorrow's plans to go to Bart-Aqua.

"You, Lars."

"What about me?"

"Tonight, I…I've never done anything like that before. You pushed me to do things, things I wouldn't otherwise do."

"I'm sorry if you didn't want to make lo…" Lars stopped short, rephrasing to avoid that word. There was no love, only fucking, he reminded himself. "It was amazing."

"It's not about the sex." She shook her head, fresh tears brimming in her eyes.

"Tomorrow is going to come fast. Brae…look at me." His palm caressed her wet cheek. Her reddened eyes went to his. "You're leaving tomorrow, remember?" The words burned like battery acid on his tongue.

"Tonight… I'd never done anything like that before. We made love," she whispered.

Lars took a deep breath, forcing an impassive expression as she used the word he'd avoided. Developing feelings for a woman who was leaving was one of the stupidest things he'd ever done.

"You…you…" she stuttered.

"I what?"

"I shouldn't say it." She shook her head and glanced to the table. "Dinner's going to get cold."

"You need to say it, Brae. We may not have much time…" Lars closed his eyes, emotion creeping into his chest. His gaze met hers, and he continued, "We need honesty. Tonight you gave me your trust and then…"

"And then you backed away." Her lips tensed. She moved to push onto her feet but he reached for her arm.

"It's true. I did, but you have to see this from my perspective. Tomorrow this all ends. We had a great time, but Brae…I can't get attached."

"I just thought…"

"Just thought what? You told me you're in serious trouble. And it appears you are. This thing with us. One weekend. That's what we agreed. If you want to stop all this between us right now we will." He paused and glanced to the table. "No more making…having sex."

"I didn't say that."

"So we have tonight? Tomorrow morning, we get what

you need and you're off. I'll make the necessary arrangements and you can disappear, if that's what you want."

"I don't want to go…you don't understand."

"You're right. I don't get it at all. And you know what, unless you're willing to tell me what the hell is going on, none of this is up for discussion. So what is it going to be, Dr. Rollins?"

"I'm hungry."

"Do I have all of you for the rest of the night? Yes or no?"

Braelynn sighed and sipped her wine. Slowly turning her focus from the fire to Lars, she nodded.

"Yes?" Lars gave a small smile.

"I can't…" Her voice trembled but her eyes shined with defiance. "I don't want to give you up. But tomorrow…"

"Tomorrow," he repeated, not finishing the thought. They both knew the score. Lars pushed to his feet. "I'll bring us dinner here."

"But Lars, I made…"

"Stay," he ordered. He hated the situation, yet he craved her, sought to consume her, knowing full well they had no future.

Piling the ziti onto a plate, he grabbed a few slices of bread, a napkin and a fork. He caught the amused smile on her face as he backtracked, capturing the bottle of wine.

"How hungry are you?" he asked, coming closer. Lars rested the items on an end table, and sat back onto the floor, still easily managing the dish. He raised a playful eyebrow at her, noting how her wild hair looked even sexier than when she'd brushed it.

"Very."

"Answers for bites, Doctor." He stabbed at the pasta and held it into the air.

"You like games, don't you?"

"Not the kind that involve lies. But in general, yeah sure. Games are fun. You didn't play them as a child?"

"I was busy learning."

"Now you see, that's no fun. You need to play."

"Maybe I don't want to play."

"Maybe you do. But you know what would be even more fun…it's getting warm in here." Lars glanced to her loose robe, looking forward to untying and retying its sash in a way that best suited him.

"I can turn the fire off. I'm sorry, I didn't think to ask…I just…"

"I love the fire. Your robe, however…" He gave a broad smile. "Well, we'll get to that in a minute. Food first, then play, then food. I want the truth. And then you get this delicious food you made."

"You're evil," she said with a flirty smile.

"Why were you really upset when I came down tonight?"

Braelynn blew out a breath and shook her head. "I already told you, but if we really are doing this truth thing, it's just that Lars…part of me, I don't know. I like you. I don't want this to be just a weekend. I want more. But I can't have that."

Her confession should have scared him. If it had been

any other woman, he'd run fast and far. But he knew she was leaving anyway, both hated and appreciated that it wasn't going anywhere. Lars teased her lips with the fork, his cock stirring as she bit down onto the food. Her fingers wrapped around the fork, and she tugged it away from him.

"You know you shouldn't ever mess with a woman's food. Like ever. If you did that in my mom's kitchen, you might end up with this fork in your arm." She smiled, yet Lars suspected she wasn't kidding. Braelynn scooped up more ziti, and grinned at him. "My turn. What's the deal between you and the redhead?"

"Jealous?" he challenged.

"I am really, really hungry." She eyed the food.

"She watches my dog."

"Wrong answer. Try again." Braelynn shoved the fork into her mouth, eating with a smile.

Jesus, the woman was fiery and he loved every fucking second of it. The desire to spank her ass pink churned within him but he enjoyed the chase.

"I could eat this pasta all day, Mr. Elliott. Red. What's the deal?"

"We fuck every now and then." Lars detected the flash of hurt in her eyes that she tried so carefully to conceal. "It's nothing serious. She watches Sasha sometimes. That's all."

"No girlfriends?"

"That's two questions." He gave a sly smile as she brushed the ziti over his lips. Lars licked at the gravy, quickly capturing the treat. With his eyes locked on hers, his fingers slid over her hand. Although he resisted his own confession, the words erupted from his soul. "There's no one else in my life. You. This weekend. You're the only one I want."

The warmth of Braelynn's smile wrapped around him, and he didn't regret his revelation. Attempting to shake off the vulnerability he'd exposed, he dug the fork into the pasta once again.

"Tonight," he reached to cup her cheek, his thumb trailing down her chin, "I want to pretend like it's just us. My turn. I get two questions now."

"Hey, that's not fair."

"Yes it is. You just had two. First question," he continued, not giving her a chance to protest further. "Why didn't you play games when you were a child?"

"My parents. They were very loving, but we moved a lot. My father was a researcher. An entrepreneur. Like you in some ways. Maybe not as successful, but still, he earned his own way. I spent a lot of my childhood in a bubble. It wasn't as if I didn't have friends, but my parents…I don't know. They were what you'd expect of your stereotypical professors…learning was a game for me. The type of games you play, Lars? I've never met anyone like you. You…you're different. You enjoy taking risks. I mean, I haven't seen you do it, but you skydive a lot, and the other things, Everest…normal people don't do those things. My parents…well, I suppose their lives weren't as adventurous. I'm sorry…what was the question?"

Lars noted the sad smile on her face, sensing her parents had passed. Although the topic had brought a somber tone to the conversation, her upbringing perhaps explained why Braelynn had been so conservative. Changing the subject, he fed her the ziti and pressed her further.

"You enjoyed tonight. Watching the threesome in the club?"

"Maybe," she hedged.

Lars sipped his wine, and continued. "Seth enjoyed watching us, too. I've shared women with him. Had threesomes."

"I'm sorry, what?" Braelynn choked on her food, and blinked her eyes.

"Would you like to have Seth join us?" Lars couldn't be sure if he'd share Braelynn. Still the fantasy rumbled within him, and his cock hardened.

"I didn't notice he was watching," she responded, not directly answering the question.

"No lying, little fox." Lars reached for her robe. His fingers drifted between her breasts, and with one smooth movement he separated the fabric, exposing her skin.

"I...I...wasn't sure who saw us," she continued.

Lars brushed the garment off her shoulders, leaving her completely bared to him. She didn't make a move to cover herself. As Braelynn struggled with her answer, he brushed the back of his hand over her stiff peaks, and she sucked a breath.

"Do you fantasize about being with two men?"

"What does it matter if I do?"

"Come here," he ordered. She scooted towards him, but not fast enough for his liking. Lars snatched her ankle, and she giggled in response. Setting the bowl onto the floor, he slid her away from the sofa. Spreading her legs wide open, he guided her back onto her arms, settling her onto the floor.

"What are you doing?" She laughed

"Finishing dinner, of course." Lars smiled, scooped more pasta and leaned towards her, teasing her lips open until she bit down. He rested the fork back into the bowl, and reached for the glass of wine. Taking a sip, he drank in the sight of Braelynn, his hungry eyes roaming over her body.

"Um…I don't usually eat dinner naked."

"You don't know what you're missing."

"Really? So you're telling me I haven't lived?"

"Jump out of a plane with me. Feel the wind. That, Doctor, that exhilaration, it makes you appreciate being alive."

"Lars." She smiled, licking her lips. "I don't think that's ever going to happen. I know tonight I was, well, it was unconventional. But I don't do heights."

"You might like it. We could go rock climbing."

"What is it with you? Don't you like living? You could die."

"Sure I could, but it's a calculated risk. And sometimes…" Lars trailed his fingers over her hip, onto her inner thigh. Her chest rose in arousal, and he continued his lesson. "Take skydiving. I'm less likely to die jumping out of a plane than hang gliding. Base jumping? Far more dangerous. Rock climbing? There's far less risk of death than base jumping…well, unless you're doing Everest."

"Has anyone ever told you you're insane?" she responded.

"Many times." He laughed, giving a broad smile. "Perhaps deserved. But this isn't about being rational. It's about taking life by the balls, not the other way around. It doesn't matter if you're flat broke or are a millionaire. No, it's all about perspective."

"If you have nothing, how are you supposed to do the things you do?" she challenged.

"Ever jumped off a cliff into the churning ocean? Surfed before the break of dawn? There are plenty of people, some at Altura, who aren't even close to being rich, but they're living. They're experiencing. Savoring life. You fuck the rules and do what you want. Be happy with what you have. Be present." Lars glanced to the burgundy essence in his glass, "Take this wine. It's two hundred dollars a bottle."

"Holy shit." She choked. "I'm sorry, I just picked a red off the rack in the kitchen and opened it. I had no idea it cost so much."

"No, worries. It's not about that. You did good. It goes great with pasta. I keep the more expensive ones in the cellar anyway."

"But…"

"Brae…it's not about the cost. You're missing my point. It's not about the cost. It's about perspective." He held the wine up to the light. "I can drink it properly, smell its bouquet. Taste the notes of berries. Observe the legs. Sip it slowly, savoring the flavor. Now I'm not saying all that fancy shit isn't worth doing. But I have a beautiful woman in front of me, so it's not about the wine per se." Lars moved closer and dipped his fingers into his glass. Withdrawing them, he brought them to her lips. "We can play. Break whatever notions society has set for us." He slid his thumb over her parted mouth. Blood rushed to his cock as her tongue darted out over his fingertip. He took a deep breath and continued, his voice low and soft. "The wine, it tastes even more brilliant than ever. You've let go. And fuck if I'm not enjoying the feel of your sweet little mouth."

As he removed his hand, she licked her lips. "I can think of other things I'd like to pair with that wine."

Braelynn squealed as he slowly tilted his glass, the red liquid flowing over her breast. A stream ran down her stomach.

"Lars…" she said, stilling so as not to spill the wine onto the carpet.

"Tonight, Brae, how about we see how far we can go?" Lars never broke eye contact as his mouth lowered to the swell of her breast. Warmth radiated from her skin, and his cock stiffened as his lips brushed over her sensitive peak.

Something about the lovely doctor drove him to test her boundaries. Over a lifetime, he'd taken risks, yet with Braelynn, he played with fire. Introducing her into his erotic world sent his adrenaline soaring. *Keep her forever*, his heart told him. *She's leaving*, his mind argued. In this moment, none of it mattered. They'd enjoy each other, and he'd deal with the consequences in the morning.

His tongue darted out over her nipple, lapping the wine off her skin. Circling her areola, he licked and kissed his way down toward her belly. His mouth hovered above her hip. As he gently bit at her flesh, she cried his name.

The sound of her pleading voice turned his dick to concrete. Jesus, no woman had ever made him so fucking stiff. As his shaft rammed against the constraining fabric of his shorts, he thought he'd come. He shucked them off, and his cock sprang free. Lifting his head, he sucked a deep breath, composing himself.

She sighed, her heavy-lidded eyes gazing at him. As she brought her fingertips to her mouth, Lars thought he'd lose it. But with the careful restraint he'd honed over the years, he simply let his eyes roam over her, taking in every inch of her creamy skin.

"And so you want me to experience?" she breathed, her palm falling to her breast.

"Experiences are special. Like snowflakes, each is unique. Unforgettable. Beautiful."

"But snowflakes melt. Disappear forever."

"True, but it's the moments in time that count. We can never capture a memory. You can take a picture. A video. But that feeling inside your chest, the one you felt when your heart was pounding? Fear. Excitement."

"And what memories are we making tonight?"

"We watched fireworks. Made some of our own." His fingers brushed over her hip, teasing her skin. "We ate a meal."

"True, but it wasn't at all what I expected."

"Better than what you expected? That is the question."

"Yes." She smiled.

"Then about this wine. We shouldn't waste it." Lars brought the rim of the glass to her lips, but she laughed, recoiling slightly. Her eyes went dark with desire as he persisted, her mouth parting to accept it.

"Lars," she breathed.

"Did you enjoy Seth watching?" His palms slid toward the crease between her legs. Lars detected her trembling as his fingers trailed a line over her mound.

"Yes." Her hips shifted upward, seeking friction. Denying her control over the sensation, his fingers hovered over her skin. The games had begun, and little did she know all he'd planned.

"Do you want to fuck him?"

"No."

Her quick response held an air of truth, yet he suspected a latent desire to explore her sexuality existed. "Would you play? Just the three of us?"

"I...I don't know. I don't think I could make love to anyone else." She paused as he dragged a finger through her wet folds, rewarding her for her candid response. "But...the way you make me feel. I want to do things with you Lars...things I never thought I'd want to do."

"Things, huh? Things are good." He gave a small chuckle, pleased with her response.

"I know we haven't known each other for long. But the things we've been doing, like at Altura? It was amazing. I've wanted to experiment in the past, but I've been scared," she confessed. "I feel safe with you...to do these things."

"Do you now?" Lars positioned himself between her

legs, lying on his stomach.

"The secrets, Lars…before this is all said and done, I'll tell you what I can. If it weren't for some of this being classified…just know that I want to tell you everything. As far as being with you…I want to do everything."

"This wine. You know, it tastes much better on you than it does in this glass. Stay very still, little fox."

Lars slowly dribbled the burgundy spirit below her pelvis, delighting in her compliance. He noted how she resisted the urge to move, tensing as the cool liquid rushed between her legs. He set the glass aside, and pressed his palms to her inner thighs, his tongue flitting over her wet skin. Delaying his gratification, he savored the sweet flavor, licking and sucking until he reached her glistening pussy.

"Lars, please," Braelynn pleaded.

As he dragged his tongue through her swollen lips, he reveled in her soft moans. Her sweet delicious juices tasted of rich berries, but it was her begging that left his rigid shaft throbbing. Flicking over her swollen nub, he pressed his fingers into her tight core. She contracted around him, and he added another thick digit. Pumping into her, he smiled as her core clamped around him. Lapping at her clit, he sucked it into his mouth, continuing his relentless assault. His fingers curled up into her slick heat, tantalizing her sensitive skin.

"Lar…fuck…please," she screamed, shivering as her release rocked through her.

Lars withdrew his fingers, but still focusing on his task, he leisurely lapped at her pussy. As he milked the last sensual shudder, he lifted his gaze to meet hers. Smiling, he rose and pressed onto his feet, and Braelynn moaned in protest.

"Be right back, sweetheart. We're just getting started." Lars licked his lips, and gave his cock a firm stroke. As he strolled into his office and retrieved his special gifts, he smiled, delighting in the anticipation of his surprise.

⋘ Chapter Sixteen ⋙

Braelynn's mind raced as Lars left her shivering in the haze of her climax. After she'd made dinner, she swore she wouldn't make love to him again. Having sex in front of everyone at the party had been exhilarating. But the immediate distance he'd set between them tore her apart. After he'd pawned her off to a staff member, she'd fought the tears through her anger.

She'd made an ass of herself tripping and tumbling down the yard, but it had been a blessing in disguise. Seth had come to her rescue, lifting her mood by joking about the fireworks. While their conversation had been laced with sexual innuendo, he'd helped her to the car, careful not to cross any lines. A small touch, a gentle laugh, a seed of intimacy had been planted.

Her thoughts returned to Lars. She was addicted to him like a drug. Although she was conflicted about what had happened at Altura, he'd ignited flames that could not be extinguished. Like a cat chasing a mouse, he toyed with her, letting her go and drawing her in again, ever so slowly exposing her feelings. It crushed and aroused her at the same time. Saying goodbye would devastate her, yet she couldn't resist the game.

As she lay bared on the carpet, shuddering from the mind-blowing orgasm, she breathed deeply. *Where did he go?* She'd expected him to make love to her but he'd once again left her alone. A shuffling behind the sofa brought a smile to her face and she glanced up to see him standing above her. Like a Greek God, Lars' powerful body glistened in the light of the fire. She smiled and caught the amusement in his expression as her eyes darted to his cock and back up to him.

"I brought you a gift," he offered.

His devious grin should have been a warning, but Braelynn's body ran wild with desire, ignoring the red flag. Hell, he could have been waving a burning torch in front of her, and she'd lie waiting for his next test. She craved his touch, her heart pounding in anticipation.

"You are a brave one." Lars bent to her, concealing the item. "I've got you a toy. You see, Doctor, I hadn't planned to keep you for the weekend but luckily I have elves who happily deliver for me."

"Hmm…toys, huh. Have I been a good girl?" She laughed.

"Toys are for bad girls, too. I'd like to think you are a little of both."

"Even good girls make mistakes." She'd always followed the rules. Dotted her I's, crossed her T's. One misstep didn't make her bad. Flawed. Human. Real.

"While I'd love to spank you for flirting with Seth tonight, I'm going to let it slide. No, tonight is about us. And this." He held up a clear piece of shimmering glass, but Braelynn couldn't quite make out what it was. So pretty, it sparkled in the light. "It's for you."

"A gift? For me? You shouldn't have," she teased.

Butterflies danced in her stomach as she wondered what it was and what he had planned. It wasn't as if she hadn't enjoyed her own personal pleasure tools over the years. But she'd only visited the naughty store a few times, never venturing further than the vibrating section. Paddles and nipple clamps scared her way too much for her to even peek down that aisle.

"Time is of the essence."

"So what is it? Bigger than a breadbox?" She cocked her head, raising an eyebrow.

"You'd surely hope not, sweetheart." His sexy smile widened as he knelt before her. "You like surprises?"

"Does it matter?" she countered, suspecting that she'd accept all he had to give.

"Ah, so that's how we are playing it? I knew I liked you."

Braelynn squealed as he rushed toward her, quickly flipping her onto her stomach. She moaned as his strong fingers slid up her waist, resting on her shoulders. His low masculine voice was steeped in tranquility. With his palms on her skin, relaxation came instantly, and she struggled to listen to his words.

"My cock is so fucking hard for you, sweetheart. But sometimes we delay what we want. Practice patience, knowing all the while the experience will be even more amazing than we ever imagined."

Braelynn sighed as the warmth of his fingers trailed down her back, hovering ever so slightly above her skin. The denial of his touch sent tendrils of desire rippling through her body. By the time he reached the swell of her bottom, her pussy flooded in arousal. She buried her face in her arms, gasping as he speared a finger inside her wet core.

"Ah…yes."

"Jesus, Brae. This pussy of yours…hmm…so nice."

"Lars…" Braelynn's cheeks heated. The way Lars spoke to her both shocked and aroused her.

"And this." He dipped his thumb into her wet heat, withdrew it and probed her puckered hole.

"This pretty little ass of yours. I want to fuck you here but that's not something we can rush into. No, the best we can do…a little training is in order. Lift up, easy now."

"A little what?" She complied as he settled a cushion under her pelvis, raising her bottom nearly a foot off the floor. Her knees grazed the carpet, and the cool air brushed over her as he spread her legs further apart.

"Your pussy…I just need another taste." His shortened beard brushed over her inner thigh, his breath warm on her skin.

She sighed as the tip of his tongue darted inside her wet heat. He teased open her aching lips, pressing it inside her core. A thumb circled her anus, and she briefly tensed at the foreign sensation. As the tip of his finger dipped inside her ass, she released a sigh. Her tight little hole clamped down on his finger, and she sucked a breath as he lapped at her clit.

The rush of another orgasm edged closer as he seated his thumb deep inside her bottom. She moaned, tilting her hips back and forth, his fingers stroking her bead.

"Aw, sweetheart," he whispered into her pussy, giving it a final kiss.

"Oh God, please, no. Don't stop."

"I'm not going anywhere. Just going to make this a little easier."

As he continued to pump inside her tight hole, she startled as the cool liquid drizzled down her cleft.

"Lars, I don't know…" He withdrew his finger, and she immediately sensed the loss and protested. "No, please…I liked that."

"You like this, little fox, don't you? Would you like me to fuck you in the ass?"

"No, no, I just…"

She cried out loud as a sharp slap landed on her bottom. "No lying."

"I wasn't lying…I just…" Confusion swept through her as she tried to reconcile her dark desire. The sweet sting of his palm to her ass drove her wild with need, her juices dripping onto her thigh.

"The truth," he demanded, caressing her sore cheek.

"I can't…ugh." She buried her head into her hands, crying out as he slapped the other side. The slice of the pain caused her pussy to contract, and she swore she'd come within seconds. "Ah, shit. Yes, fuck. I don't know. I just like when you had your fingers inside me."

"That's a good girl," he praised her, brushing the hair away from her face so she could see the rounded toy he planned on using.

"Please...I can't...I need..."

"Easy now, sweetheart. I'm going to go slow."

Braelynn bit her lip as he trailed the tip of the plug over her anus. Her heart pounded at his touch. The only anal play she'd ever engaged in had been with Lars and never in her life had she put anything inside herself.

"I don't know...maybe we shouldn't." Panic rose in her voice.

"It's okay, sweetheart. I need you to breathe. It might sting a little at first but I promise it'll pass."

Braelynn sucked a breath as the slick glass slowly pressed through her tight ring of muscle. Concentrating on his voice, she lost focus as his fingers began to circle her clitoris. Pleasure and pain mixed in delicious harmony as he continued to insert it deeper.

"That's a girl. Push back on me."

"It feels...please...just...I need..." Her hands went to her breasts as she begged him for release.

"You're so fucking beautiful, Brae. I could come just watching you. There you go. It's all the way inside you."

"Oh God, Lars...I need you to fuck me now... please, I'm going to come."

"I just need you a little higher."

"What? No. I need you inside me now," she cried

"I want you to stand up for me."

"Why?" A rush of air expelled from her lungs. The sting of the plug began to subside but her orgasm grew ever closer. Her hips pumped into his fingers, her swollen nub tingling.

"I want to see you, all of you," he told her.

As he removed his hands from her pussy and gently slid them under her belly easing her upward, she cried for mercy. "Lars, I can't. I'm so close."

"Oh, I know you are. That sweet little pussy of yours is so ready for me but first I want …this…your lips."

Braelynn knelt, the plug tight inside her ass. Her body screamed for his touch, yet he was nowhere. Uncomfortable and aroused, she closed her eyes and attempted to breathe deep and slow, feeling as if she'd come undone. As she blinked them open, the heat of his body was immediate. Lars towered above her. She caught sight of his enormous erection and smiled.

"Suck it," he told her, dragging its tip along her lips. As she went to reach for him, he corrected her. "No hands. Just your mouth. Open for me….that's it."

Her heart sped at his demand. Without hesitation she dragged her tongue over his slit, tasting his salty essence. His hand fisted her hair as he pressed his cock deep into her mouth. Her eyes looked up into his, as she swallowed him down to the root. Her ass tightened around the toy, and she shivered at the sensation, craving him inside her.

She moaned, sucking and licking every inch of his hardness. Aware she was on her knees, allowing him to fuck her mouth, the control was all hers. The sting on her scalp told her she'd brought him to the edge like he did to her. As her head tilted backward, she gave a small laugh, hearing the sound of his panting above her.

"Fuck, Brae. You feel so good. I need you up here….now."

With his fist still wrapped around her thick locks, she accepted his hand and he helped her to her feet. Slowly she shuffled toward the edge of the sofa, until her legs were against its arm.

Braelynn felt his possession down to her soul as he held her tight, his mouth crushing onto hers. Rough and passionate, he kissed her. Lust morphed into love, and she grew dizzy from her churning emotions. She lost her inhibitions, the drugging sensation causing her knees to go weak. As he tore his lips from hers, she heaved a breath, unsure of what he'd do next.

"I want to watch you come again."

"What?" she asked breathlessly.

The buzz of an instrument caught her attention and she glanced down to the long thin device. She had no idea where he'd hidden it but knew he'd deliberately kept it a surprise. Its rounded tip grazed over her slippery folds, and she jumped, her hand clutching onto his shoulder for support. Her forehead lolled onto his chest as her back hole contracted around the plug.

"Look at you. You're amazing," he said, his head dipping down to capture her nipple in his mouth. His eyes flared with sensuality as he kissed her breast.

Braelynn trembled, heaving for breath as the intense vibrations rippled through her pussy. Her bottom, so full, tightened. He teased over her clitoris, bringing her to the edge until tears streamed down her face.

Never in her life had she known a man like Lars Elliott. He was a hurricane, sweeping her out to sea and slamming her back against the shore. He pushed every button, giving her no quarter, bringing her a surreal pleasure she'd never experienced.

"Please, Lars…I've got to come…I can't…" Her fingernails dug into his flesh, holding on for dear life as he hovered it over her sensitive bud. Exploding, she came hard and fast. Screaming his name, she shook in his arms. Her mouth found his shoulder, and she bit down onto his flesh, a fresh orgasm rolling though her.

"Aw fuck," he cried.

Her mouth parted, releasing him, and she gasped as he spun her around, bending her over the sofa. She fell over the side like a ragdoll, her fingertips brushing the cushions. As he slammed inside her pussy, she gave a guttural sigh, her tight channel expanding to accommodate him. With the plug lodged in her ass and his cock deep in her core, she panted, delighted with the sweet invasion.

Braelynn pressed onto her tiptoes, and flattened her palms against the cool leather, bracing herself for each deep thrust. The room smelled of sex, her breath quickening as he increased his pace. He gripped her with such force she expected he'd leave bruises on her hips. The thought of wearing his prints tattooed on her skin, thrilled her, a memory of the most spectacular sex she'd ever experienced.

Faster and harder, she knew he was close. As he twisted

the toy inside her back hole, she shuddered. The tip of his cock stroked her sheath, leaving the sensitive nerves dancing.

"Yes! Fuck, yes! I'm coming, oh God." Braelynn's head thrashed from side to side as she convulsed around him, submitting to the intense release.

Lars bent her further over the sofa, and with a final thrust, he grunted, spilling his seed deep inside her. With his glistening body bent over hers, he pressed his lips to her back, peppering her with kisses.

"Ah, Jesus Christ, Brae," she heard him say. Remaining listless in the warmth of the sexual afterglow, she didn't want it to end.

"I don't know how…"

"What?" she managed, her breath ragged.

"Shit. I didn't use protection," he cursed.

Braelynn's tired eyes flew open. She'd been using a birth control shot for several years, had even stopped getting her period, but with her recent injury and working for her uncle, she was overdue for another one.

"It's okay. I'm clean," she offered.

"So am I, but fuck…I never ever forget. Are you on something?" he asked, slowly removing himself from her.

"I, uh, I take a shot."

Lars gently slid out of her, his hands never leaving her skin as he scooped her up into his arms. She buried her face into his chest, wrapping her arms around his neck. Her heart squeezed as he tenderly carried her upstairs, laying her onto his bed. Aware that she still had the toy inside her, she moved to stand, but he insisted she stay on the bed.

"Stay here. I'll be right back. I'll take care of you," he promised, smiling down upon her.

Take care of me? She couldn't remember the last time anyone had uttered the words. So long on her own, she'd embraced her independence, yet within Lars' embrace, the temptation of wanting more lured her.

He returned in silence. Sitting on the edge, he slowly turned her, and gently tugged it out of her. As he cleaned her with a warm washcloth, she breathed in the soothing scent of him on his sheets. Within seconds, he'd slid into bed, covering them with the blankets.

Waves of emotion rolled over Braelynn as his strong arms circled her, spooning her small body into his. His lips pressed to the back of her head, and she brought his hands to her chest. Within hours, his kiss would be a final goodbye. Never again would she hear his voice. Never again would she feel his touch. A tragic ending to a story that should never have been written.

Tomorrow, she'd recover the research and return it to Emerson Industries. Braelynn replayed the plan in her head, each carefully calculated action ready to be implemented. She'd go to the airport with the few belongings she'd packed and purchase a one way ticket to the Caribbean, where she'd begin the search for a remote research position. She'd saved enough money to live for months on her own, and Garrett had promised to help her with the move. As long as she stayed far away from the States, she'd have a chance at living.

She sighed, snuggling closer to Lars. Bringing his fingers to her lips, she kissed them. She prayed whatever she was feeling was simply lust but she knew it was a lie. Whatever chemistry sizzled between them, it was real, and utterly intense. Braelynn closed her eyes, falling into a deep slumber, dreaming of a life with Lars.

⤙❦· *Chapter Seventeen* ·❧⤚

As the SUV rolled to a stop at the light, Braelynn took a deep breath, their earlier conversation playing through her mind. After she'd showered, she'd gone downstairs and found Lars fully dressed. He'd kissed the top of her head, directing her to sit and eat breakfast. Never speaking of their feelings or lovemaking the night before, they'd sat on opposite sides of the kitchen table. It was as if they'd both made the unconscious decision to put distance between them.

Although Braelynn had argued to the contrary, Lars had refused to let her go to Bart-Aqua alone. She hadn't disclosed to him specifically what she planned on retrieving, but she'd explained that it was data. They both knew that it was dangerous; her uncle was already suspicious. Killing her cat had been a warning to do as he'd ordered, yet she'd disobeyed. He was monitoring her every move, and would have known she hadn't gone to the office as he'd instructed. It was likely Shane had passed by her condo, looking for signs that she was there.

Lars had insisted they take his car, which was both newer and faster than hers. As a precaution he'd arranged for fake plates, disguising the vehicle as a rental. Since it was Sunday, the regular security team would be off duty, and those attending to the gate probably wouldn't recognize her regular car. She'd drive the vehicle, and he'd hide beneath a comforter in the large back seat. They'd thrown in a chair and tote bag, and she planned to tell the guards she was going to the beach if they questioned her.

Guilt teemed through Braelynn. She'd avoided telling Lars she was related to Armand Giordano, that the data was going back to Emerson Industries. But she couldn't risk getting him involved any further. Given that she'd be on a jet before the sun set, she told herself that he didn't need to know anything else.

"Here we go," she said, turning into the corporate facility's entryway.

"Remember what we discussed."

"I can do this. In and out. You drop me off at my house. I get in my car and I leave."

"One more time, let's hear it."

"Forty-five minutes at my desk. Move to secured research area. Someone might stop and ask me what I'm doing. Not as many people are there on the weekend, but since my un…" she stuttered, and corrected herself, "Mr. Giordano told me to be there yesterday, I don't know what will happen. Shane could be there. They'll be watching my place. Even though we left the lights on, they could find out I wasn't there."

"Stick to your story. You were too devastated about the death of your pet to think straight. You needed to be alone. You went to a bar, drank too much and spent the night in a motel in Mission Beach."

"They might not believe me."

"Have they ever seen you when you're grieving?"

"No," she lied. Her uncle had held court at her mother's wake, never missing a beat. She'd been distraught. It had been the one time in her life she'd taken a sedative. The funeral had been a blur, and considering her state of mind, the scenario of getting drunk over the loss of her cat seemed plausible. "But I'll go with it. It'll have to be good enough."

"Just don't waver. If he asks where, tell him you went to several bars. He's not going to have time to check while you're there. He'll do it later and by then you'll be long gone."

Gone. The word stabbed her heart but it was reality. There was no use lamenting the inevitable at this point. She had to get her shit together. With her life at stake, possibly Lars' too, there was no room to fuck it up. Game face on, she continued running through their plan. "If anyone else stops me to talk, it could take longer to get to the research."

"Shake 'em off. You've got to meet friends at the beach."

"Give me twenty minutes tops to get into the room. I'll need at least thirty minutes once I get there to locate the rest of the documents, take care of the files. If I leave sooner, they'll suspect something."

"An hour and forty-five minutes," he told her. "If you take longer than two hours…"

"You'll call the police?" Her heart sped.

"I'll call my friend Dean. He can get in touch with the police, help get you out of this mess. I'm going to assume that there is an issue if you are any longer than what we agreed."

"But there could be a delay. You don't need to call that soon." Panic laced her voice.

What was he going to tell them? That she was stealing data and didn't make it out on time? He didn't even know what she was stealing. In the eyes of the police, all they'd see was a researcher, one who was committing corporate espionage at a company that had already been called to a congressional hearing for fraudulent and unethical business practices. *Jesus Christ.* She sighed, wondering how the hell she'd ever gotten herself into this position.

"Two hours. If you don't come out in two hours, I'm calling Dean. And you can bet your ass that I'll be out of this car and breaking down the damn door to get you out of there."

"But nothing is going to…"

"This is not up for discussion, sweetheart. Two hours or I'm coming to get you. That asshole killed your cat. People who do shit like that are capable of anything. And don't think I forgot for a minute about the people who shot at you. Maybe you really don't know who they are, but they're tied into this. Bad people do bad things. And right now, the two of us are about to do something that I've already told you," he paused and blew out a breath, "it's not too smart. I don't even know what the hell you're taking. I may be a fucking idiot but part of me wants to trust you. I'm trusting that whatever this is, it really belongs to you, and is a matter of national security."

Braelynn went silent, and told herself she was doing the right thing. She'd already told him too much, acknowledging the existence of the stolen research. She couldn't divulge the classified information and tell him the truth, tell him what it was, what it could be used for or who she was giving it to. He'd have no choice but to trust her.

"I can see those wheels turning, Brae. Just stop. I know you're not telling me everything but my gut tells me you've gotten caught up in something you can't control. I know behind all that cloak and dagger shit, there's some serious, life-threatening things that go on, things regular folks don't know about. I'm doing this based on my intuition and hoping like hell I'm right."

"We're coming up." She slowed the car as they approached, and her heart caught at the sight of the large modern building in the distance. "Lars, I'll be forever grateful for what you've done for me. No matter what happens today, I want you to remember that."

"You gonna be okay?" he asked.

"I just want you to know that everything, this weekend, it meant…" Braelynn went silent, realizing that if she let her emotions take over she'd lose her shit. *Concentrate*, she reprimanded herself. "I, uh, I just want you to know if I could have told you everything I would. And you're right. There are some very bad men inside that building."

"Two hours."

"Two hours," she repeated.

"Here we go. You've got this."

Braelynn's heart pounded against her ribs as she pulled up to the guard. She lowered the window and gave him a closed smile, friendly but professional.

"Dr. Rollins," he said, inspecting her ID. Typing at the computer, he looked to her car and back to the screen. "It says here you drive a Prius. That big ole truck there doesn't exactly look fuel efficient to me. What's that…hmm…an Expedition?"

"Um…yeah. I had car problems. My battery was dead. With the convention in town, this gas guzzler was the only thing I could rent at an affordable price." The lie made no sense but as she looked in the back seat, her stomach flipped, aware she had bigger problems.

"Going on a trip?" he asked, peeking around her.

"Just headed up the coast to Malibu to see a friend." She glanced to the time on her dashboard and back up to him, her facial expression stern. "I'm actually running short on time. Gotta get in and out of here if I'm going to get any serious beach time. I've got a volleyball match at three," she added.

"It says here that you were expected yesterday," he commented.

"I'm expected almost every day. I'm a researcher. That's why I have this nifty doctor label on my badge," she quipped with annoyance and tapped her fingers on the steering wheel. She looked to the parking lot and back to the guard, softening her voice. "Look, I'm sorry for being short with you. Just between us, Giordano has been running the lot of us into the ground. Oh, I know he wants us here on Saturdays, squeezing blood out of his minions, but something's gotta give. I've just about had enough of this seven day a week job. Just because I've got those letters in front of my name, it doesn't do me any favors. You and I are both here working our asses off on a Sunday, right?"

"You know it. This isn't even my weekend to work, but I got no choice." He looked to the building and back to Braelynn, giving her a grin. "You have a nice day, Doc."

Braelynn sighed in relief as he waved her on, leaving her windows down so that Lars had fresh air.

"Nice job," she heard him say but resisted looking back, careful not to have anyone notice he was in the car.

"Thanks," she whispered.

"This car gets pretty good mileage, by the way."

"Sure it does."

"And it's not an Expedition."

"Still not a Prius."

"It's a Suburban and I can fit a lot of shit in it when I go camping."

"Okay." She laughed.

"What?"

"Not exactly good for the environment."

"Hey, I use solar panels for electricity. It's not like I drive this baby every day of the week. All good things in moderation."

Braelynn turned off the car but left the keys in the ignition. "It's showtime."

"Two hours, Brae. Time?"

"Ten seventeen."

"You've got till twelve seventeen. Check your watch."

Braelynn glanced down to the Cartier watch he'd given her in the kitchen. At first she'd refused to accept the insanely expensive gift but he'd insisted she'd need it to keep track of time. Employees weren't allowed to bring cellphones, tablets, or any other computer devices into the building. She blew out a deep breath, carefully setting the alarm on the intricate moon phase timepiece.

"I'm on," she said, opening the car door.

"I'm going to be right here, Brae. Remember that while you're in there. Two hours."

"I've got this," she breathed, afraid to look at him. As the door shut, she shoved her emotions as deep inside as she could manage. *Fear. Love. Grief.* She hated that she was falling for him, yet she'd lost grip of the situation. The only thing she could do was live with the consequences.

Wearing jeans, a white t-shirt and sneakers, she'd dressed casually, hoping that others would get the impression she hadn't planned on staying in the office long. By the time she reached the front door, her mind had gone on autopilot. There were no choices, only tasks to be performed. Any mistakes could result in her death, she knew. If her uncle caught her stealing, he'd gladly hand her over to his friends to let them finish the job they'd set out to do several months ago. There would be no limit to the punishment he'd inflict on her.

Determined, she adjusted her sunglasses onto her head,

and scanned her security card onto the reader. The door beeped, and she yanked it open. The sterile scent of the weekend's floor cleaning burned her nostrils as she entered. With confidence, she approached the guard who held out his hands, reading her identification.

"Your bag, ma'am?"

"Of course," she said, willing her hands to stop shaking as she handed it to him. Braelynn didn't recognize his face but noted that he followed protocol as if he worked full time.

"No cell phones? Laptops? Recording devices?"

"No sir." She reached for the sunglasses and handed them to him. "Oh sorry...forgot."

He took them from her and set them aside on the table. "Tablets? Thumb drives?" he continued, searching every last pocket. "How long are you here for?"

"Just a few hours," she responded, positive he wouldn't find anything in her satchel. She'd packed only empty folders and a notepad, as well as a banana and a bottle of water, her typical morning snack.

"Whatcha doing here on the weekend?"

"Workin'." Braelynn's eyes darted to his gun. "Just catching up is all."

"Go on through," he instructed, nodding to the metal detector.

Braelynn strode through it, like she'd done every work day for the past nine months. But this time, every hair on her arms stood up as she did so. Relief flooded her as the alarm remained silent.

"Okay, then. Looks good." As he went to return her bag, he hesitated. Braelynn remained calm, summoning courage. "You might want to be careful. The floors are wet all the way up. They waxed em' good this time. Almost slipped and broke my neck earlier today."

"Yeah, thanks. I know, right? They need to be a little more careful." She gave him a warm smile and accepted her belongings.

Slinging it over her shoulder, she forced an impassive expression, and quickly made her way over to a bank of high-speed elevators that shot directly to the twentieth floor. The office building itself was located on the outskirts of San Diego city proper, and she often wondered who her uncle had had to pay off in order to build a tall building in the midst of a suburban area.

Braelynn entered the elevator, brushing her security card to the sensor. As the doors closed, she desperately yearned to collapse against the wall, but out of her peripheral vision she spied the small circular camera in the far corner. Not an inch of the building's interior went unsupervised; all areas were recorded. She suspected even the bathrooms were monitored, since key cards were required for their use. Although she hadn't seen it with her own eyes, she was aware that her uncle ran a central security office. The security team regularly roamed the hallways, wearing earpieces and firearms on their hips.

A ding sounded and the doors opened to the stark white interior of the hallway, its blinding bright lights causing her to squint. Composing herself, she looked in both directions before proceeding to her office. On a routine work day, the hallway was filled with the chatter of lab assistants and interns, but today, save for the soft squeak of her shoes, silence echoed throughout the empty space.

As she reached her office, she stilled, listening for errant noise. While she didn't hear voices, the distinct sound of shuffling footsteps alerted her that she wasn't alone. She quickly tapped her card to the reader and entered her office, the motion detection lights instantly illuminating its interior. Braelynn went straight to her desk, sat down and booted up her computer. *Just another day at work*, she told herself silently. *I can do this. I can do this.* She reached into her bag, retrieved her bottle of water, sipped it, and set it aside.

Braelynn glanced up to the fish-eye security camera located in the ceiling, and proceeded to work, all the while knowing she was being watched. She'd run through the scenario a million times in her mind. Retrieve the research. Destroy the remaining files following the instructions Garrett had given her. He'd promised that the sophisticated technology he'd given her would ensure that Bart-Aqua would have no way of recovering the files. In reality, she doubted her uncle or Shane had thought that far ahead. While they invested heavily in the manpower and physical resources, they slipped when it came to ensuring computer security. She was aware of at least one breach in the past month that had occurred in acquisitions, exposing data to customers who shouldn't have had access.

Braelynn tapped on her keyboard, opening a few emails,

and quickly responded. She opened the report her uncle had asked her to review. It was being sent to a group of investors on Monday, and needed her attention. She glanced to her watch, noting that nearly thirty minutes had passed since she left the car. *Ninety minutes. Tick tock. Tick tock.* She returned her attention to her screen. Pretending that she was reading, she stared at the words, yet the only thing that ran through her mind was the next steps. Ten minutes passed and she stretched her arms above her head.

With eyes on her every movement, she casually picked up the water bottle and stood. She glanced at the shriveled Boston fern that hung from the ceiling and shook her head, feigning concern. Reaching onto her tiptoes, she tilted its basket, sliding her fingers into its dry dirt. Braelynn dribbled water into the plant, searching for her hidden prize. Within seconds she located the tiny coin. The size of a dime, it had remained buried yet near the surface. Edging it upward, she carefully lifted it out until it dropped into her palm. As she closed her hand around it, she gave a fake cough, fisting it tightly.

She reached for a tissue and blew her nose, using the paper to dislodge any dirt around the disc's surface. Bunching the tissue up into a wad, she threw it into the trashcan, keeping the coin concealed between her fingers. She sat back down at her desk, focusing on the computer. Sliding the small object into her jean pocket, she slowly exhaled, her heart pounding in her chest.

As she went to close the document, she startled as a knock sounded on her door. *Shane.* Braelynn calmly lifted her eyes to meet his, unable to conceal her contempt for the man who stood by and did nothing while her uncle killed her pet. When she'd first come to work at Bart-Aqua, she'd mistakenly thought he possessed a soul. With his striking good looks and amber eyes, the women in the office fought over him. Tall and muscular, he'd initially been like a dark angel. She'd observed him performing small acts of kindness on occasion. But Braelynn's initial instincts had been proved wrong.

When it came to Armand Giordano, there was no grey area. Watching Shane kiss her uncle's ass made her ill. Under no circumstances would Shane go against him. Leaving bruises on her arm had dispelled any notions that he could actually be a decent human being.

"You were supposed to be in here yesterday," Shane stated.

"You killed my cat," Braelynn replied with an icy tone. She supposed she could have pretended to care otherwise, but Shane knew her too well. It would have been out of character to respond any other way, and doing so would have raised his suspicion.

"I didn't do it." He took a step forward.

A sliver of confusion stabbed through her as she detected a hint of regret in his eyes. But even monsters could disguise themselves behind their beauty. *Shane is a monster. A predator.*

"You were there."

"I was, but I didn't do it. Braelynn, I…" Shane appeared to soften but a stern expression swiftly replaced his concern.

"You should have learned a lesson. Your uncle wanted you here."

"Fuck you. Seriously, Shane. Just get the hell out of my office. I have work to do. I don't need to explain myself to you." Braelynn trembled with anger. Tempted to spring up out of her chair and slap him, she gripped the edge of her desk.

"That's where you're wrong, Dr. Rollins. I work for your uncle. He wanted you here yesterday. We went back to your place and you weren't there. So now," he leaned toward her, flattening his palms on her desk, "I want to know exactly what happened and where the hell you've been."

Braelynn sucked a deep breath and closed her eyes briefly, then blinked to meet his hard stare. She generally wasn't a violent person, but after they killed her cat, she wanted to inflict the kind of pain on them that they'd done to her. She glanced to her long silver letter opener and slid her fingers over it, gripping its handle.

"You…you are the biggest asshole I have ever met," she began, lifting the sharp knife an inch off the surface of her desk. She saw his eyes dart to her hand but he didn't move to reach for her. Her voice trembled as she spoke in a slow deliberate manner. "After you killed Benny," she paused, reaching for a piece of mail and inserting the tip into its crease, "you may not understand this since you and my uncle seem to be devoid of any emotion, but I was devastated. Like any normal person, who had a pet die, I could hardly get up off the floor let alone go into work. So I uber'd my ass down to Mission Beach and got fucked up.

Spent the night down there. And before you ask, I don't know his name. Don't particularly care either."

The envelope tore open as the knife ripped through it. Braelynn hadn't intended to embellish her story, but she knew he liked her. A flicker of pain registered in his eyes, and she secretly delighted, knowing he'd never have what he wanted.

"You should have texted. We couldn't reach you."

"Yeah, well. The next time you kill someone's cat, just remember that you aren't just killing their pet. You killed a tiny part of me. And no, I am not just going to get over it." Braelynn shook out the letter, giving it a quick glance before inserting it into the shredder. Her eyes flashed to his and she continued speaking to him, this time with a nonchalant lilt in her voice. "My uncle wants me to work. I just looked at the Mead report, and am getting ready to approve it. But I have some research I need to get to before I leave this hellhole. Is there anything else I can help you with? I'd like to get what I need to get done so I can enjoy what is left of my weekend."

"You need to be careful," he warned, standing tall, his arms at his sides. "Your uncle is a powerful man."

Braelynn stared through him to the clock on the wall, her eyes noting the time. She was five minutes over schedule. *I'm going to be late. Get out now, Shane.* She impatiently tapped her heels, waiting on him to leave.

"I'm not kidding, Braelynn. You need to watch your step. You understand me? The next time he tells you to get in the office," he shook his head and turned to leave, "you get in the office. Believe it or not, I don't want anything happening to you."

Braelynn watched in silence as he left. She resisted the urge to bang her fists onto her desk, but instead sucked a breath before quietly releasing it. Standing, she looked around her office, knowing it was the last time she'd ever be here. Any knick-knacks or pictures would remain. If she had her way, her uncle was going down, and everything in his Godforsaken building would eventually be destroyed as well. She stood, leaving all her belongings, and set off to collect her research.

She strode into the hallway as she would have any other day. An inconspicuous glance over her shoulder was the only hint she provided as to her intention. Braelynn's adrenaline surged as she approached the secured room, noting that her uncle's mistress, Jeannette, stood flipping through a manila folder outside the secured room. The icy bitch had a heart as dark as coal. A match made in hell, she and her uncle were the perfect couple. He'd killed her cat as punishment but she imagined that Jeannette strangled puppies for fun.

"Dr. Rollins," she said, not looking up from her work.

"Good morning." Determined, Braelynn hid her emotions.

"Your uncle was expecting you yesterday." She raised her lids, giving Braelynn a cold stare.

"So I hear." Braelynn balled her fists and dug her fingernails into her palms.

"Did you review the Mead report?" Jeanette tapped the

pen against her chin, delight flickering in her eyes.

"Yes. I just have to check on something before I give approval." Braelynn's entire body went tense, but she forced herself to release the breath she'd been holding and reached for the doorknob. *Get in, get out. You're running out of time.*

"We need it today. It has to go to the client tomorrow."

"I'll have it to you within the hour. Like I said, I've got to check on something."

"It would be a shame if something happened to you…if you ended up having another accident like you did a few months ago," she added, turning to leave.

"Excuse me?" Braelynn's eyes widened at the veiled threat. Her thoughts spun out of control. *Did Jeanette have something to do with my attack?* Braelynn fought her rage, attempting to focus on her mission but shock washed across her face. "What did you say?"

"I think you heard me quite clearly, Dr. Rollins. Just remember, you've only been working here for a very short time. Loyal employees remain. The others? Well, you do know the expression, 'heads roll'?" Jeanette's expression remained flat, her voice as calm as if she was ordering a sandwich. "The weather here in California is lovely, but the sea? Such a dangerous place, you know. The cliffs, the currents…people go missing all the time."

"I'm well aware of what happens on the beach," Braelynn spat. She gripped the metal knob for dear life, knowing if she let go, she'd lose it and knock Jeanette to the ground. "You'll have the report in an hour. Give my dear uncle my best."

Braelynn turned her attention to the vascular biometric device on the wall. As the yellow light flashed, she placed her finger onto the screen, counting the seconds as it scanned her vein pattern. A click sounded and she opened the door, relieved as it shut behind her.

She scanned the area, noting the seven security cameras in various locations throughout the room. Making a beeline for the large central file unit, she held her security card to the sensor and waited for the mechanical door to unlock and rise. While thousands of files were kept inside, she knew the exact location of the folder she sought. Flipping through the last shelf on the right, she quickly slipped the half inch sleeve out of the cabinet. Following protocol, she scanned the barcode on its exterior, recording its departure, and waited for the shelving unit to relock.

Braelynn glanced at her watch, noting the time. Eleven fifty-seven. In exactly twenty minutes, Lars would call the police. A fine sheen broke out on her forehead as she sat at the desk. She fingered the folder, aware that seconds after she left, she'd be at risk. Laying it onto the desk, she spied its embedded security chip that tripped the alarm.

She set her fingers to the keyboard, typing in her password and ID, and breathed a sigh of relief as she entered the system without an issue. It had only been the third time she'd accessed the file. The first time that she made an attempt, she merely verified the existence of the stolen research and reported it to Garrett. The next time, she'd utilized first generation technology he'd given her, but it had failed, only copying partial files. The second generation single layer cell drive he'd recently provided, was as thin as paper. Garrett had guaranteed her that it would work.

The lab computers deliberately lacked USB or other ports, so that files could not be imported or exported. Yet the specialized chip was designed with state-of-the-art technology that gave it the capability to secure a connection to any device within five feet, copying files without detection. Special coding within the device erased any evidence that she'd accessed the files. Emerson Industries held the patent on the top secret technology, and its existence had not been disclosed to the general public.

Braelynn clicked on the Mead files, pretending to scroll through them. Sliding her hand into her jeans pocket, she dug her nail into the coin's edge, and depressed the mechanism that opened it. When she'd first received it from Garrett, she'd practiced opening it a hundred times in the privacy of her home. It had taken her several attempts before she was able to do it without looking. As it clicked, and she fingered the freed drive, her eyes flared with determination.

Braelynn blew out a breath, and switched screens. Continuing her task, she tapped the tiny button, activating the device, and prayed it worked. Leaning closer to the desk, she hoped to block the camera's view of her clandestine activity. Her heart caught as the display flickered, finally retrieving the list she needed. Clicking on HWB614, she counted thirty files. Braelynn set her cursor at number one and double clicked. As each file copied, it lit up in succession. Ten seconds passed, and it moved onto the next one. Running through the math, she realized she needed approximately five minutes, then the elimination program would initiate, scrubbing the server and any virtual locations of the data. At five after twelve, she'd run out of time, and if Jeannette returned, she'd be caught in the act.

Hurry up, hurry up, she repeated silently, still attempting to appear as if she was reading the report. Nonchalantly, she picked up the folder and began to loosen the pages. Surprisingly, they easily separated from their binding, but as she did so, one fell onto the floor. As she bent to retrieve it, she caught sight of Shane passing by through the door window. Quickly snatching the sheet, she glanced at the list of names of people who appeared to be working with foreign investors. Projects. Dollar amounts. Names. *What the hell is this?* She glanced to the screen, remembering the download, noting the files had begun disappearing into oblivion. Ten remained. Five. Three. Two. The black display teased her, and she clicked the screen, attempting to find HWB614.

Braelynn gave a ragged breath at her small victory. Emotion bubbled inside her chest but she shoved it away, maintaining her focus. She glanced to the door. Seeing no one, she closed out her session. Her life was at stake, and she was still inside the walls of Bart-Aqua, a prisoner of her circumstances, but freedom beckoned.

With the cameras recording, she'd have to perform a sleight of hand: a deliberate accident. She loosed her fingers, the entire folder slipping between her legs. As it fell to the ground, the dislodged contents spilled out. She bent over, her head barely missing the edge of the desk. Reaching for the documents, she tugged the remaining leaflets from the sleeve, and shifted them underneath it. As she sat up, she folded the papers once over. Keeping the folder close to her chest, she slipped the documents under her shirt, giving a firm tuck into her pants.

Three minutes, and Lars will call the police. She quickly stood, using her key card to open the file cabinet. Haphazardly shoving the emptied folder into its slot, she didn't wait for it to shut, and headed toward the door. As she wrapped her fingers around the knob, she checked the hallway, making sure no one was watching before heading toward the fire exit.

Braelynn had ruled out taking the elevator, suspecting that security could suspend it, trapping her. She pushed through the doors to the stairway, aware that eyes in the sky tracked her every move. With the chip in her pocket, she began her descent. She traveled quickly but not too fast, attempting to maintain typical behavior. It wasn't unheard of for employees to take the stairs. Exercise was encouraged and practically everyone who worked for her uncle was in good shape. She imagined he cherry picked the healthiest and youngest applicants, discriminating but ensuring lower insurance costs.

By the time Braelynn reached the tenth floor, she had begun to increase her pace. Holding onto the rail, she loped down the steps. Fifth floor. Fourth. Third. Her pulse raced, adrenaline surging through her veins. Soon she was running, noting she was out of time. *Twelve seventeen.* Her spirits dropped. So close, but not good enough. The police would come for her. There was no explaining her actions. As her feet hit the landing, alarms sounded, and she burst through the exit door, sprinting through the lobby.

Braelynn flew by the guard, whose back was turned. Her lungs burned, but running out of sheer terror, she pressed onward. As she slammed through the front entrance doors, shots rang out, whizzing past her head. Sucking air, she didn't look back as she tore down the path to the parking lot. She spied the black SUV fifty feet away. Lars shouted to her but she couldn't hear what he was saying. Bullets sprayed into the air, and she covered her ears. The trauma of her terrifying ordeal on the beach flooded her mind. Anger and determination set in and she began to run even harder, her thighs searing.

She ducked as bullets ricocheted off a steel lamp post. The passenger door flew open, and she dove into the car, grasping at Lars' waist. The car jolted forward, and the door flapped open. She leaned out, reaching for the handle. Her fingers slipped and she cried out in frustration.

"Leave it!" Lars yelled as they barreled toward the gate. The guard stepped in direct line of being hit, firing off shots at the front of the car.

"No, I've got it." Braelynn held tight to the seat and lunged forward. With a grunt, she clutched the handle and yanked inward, slamming it shut. Lars and Braelynn slid to the right as he swerved to avoid the security guard, rolling the SUV up over the concrete barrier and onto the grass.

"You okay?" Lars wrestled the car under control and drove it onto the main highway.

"They won't come for us out here." Braelynn stared out the windshield, stunned by their escape.

"No, they'll do it far away from their nice little corporate center."

"He's going to kill me." She shook her head.

"He's going to jail."

"We have to get this data to…" *Don't say it. Leave him be*, her conscience warned.

"To who? Jesus Christ, I wish you'd fucking trust me." He banged the heel of his hand on the steering wheel.

Braelynn shook as he yelled at her. She deserved it, she knew. *Maybe it's better he's angry. I'm leaving.* As soon as they returned to his house, she'd collect her things, and drive to Emerson Industries. Lars had told her he'd help her leave San Diego but they hadn't discussed the specifics. She couldn't bear the thought of long goodbyes at the airport. In her mind, the plan was set; turn over the data to Garrett, and drive straight to the airport.

"Brae," she heard him say, breaking her contemplation.

"You know I can't talk about it." She reached up into her shirt, revealing the papers. Tugging them from her clothes, she shuffled them into a neat pile and laid them on her lap. She stabbed her hand into her pocket and fished out the tiny chip. "I have all the files. The program worked. Everything's deleted. And they can't claim to have had something stolen that never belonged to them to begin with."

"But the question remains…who gave it to them? If they stole it once, they could take it again."

"True, but they don't have me." Braelynn wasn't sure what Garrett Emerson would do with the information. Although she'd theorized the practical implications of her research, she couldn't be certain others would draw the same conclusions. At least at Emerson Industries, she could be assured that if it got stolen again, she would not be there. *I can't save the world.* In truth, she would have given her life for it, almost had, but losing Lars would be penance for her mistakes. She'd never be the same.

"You need to tell me where it's going."

"You know I can't. I'm sorry, Lars." She buried her face in her palms. If she made eye contact, she'd burst into tears. He and Garrett were good friends. She didn't need him to fight her battles. And she had no intention of causing a rift between them. "You don't need this trouble. You don't need me. You've got yourself a nice life. Great dog. Beautiful home. And you've worked hard and deserve it. I appreciate everything you've done for me but you have an amazing future in front of you and don't need to worry about me."

"Really. That is your answer?" He blew out a breath and shook his head.

"Lars, you know I can't…"

"No," he interrupted, anger in his voice. "It's not that you *can't*. No, Dr. Rollins, you *won't* tell me. Can't and won't are two entirely different things. Now you can pull this clearance shit with me all you want but somewhere along the line, despite everything between us, I earned a little trust. I was on that beach getting shot at that day. But

I still respected this bullshit clearance excuse. I get it. I work for the government. But guess what? Today I got shot at again. So fuck clearances. No, I deserve to know what the hell is going on. But I guess if you won't tell me, if you really plan on getting in your car when we get back...on leaving...hey, I wish you the best of luck. I'm getting off this fucked up carnival ride. I thought maybe you and I..."

"You thought what?" she asked, trembling.

"Nothing. You and I nothing. It was a memorable weekend. Nothing more. Nothing less." He let out a loud exhale, and tapped at his cell screen.

His words speared through her heart. *Nothing.* She was nothing to him. Even if he'd said it out of anger, perhaps there was truth in his words. His disdain was welcome, making it all the more easy for her to get in her car and roll away.

"Fuck, Seth. Pick up, man. Where the fuck are you?" Lars slammed his phone onto the seat and turned into his driveway.

As they approached the house, Braelynn caught sight of a man running across the side yard. By the time they pulled into the carport, he'd disappeared down to the beach. The front door, wide open, swung in the wind. Bright red streaks were smeared across its white surface.

"Stay here," Lars ordered.

Without another word, he tore out of the car and into the house. Braelynn opened her door and called out to Sasha, who romped toward her. She fell to her knees, wrapping her arms into the dog's warm fur. She craned her head, stretching to see a black sedan parked along the left side of the house. Her heart sped as Sasha growled. The crackling of footsteps along the dry stone landscaping alerted her to his presence. As she turned, she flinched as the blow landed across her jaw. A sharp pain to her skull registered seconds after he'd hit her, and as she lay up looking at him, her world blurred.

"Lars," she breathed. As her world went dark, she pictured herself in his loving arms, and swore if she survived, she'd never leave him.

Chapter Eighteen

"What the hell happened? His home had been torn apart, and shattered glass scattered across the floor. Lars found Seth inside the kitchen, blood sprayed onto the wall. "Are you okay?"

"No worries, dude." Seth gave him a broad smile and held out his arms. He held a cast iron pan in one hand and a knife in the other. "I'm the kitchen ninja."

"Yeah, okay." Lars shook his head, relieved Seth wasn't hurt. He was one of the few people who had the code to his house. Lars knew that although his friend joked, he could have been killed. "Is there anyone else in here?"

"I don't think so. I was just stopping by to see if you wanted to go to the beach. Sasha girl…she was barking up a storm. Thought I'd let her out before I went, so I took her out back. You know how I do. While she was doin' her business, I got caught up checkin' my email. Next thing I know she's growlin', and I knew there was no way in hell she'd be actin' up like that for you. Then I hear someone in the house, and this guy, dressed all 'men-in-black', comes out of your office. He came right at me with his gun. I was going to use the knife but you've got those nice expensive pans hanging right there. I'm fast, bro. Smacked him hard." He plowed his fingers through his hair. "Yeah, pretty sure I broke his nose. I heard that sweet li'l pop. Anyway, he ran out the back door. I heard you pull up and I was just coming out."

"Jesus Christ."

"Yeah, sorry about the mess. Hey, uh, where's Braelynn?"

"Fuck!" Lars cursed, realizing she was alone in the car. He didn't have time to get his Glock but he'd send Seth. "Go grab my gun. Second desk drawer. It's unlocked."

As he tore through the living room and thrust through the front door, Braelynn released a piercing scream. Rage surged through Lars at the sight of the intruder hovering over her. He gripped her attacker by the collar, and shoved him onto the ground. The stranger stumbled upward and lunged for Lars, but he'd already swung his fist, landing it square across the man's jaw. Blood sprayed into the air, and Lars hit him again and again, pummeling his face.

"Lars," Seth yelled. "Yo! Stop! Lars! You're gonna kill him."

"Fucking right I am," he huffed, throwing him onto the driveway. The crumpled body went still, and Lars rushed to Braelynn.

"Jesus Christ, man. You beat the shit out of this guy." Seth poked him with his foot and bent to check his pulse. "Still alive."

"Brae. Sweetheart. Come on now." He scooped her body into his arms and his stomach dropped as soon as he felt the lump on her head. Gently turning her head to face him, he observed the handprint across her cheek. A trickle of blood spilled onto her chin. "Goddammit."

"Is she okay?" Seth asked, rummaging through the intruder's pockets.

"Brae, come on, baby. Say something," Lars urged.

Braelynn stirred. She gave a moan and brought a hand to the back of her head. "What the fuck?"

"You're going to be okay," he told her with a kiss to her forehead. His attention quickly shifted to Seth, who stood over the body. "You find anything?"

"Not a damn thing. No wallet. No ID. Nothing. Who the hell are these guys?"

"We've got to get her outta here." He needed to get them to a secure location as soon as possible. "I have no right to ask you…"

"Dude, you don't have to ask. I'll help you." Seth stood, brushing his palms on his thighs.

"Come with us. I'll tell you everything in the car."

"Where are we goin?" Seth gave him a smile, knowing that when Lars asked to go on a trip it could be anywhere on the damned planet.

"The cabin," Lars responded.

"Big Sur?"

"Yeah, we can hold up there for a few days." Lars stood, cradling Braelynn to his chest. He was a fucking idiot for leaving her alone. He should have known better.

"Let me just grab my backpack." Seth ran over to his ragtop Jeep and snatched his satchel off the front seat. "You need anything else out of the house?"

"I just need to grab some ice." He glanced to Braelynn's reddened face, then focused on the car, surveying the damage from the gunshots. Only a few nicks on its exterior were visible, and he reasoned it wouldn't draw the attention of others. "We've gotta go now. Whoever sent these guys is going to come looking for them. You have the gun?"

"Got it." Seth lifted his shirt, displaying it tucked into his waistband, and looked to the beaten man on the ground. "Hey, maybe we should call Dean. Let him deal with this."

"I'm going to call him all right, but first we're getting the hell out of here. I want to see exactly what's in this shit Braelynn lifted from her former employer. I'll drive." Lars approached Seth and shook his head. He wanted the truth and he wanted it now. Guilt for leaving Braelynn ran deep but her secrets brought danger to their feet at every turn. He looked down to her tearstained face, her tiny hand clutching his t-shirt. Letting go of her in any sense was going to rip his heart out, but she was trouble. The kind of trouble that would get him killed. "Can you take her for a minute?"

"Of course." Seth rushed over, reaching his arms underneath Lars'.

"No, I don't want to," she protested. "Please, I think I can stand…maybe…"

"I'm sure you can, sweetheart, but you know that? That's not happening right now. We've got to get going, and I want Seth to keep an eye on you."

"Lars, I'm sorry." Her voice trembled.

Braelynn's eyes fluttered open, gazing up at him, and his heart melted at the sight of her tears. Anger. Sympathy. Desire. He hated the rush of emotions streaming through his chest. *Not the time. Get your shit together. She's going to be all right.* Lars broke eye contact with Braelynn and continued to gently place her into Seth's arms.

"Hey there, darlin'," Seth said, his voice warm. "I promise I'm going to take care of you. Lars is going to be right back. We've gotta get out of here and then you guys can talk."

As Lars walked back into his house, he glanced back to Seth. His friend carefully lifted Braelynn into the car, keeping her against his chest, stroking her hair. The comforting act gave Lars confidence that in the middle of this shit storm, everything would be all right. He hated that someone had violated his home. But a sliver of hope flickered in his mind, knowing that he was about to discover the dangerous secrets that had resulted in her being shot.

Lars stood over Braelynn, who slept in his bed. It had been a seven hour ride up the coast, and he'd been relieved when they finally reached his cabin. He'd built his sanctuary on several acres of oceanfront property off Pacific Coast Highway. An intricately designed ten foot bronze gate guarded the entrance, a stone wall blocking further access to the heavily wooded plot of land. With breathtaking views of the rugged coast and enormous cliffs, it was secluded and quiet. Few friends knew about the cabin; only Garrett and Seth had been invited. With a state-of-the-art security and camera system, intruders were easily detectible. It was nearly impossible to infiltrate the barriers. Given the instability of the three-hundred-foot cliffs, it would be foolish for anyone to attempt to climb them.

Lars glanced out the floor-to-ceiling windows in the master bedroom. Although the sun had already set, the gorgeous sky exploded in pink puffy clouds resembling cotton candy. He scrubbed his hands over his scruffy beard, considering he should have called Garrett right away. While Braelynn and Seth had slept during the long ride, he'd vacillated, finally settling on texting him in the morning. While Lars needed help, he wanted time to find out exactly what was in the files without interference.

He'd briefly flipped through the stolen documents. With nearly a hundred papers, it would take several hours to pore through them. He planned to let Braelynn sleep through the night before questioning her. While undressing her earlier, he'd found the chip in her pocket.

He fingered it, and shook his head. The one thing Braelynn hadn't lied about was the level of her clearances. Whoever had given her the data chip was either in national intelligence or had worked directly with them. The technology hadn't been published nor was it generally known it existed. But what he held in his hand was real, and he knew very few people who had access to that kind of classified information.

Garrett Emerson. Lars had overheard him discussing it with Evan over a year ago, when he'd accidentally interrupted an after-hours office conversation. When pressed, Garrett had denied possession of such technology. The connection, if any, between Garrett and Braelynn, however, wasn't apparent.

Lars' mind spun as he paced the floor. *The party at Altura. Garrett didn't just know her from the shooting. He knew she'd worked at Bart-Aqua, knew of her research.* When Lars had gone to the bar, he'd observed Garrett deep in conversation with Braelynn. Given his friend's abhorrence for Giordano, Lars had assumed he was drilling her for any kind of tidbit that would help him reopen the congressional hearings.

No, no, no. Lars shook his head, the betrayal hitting him in the gut. Garrett hadn't been asking her about Armand Giordano. He'd been interrogating his corporate spy, enraged that she'd infiltrated his precious Altura. Lars pinched the bridge of his nose, sucking in a deep breath. Braelynn's involvement didn't reconcile with espionage. It hadn't appeared she'd been doing this willingly. She may have held top level clearance but the woman was no spy. Hell, she'd practically killed herself the night she'd attempted to break into his home. Had she been coerced by Garrett?

Lars laughed to himself, stretching his neck, as all the pieces started coming together. He'd done the background checks on Dr. Braelynn Rollins. Significant chunks of her history information appeared scrubbed from existence.

He'd wrongly assumed she'd been unemployed during certain periods. .

Garrett's constant warnings about staying away from her made perfect sense. She'd worked for Emerson Industries, and he'd covered it up. His friend didn't want him discovering whatever bullshit the two of them were involved in, stealing data from Giordano. But why would Garrett enlist an amateur like Braelynn to steal it when she knew little of technology and clearly wasn't a trained spy? What could he possibly have on Braelynn to force her to steal it? With the stringent hiring practice Giordano implemented, how had Braelynn got a job so easily? Sure she was qualified but so were several other scientists. She wasn't in a position that necessarily utilized her skills as a marine biologist. Did she have an inside connection? And why did Giordano go to her house and threaten her, an average employee? Maybe he knew her? But what was the connection?

Lars blew out a breath, lifted the papers off his dresser and entered his walk-in closet, flicking on the light. He crossed the large space to a keypad on the wall and typed in a code. As he did so, a wall mirror flickered with a yellow neon glow. It clicked open, revealing a hidden safe. Placing the documents and chip inside, he pecked at the keys, entering the lock sequence. As easily as it had opened, the mirror dimmed, returning to its prior state.

When he reentered the bedroom, Seth had joined them. Lars noted how his friend held Braelynn's hand and observed the intimacy as he spoke softly to her. Her eyes blinked open, and her gaze went to Lars. Although his mind churned with questions, her sad smile caused his heart to crush.

Jesus Christ almighty, he yearned to keep this woman in his life. He wished he had a reasonable explanation for his out of control emotions. Never in his life had he lamented over a woman. Dating had been easy. He'd fuck women, and either they'd end up friends or not, but only a few remained in his life.

"Lars," she whispered.

"Hey, sweetheart."

"I'm sorry. Your house. I should have…" she stammered. Confused, she looked to her surroundings. "Where are we?"

"My cabin."

"This doesn't look like a cabin. It's a house."

"You like how he does that, right? I've told him a million times this ain't no cabin but he likes to think he's camping," Seth joked.

"It's a cabin." Lars shrugged.

"Where's the papers?" she asked, panic in her voice. She shoved up onto her elbows. "Wait…my pants. Where's my…"

"I've got the chip, Brae." Lars rounded the bed and sat down, giving a long sigh. "I found it when I took off your jeans…they were dirty. You'd fallen."

"I've got to go. Lars…" As she went to push up from the bed, she grabbed the back of her head and fell back onto the pillow. "Fuck. What did that dick hit me with, a rock?"

"I think you may have hit your head when you fell on

the driveway. It's just a little bump."

"My face." Her hand went to her lip, and she gingerly tapped her fingertips to it. "Am I swollen? How bad is it?"

"No, Seth kept you iced down in the car."

"He must have just clipped you. Didn't get a clean shot. Pussy," Seth growled.

"Brae. We're not going anywhere for a few days. Not you. Not me or Seth, got it? Tomorrow we're going to sort all this out. I've been understanding and kept my word, haven't called the police, but that chip in there…that's not the kind of technology you can buy online."

Braelynn lowered her eyes, exhaling. She bit her lip and met his gaze. "I know. I told you. I'm involved with something very bad."

"I'm tired and you know what, Brae? This conversation is for the morning. We aren't doing this tonight."

"Okay," she quietly agreed.

"Right now, I think we should wash up, get something to eat. Get some rest." Lars looked to Seth, and gave him a closed smile. "You wanna take the guest room? I have extra clothes in the closet that should fit you."

"Take your time." Seth nodded. "I'll get a quick shower and get some grub going."

"I keep the freezer stocked, but I'll need to call in some more supplies tomorrow. There should be some steaks in there."

"I'm on it, man." Seth stood and turned to them. "I texted work that I wouldn't be in tomorrow. I was supposed to be at the beach testing out some equipment anyway. No big deal if I'm gone for a few days. You know me…a good surf going and I'm hittin' the waves. I figured you could give Garrett the run down tomorrow. Did you text him?"

"Yeah, Garrett." Lars hedged, unsure if he could trust his lifelong friend. He needed to confirm the connection between him and Braelynn, before he called him. "I'll text him in the morning. I called Dean about the break in at my house. He asked me a million fucking questions I wasn't ready to answer. Told him I was fine and I'd call him in the morning too. So if G contacts you, do you mind just holding off the conversation until tomorrow? It's too fucking late for this shit."

"Hey, I wasn't planning on saying anything. Aside from the shit that just went down, I don't know anything anyway."

"This isn't your battle."

"I got your back, Lars. You know this."

"I appreciate it, man."

"And, I've got dinner. K'?"

"Thanks." Lars nodded.

"Hey, that's a killer drive. I know you must be beat to hell."

"Pretty much."

"Right. See you in a bit," Seth said, leaving them alone.

Lars turned his attention to Braelynn, whose heavy eyes stared through him. "I'll be right back."

Braelynn remained silent as he went into the bathroom. He flipped on the dim lights, and moved toward the oversized granite tub. Switching on the spigot, he glanced around the open area. Lars had helped design his home, ensuring that the bathroom overlooked the Pacific. As he stared toward the ocean, dusk had evolved into darkness. An array of twinkling stars was painted across the evening sky. The moon shone onto the rolling white breakers that crashed into the rocks along the cliffs. He loved the rawness of Big Sur. The dichotomy of its brutal environment and spectacular beauty existed in perfect accord.

The hot water bubbled upward and Lars reached to turn off the flowing stream. Opening a decanter, he shook Dead Sea bath salts into the tub. Steam swirled into the air, the scent of lavender wafting into his nose. He stripped off his shirt and crossed the room. As he strode through the doorway, he spied Braelynn sitting on the edge of the bed, her face buried in her hands. A soft whimper came from her lips.

"You okay, sweetheart?"

"I can't do this…" she repeated over and over, shaking her head.

Lars knelt before her and slid his hand onto her cheek. She closed her eyes, refusing to look at him. "We're going to get through this. Together."

"I want to believe you." Her reddened eyes opened, giving him an empty stare.

"First things first. Let's get a bath. Yes?" He nodded, seeking her agreement. She'd already had enough taken from her today, had experienced a total lack of control. The last thing he'd do was ignore her wishes.

"Yes." She sighed.

"Let me help you."

"I can do it," she protested, lifting the hem of her shirt.

"Here. I've got it." As he took the fabric from her fingers, she acquiesced.

"That's a girl." Lars easily tugged it over her head. Reaching behind her, he unsnapped her bra, and it fell down her shoulders onto the floor. He kissed her knee, sliding his hands up onto her hips. Tenderly slipping his fingers underneath her panties, he eased them down her legs.

Silence fell between them as he gazed upon her bareness. His heart broke, as he caught sight of a large scratch on her knee. A small bruise blotted her forearm where her assailant had grabbed her.

Lars pressed upward onto his feet, and removed his shorts and shirt, standing nude before her.

"I've got you, okay? Trust me." He wasn't sure if it was a statement or a question as he reached to cradle her to his chest. She nodded, wrapping her arms around his neck.

Lars sighed. It was a small victory. No argument. No protest. One small step toward her accepting his help. She'd learn that she had someone in this world who gave a damn, someone who she could trust with her life.

Lars made his way into the bathroom and stepped into the tub, carefully easing them into the water. Settling her in between his legs, he rested the back of her head onto his chest. He slid his arm around her belly, and rested it under her breasts. He felt her muscles relax against his and released a breath. The heat seeped into their pores, washing away the pain and stress.

As he brought his lips to the back of her head, he acknowledged the feelings he'd been trying to deny. Whatever lust he'd held for the once mysterious stranger had evolved over the course of a weekend into something stronger. His feelings for her scared him. Losing her would tear him apart, and despite everything he'd discovered about her, the chip, Garrett's involvement, the deception, his intuition told him she was innocent.

"Lars," her soft voice spoke.

"Hmm…"

"I know we're going to talk tomorrow but I want you to know…well, I know you have no reason to believe me, but what I did today, I had no choice."

"I know."

"Lars."

"Hmm."

"I know it's just a weekend…"

"Was. Was just a weekend. Tomorrow makes three days." He gave a small chuckle.

"I love…I loved being with you," she confessed. "You know, last night…yesterday…now."

"I loved it too." *Love.* Lars couldn't remember the last time he'd told someone he loved them, but he tasted the words on his lips, and an odd sense of comfort came over him. *Am I falling for her?*

"I want to stay."

"I want you to stay." Lars didn't want to talk about tomorrow. It would come soon enough. Without warning she wrapped his arm around her tighter, cupping his hand to her breast. His cock stirred as his thumb brushed over her nipple. Her hand slid down his outer thigh, caressing him, and he smiled. "You sure you want to be doing that?"

"I need you in my life," she whispered. "You're the only one I can trust."

Lars' heart melted. The words shouldn't have meant anything. But she'd fought him, denied him the truth.

"Ah, yes." Her head stretched back onto his chest.

"I can't get enough of you. You know that?" As he glided his palm down her stomach, his fingers delved into her slippery folds. His teeth sunk down onto the soft flesh of her shoulder and he murmured onto her skin, "We shouldn't be doing this. You're hurt."

"No, I'm okay. I need this. I need you. Please."

His hardened cock prodded her back, and he cursed his lack of discipline. He peppered kisses along her neck, his fingers spreading her labia open. She cried out with pleasure as he plunged a thick finger into her core, circling her clit with his thumb.

Lars fucking loved how alive she came under his touch. His sweet little fox demanded attention and he couldn't deny her.

"You're such a naughty girl, you know that?" he breathed into her skin.

"Fuck me just like that. Yes, harder."

Lars opened his eyes, smiling as she talked dirty to him. His lessons had taken root, and he loved how she opened her body and soul to him.

"Yes, oh my God. I need this. My pussy…" Lars added

another finger, plunging it deep inside her. As she arched her back, Braelynn's full breasts breached the water.

"That's it. Just…" Lars kissed and sucked her shoulder. Having forgotten he hadn't shut the door, he heard a small creak in the floorboards.

"Hey guys, I just thought you all might want some…" Seth wandered into the bedroom, oblivious to their actions. With three glasses of wine in his hands, he stopped short of the dresser.

Lars caught his gaze but didn't pause for a second, continuing to finger her. He felt Braelynn tense but she continued to tilt her hips up into his hand. Certain she'd seen Seth, he spoke softly, keeping his lips on her skin.

"It's just Seth, sweetheart."

"It feels so good….please," she begged.

"I've got you." He gave a small laugh, pleased at her demand. "I want him to see how beautiful you are." Braelynn raked her fingers up into his hair, and moaned. He gave Seth a small smile, acknowledging his presence. "That's it. You want him to come play?"

"Hmm…" she responded.

"He watched us before. You liked it, didn't you?" He slowed his pace, forcing her to concentrate on the question.

"Yes," she breathed. "Don't stop…I'm so close."

Seth gave a warm smile as he entered the dimly lit room. He pulled up a settee next to the tub, bringing his glass to his lips.

"Tell her, Seth. Tell her how beautiful she is." Lars glanced to his friend, knowing he'd have to put them both at ease. Braelynn wasn't a club girl who they'd picked up on the dancefloor. No, she belonged to him, and his decision to share her would come on his terms.

"You're gorgeous." He moved closer with a smile.

"Seth," Braelynn whispered.

"Do you want him?" Lars asked.

In silence, she reached her hand over the tub, her fingers brushing Seth's knee. Lars' cock turned to concrete at the sight. Maybe she wasn't ready to have sex with his friend, but she was open to his touch.

Seth set his wine down onto the counter and leaned to take her hand in his. He sucked her fingers up into his mouth, his eyes locked on hers. She sighed as he released them and kissed her palm.

"Do you want me to touch you?" Seth asked, his voice low and rough.

Lars plunged a third finger up into her heated core, and she cried aloud, "Ah God...yes."

Seth removed his shirt, revealing his tan chest. Braelynn's hand drifted onto the stiff bulge in his shorts, but he reached for her wrist, moving her palm onto her stomach and glided his hand over hers.

"You just relax now," he told her. "This is about you, darlin'."

Lars nodded in approval, aware Seth wouldn't make a move without him. As his friend caressed Braelynn's breast, he let out a small groan. She mewled as he rolled her nipple between his fingers. Lars' cock thickened, aroused at her hot as fuck reaction to Seth's touch.

"Lars," Braelynn called to him. He increased his pace, pumping inside her tight core and stroking her clit. "I'm so close."

Seth fell to his knees, brushing his lips to the swell of her breast. His eyes darted to Lars, who thought he'd explode watching them. Completely in control, Lars' eyes flickered in approval. As Seth's mouth descended on Braelynn's stiff peak, he increased pressure to her sensitive nub, curling his fingers up into her.

"Fuck yes!" she screamed. "Don't stop...oh my God...yes!"

Lars held tight as she shuddered underneath his command, water splashing onto the floor. Her hands clutched the sides of the tub, as she braced herself for the next wave of her climax. Seth dragged his tongue over her nipple, biting gently down onto her tip.

"Look at how gorgeous my girl is." Braelynn arched her back, panting for breath as Lars continued to fuck her. He milked her orgasm, delighting in how responsive she was to both him and Seth. He'd expected that he'd enjoy sharing her at least once.

"Fucking amazing," Seth praised her.

"Lars," she gasped.

"Can you get us a towel?" Lars asked. Jesus, he was as hard as steel, couldn't wait another minute to be inside her.

He wrapped his arms around her waist and pressed to his feet. Braelynn lolled forward but he easily maneuvered her around so she faced him. Seth backed out of his way, giving him a wide berth as he stepped out onto the rug.

Water dripped onto the slippery cold floor, and Seth draped a towel over her shoulders.

"I need you...now," she told him, her eyes on his.

"Way ahead of you there," he said, lifting her into his arms and striding across the room.

As Lars laid her onto the bed, he glanced to Seth. Lars nodded to him and contemplated how far he'd take this first interaction. He suspected she yearned to experience sex with two men, but given it was the first time they'd played with Seth, he'd err on the side of caution. She'd want more, he knew, but right now, if he didn't get inside her, he'd lose his shit.

Braelynn arched her back, spreading her legs to him and he climbed onto the bed. Her hungry eyes went to Seth, who slowly made his way toward the bed. Pressing her thighs open, Lars tapped his dick on her mound, garnering her attention. Seth eased next to them and lay on his side next to Braelynn, resting his head on the heel of his hand.

"You ready, sweetheart?" Lars asked, gazing upon her. She gave a sexy smile, wearing the sultry haze of her orgasm.

"Ahh...." Braelynn reached to support her legs, as he slammed inside her.

"Fucking hell, Brae. Holy shit, you feel so good." Lars stilled. Like a teenager he fought the orgasm that threatened to roll through him. Her tight little pussy quivered around him, still spasming from her earlier climax.

She tilted her pelvis up into him, and he scolded her. "No, don't move. Just...just..." He blew out a breath, willing it to subside. "Slow, baby, slow."

Braelynn smiled up at him, and he sensed she was altogether aware of the effect she had on him. He withdrew slowly, his cock throbbing in arousal. Making love to Braelynn had been like no other experience in his life. A part of him knew the thrill lay within teaching her, pushing her limits. Yet it was her pure openness to him, the trust she gave him in her actions that attracted him to her. Like the tide being drawn by the moon, he couldn't fight it.

"Come help me." Lars detected Braelynn's desire in the glance she gave to Seth, who'd begun stroking his stiffened dick. "I think Brae…she needs a little more."

"I…I…" Braelynn's words were lost as Seth reached between her legs, spearing his fingers through her swollen folds.

"Take his cock." Braelynn's eyes lit at his demand, but she hesitated. Lars released her legs, caging her with his arms. Seth was merely an exploration into her sexuality, and he sought to reassure her. "This is just play. It's okay to touch him."

As Lars pressed his lips to hers, she reached for Seth's dick. Seth fell onto his back, groaning in pleasure, as Lars ground against Braelynn, edging him out of the way. As he deepened the kiss, she speared her fingers through his hair and wrapped her legs around his waist. With a frantic pace, he thrust inside her, tasting and sucking her mouth. The warmth of her body surrounded his, and he struggled to conceal the passion swirling inside him.

He heard Seth grunt loudly, and as Braelynn's hands clutched at his back, he knew she'd released him.

"Lars…I need this….need you. Please," she pleaded as he pounded into her.

"Only you." Lars' explosive release rocked through him, and he kissed Braelynn desperately, not wanting it to end. She convulsed underneath him, her pulsating sheath wringing the climax from his body.

As Lars tore his lips away, she gasped, and her eyes locked on his. The ease of her smile clutched at his heart. The terrifying thought that he was falling for a woman who could be out of his life within hours struck him, and he groaned in both pleasure and agony. Lars sensed the shift in the bed, cognizant that Seth had left, but he couldn't tear his eyes off of Braelynn. He studied every contour of her face, his heart pounding in his chest. When tomorrow came, he'd know every dimple, freckle on her beautiful face. Braelynn Rollins was his, and he'd kill to keep her in his life.

Chapter Nineteen

"Are we going to talk about last night?" Seth asked with a laugh.

"What about it?" Lars replied, seasoning the defrosted steaks. Although they'd been starving last night, making love had both sated and exhausted him. When he'd awoken, it was nearly seven in the morning. He'd left Braelynn sleeping in his bed, and as he'd glanced back to her, he'd considered that he'd never tire of having her in his home, in his life.

"The thing is, Lars." Seth laughed, pouring coffee into a mug.

"What's the thing?"

"You know she's not like us, right?" He opened the refrigerator, and cursed. "Aw shit. No cream."

"Cabinet to the right." Lars pointed. "Powdered stuff."

Seth reached for its handle, opened it, rummaging through the containers until he found the jar. He opened it and sniffed.

"What the hell are you doing?" Lars asked, shaking his head with a grin.

"I never trust this shit. It's got a million chemicals. Hydrogenated vegetable-based fats. It'll give you a heart attack."

"Yeah, well, number one…it's not like you're eating the whole container. A spoonful is all you need."

Seth opened the refrigerator door and pulled out a carton. "Hey, you've got eggs."

"They keep pretty long. I was just up here a few weeks ago. You know I drink it black."

"This stuff is not good for me," Seth complained, digging at the hardened substance.

"Number two. You jump out of planes. Hang glide. Surf killer waves. Call me crazy but if you're gonna go, I don't think that stuff is going to contribute to the cause. Just sayin'."

"You never know, man. I like clean living. Be one with the environment. Live and let live."

"You want coffee? Powder it is."

Seth mixed it in, grimacing as he attempted to dissolve the clumps. He set the spoon on the counter and sipped it, exhaling loudly. "Hmm. Not bad. Good enough."

Lars laughed. "Live in the moment, bro."

"Speaking of which," he raised an eyebrow at Lars and gave him a sideways smile, "so…Brae. What's going on there?"

"What do you mean, what's going on?" Lars shrugged. He set the spices onto the counter and washed his hands.

"So aside from the shit that went down at your house yesterday, and oh yes, I will come back to that topic, you and her…what's up?"

"What do you mean, what's up? You know the deal. We, uh, we met on that beach."

"Hey, don't take this the wrong way, but that's kind of a lame 'how we met' story. Once upon a time, I met a beautiful girl in a hail of bullets. She was bleeding but you know...she was kinda hot."

"Fuck you. She's not kinda hot. She's smoking hot. If anyone asks...I'll say we met on a beach. It's romantic." Lars laughed.

"You are so full of shit it isn't even funny." Seth shook his head and gave a chuckle.

"Scrambled or quiche?" Lars retrieved a bowl from a shelf and began breaking eggs into it.

"Are you serious?"

"What?"

"You're making quiche?"

"I just asked if you wanted scrambled."

"I'm just sayin' like who just whips up quiche for breakfast?"

"I do. You know I like to cook."

"I can barely boil an egg."

"Yeah well, I'm awesome." Lars smiled and went in search of cheese and an onion.

"Hey mister perfect. You make me sick, you know that."

"Don't be a hater. I can't help that I am a catch." He shrugged, and began whisking the eggs. "Quiche it is. Sounds like big man needs food, right, Sasha?"

The dog whined, sitting up, waiting on a treat. He tossed her a chunk of cheese.

"Speaking of which, big catch that you are...stop changing the subject."

"I don't know what you're talking about."

"Braelynn. I asked what's going on with her. I know damn well where and how you met her, but bringing her to Altura? When I saw you guys there," he sighed, pausing as he opened the large sliding doors to the atrium, "it's just...I get the part about her being in trouble."

"She didn't do this. I don't know how but Garrett is involved. And before you say anything about Brae, I'm more convinced than ever she was coerced into going to work at Bart-Aqua. That chip she used to retrieve the data?"

"Yeah?"

"That's spy shit. Above top secret. It's not available to anyone. There's no fucking way someone like Braelynn should even know about it, let alone be using it. No, someone gave it to her to use. Government contractors don't even know about it. At least not most. Only those with access to sensitive compartmented information would know of its existence. But guess who I heard discussing it?" Lars shook his head, and selected a large Chef's knife from its wooden block. Setting an onion on the counter, he began chopping. "Garrett, that's who. And Dr. Braelynn Rollins? I told you that I'd looked up her records. She hasn't worked for Bart-Aqua very long. Nine months. And before that, she's got a big gap in employment. And you know who is capable of making records disappear? Emerson Industries, that's who."

"Why would Garrett be involved in this?"

"I don't know. When Braelynn comes down this morning, we're going to find out. Because I'm telling you that he's involved up to his eyeballs in this fucking mess. And Dr. Rollins? She was forced to become some kind of corporate spy, which to be fair, she doesn't completely suck at. Somehow she got a job at Bart-Aqua. You know that couldn't have been easy, which makes me think she has an in somehow. Not sure how. Not sure who."

"You know I respect you, but Lars, this is all a little out there."

"Oh, trust me, man," he pointed the knife into the air and shook it, then resumed cutting, "this is some fucked up shit. And I'm not saying I have all the answers. But I do have that high tech chip. And there's those documents there," he glanced to a neatly stacked pile of papers on the kitchen table, "I didn't get a good look at them all, but Garrett's name and some of our other friends…their names are splattered all over them."

"You're shittin' me?"

"Oh no I'm not. I wish I was."

"But why Braelynn? How's she connected to Garrett? I know Chase has got some marine biologists on staff, but I don't…"

"He probably knows her. I don't know. He was just as adamant as Garrett that I stay away from her."

"Maybe she worked for him?"

"Possibly."

"I'd like to say I would have known, but honestly, there are a lot of faces I don't know at Emerson."

"You're practically part time," Lars joked. Seth spent at least half the year vacationing and chasing the next big wave. He'd earned his fortune developing specialized scuba equipment. He'd sold the patent to Emerson Industries, and later developed other types of marine technology that were sold specifically to government agencies.

"True, but I don't know. I guess she does look a little familiar, but she's hot, and there're a lot of hot women in Cali."

"Not like her," Lars corrected.

"But wait…if you brought Brae to Altura, wouldn't you have known if she and Garrett knew each other? I mean if Garrett didn't say anything to you, that means he would have…"

"Lied." Lars blew out a breath, gathering the onions and throwing them into the bowl. "I do believe that is the term you are looking for."

"Why would he do that? You guys are tight."

"I don't know." He shook his head, removing a defrosted pastry crust from its box. As he pressed it into a pan, he continued. "I'm really pissed, and I might be making excuses here for both of them, but maybe it's as simple as clearances. The thing with Braelynn. She's been honest that she hasn't been telling me the truth, or at least the whole truth. The entire time she's been telling me that whatever this is it requires specific clearances. And even though I have access to top secret information, you know how it works. Just because I work on certain government projects, that doesn't mean I do or even should have access to everything that goes on at Emerson."

"Yeah, but still. Garrett, you'd think he'd say something, or at least hint to you that he knew her or was helping her."

"Or was hurting her," Lars interrupted. "Who knows? All I know is the night of the party, he had a long conversation with Brae. And at the time, I don't know...I just thought he knew about her from the shooting, that she worked for Bart-Aqua. I had no idea he actually *knew* her. And you know," he paused, a thoughtful expression washing over his face, "he kept warning me off of her. Telling me not to talk to her. To keep away from her. Even that night at Altura, he was really pissed I'd brought her. And at the time, I just chalked it up to him being mad I'd brought someone who worked for Giordano. No, no. This is much more personal. He knew her. And he lied to me."

"And she lied to you too," Seth pointed out, looking into his mug. "Which brings us back to me asking what's going on with you and her. Last night..."

"She's amazing, isn't she?" Lars took a cleansing breath. He was angry about everything that had gone down, but making love with Braelynn had been incredible. In spite of the secrets, he admired her courage and determination. Sexually, she'd been adventurous, trusting him to introduce her to forbidden pleasures.

"Are you serious? You're in love with her, aren't you?" Seth laughed. "No fucking way!"

"What the hell are you talking about? I am not," he huffed. Opening the oven door, he slid the pan inside and slammed it shut.

"You totally are."

"You don't know what you're talking about." Lars reached for the oranges he'd picked off a citrus tree in the yard earlier in the morning. He began slicing them in half, attempting to ignore Seth's accusation.

"Oh you do. But whatever, man. Deny it all you want." He gave a broad smile. "I have to say, I never thought I'd see the great Lars Elliott going down. The girls at Altura are going to be pissed. And you fell for a civilian. She doesn't even jump."

"Yet," he countered.

"Ah ha! I knew it. You think you're going to keep her, don't you?"

"Keep her?" He cracked a small smile. It was ridiculous that he'd begun to fall for her, he knew. "She's a grown woman. She's leaving me anyway."

"What do you mean, she's leaving you? She just got here."

Frustrated, Lars set the knife down and pressed his palms to the cool granite. "The people she stole from. Giordano. He's a very bad guy and so are the people he hangs out with. She thinks they'll come for her again, try to kill her. And to be honest, if he doesn't go to jail...like if there isn't anything incriminating on that chip or in those papers, he could very well go free." Lars stretched his neck to either side and turned to face Seth. "Giordano is a small-time corporate thug. He won't leave the country for her. His reach won't go that far. Whoever shot at her the first time, whether it was him or maybe he has business associates, I don't know…doesn't matter…if she stays here, and he's free, he'll go after her. He almost killed her once. He'll try again. But if she's out of the country, she'll most likely be safe."

"So let me get this straight. You, someone who like never falls in love, just found a woman who he's into, and you're just going to let her go? Just like that?" Seth snapped his fingers.

"It's complicated." It would crush him. But to protect her, he might have no other choice but to let her go.

"And last night?"

"What about it?" Lars plugged in the juicer and began pressing the oranges into it, the juice spilling into a pitcher.

"I know we've shared women before, but Lars…"

"I'm not saying I can do it forever, Seth." Squeezing fruit, he continued his task.

"Why are you doing it with Brae? She's not like us."

"This thing we do," Lars began, turning back to Seth, "we work hard. Then we turn around and do this fucking crazy shit. You know I love it, but it's out there. And Braelynn, maybe she'll never understand that rush, but you saw her under the fireworks. Even though she'd never even been to a place like Altura, she enjoyed it. And that's what I lo…like about her." Lars cursed his own choice of words, refusing to say how he felt. "So last night, we were just kind of bending rules, pushing a few limits. She's never been with two guys. I'm not saying she's going to always want to do this but right now, she's safe with me. She trusts me."

"So you're cool with sharing her? Because you are falling for this chick."

"I don't know. It's not like the other times. I'm not going to lie, this is different. She's…she's special."

"You sure about this?"

"I'm just living life one day at a time, Seth. For all I know, this whole thing could come crashing down today, and if it does, she's gone. But until then, we're still getting to know each other, and Brae…if she's into it, wants to explore, then I'm into it."

"So you're saying I have a shot at her?" Seth joked.

"Not a chance in fucking hell," Lars stated, his expression serious. "Make no mistake. That woman upstairs. She's mine. So if something happens, don't go getting any ideas."

"Ha! See…I told you." He laughed, pointing at Lars. "You're totally in love. This is so funny. It'd be even funnier if Garrett was here to see it."

"Fuck you. And G? Fuck him too. He's got some serious explaining to do. Because this is some shit he's got us in. I'm going to punch him as soon as I see him and then we can talk."

"He kinda deserves it."

"You know I love him. There's no way he's crooked. Not a chance in hell. But he made a bad call with Braelynn. I don't know what his issue is with her or why he picked her to do this, but it's some bullshit. Brae…fuck…she almost killed herself trying to break into my house. She's no James Bond."

"He's got something on her."

"Yeah, and I want to know what it is." Lars heard

footsteps above and he pointed upward to the stairs. "She's awake. Let's just get through breakfast and then we'll get into it."

"Lars," Seth commented. He stood and stretched his hands over his head and then blew out a breath.

"Yeah?"

"I like her, too. I don't know her well. But this is just a gut feeling. She's not like the other girls. I mean here she is in this shitty situation, and it seems like she's tried her best, maybe not successfully, but she's tried to keep you protected. At least that is how it seems to me."

"That's how it seems to me too. I'm so pissed at the situation but I'm having a hard time staying mad at her. I don't know what happened, but there's part of me that thinks whatever she did, she didn't deserve what's happened to her. She certainly didn't deserve being shot at."

"I want to keep her." Seth smiled.

"Yeah, me too." Lars held his finger to his lips as he heard her padding down the steps.

"Hey, Lars."

"Yeah?"

"Can I call you loverboy from now on? Because I am feeling the love." Seth held his hands to his chest and blew him a kiss.

"Hey, Seth." He wagged his eyebrows at him. "How about you kiss my ass?"

"Any day of the week, big boy."

Lars went still as Braelynn came into view and gave him a sleepy smile. His heart caught in his chest at the sight of her dressed only in his t-shirt. She gave a sideways glance to Seth, a demure expression crossing her face. As she wrapped her arms across her chest, her full breasts perked upward, her peaks straining through the soft white fabric.

His cock stirred, and he sucked a deep breath. Going one minute without a fucking hard-on was going to become the single greatest challenge of his life. He reached for Braelynn, taking her in his arms. The silence between them was replaced by the beats of their hearts, and he knew for certain Seth was on point.

Chapter Twenty

Braelynn woke, and reached across the bed. *Lars.* He was the first thought in her head when she woke and the last when she'd fallen asleep. Every time they made love, he claimed another piece of her heart. *Love.* The word danced in her head, yet the devastating prospect of losing him loomed over her like a foreboding storm. An impossible relationship, it'd never work.

Her eyes fluttered open and she scanned her surroundings. Bright light streamed into the bedroom, and her breath caught as she took in the breathtaking sight of the Pacific. She'd only visited Big Sur once before in her lifetime but the distinctive view of its majestic cliffs captivated her.

Realizing she was naked, she spied a folded white t-shirt on the dresser. She stepped out of bed, crossed the room, and took it into her hands. Braelynn sighed as she brought it to her nose, inhaling the sexy aroma of Lars' cologne. His delicious scent reminded her of the night before, his hands on her skin, his lips on hers. Her nipples hardened as she

279

recalled how he'd made love to her. Although she wasn't attracted to Seth in the same way she was to Lars, he'd been kind and gentle. Her dark fantasy of being overwhelmed by two men had almost been fulfilled, and she considered how Lars had encouraged their play with no jealousy. He'd controlled the situation, giving her just enough leeway to test the waters without drowning.

Braelynn sighed and yanked his shirt over her head. Walking toward the window, she pressed her palms against the cool glass. Like an ominous warning, the waves smashed against the rocks with force. The coastline along Big Sur was both dangerous and gorgeous. The average swimmer would struggle to survive its cold water and strong currents. With both unpredictable weather and wave sizes that could change on the flip of a dime, even experienced surfers would be challenged in the rough surf.

Braelynn took a deep breath, having made the decision to tell Lars everything. Up until this point, Braelynn hadn't compromised her clearances by divulging the discovery she'd made or the implications of the data. But this morning, Lars planned to call Garrett and ask for his assistance. All the secrets would come to light, including what was contained in the chip and documents. She'd decided that when Lars found out the truth, it would come from her lips. Whether he left her to the wolves or chose to believe her, she'd live with the consequences. She prayed he'd understand how she'd been given no choice but the path she'd taken.

The clank of pans resounded from below, breaking her

contemplation. Braelynn padded into the hallway toward her sentence. The time of reckoning was upon her, and she'd face it with courage. In the same way she'd bared her body to Lars, she'd reveal all her secrets.

As she stepped into the kitchen, Lars stood waiting. Braelynn fell into his outstretched arms. Lars provided the refuge she'd sought, his embrace assuring her that everything she'd experienced the night before was as real as the man holding her. A delicious scent filled the kitchen and her stomach growled. His low laugh warmed her from the inside out and she closed her eyes, listening, attempting to remember exactly how it sounded, felt. After today, she'd never hear it again.

"How's your head?" Lars gently brushed his fingers over the tiny bump.

"I feel great."

"You sure?"

"Hmm…yes. My lip, though…" Her voice went soft as she recalled the slap to her cheek. "He hit me."

"I'm so fucking sorry, Brae. I should never have left you alone."

"It's not your fault. It's mine. I…"

"Let's eat something before we get into it."

"No Lars…"

"You must be hungry, sweetheart."

"Hmm…yes." Braelynn snuggled into his chest one last

time. She was starving but couldn't decide what she craved more, food or Lars. "But I need to tell you…"

"The quiche is cooking. I'm going to throw the steaks on in a bit."

"You made quiche?" she asked, a smile breaking across her face. His lips pressed to her head and he tilted her chin, so that her gaze met his.

"Why is everyone surprised I can cook?"

"Because we don't, that's why," Seth joked from across the room.

Braelynn's eyes went to his and her face flushed with heat, recalling Seth's touch.

"You don't need to be embarrassed," Lars told her.

Her stomach flipped as he brought up the subject. She'd loved having their hands upon her skin, but admitting it in front of both of them was difficult. All she knew was that she'd enjoyed the experience.

Glancing to the pitcher, she wrenched out of his arms and attempted to change the subject. "Good morning, Seth."

"Morning, darlin'."

"I…" She began pouring juice into a glass that had been set out on the counter. "I need to tell you both about the chip. The papers I stole."

"Brae…" Lars attempted to interrupt her.

"I need you to know what I know," she pressed.

"Do you really want to do this now?"

"I have to tell you…yes. You shouldn't mess with the chip. It might self-delete." She sipped her drink, and her eyes lifted to his.

"Okay, fine." Lars sighed. "Brae, I've run through all of this, and I'm going to tell you what I think."

"All of it is confidential," she told him, setting the glass on the counter. "I know you both have clearances but we all work on different projects."

"Did Garrett make you do this?" Lars asked point blank.

Braelynn forced down the emotion that rushed up through her chest, her lips tightening at the question. "Yes." She crossed the room to the kitchen table and sat, shaking her head. "I worked for Garrett. Well, technically I worked for Chase but I was at Emerson Industries."

"No way, I would have seen you there." Seth reached for a chair.

"I worked with Chase in the lab. I'd met him when I worked in the Caribbean. During my postdoctoral work. He was, you know…larger than life. I was young. Impressionable. You could even say I had a small crush."

"Do you sleep with him?" Lars' eyes widened.

"No, I didn't sleep with him. I mean, we…" she paused, turning her head to stare onto the veranda. *Tell him the truth.* "We dated, okay? We did things people who are dating do. But it wasn't serious. He's the one who got me a job at Emerson Industries."

"What does Garrett have to do with this?"

"Chase and I found something in the Caribbean. An undiscovered species. We'd only seen maybe five of these creatures in the water over the course of the day. Once we'd brought them to the surface to test their blood, it was clear they wouldn't survive. We found a protein. I mean this protein, it's not like other animals don't have it but in this creature, it was different. We could see the potential almost immediately."

"What was so important about it?"

"Myoglobin. It's a protein that allows cetaceans to breathe underwater." She registered the confusion on their faces and continued. "Whales, elephant seals, they can dive for long periods of time without surfacing. Some whales can stay down for a couple of hours. Now this research, scientists have already been looking at its potential for medical uses."

"So what's the big deal about this fish?"

"HWB614. It's a mammal like other cetaceans. But when we tested the blood, we found an extra protein...a very special one."

"What's so special about it if they are already looking at it for medicine?"

"No, this was a unique protein the others don't have. Imagine if we could somehow use these oxygen-binding proteins for soldiers...if they could take a pill or a shot and dive for hours without scuba gear? The implications are limitless. For the military. Industry. We think it could even provide the ability to survive at higher elevations where most species are no longer able to exist. Mountain climbing. Fighter pilots."

"Everest, baby." Seth gave a disbelieving smile. "No offense, but this sounds like science fiction."

"But that's the thing. It's not real yet. It's just a theory. But it's solid. And it's mine. It's my theory." She went quiet, aware of Lars sitting next to her. Chase hadn't believed her at first, but within weeks, he'd given her project the green light. "This creature's blood was special. Nothing had been tested yet. We'd been working through the case, still dissecting the sample, cell level testing."

"Okay, let's say all this is true. How does it end up missing?"

"Lars. I need you to believe me on this, because Garrett," she sighed, frustrated, "he never believed a word I said. I'm telling you. I didn't steal the data. Or the samples. But one day…it was gone. The paper files too." She shook her head with a grimace. "And at Emerson, you know you can't just take in a USB flash drive. You can't save anything. But it disappeared."

"And Garrett accused you of taking it?"

"Chase at first. There was no explanation for it. And Chase, I mean, part of me doesn't blame him. I was new. The discovery technically belonged to Emerson Industries, since the expedition had been partially funded by them, and then one day…poof, it's gone. They said they had me on video but I was nowhere near the office when they claimed I was. Of course I had no alibi."

"They blamed you." Seth leaned back into his chair.

"Yeah, and then worse, they questioned the discovery of the protein, which is bullshit, because Chase was there. But since the samples were missing too…look, I swear to you I did not take them."

"What happened?"

"They searched my office, my car, my house. Even

though I didn't have anything." She knew the disclosure would come as a shock to Lars. "When I went to get my clearances, I lied during the interview."

"Lied about what exactly?" Lars pressed.

"Armand Giordano."

"What does he have to do with you besides you working for him?" he asked, pressing the bridge of his nose with his fingers. He lifted his lids, pinning her with his stare. "You know him, don't you? What is he to you, Brae? A lover?"

"No. He's my uncle," she whispered, having not admitted the lie to anyone.

"What?" Lars shook his head. "No, don't tell me this. Garrett has had his ass in congress, been trying to take him down for over two years."

"He's my mom's brother. I have a different last name. I think…I have no proof. I think he may have killed her or had her killed. My dad is missing. It's been five years. But before I went to work at Emerson, before they made me work at Bart-Aqua, I had nothing to do with him."

"So Garrett found out and accused you of stealing for your uncle?"

"Yes. But I swear to God, I've had nothing to do with that man since my mother's funeral. You saw what he did to my cat. He's been like that forever and I just…"

"This is what he had on you, how he got you to steal it back? And he scrubbed any records of you being related to him in case anyone started poking their nose around?"

"Yes, but Lars, he had no proof my uncle took it."

"So he sent you in to find out?"

"My uncle was suspicious of me at first, because I hadn't talked to him in years. But I managed to convince him that I hated working at Emerson. I have no other family, and I think he thought he could use me against Garrett. But you know…he's dangerous."

"Well, yeah, you were shot at. We all were shot at."

"Those men who shot at us? I'd overheard him talking about HWB614. It was late in the day, and I followed them."

"They caught you," Seth surmised.

"They saw me tailing them. Chased me. Shot at me. But at the hospital…I lied to my uncle. I told him it was a coincidence. That I was going to visit a friend. They couldn't prove anything."

"You refused to see me."

"I had to protect you. If you'd stayed, they could have killed you."

"But we didn't know each other."

"I knew you," she confessed, a rosy flush rising in her cheeks.

"I don't work at Emerson. We'd never met."

"You gave the employee speech once. Do you remember?"

"Everest." He gave a small laugh. "So there was no friend, was there?"

"Every girl in the office knew who you were. But that day, everything about your speech, your eyes, your lips…I just…I…" she stammered, embarrassment coursing through her. "I recognized you…your blue eyes…that day on the beach."

"You said my name."

"Yes. I was afraid they'd kill you too."

"And the key? What does it open?"

"There's a duplicate chip. A prototype. It failed. It only has partial files on it. I hid it in the sea caves. It's nearly impossible to find. But the key opens its lockbox. Garrett was so angry I'd lost the key but I don't know what I'm doing. They sent me to retrieve it, told me you'd be out of the house. And I wanted it back. I didn't want any evidence. The keychain has my initials on it."

"You were expendable."

"Yes. No," she said, confused. "I was the only one with clearances who even knew about the research besides Garrett and Chase. And Garrett, and you can't blame him for this, he felt that the fewer people who found out about it, the better."

"Who are the people who shot at us on the beach?" Lars asked, blowing out a breath.

"I don't know who they are. I just know they were talking about it with my uncle. I haven't seen them in the office since that day. When I followed them, it looked as though they were headed to the border."

"Garrett knows you aren't a spy," Seth stated in anger.

"But she has top secret clearance and understands the research. And he thinks she stole it," Lars countered.

"I didn't steal it," she protested. *Dear God please let him believe me.* Leaving him would be hard enough but if he didn't trust her, she'd be devastated.

"I'm not saying you did, sweetheart. Honestly, even

though you did try to break into my house, you weren't very good at it."

"I was just so stressed out. I didn't want you to see me." Braelynn exhaled. "I'm sorry, Lars. I'm sorry for all of it. You don't know. I've never been accused of something like that before. Garrett and Dean...they wouldn't believe me. My uncle, he never left me alone. It took me months before I had access to the room I needed, where they keep the data. The samples though...we still don't know where they are. From what I can tell, my uncle doesn't have them. My guess is that if they weren't stored properly, they'd be compromised anyway."

"But still, how did the data get stolen?" Lars scrubbed his hand over his beard.

"It's not the first time there's been an inside job," Seth offered.

"It's possible," Lars agreed. "There was a guy who tried to infiltrate Emerson's entire network with a virus. He was a mole."

"I've thought about this over and over again. When we made the discovery, we were on a yacht. Maybe thirty plus staff onboard. Most of those people knew about the discovery. We were celebrating a new species. It wasn't exactly a secret but we had no idea of the implications until maybe a couple of days afterward. Maybe someone overheard Chase and me talking? My uncle...he's not working alone."

"Someone else obviously knows what your uncle is doing. He could have financial backing from a terrorist organization. Who knows? Or it could be as simple as one of the other large countries looking to steal secrets," Seth speculated.

"It wouldn't be the first time." Lars shrugged. "Those guys in the helicopter, the ones who went after Garrett, they were never caught. Maybe it's all connected."

"That discovery…it was ours. Chase and I found it together. But the theory, how we could use it, not just use it but proving its use, that is my idea. And some of that isn't anywhere but inside my head." Braelynn bit her lip, terrified Lars had chosen to believe Garrett. The painful truth lay out there, and with the guilt lifted, she blinked away the tears on her lashes. "But now? Honestly, I don't want anything to do with the data or Emerson Industries right now. I just want to be safe."

"But if your uncle isn't arrested, you'll need to leave San Diego." Lars shoved to his feet, clearly frustrated.

Braelynn jumped as he slammed his hands onto the granite countertop in frustration and grabbed a potholder. Lars swung open the oven, and retrieved the quiche, letting the pan drop on the counter, and slammed the door shut.

"This is what we are going to do," he began, without looking at her. His disappointment in her crushed her spirit but her mind told her she deserved it. "I'm going to go through the documents and that chip. I don't know how it works but I'll call in a few favors with a few buddies in the NSA. My company works in data, and if Emerson Industries has clearances for it, I'm calling them on the carpet. I want to know how it works and how to read it so we can figure out how bad this shit is."

Although Garrett had warned her that under no circumstances should she try to tamper with the chip, Braelynn remained silent and hoped Lars could pull strings and read it before Garrett arrived. Exposed to so many lies and accusations, she no longer knew who to trust. Braelynn's eyes flashed to Lars, and her heart caught in her chest. His feral expression laced with both anger and desire, reminded her that this man had risked everything for her when no one else gave a shit. The only thing he'd ever asked for was the truth, and with it finally out in the open, there was nothing left to do.

"I'm sorry." There was no apology that could make up for the lies.

"You should have told me." Lars sliced into the quiche and then glanced to the steaks. "Fuck, I forgot these."

"No worries. I'll start up the grill." Seth jumped up from the table and snatched the plate.

"Thanks." Lars nodded

"I didn't even know you very well. How was I supposed to trust you?" Braelynn asked.

"I get that maybe you didn't know me in the beginning, but Brae, I've never given you a reason not to trust me. I have given you every opportunity. Everything that's happened between us." Lars dropped the knife onto the counter.

Braelynn cringed. "A weekend. You said that. That's all it's been."

"It hasn't been just a weekend. That's the thing. It's been

months. That's how long I've known you." Lars crossed the room to open the sliding glass doors, and stared out into the glass solarium. "I was there for you in the hospital. I came to that event the other night specifically looking for you, for answers."

"Aside from clearances, if I'd told you, I could have put you in even more danger," she countered.

"I was already in danger. Those guys, your uncle's pals? They probably knew exactly who I was after I took you to the hospital. Now granted, you kept me out of it by saying you didn't know who I was, and they didn't go after me again. That's probably why Garrett didn't want me near you at the party. He kept warning me off, but he still sent you to get that key after I told him I'd found it." He flattened his palm against the doorjamb. "You lied to me. You both lied to me. At Altura. He was right there. How could you not say anything?"

"I told you...clearances."

"You know what? It doesn't matter.' Lars raised his voice.

"They were threatening to put me in jail. Do you really think I had a choice? Because I'm telling you right now that I didn't have one. Not only did Garrett accuse me of stealing, he'd brought in the Assistant District Attorney to pressure me into doing what they wanted. There's no way I could have told you. I have no evidence to prove my innocence." All Braelynn had ever wanted was to be a scientist, work with animals and plants in the ocean. Chase had offered it all to her on a silver platter, giving her a chance to expand her knowledge, work for a prestigious company.

"We made love right there at the club. In front of everyone. Jesus Christ." He raked his hands through his hair.

Made love. Braelynn's heart contracted at his words. "It was special. You trusted me to go there and I trusted you. You know what we did…"

"I don't even know what to think. I'm just frustrated as hell over this whole situation. You have to see this from my perspective."

"I do. And I'm sorry." Braelynn knew that in the heat of the moment, her words brought him little comfort. Lars needed time to process everything she'd disclosed.

"We've got to eat before breakfast gets cold," he replied, not acknowledging her apology.

"Lars…I didn't want to lie to you. I would never hurt you. The club…everything. This whole weekend…"

"Seth will be in with the steaks soon. I'm going to text Garrett. Don't leave the property."

"What?" Her voice trembled.

Lars served the quiche onto large plates, focusing on his task. She wiped a tear from the corner of her eye, attempting to choke down the sob that rushed to her throat.

"I said, don't leave," he repeated.

"Why would I leave?" she asked, shocked he'd think she'd try to go anywhere.

"Because you've been telling me since the day I met you that you're leaving San Diego. And I got news for you, sweetheart, this isn't San Diego. You're in the thick of Big Sur. Strong winds and stronger currents. There is only one way down to the ocean and you won't survive. The terrain is rough. We've got mountain lions, dangerous roads and cell service won't work. Garrett will be here by the afternoon and he can copter you back to an airport where you can catch whatever flight you want to whatever shitty country you're planning on going to."

"I can't believe you are even saying this." Braelynn pressed her face into her palms, looking up as Seth entered.

"Steaks are ready."

"I'm not hungry," she said and stood up, pushing away from the table.

Lars sighed, and set a plate in front of her. "You need to eat something."

"Gotta agree with the boss here. You didn't eat anything but breakfast yesterday. Eat." Seth poked a fork into a steak and placed it on her dish.

Braelynn shook her head, and sucked a breath. Wiping another stray tear, she sniffed, aware she was seconds from losing it.

"I'm taking mine in the office. I need to get started on this right away," he told Seth. Walking out of the kitchen, he paused and turned to her. "Look Brae. I'm just…I don't know. Part of me, I get why you did what you did. I know about clearances, but you could have trusted me. You need to give me time, okay?"

Braelynn grabbed her fork, and nodded.

"He's right, you know. All of this today, some of it he

suspected. But the rest? Not so much. Just give him some time," Seth told her once Lars had gone.

"But the thing is…we're out of time." Braelynn sat and slid her fork into the quiche. As she held it to her lips, regret washed over her. Lars had always been larger than life and today was no different. *Scaling Everest. Skydiving. Mindblowing sex. Cooking.* She wondered what the man couldn't do. *Relationships. Love.*

"He understands you had no choice. He's just pissed. Lars knows all about government secrets. Hell, we all do. It's our business." Seth shrugged. "It's not like it's the first or last secret Garrett will have. Same with Lars. He's just frustrated that two of the closest people to him didn't tell him what was happening."

"He's not going to forgive me." As she bit into the flaky mixture, she resisted releasing an audible moan.

"Yeah, he will. He's got it bad for you. You know that." Seth laughed and stabbed a piece of steak, pointing it at her before popping it into his mouth. "Lars Elliott. You know he could have anyone. No offense, but he's had a million girls. And this is the first time in a long time I've seen someone get him tied up. He could have easily shaken you off, but he didn't. The three of us, though? We'll get through this. I promise we'll keep you safe. But Brae, you've got to give him a little space."

Braelynn sighed, contemplating Seth's words. She'd give anything to have Lars' forgiveness. Her mind warred, telling her it would be easier to leave if he was angry. Yet as she tasted another perfect piece of her meal, she was reminded of everything she loved about him. Her stomach clenched in a knot; she was devastated that she'd disappointed him. Braelynn set down her utensils, and gave Seth a sad smile.

"It's going to be okay," she heard him say, but she'd already left the kitchen and walked into the solarium. The view of the ocean was the only drug she sought. No one would ever replace Lars. Her heart broke into a million pieces, knowing that within hours, she'd never see the man she was falling in love with again, he'd be forever gone to her. As sure as the waves crashed into the rocks, her life would never be the same.

❧ *Chapter Twenty-One* ❧

The day had passed with few words between Lars and Braelynn. He'd pored through the papers, discovering an internal memo on a Bart-Aqua letterhead, naming at least a dozen contacts of interest. Three were dead, each of whom had worked for Emerson Industries and had been members of Altura. *Evan McMillan. Cormac O'Malley. Beckett O'Malley.* Other names on the list weren't recognizable to Lars but on a search, he discovered that all the individuals worked for affiliates of Emerson Industries.

Lars recalled Beckett's recent criminal activities. He'd killed both Evan and his own brother, Cormac. After a failed attempt to plant a virus at Emerson Industries, he'd kidnapped Selby and set fire to Altura. During a final altercation, Garrett had shot and killed him. They'd suspected that he hadn't been working alone, but the police never caught his accomplices.

After calling in a favor to a NSA contact, Lars was given the sequence and clearance to read the stolen chip. It appeared that Bart-Aqua had indeed been analyzing

Braelynn's initial data. Her discovery, how and where it was found was documented, indexed within the files. Braelynn's claim that the research was of little use without her knowledge, appeared to be true. With marked notes scattered throughout the files, Lars surmised they'd made no progress in their attempt to develop testing of the theory.

They'd speculated on the protein's applications but without the samples, which it appeared they didn't have, they'd been unable to proceed. Although Lars wondered who'd stolen them, her uncle had set plans in motion to put together a search team for the elusive cetacean. It was entirely possible he'd already sent scientists to the location, but given the creature's ability to remain hidden all these years, he speculated discovering it would be a shot in the dark.

After Lars completed his review of the chip and documents, he texted Garrett one word: HWB614. Garrett's response had been immediate, calling him. Lars told him about Braelynn and their run in at Bart-Aqua. Garrett planned to call in support from Dean and the feds to meet him at Big Sur so he could collect the research and Braelynn. Lars had insisted Garrett make another review of the security footage that had implicated Braelynn. He'd expressed concern that whoever had stolen it from Emerson Industries might have access to the same high tech chip they'd used to steal it back. With a mole in the organization, it was unsafe to return it.

Several hours later, Garrett contacted Lars, explaining that a more thorough analysis of the video had revealed an anomaly.

Although facial recognition software had initially identified Braelynn, further scrutiny had exposed a slight height difference between her and the thief. They'd suspected the intruder, who appeared female, had worn a prosthetic mask.

Lars had cursed at Garrett's revelation. Dean's goddamn sloppy investigation of the breach had nearly destroyed Braelynn's career. Worse, she'd almost been killed, shot at on more than one occasion. Lars had briefly relayed this news to both Seth and Braelynn, then continued on for hours at his desk, searching for answers.

Lars sighed, needing a break from his thoughts. As he set the papers on his desk and went to leave his office, he noted the deafening silence inside his home. He descended the steps, noting that neither Braelynn nor Seth were in the family room or kitchen. He glanced out the solarium, where he found them both staring out onto the sunset.

With its stunning views, the serene sunroom provided a tranquil sanctuary any time of day. Due to the cool temperatures and often foggy coast, Lars frequently kept it closed to the elements, opening the cathedral ceiling windows on warm days. An oversized chestnut-wicker day bed with YinYang-shaped azure-colored cushions added peaceful respite alongside the hot tub. Modern chaises longues lined the edge of the pool.

Seth caught his gaze and crossed the room to join him at the bar. Lars set three glasses onto the counter, aware they had a long conversation ahead of them.

"What's up?" Seth asked. He'd changed into his swim shorts.

"Garrett's on his way over tomorrow." He retrieved a wine opener, sliding the knife up along the neck of the bottle. Slicing away the foil, he peeled it away. He inserted the screw point into the cork and began to twist.

"Hey, I know you're pissed." Seth took a seat, glancing to Braelynn. "But dude, I don't think Braelynn did anything wrong."

"I don't disagree." He sighed. "I'm just frustrated with the whole damn situation. It's not that I don't get the deal with clearances. But the video? They fucked up. If she was telling them it wasn't her, you would have thought they'd take another look at the video. Facial recognition is good but you and I know it can be fooled."

"It's kinda shitty if you ask me. Don't get me wrong. Garrett is always careful, and it did look like her. To be fair, it was Dean's job to verify it was her."

"Yeah, but they didn't question it. After he found out about Uncle Fester, she was done."

"Garrett doesn't fuck around, you know that."

"Takes no prisoners."

"He's one ruthless motherfucker sometimes. But that's the nature of this game."

"It is. You know I'd be the first one to defend him. But right now," Lars hedged on his words, "I care about Brae."

"Just a little." Seth rolled his eyes.

"A lot, all right. I'm conflicted. I know the things we do, they're bigger than the whole of us. Sometimes you have to sacrifice, and unfortunately for Braelynn, she was the lamb."

"The trouble is that she's not like us."

"She was pretty bad ass stealing it back, though." Lars carefully poured the burgundy liquid into the glasses.

"She got out alive."

"She's brave. And she's beautiful."

"Tru dat. Last night was rockin'." Seth waggled his eyebrows.

"She's open to new experiences." Lars shrugged and smiled. "I like it."

"You do have it bad, you know that?"

"She's special to me. I don't want her hurt."

"A little too late for that."

"She wasn't too smart about the tides the night she tried to break into my house. But I'll give her this, she's got brass balls."

"Garrett and Dean," Seth sighed.

"Their idea. And honestly, the key, I don't even know where the other chip is but she said she hid it in one of the sea caves. Kayaked in and submerged it. At this point, it's either still there or washed out to sea."

"She's tough."

"She's leaving." Lars glanced to Braelynn, who dipped her toes into the hot tub.

"Giordano's going to claim he knew nothing about the espionage. That's a woman on video, not him. It looks bad that it was at his company but unless you can tie him in directly, he's getting off."

"He's got all these bad things going on around him but there's no evidence. As long as he's out, Braelynn's at risk. He knows she took the data and don't think for one second he won't come after her. He might not do it himself, but he'll make a move. No, she's got to leave."

"I see your point." Seth glanced to her.

"The good news is that the research is going to be back where it belongs. We have the key and can try to get the other chip. Braelynn will disappear to wherever the feds are sending her. She'll be set up somewhere safe." Lars' stomach dropped as he talked through the scenario like the calm rational person he usually was. But inside his chest, a tornado of emotion swirled.

"So you're gonna let her go?"

"Yeah." *No choice.*

"Just like that?" Seth raised an eyebrow at him.

"Just like that." The lie lingered on his lips. Setting her free, ensuring her safety would come at a steep price. "Can you do me a favor?"

"Yeah."

"I've got lasagna in the freezer. Can you pull it out for me?"

"Homemade?"

"Hell, yeah. Is there anything else?"

"You know, I love you, right?"

"I love you, too. But this relationship seems a little one sided," Lars joked.

"No, no, no. I provide you with endless hours of entertainment and you feed me. I think I might move in when we get back." Seth gave a wave and set out to tend to dinner.

Lars scooped up two glasses, watching as Braelynn

stretched her arms above her head. The sunset waned in the distance; a cascade of light danced upon the waves, its final beams streaming from the pink and blue sky. The thin marine layer skimmed the horizon, and the sun disappeared within seconds.

His cock twitched as she raked her fingers into her dark hair, twirling the silken strands. The draping fabric of his robe did little to conceal her raw beauty underneath it. He laughed, considering that she could be wrapped in burlap and he'd still get hard. *I want to keep her in my life.*

"Brae." As she turned, the sight of her puffy, reddened face gutted him. Although her eyes had dried, she wore the pain of the day like a mask.

"I'm sorry for everything. But you see," she gave a sad laugh, "it wasn't me. Finally, *finally* someone saw it. And it wasn't me."

"We need to talk." He set down the wine onto an end table.

"I've already said I'm sorry, Lars."

"How long have you known me? You said you saw me speaking? That was months ago. This thing between you and me? It's not about just this weekend. Ever since the beach, you've been the only thing on my mind." He slipped his arm around her waist. "How long? Truth."

"Why does it matter?"

"You seem to be having a little trouble with the concept of trust. Do we need another lesson?"

"Maybe," she said with a flirtatious lilt to her voice. His dick hardened, her eyes flashing to his.

"How long?"

"Soon after I started working at Emerson Industries. The girls, they all knew who you were. I was working. For Chase."

"You got with him, right?" Lars regretted the jealousy that laced his words.

"I told you. We didn't have sex. I dated him. Big difference." She cocked her head, keeping eye contact. "You and I…this is something else."

"Something else."

"Complicated. Intense."

"True."

"The first time I saw you…I'd just started working there," she said, changing the subject. "I passed you in the hallway, and I can remember I was in a hurry, following Chase around like a new puppy. Your arm accidentally touched mine, and I turned back, like just a second, and I remember thinking, who is that guy?"

Lars slid his hand around the nape of her neck, his thumb trailing behind her ear. He brushed his body against hers, closing the distance between them. The temptation to taste her was great, but he resisted. He tilted her head backward, and his lips hovered over her delicate neck. Warmth radiated from her skin, her feminine scent ingraining itself in his memory.

"I…I couldn't ask him who you were but then I heard the rumbles in the lunch room about the sexy playboy, Lars Elliott. The rumors about the adventurer, Garrett's dangerous friend…he dated a different woman every week, could be cocky. That kind of guy…he wasn't for me. But then…" She gave a sigh as his lips grazed over her ear.

"So you didn't care for me?" He fought the urge to take her.

"No, but I…I didn't know you. It was when I heard you speak…Oh God." She sighed as Lars' fingertips glided down her chest, untangling the tie of her robe. He cupped a firm breast, caressing her creamy flesh. "I was inspired. You…you were amazing. How you described the journey, how difficult it was on the way down the mountain, but you never gave up."

"No, you should never give up. Practice makes perfect." Lars shoved the fabric down her arm, letting the robe pool onto the floor.

"That's when I knew."

"What's that?"

"I needed to meet you, but then I never got the chance. Not until the beach. When I saw you…you have no idea…I never wanted to send you away. You have to believe me."

"You're beautiful," he told her, pressing his lips to her shoulder.

"I wanted you so much," she confessed.

"I'd give anything to keep you here with me. If you could stay…" As he kissed her neck, he caught sight of Seth returning. "How far are you willing to go?"

"You make me want it all." Her response came without hesitation.

His eyes met Seth's. He'd push her final limits, make love to her all night, and give her up in the morning.

"Hey." Seth approached, set his beer onto the floor and flicked a switch on the wall. The gaslit fire pit roared to life, illuminating the dimly lit solarium.

"Our little Brae is gorgeous, isn't she?" Lars smiled.

"She's amazing," Seth replied, his tone sultry.

"But you know," Lars held out her hand, stepping back so he could view her. She blinked at him with a hazy smile, "she's been very naughty. Didn't trust me. Didn't tell me the truth."

"True." Seth gave a broad smile.

"She needs to learn that I will always take care of her. We both helped save her that day on the beach." Without warning, Lars scooped her up in his arms. As he heaved her over his shoulder, she squealed, kicking her feet. His cock hardened to concrete as the sensual plan formed in his head. "Settle, sweetheart."

"Lars…what are you doing?"

"She has a beautiful ass, don't you agree?" he asked Seth, palming her fleshy globe. "But she's so very bad."

"I…I…ah…" She lost her words as his fingers trailed between her legs.

"I do recall that when we first met I needed to cuff you to my bed, but since Seth is here with us, he's going to give me a hand." Lars sat, adjusting her onto his lap. Lying on her stomach, she rested her face onto Seth's thigh.

"Last night was just the beginning of this experience, and since your actions brought both Seth and I into your world, I think it's only fitting we have a final lesson with him here." Lars ran his hand over her ass, gliding it down between her legs. Her hips tilted against his thighs, seeking contact. "Not just yet. I want you to open up and show us your pretty little pussy."

"What are you doing?" Her lips parted in a soft but audible gasp.

"Wider. Let's see you. That's it. Look at how wet she is, Seth," he said, spreading her legs and revealing the glistening cleft between them. Braelynn gave a moan as his fingers played along the crease of her thigh. "I need your trust, Dr. Rollins. This isn't about a weekend. As we've established, we've known each other much longer."

"Lars, I don't know if I can…" she mumbled, Seth's fingers brushing over her lips.

"Both Seth and I…we're going to give you this lesson. And you, my little sweet fox, you are going to love it. With pain comes pleasure. You should not be surprised by what we're about to do. And I'm going to warn you, my naughty girl, that this is going to sting, but I promise we're going to take care of you."

"That is for lying to me," she heard him tell her, his deep calm voice radiating into the night air.

Braelynn screamed as he slapped her bottom, the heat rippling throughout her body. She gripped the cushion, gasping for breath. Confusion swept through her, as she processed the bliss that followed the fiery burn of his palm to her skin. Lars encouraged her forbidden fantasies, all the while remaining very much in command of the situation. *Two men, one love.* Open to both of them, she released her inhibitions. Another slap landed on her other cheek, the sting causing her pussy to clench around his finger.

"And that is for lying to Seth." Braelynn went to protest when his finger slid through her folds. "Oh God…"

Braelynn's body lit on fire in arousal, and she struggled to respond. Craving their touch, she simply accepted what she was given, trusting him. Lars glided a hand over her back, continuing to fuck her. He gave two more lashes to her bottom, and she trembled, her orgasm rising. Seth slid his hand under her chest, pinching a swollen nipple, sending a tingling jolt to her core.

"Look at our girl, Seth. I think maybe she needs to come."

"I want to taste her," she heard him comment.

"Say it Brae. Say you trust me," Lars told her.

"Please," she managed, her voice shaky. "I'm so…so…"

"I'll stop right now. Say it," he demanded, his tone firm. As he spanked her again, her cheeks turned a rosy shade.

"Jesus…that hurts."

"I know it hurts. And I want you to remember it hurts. Now say it or I'm taking my hand away."

He withdrew his fingers, leaving her with a cruel sense of emptiness. Her clit ached for his touch and she cried for him. "Yes, goddammit. I trust you. I'm sorry."

As he plunged three fingers inside her quivering sheath, her body shuddered. His thumb circled pressure onto her sensitive nub, and she rocked her hips into his hand as he fucked her. Seth held her hair, and she bit his thigh, her fingernails digging into the cushion.

"Yes… I'm, I'm com…ah, yes."

"That's a girl. See how it feels to trust us," Lars praised her.

As his fingers slipped away, he lifted her onto the day bed, leaving her gasping for breath.

"Hands and knees." Braelynn struggled to obey but did as he said. Her hair spilled onto the cushion as her head lolled forward.

Lars swiftly tugged off his shorts and settled in front of her. He stroked his stiffened dick with one hand while fisting her thick brunette hair into the other. Braelynn went to move toward him, but the tight pull on her scalp reminded her he was still very much in control.

Her eyes darted to Seth who'd undressed. He was lean and muscular, his blond hair hung down over his dark skin.

"As much as I want to see Seth inside you, I'm only ever going to share you once," Lars said, his voice deep and sensual. "Truth. I need to know if you really want this. Because, Brae, there's no going back. Do you understand?"

Braelynn's eyes locked on Lars'. She nodded, the words stuck on her tongue. Admitting the dark fantasy brought a surge of emotions, untold arousal dancing over her skin.

Lars spoke as if they'd be together forever, and her heart wept knowing it would never happen. There'd never be another man she'd trust to make love with her, and her attraction to Seth was undeniable.

Braelynn could only see Lars, whose penetrating gaze

held her frozen. She gasped as Seth lifted her hips and widened her legs, readying her from behind.

"Let me in, darlin'," he told her, sliding on his back underneath her.

Still focused on Lars, she inhaled sharply as he spread her thighs open, the cool air brushing her wetness. The warmth of his breath on her belly sent her reeling in anticipation, her juices dripping onto her inner thigh.

"I'm going to let Seth taste how sweet you are. And I want to see the excitement in your eyes as he licks you senseless."

"Ah…" With Lars' approval, Seth suckled her throbbing nub, his hands firmly clasped to her ass. "Oh my God. Oh my…ahh."

"That's right, sweetheart. Now open up those beautiful lips." He guided her down between his legs, and she braced herself on her forearms.

Braelynn breathed in his clean scent and tasted his salty essence as he teased his head over her lips. He tapped his thick crown onto her tongue, and she opened to him.

Her breath went ragged as Seth plunged a finger deep inside her, breaking her concentration. "Oh my…"

Lars guided her onto his shaft, muffling her words. Craving his cock, she swallowed him down her throat. Lars controlled her movement, never allowing her to release him.

"Fucking unbelievable," Lars grunted as she gave a hard suck. "Seth is going to lick your pussy so hard. Are you ready for this? 'Cause I'm not going to let you go now."

Lars groaned as she continued lapping her tongue over

his shaft, never giving him quarter. Although she couldn't see Seth's face, she shuddered as he drug his tongue through her labia, flattening it against her clit. Relentless, he lapped at her, and she writhed her mound onto his face. Her climax roared, and she heard him gasp for breath. He speared another finger inside her, his lips surrounding her clitoris.

"Ah Jesus...no, no, no. I'm coming inside you, sweetheart." She heard Lars cry. He grasped her by the hair. Lifting her head, he forced her to release his straining shaft.

"Come on, baby. Give me that pussy," she heard Seth urge. Her hips rocked uncontrollably, her pelvis grinding into his lips. Relentless, he lapped at her swollen bead, and Braelynn splintered apart, shaking and panting Lars' name.

"Come here, Brae," Lars demanded, crooking his finger at her.

With heat in her eyes, she crawled up him, until her chest hovered above his.

"I love to watch you come," he said as he crushed his mouth onto hers and rolled her onto her side.

Consumed with passion, Braelynn kissed him back as if it was her last night on Earth. Hungry for Lars, she tasted her lover, his intoxicating essence racing through her. Although he'd shared her with another, he claimed her with his touch and direction, and she reveled in his embrace. Whatever Lars had planned for her, she trusted he'd lavish her with limitless pleasure.

Seth's lips brushed her shoulder, and she shivered in anticipation. His hands drifted to her waist, and she arched her back, delighting as his hard shaft brushed her bottom.

Braelynn moaned into Lars' kiss, his strong fingers slipping through her wet slit, flicking over her swollen bead. Seth's palm gripped her bottom, his pinky grazing down her cleft. She gasped as his finger circled her puckered flesh. Surrounded by masculine strength, she quivered, Lars teasing over her clit.

"Lars," she breathed.

"Look at me, sweetheart," he whispered, his lips against hers. His hand guided her chin, drawing her attention. "We're going to do this. Right here. Right now. Are you ready?"

Her eyes blinked open, catching his heated gaze. The thought of them inside her, commanding her body spiked her arousal. "I…" Afraid to say the words, she stuttered but as he drove two fingers inside her pussy, she found her voice. "Yes. Yes…ah, please."

"Seth." Lars' eyes darted to him, and he smiled. "Let's take care of my girl."

"We're going to make you feel so good, darlin'." Braelynn sucked a breath, as the pad of Seth's finger circled her back hole.

"I don't know if I can…"

"It's okay, Brae. Just feel us…." Lars tore his mouth from hers, dipping his head and capturing a nipple.

Braelynn flooded in arousal as Lars grazed his fingers through her slippery folds, stroking in and out of her pussy. She gasped as Seth's pinky slipped inside her anus. She let the back of her head rest onto his sculpted chest, panting as the dark sensation rolled through her. Every inch of her body lit up in excitement, and she begged for release.

"Please, oh God, please…I need to…So close…"

Lars released her taut peak, eliciting an audible breath from Braelynn. As they both withdrew their fingers, she moaned. Confusion swept over her at the loss of their touch. Lars raked his fingers into her hair and brought his lips to hers.

"Always remember that I'm doing this for you. One time, little fox, because you are mine," he promised, his strong lips crashing onto hers.

Braelynn's heart nearly exploded, his fierce kiss branding her. *I love you.* Never in her life had she been so sure of anything. In that moment, she knew she belonged to him. No matter what experimentation they enjoyed with Seth, Lars possessed her body and soul. As he tore his lips from hers, he gave her a sultry gaze and winked before he lifted her into the air.

She trusted Lars, as he set her onto her knees and straddled Seth, who lay on his back, his gentle smile reassuring her. His jutting cock slid between her legs. Out of her peripheral vision, she caught sight of Lars reaching into a drawer behind the bar. Her attention quickly focused on Seth who rested his hands onto her knees.

"You sure about this, darlin'? As much as I fucking want to be inside you, I know you love Lars."

"I don't…" Her heart sped as he said the words she hid deep inside her.

"No lying now." He cocked his head, and gave her a devious smile. "Not unless you're up for another spanking.

But I'm pretty sure that li'l ass of yours is a bit sore already."

"Yes…I want…I want this." The partial truth rolled off her lips, but she chose not to address his accusation of love. She gave him a sexy closed smile and reached between his legs, taking his steel-hard dick into one hand and his velvety sac in the other. He groaned, his eyes closing and she gave a small laugh, pleased to be in control. As she massaged his balls, she swiped her thumb over his weeping slit, stroking the wetness over his shaft.

"That's hot as fuck," Lars commented as he came up behind her, a hand finding her breast.

"I'm so horny." Braelynn gave a small flirty smile. "I need him inside me now."

"Look what you are doing to my woman, Seth. And you're keeping her waiting."

"I…I'm sorry, but…oh…" He gave a heavy sigh, pumping his pelvis into her fist.

With his chest against her back, Lars embraced Braelynn, handing her the condom. As she reached for it, Lars slipped his hand over hers, palming Seth's dick.

"I've got him now. You put it on," he told her.

Braelynn flooded in arousal at the sight of him holding Seth's cock. She'd never given a thought to his sexuality. His dominance emanated as Seth's eyes met his.

"Go ahead," Lars directed, holding Seth in place as she rolled it onto his shaft.

"That's so…," her voice trembled.

"I think our girl likes me touching you, bro. What do you think?" Lars pumped his fist up and down his friend's shaft, and Braelynn brought her fingers to her breast.

"That feels so…yes. Come on, you're killing me now." Seth threw his head back in frustration. "Jesus Christ, you two. Stop fucking around before I come."

"He's a little impatient." Lars laughed.

"Maybe he's the one who needs a punishment." Braelynn gave a wicked smile as she locked her eyes on Seth, and licked her fingers. Plunging them through her pink lips, she sucked them, twisting and moaning. She focused onto Seth, who pumped his hips upward into Lars' tight grip. Braelynn arched her backside into Lars, and he rocked his cock up against her ass.

Braelynn reveled in her command, teasing them with her slow delicious torture. Driving both men mad with desire, a rush of erotic satisfaction crested over her, as she enjoyed every second of their attention. Withdrawing her fingers with a pop, she lazily dragged her hand between her breasts and over her belly. With deliberate hesitation, they hovered above her mound. Seth's eyes tracked her movement with a vigilant intensity.

As she drove her fingers up inside herself, he groaned. "You are so fucking hot." His pleading eyes darted to Lars. "Please…I need to be inside her. I wasn't kidding. I'm gonna fucking come right here."

Lars turned her chin towards him and leaned to claim her mouth, sucking her bottom lip. She gave a small laugh, continuing to touch herself.

"Hmm…sweetheart. As much as I'm enjoying this, I'm so fucking hard right now it hurts." He kissed her lightly and wrapped a hand around her waist adjusting her into place. "Don't move."

Braelynn moaned, aching with need, as Lars glided Seth's crown through her labia and over her clit. He positioned the broad tip at her entrance, and she fought the urge to slam herself down onto Seth. "That's a girl. Right there. Now."

"Oh my God. Lars. Yes." Braelynn's body shook with ecstasy as she impaled herself onto Seth. Falling onto her palms and writhing her pelvis onto him, she let waves of rapture roll through her.

Her sensitive nipples brushed his muscular chest, and her eyes widened. Seth reached up into her hair and brought her closer, brushing his lips to hers. Contrary to Lars' commanding presence, his was a gentle gesture, a borrowed kiss. As she looked closer at his handsome face, she smiled, knowing that although she was attracted to him, there was no comparison. Lars had stolen her heart.

Braelynn sighed, her lips parting in surprise as a cool liquid dripped down the cleft of her bottom. Her body already on fire, she anticipated Lars' touch. As he swirled his fingers over her puckered skin, she widened her legs.

"I'm going to get you ready for me," she heard him tell her, his low confident voice sending a thrill through her. As he pressed a finger into her anus, she sucked a breath. Lars added a second digit, plunging the pair into her ass. So tight, a slight burn radiated through her bottom, yet she couldn't deny the sweet sensation.

"Lars... I don't know...I'm not sure..." Uncertainty

swept through her, as he scissored his fingers, spreading her back hole, preparing her. "Ah…I…"

"That's it. I promise you we'll go slow. You ready?"

"No, no, no…don't take them out," she panted as he removed his fingers.

"I'm not going anywhere. Now I want you to look at Seth, sweetheart. He's sliding in and out of you so nice. I can see him. Just breathe."

The idea of Lars watching another man's cock inside her excited her. While reason told her it was wrong, the sheer sexual excitement of the situation urged her to go further. Her mind swirled with erotic thoughts, but her focus was brought straight back to Lars as he pressed his crown to her back hole. She moaned through the sting as he penetrated her tight ring of muscle.

"Hmm…too big…fuck…I…I…" She gave short jagged breaths, stilling as Lars continued to press into her. His firm hand caressed her cheek, warming her skin.

"Easy now, sweetheart. Just push back onto me. That's it. Ah…God…I'm almost…yes…" Lars grunted.

"Lars…Lars…" So full with Seth in her pussy and Lars in her bottom, the pain and pleasure twisted, arousal streaming through her entire being.

"I'm all the way in. Are you okay?" he asked, his voice gentle.

"I…yes. I need…I need…fuck me now…I can't…please just…fuck me."

Unable to wait, Braelynn slammed down onto Seth's cock, causing him to give a loud grunt. Filled completely and overwhelmed with the dark invasion, she leaned onto Seth's chest, allowing him to embrace her. He cradled her head, brushing a lock of hair from her eyes. Her lips pressed to his nipple and she bit down as Lars thrust deep into her. Moving in tandem, her lovers merged with her body as one. As they increased their rhythm, she rocked her hips upon Seth's, seeking friction. He tilted his pelvis, brushing the root of him onto her clitoris. She cried Lars' name with each stroke to her swollen bead.

"I'm going to...yeah...fuck me...fuck..." she demanded, her thoughts incoherent as her body shuddered around Seth's cock. "Lars...please."

"Ah God, yes...you feel so good."

"Harder...fuck me harder. Now." Braelynn sensed Lars held back, afraid he'd hurt her, but her body accommodated him. He pounded into her and she braced herself on Seth. "Yes, yes, that's it...oh yes."

"Fuck, yeah." Lars gave a final jarring thrust, grunting in satisfaction.

Braelynn's orgasm roared through her, leaving her trembling. As Seth drove up inside her, his hips wildly pumped as he rode out his hard climax.

Shivering from the last tendrils of her release, Braelynn sighed as Lars withdrew from her. She fell limp onto Seth, her arms resting on his shoulders.

"Lars," she managed, as she felt a warm cloth on her bottom.

"You're amazing." Lars' comforting voice surrounded her.

"That was unbelievable, darlin'." Seth's lips brushed her forehead as he carefully removed himself from her.

Within seconds, Lars' strong arms wrapped around her waist and he cradled her into his embrace. Barely cognizant of her surroundings, Braelynn nuzzled her face against his chest, reveling in his scent. Never in her life had she submitted her body to the domination of two men, fulfilling sexual fantasies she'd never been safe to indulge. Yet, trusting within Lars' command, she'd maintained control of the situation. Her body spent, her mind wandered back to the raw emotion that lingered in her heart.

By the time he'd taken her upstairs and settled them into his bed, the sensual haze of their encounter had morphed into exhaustion. Lars embraced her and pillowed her head on his chest. Braelynn's love for him danced in her heart as she snuggled into his warmth.

I love you, she whispered, falling into a deep slumber and dreaming of a lifetime with Lars.

❧ Chapter Twenty-Two ❧

I love you. Lars' chest ached. He'd gone most of his adult life without ever uttering the words, but as she revealed her greatest secret, Lars couldn't have been any more certain of his own feelings.

"I love you, too." A surge of melancholy seized him, as his lips brushed her hair.

Telling her while she slept was the best he could manage, given it'd be likely she'd leave in the morning. With little evidence to convict her uncle, she'd most certainly have to go into hiding. Lars struggled to work through a scenario where they could stay together. Giving up his life and company in San Diego to follow her out of the country simply wasn't an option. People counted on his leadership, their careers, livelihoods and families depending on his innovative direction to ensure the company's solvency. While he often worked out of the office, he'd been a committed presence at DLar-Tech.

A weekend. It'd been all he promised. But as he'd discovered her playful, trusting nature, he'd grown attached.

The thought of letting Braelynn walk out of his life ravaged his soul. The devastating loss would come swift and hard.

Lars closed his eyes, attempting to memorize every contour of her body, the touch of her skin, her laugh. He sighed, allowing the scent of his woman to infiltrate his senses. With her in his arms, he was home. He pressed his lips to the nape of her neck, praying that a solution would come to him in a dream. As sleep captured Lars, drawing him into her thick web, he drifted into a fantasy where she was his forever.

"Hmm." Lars stirred. He blinked his eyes open to find Brae, curled onto her side, smiling at him.

"Hi." Her palm brushed over his rough beard and he grinned.

"Hi." Lars reached over her waist and jerked her toward him. "How do you feel?"

"I feel so good when I'm with you." She pressed her lips to his, peppering his face with kisses.

"God, I love…" Lars hedged, retracting the confession that had almost passed through his lips. "I love being with you."

"I don't want this to end." Although he couldn't read her expression, the tremble in her voice gave her away.

"No matter what happens, Brae, it's only temporary."

"But I won't see you," she began, her words trailing into silence. Warm tears brushed his shoulder and guilt pierced his chest.

"Please don't cry." Lars silently admonished his lack of empathy. *Is that all you have? God, I'm an asshole.* He was a problem solver, and couldn't accept that he hadn't yet figured out how to keep her safe and in his life.

"I'm sorry. It's just...Lars..." She paused, and lifted her gaze to meet his. "I want you to know. This weekend, I loved being with you. I know it's crazy for me to say that. I broke into your house...tried to break in." She gave a small laugh. "We stole research. Got shot at. I don't mean that stuff. But everything else? I'd do it all again if it meant getting to be with you."

"Aw, sweetheart, I don't know how things are going to play out but this is not the end. I just need some time." Lars knew Garrett would arrive within hours, take the data and Braelynn would have to go with him. He expected after it was all said and done, they'd come up with a plan to see each other. But at the moment, getting her to safety was paramount.

"You really think so? Because I'm not sure. Garrett, I know he's your friend, and part of me knows why he did what he did, but when I've talked to him and Dean, they've always been pretty sure I couldn't return. My uncle, he's not going to take this lying down. I wish I had something on him, but aside from killing my cat and roughing me up...it's not enough."

"It's going to be okay," he told her.

"I know I can't stay. This is the way it has to be."

"You won't be alone."

"It's okay. Really. I know what's coming. I can do this."

Braelynn nodded. With the back of her hand, she swiped at the tear that streaked down her cheek.

Lars tensed as she pulled out of his embrace, noting the change in her demeanor. A switch had gone off inside her. The light in her eyes dimmed, and she averted her gaze. She pushed out of the bed onto her feet and set off toward the bathroom without saying another word.

Lars leaned against the headboard and closed his eyes. *Fuck.* Anger exploded through him, and he shoved out of bed. Swiping a pair of shorts out of his drawer, he made quick work of dressing. He took a deep breath, glancing at the stream of light that spilled through the crack onto the bedroom floor.

The sound of running water tempted him. He wanted to go to her, to comfort her, but he resisted. Reality had set in and giving in to emotions was a futile use of energy. The only solution was to stop her uncle, to find enough evidence to put him away. He'd found an adventurous woman to match his fire, and there was no way in hell he'd give her up without a fight.

Lars took off down the hallway and made a beeline for his office. Flipping on the light, he slammed the door and a painting fell off the wall, the glass shattering onto the floor. Disgusted with the situation, he tore open the file and began to pore through it one more time. Inspecting each page, he searched for answers.

Lars pounded his fist onto his desk, frustrated he hadn't found one shred of evidence to tie Giordano to the stolen research or the shooting. A loud rumble echoed through the windows, the familiar whirl of helicopter blades tearing through the wind. *Garrett. What is he doing in a heli?* Garrett had told him he was driving up with Dean, feds in tow. As much as he loathed the thought of Braelynn's departure, they'd assured him that he'd bring his people to shepherd them to a secure location.

Lars shoved to his feet, closing the file and sealing it. His eyes went to the safe, where he'd kept the chip. But as he strode across the room, the roar of the blades continued, sending a chill up his spine. Garrett had planned on staying for at least the morning, and would have immediately cut the engines. His mind rapidly processed the inconsistency, registering alarm. Without hesitation, he slid open a hidden compartment underneath his desk drawer. Retrieving the loaded Glock, he slid out the magazine, examining the seventeen rounds. Satisfied it was fully loaded, he clicked it back into place, and jammed three extra cartridges into his pocket.

He glanced to his bare feet and cursed, wishing he'd worn shoes. Not a floorboard creaked as Lars skirted across the hardwood floor with stealth movement. He wrapped his fingers around the door handle, slowly twisting it open, and stole a glimpse down the hallway, checking for intruders. Quietly, he descended and prayed like hell that Braelynn was locked in the bedroom. But as he heard her and male voices echo up the stairway, his stomach dropped. Their loud argument resonated through the house. An ear-piercing scream ensued, spearing terror through his chest.

As he tore down the steps, Lars' heart caught as he spied Armand Giordano dragging Braelynn by her hair, holding a gun to her head.

"Get the fuck off me," Braelynn yelled at him. She struggled, her hands around his wrists.

"Shut the hell up, you little bitch. I should have never let you into my company." Giordano kicked open the door and called out to a tall man in a black suit who followed. "Stay and look for it. Five minutes and she's done."

Lars recognized the second male. He'd seen him exiting Braelynn's condo. *Shane.*

"Let her go." Lars drew his weapon and pointed the barrel at Giordano.

"Don't press him," Shane called to him, his voice firm but not threatening. "He'll shoot her."

The statement struck Lars as odd but he ignored it, and took off after Braelynn. By the time he'd passed through the atrium's back door, Giordano stood precariously close to the edge of the cliff.

"Get back, asshole or the cunt goes bye-bye." Giordano gripped her chin, still holding the gun in his hand.

"Easy now." Lars raised his hands into the air, holding them in a defensive posture. Well-trained and confident that he could hit Giordano, he chose a calm approach. The cliffs were notoriously unstable and one couldn't predict the shifting earth. If he got any closer to the edge and slipped, they wouldn't survive the two-hundred-foot drop into the churning Pacific.

"Fuck you, asshole. You're the reason she's going to die today. You really think this little whore is worth it? Her mother…"

"Shut up! Don't you talk about her!" Braelynn screamed.

Giordano kneed her in her back and she cried out, falling to her knees. Holding her up by her hair, he dangled her like a puppet. Braelynn heaved a breath, and Lars fought the urge to go to her.

"If she dies, you're going to die. This," Lars waved his pistol, reminding Giordano of his weapon, "I'm going to take you the fuck out. The research you want? Your friend isn't going to find what he needs. That chip you used to steal the research, there's an improved version. Erases everything. You won't get it back." Lars glanced back to the house as a chair smashed through a pane of glass. Ignoring it, he refocused his attention on Braelynn, who looked as if she was gathering her strength. She stared at him with an intensity he'd never seen. He couldn't be sure how or when but his girl was going to make a move.

"If you haven't noticed, the helicopter's running." Giordano glanced to his watch.

"You won't make it."

"I'm going to fucking make it. You know, Braelynn here, she's as stupid as her mother."

"You killed them," she accused. Her toes dug into the ground, seeking a firm purchase. "Where's my father?"

"Ah, he's been of use. Your mother, though, she never got the meaning of family. I always wanted to have a daughter." He tugged her hard, wrapping his arm around her waist. The T-shirt she was wearing rode up, revealing her bare skin.

"With that little dick of yours, you probably couldn't get it up," she spat. "Jeannette fucked every guy in the office, you know that, don't you?"

"I should fuck you right here in front of him. You were mine to have. Mine."

"Get the fuck away from her!" Lars screamed as Giordano pressed the barrel of his gun to her mound.

"Get off me." Braelynn elbowed her uncle, breaking free of his grip. She stumbled over a rock, losing her balance, and toppled over the edge of the cliff.

Bullets whizzed by Lars' head as he barreled into Giordano. They wrestled into a bush of golden flowers, and Lars swiftly landed a left hook to his jaw. He caught the sound of Braelynn's deafening cry as he threw another punch at Giordano, knocking him unconscious. Lars shoved to his feet, carefully searching the bluff. Braelynn's scream carried to him in the wind, and Lars craned his neck over the precipice, searching for her. Terror set in as his worst nightmare was realized. Nearly thirty feet down from the edge, Braelynn clutched onto a small jut in the rock.

"Help me!" she cried.

"I'm coming," Lars told her. An avid rock climber, he was well aware that this was not the kind of cliff that was safe for recreation.

His eyes darted to Seth, who fought Shane inside the solarium. Shots rained down, and he caught sight of his assailant aiming the rifle from the inside of the helicopter.

Lars took aim with his pistol and clipped the shooter's leg, momentarily gaining a reprieve.

With Giordano still down on the ground, he needed to work fast. Carefully descending, Lars gripped the precipice, his feet dangling hundreds of feet above the ocean. With no equipment, he searched blindly with his fingers, navigating the bluff. His hands like vises, he lowered himself, deliberately selecting his next hold. With each move, he tested the unsteady rock, aware it could break away at any second.

He glanced to Braelynn. She'd managed to support herself along an edge. Lars prayed that Seth had seen him climb down, and would bring rope. Getting her up the embankment with no gear would be nearly impossible. The best he could do was to keep her safe against the face.

"Easy, sweetheart. I've got you." Lars sidled up next to her.

"Lars," she wept, her cheek pressed flat to the rocks. Her bloodied fingers gripped the gray boulder.

"You've gotta just hold on here. Let me see what we're working with." Lars inspected the crag, securing a firm bucket hold on a ledge.

"I can't do this." Her eyes darted down to the rough surf. The early morning fog had begun to burn off but a brisk wind blew through and she shuddered.

"Don't let go, Brae. No matter how cold you get. Do not fucking let go," he ordered. If she released her grip for any reason, she could easily plummet to her death.

"Hey! I'll be right back," Seth called and quickly disappeared.

"We're going to get you up." Lars tilted his head upward, relieved they'd been discovered. He could easily climb the short distance back up but even with gear, he'd have to assist Braelynn.

"I've got it." Seth's voice was like a guardian angel from the heavens. "You ready? Here it comes. Heads up."

"Don't let go." Lars snatched the rope out of the air as Seth flung it down into the abyss. Using his mouth and one hand, he opened the harness. "Now listen carefully, Brae. You're going to have to lift your leg. One at a time, okay."

"No…I can't move. I can't move," she repeated.

"You can do this and you will do this." With no time for coddling, he stood firm and pressed her. "I'm going to keep you safe but you have to do what I say or else you will die. Exposed to the elements out here, it's only a matter of time before you go into shock. Even if a helicopter manages to get down to us, you still need to put on a harness. Now listen to me. We're going to put this on. Easy peasy. Once it's on, Seth is going to haul your pretty little ass up the cliff. You'll be up in less than a minute."

"Lars, please," she begged, tears streaming down her face.

"Trust me?" He nodded.

"Yes," she whispered.

"Yes. I'll take care of you."

"Promise." She blinked, exhaling a deep breath.

"Promise. Now don't move until I tell you to." Lars adjusted his grip downward, reaching toward her right foot. "Hold on tight and just lift your toes up an inch or so. No big balance act here. I'll have it on the second you lift up."

"I…I…Oh God, Lars…please don't let me fall." She did as he asked, the leg loop slipped on easily, and he held it until she set her foot back onto the edge.

"Good girl. Now the other one, go ahead," he instructed. As it slipped on, Lars dragged the harness upward, the waist belt sliding over her hips. "Look at you. You're going to be rock climbing with me soon."

"I highly doubt it." She gave a nervous laugh. "You are crazy, you know that right? I can't believe you seriously do this for fun. This is not fun."

"Skydiving then?" he joked, tugging the straps.

"Maybe."

"It's a date." He winked.

"A date?"

"One of many, sweetheart. We haven't had a proper one yet, but we will."

"I'd like that." She smiled.

He tugged on the belay rope, giving a firm pull. Unable to properly load test it, they'd have to hope it held. Although the harness was for a man, he reasoned it would work for the short distance.

"Lars." Braelynn's voice softened. Her eyes darted up to Seth and back to Lars.

"Wrap your hands around this rope here and lean back for me now. On your way up, push away with your feet if you feel you're getting too close. No matter what happens, just hold on. Seth will haul you up."

"Lars," she repeated.

"Trust me." He nodded, breathing a sigh as she gripped it. Lars locked his eyes on hers. "You've got this."

"I love you." Braelynn shook her head, glancing over her shoulder to the ocean and back to him. "I, uh…I know I shouldn't tell you like this. But I want you to know. Okay? I love you. And I know it seems soon but I…I need you to know, okay? No regrets?"

"I love you too, sweetheart." Lars smiled, and as he confessed his own feelings, the rush of the moment threatened to overwhelm him. Forcing himself to concentrate, he took a deep breath. "No regrets. Now don't let go. See you on the flip side."

Lars pressed his lips to hers. A gentle kiss, it felt like their last as he gently guided her away from the cliff. As she fell back into the harness, he looked up to Seth and whistled, giving him a thumbs up. Lars had climbed hundreds of times, yet as he watched her ascend, apprehension set in.

Shaking off fear, he set out up the cliff. Testing each jutting rock, he easily scaled it. *Ten feet. Five feet. Two feet.* A shot rang out, and Braelynn's distinctive voice reverberated in the crisp morning air. Clasping onto the ledge, Lars watched, in shock, as Seth toppled over the precipice.

"No!" Lars roared, helpless to save him. Blood sprayed into the air as his friend tumbled down the cliffs. With one hand, Lars hung, struggling to locate him. As the possibility of Seth's death slammed into him, tears sprang from his eyes. Even in the rare chance he'd survived the fall, Lars knew that he'd never be able to reach him. The unstable cliffs could slip anytime during his descent, killing them both.

Gunfire sprayed, and Braelynn went silent. Anger and grief surged through Lars. He swung his arm over the ledge, digging into the dirt and hauling himself over the edge. In the distance, he caught sight of Garrett dragging Braelynn by her arm into the house. Although relieved she was alive, he hated seeing her distressed and swore he'd kick Garrett's ass. Both Dean and Shane took cover behind redwoods, firing off shots at Giordano, who stumbled across the lawn toward the helicopter. Giordano spotted Lars from twelve yards away, and turned his gun toward him.

It wasn't as if danger didn't register, but Lars simply didn't care. Giordano had killed Seth. Eye for an eye, the man would die by his hand today. A gunshot exploded from behind Lars. He dove to the ground, never taking his eyes off Giordano, whose body jolted, wavering like a flag as he took a clean hit to the arm. Still holding his gun, Giordano staggered back, but kept his eyes trained on Lars. Springing to his feet, Lars lunged at him like a striking cobra. The gun flew across the lawn, and Lars smashed his fist into Giordano's face. The sound of crunching bone sounded in his ears as he lost control, pummeling him.

"You're a fucking dead man!" Lars screamed as his bloodied fist slipped off Giordano's lifeless body.

"That's enough," Dean yelled through the roar of the aircraft. "You're going to kill him."

Exhausted, he fought as Dean restrained him. "Get off me," Lars demanded.

Lars caught sight of the helicopter spinning off into the distance, wind blowing dust into the air. Heaving for breath and devastated, he fell onto his knees. Through a heavy sob, he pleaded. "Dean. Get my fucking heli. It's in the hangar. Call the coast guard."

"I'm sorry." Dean's voice cracked as tears came to his eyes. "Seth. Giordano shot him, shoved him off. We got here just as he was going after Braelynn again."

"I'll fucking do it myself." Lars shoved upward, and stumbled.

Dean held out his hand, supporting him around his waist. "Look. The feds are already here. They'll find him."

"No. I've gotta go down. Just hold the rope."

"No way, man. You know it's not safe. If those rocks slide, we'll be picking up both your bodies. Just let them do their job. Garrett. My office. We'll exhaust every resource looking for him."

"This is my fault," Lars cried, brushing his hand over his face. Realizing he was covered in blood, he opened his palms and sighed. "Where's Braelynn?"

"Garrett's got her."

"I saw him take her. Where the fuck are they?"

"She's gone by now."

"What?" The words hit him like a punch in the stomach. Lars bent over, his hands on his knees, trying to comprehend the overwhelming loss. *Seth. Braelynn.*

"The ambulance. They'll be here soon." Dean glanced to Giordano. As Shane approached, he gave a brief nod. "We need to keep him alive so we can question him. We don't know how far Giordano's reach is, who he's working with."

Confusion swept through Lars as he caught sight of Shane cuffing Giordano. Quickly processing the situation, Lars realized that he must have been working undercover for the DA's office.

"Let him die. He's a fucking murderer," Lars yelled.

Dean took a deep breath, and held his hand to his pursed mouth. He coughed away a sob, attempting to keep his composure.

"I'm sorry. Dean. I know he's your friend too. Garrett. Does he know about Seth? Jesus Christ. I can't do this…I can't." Grief rolled through Lars as Seth's death registered.

"We're going to look for him," Dean managed but Lars knew the truth. Even if Seth had managed to survive the three-hundred-foot fall, it'd be likely he'd been sucked out into the Pacific.

"I've…I've got to call Garrett. I'll be in the house."

Braelynn Rollins, the only woman he'd ever loved, was gone. And as much as he loved her, the guilt of knowing they'd killed Seth left him reeling. Seth had been like a brother, and he'd brought this mess to his feet. Lars trod into the house, knowing that when he returned to San Diego, he would never see Big Sur again.

❧ *Chapter Twenty-Three* ❧

Sixty-five days had passed since Seth's funeral. Despite the two-week-long search, they'd never found his body. His closest friends had held a paddle out in La Jolla. The ritual had been meant to provide closure, to honor a great man, surfer and friend. With the soothing sound of a conch shell and flowers in hand, they'd said goodbye in a way that would have made Seth proud.

Racked with guilt, Lars hadn't forgiven himself. He'd spent hours contemplating the events, unable to come to terms with Seth's death. Reason told him survival was unlikely, but Lars had seen him live through wicked wipe outs over the years. Lifeguards would Jet Ski out only to find Seth happily bobbing at the surface giving a shaka to his would-be rescuers.

Garrett and the feds had insisted that Braelynn stay isolated until her uncle had been indicted on several counts of attempted murder and corporate espionage as well as Seth's murder. Giordano had claimed a terrorist organization had been paying him to steal national secrets including the data he'd taken from Emerson Industries. Although evidence of the transactions existed, he'd been unwilling to provide specific names. He claimed that his one-time girlfriend, Jeanette, had been responsible for bringing the associates into his inner circle. They'd been unable to locate her, and he insisted that she continued to work for and was protected by her unidentified accomplices.

A more disturbing fact revealed during the investigation was that his longtime girlfriend had been related to him. DNA testing proved she was his half-sister. Giordano confessed that Braelynn's mother had threatened to expose him, but he refused to confess that he'd killed her. Dean's team was still building a case, digging into the circumstances of her death. Braelynn's father, still missing, was a wild card. Giordano denied any knowledge of his involvement in his disappearance despite claiming otherwise the day he'd attacked them in Big Sur.

Eighty days, and Lars hadn't spoken to Braelynn. After Giordano had been arrested, her internet access had initially been limited to contact with Emerson Industries, working with Garrett and Chase to document her theories. But after a few weeks, she could have easily contacted Garrett. He knew why she hadn't, and with depression over Seth's death fresh in his mind, he hadn't been ready to see her either. But today, one week after her uncle's indictment, Lars planned on bringing her home, to his home, their home.

Eighty days and he hadn't gone a morning without dreaming of her smile or her laugh. Eighty days and he hadn't gone a night without fantasizing she was still in his arms. Whatever fear or guilt she carried would be lifted and today, he'd be the one to save her. And if he was lucky, she'd save him right back.

Lars' cell phone sounded, breaking his contemplation. He glanced to Garrett's text, double checking the address. Lars settled his nerves, and approached the beach bungalow. He suspected she'd fight him. She hadn't returned his texts or calls, and while he understood to some extent, there was no way he was leaving without her.

Lars knocked on the door, but no one answered. Although he didn't think she suspected he'd come for her, he'd taken no chances. Garrett had given him the digital code to the security system. He typed it in, and promptly cursed, as the light flashed red.

"What the hell?" He tapped at the keys, his stomach sinking as it once again refused to open for him. "Fuck."

"Are you trying to break into my house?" Lars heard Braelynn call from behind him.

"No, I'm just…" He lost his words as he took in the sight of his beautiful little fox. Her dark hair had lightened slightly, reddish streaks shining throughout her mane. Tanned and radiant, she stood with a basket cocked on her hips. Dark sunglasses hid her eyes but her trembling voice gave her excitement away. Her long white skirt brushed her ankles, the matching tank top hugging her full breasts.

"You know, I think I should call the police," she began.

"Really?" He raised an eyebrow at her.

"It's a federal crime, you know? Breaking and entering."

"This isn't the States. I don't think that applies."

"Doesn't matter. My house. My rules." She lifted her sunglasses onto her head, brushing her hair out of the way.

"I wasn't breaking in. I was just typing in a code," Lars protested, recalling her excuse.

"I don't think the authorities will see it that way. There's video." She took a step closer and set her basket onto the ground.

"Then I guess you'll have to arrest me." Lars slowly approached. Jesus, she was more gorgeous than he'd remembered.

"I have handcuffs," she stated with a flirtatious flicker in her eyes.

"Hmm…do ya now?"

"I know how to use them." She gave a small smile.

"Well, I guess you'll have to take matters into your own hands." Unable to resist, he closed the distance.

"I'm sorry." She averted her gaze briefly but then locked her eyes on his.

"For what?" Lars knew the answer but he asked anyway. She had to say the words and he needed to listen.

"Seth." Her voice cracked, and she pressed her lips together, struggling to contain the emotion. "I've cried so many tears."

"It's not your fault, Brae." *It's not my fault.*

"We…he would have never been there if it weren't for us."

"True, but Seth, he lived in the danger zone. If he were with us right now, he'd tell us that we shared the most amazing night, that sometimes we've got to take risks to live life the way it's meant to be lived. I've seen him ride fifty-foot waves in Portugal, knowing there was a chance he wouldn't survive, that he'd drown. But not riding them? It wasn't even a factor in his mind."

"But this wasn't fun for him. He did this for us," she countered.

"True, but Seth cared about you. And he cared about me. That was his life. We didn't kill him." *If he's even dead.* Lars dare not speak the words. On the plane ride down to the island, Lars had arranged to have a private rescue organization search the cliffs for evidence of his death. "A psychopath killed him. He took his life, not us. Not me. Not you."

"Lars." She fell into his arms with a small sob.

"Aw, sweetheart, don't cry…please don't cry."

"I missed you so much. I wanted to call you. I wanted."

"Speaking of which," he kissed her hair, his lips pressing to her forehead, "I'm taking you home."

"Home?" she responded, her eyes on his.

"My home. Our home."

"But…do you mean…"

"I mean I'm here to bring you home. And I'm never letting you out of my sight again." Lars leaned into her, capturing her lips. Tasting her familiar honeyed essence, he swept his tongue against hers. The gentle kiss turned urgent, and she clutched at his shirt, her leg wrapping around his waist.

"Brae. Sweetheart," he panted, never taking his lips from hers. "We've got to continue this discussion inside before I fuck you right here on the patio, and I have a feeling that could get us arrested. Don't get me wrong. I love the island but I'd much rather spend the holiday in bed than jail."

Braelynn laughed and broke away from him, frantically typing in the code. Lars shoved the door open and threw his backpack onto the floor. She squealed as he lifted her up into the air, and kicked the door shut.

"Bed now," he stated, crushing his mouth onto hers.

"Hmm…there." Braelynn pointed.

As they stumbled into the bedroom, he tore his lips from hers and tossed her onto the bed. She laughed, crawling back onto her elbows.

Lars grabbed her ankles, knowing that he wouldn't last long. His cock throbbed, and he'd struggle not to come as soon as he slid home. He dropped to his knees, and yanked her bottom to the edge.

"This is mine."

"I'm sorry, what?" She cocked her head, giving a sexy smile.

"Skirt off. Now." Lars reached up to her waist, tugging the stretchy waistband over her hips, delighted to see a pair of rainbow boy shorts. "What's this?"

"Underwear." She laughed.

"This," he pointed to a large fish.

"It's a shark."

"You like to get bitten, huh?"

"Maybe." She giggled. "Maybe I like sharks."

Hooking his fingers over the fabric, he tugged them off, leaving her bared to him. "Now this…God, I missed you," he stated, sliding his fingers through her slick folds.

"Ah God." Her head fell back, momentarily, then she lifted her eyes to meet his.

"You belong to me, Dr. Rollins. And I belong to you. Am I clear?"

"Yes…please."

"Tell me," he demanded, his lips falling to her inner thigh. Nibbling her sweet flesh, he took his time, lapping her skin, and drove a finger inside her wet core.

"I'm yours. Lars," she breathed as he dragged his tongue over her clit, making love to her. "Ah…yes."

Braelynn shook as he plunged a second digit into her pulsating channel. He sucked her sensitive bead between his lips and flicked his tongue over it, increasing his pace until she screamed. As she shook in release, Lars unbuttoned his shorts, quickly yanking them off his legs.

Unable to wait a second longer, he lifted her legs wide open, positioning himself at her entrance. As he slammed inside her, he knew in that moment that no matter where he was, as long as he was with Braelynn, his life was complete. This spectacular woman was his and his alone. Trusting and loving him with her body and mind, she met his adventurous nature with a passion no one could match, giving him the greatest gift he'd ever known.

Braelynn's body quivered in arousal, still shocked he'd come for her. So many weeks had passed since Seth's death.

There'd been days she'd barely been able to lift her head off the pillow, let alone answer a text. *All my fault.* The words had pounded a beat in her psyche, and the guilt smothered her. Although she hadn't been in love with Seth, had only known him for a few days, she'd made love to him, and she couldn't forgive herself for bringing her uncle into their lives. Remorse over his death had consumed her, and she couldn't bear the thought of Lars' rejection.

After documenting her research to Emerson Industries, Braelynn had been left waiting her days out until they'd told her it was safe to return. Not a second passed when she didn't think about Lars. She'd replayed their last kiss a million times in her mind. With no regrets, she found consolation knowing she'd told him that she loved him. Dreaming of Lars, his touch, she'd been in agony without him.

When she saw him at her front door, her pulse raced. He'd told her he'd come for her, that they'd be together again. So many people in her life had delivered empty promises, but Lars, a man of integrity, kept his word.

His possessive kiss sent desire throughout every cell of her body. Happiness bloomed inside her chest and she reveled in his erotic touch.

"I missed you so fucking much," he told her, and she smiled into his kiss.

"I missed you too. Don't ever let me go."

"We've got all weekend."

"A weekend?" she panted as he pinned her arms to her side. His sleek muscular body covered hers, immobilizing her.

"Forty-eight hours." His lips brushed hers, as he slowed his pace.

"Just a weekend?"

"A weekend here in paradise, sweetheart. A lifetime together. You'll come home with me?" His eyes locked on hers.

"God yes," she replied, her voice breathy. She'd give him anything and everything. "I love you."

"I love you, too." Lars captured her mouth with his once again, branding her with his searing kiss.

Braelynn wrapped her legs around his waist, drawing him deeper. With deliberate thrusts, his pelvis brushed against her, and she rocked up into him.

"Lars…I can't….I'm going to…ah…" As his cock teased over her delicate strip of nerves, she shuddered in an uncontrollable release, contracting around him. Restrained, she submitted to the longest climax she'd ever had, rolling waves of ecstasy claiming her body.

"Ah…yes. You're killing me….you feel amazing." Lars pounded into her tight heat, making love to her mouth with a fierce intensity. With a final thrust, he came.

As Lars rolled onto his back, he brought her to his chest. Braelynn embraced him, reveling in the moment.

"I love you so much." The happiest she'd ever been in her life, her heart skipped a beat.

"I love you too, sweetheart."

"Trust," she whispered.

"Hmm…what?"

"Trust. I…I…I have something to tell you."

"What's wrong, Brae?" He pressed her, meeting her gaze. "Tell me."

"I'm sorry...I took that shot, but I'm not sorry. You see...I'm older. I'm not in my twenties."

"I'm not either. You're scaring me...what's going on?"

"You like adventure, right?" She closed her eyes, praying he wouldn't leave her. Her fragile heart couldn't take the loss of his affection.

"You know I do."

"I wasn't sure how to tell you. And I...you know I never wanted this to happen but now...I want this...and not just because of it, because it's with you."

"What is it?"

"I'm having a baby," she confessed. As the words left her lips, she held her breath, terrified of his response. She'd only discovered the pregnancy a few days ago.

"You clearly need more lessons, sweetheart." He laughed, pressing his lips to her head.

"You're okay?" she asked.

"I'm more than okay. Was this expected? Hell no, but Jesus, Brae. Don't you get how much I love you?" He kissed her again.

"I love hearing you say those words."

"But you know, my little fox," Braelynn giggled as he flipped her onto her belly, and caressed her bottom, "I'm going to look forward to more of these lessons."

"Are you now?" she purred, arching her back. "You know I can't be tamed?"

"I'm not looking to tame you, sweetheart. Enjoy you.

Love you. But never tame you. You're the best adventure I've ever had. That rush?"

"Yes," she smiled.

"You're it."

─❀· *Epilogue* ·❀─

His body burned hot with fever, every muscle in his body aching. Seth's swollen eyes cracked open, and he saw the flames of a fire dancing in the corner. His vision blurred, as a figure brushed past him.

"You're okay," he heard the voice tell him. His dry lips parted, but no words would come. *Who are you?*

Squinting, his eyes adjusted to the dim light. His adrenaline surged as the dancing shadows came into focus. Rows of military grade weapons hung from neatly organized racks of the log cabin walls. *Where the fuck am I?*

He moaned, and the figure returned to his side. "Hey, here." A sharp object probed his mouth and he coughed. "It's a straw. Can you get any? Shit. Sorry…you need to try to drink something."

Seth concentrated, attempting to seal his swollen lips around it. As the cool liquid coated his tongue, tears ran down his face.

"Hey, now. You're going to be okay. You took a beating going down that cliff, but I don't think anything's broken.

You got shot, too. Clean through. The bleeding's stopped."

Drowning under monster waves, he'd never allowed fear to creep into the recesses of his mind. Live or die, what was meant to be would happen. The struggle, the fight for life, however, that was a choice that every individual at one point in their life made. It didn't guarantee you'd live but rather increased the probability. Risk. Chance. No one was safe. You could die on the top of a mountain or sitting on your sofa watching TV.

At a loss for control, Seth fought the dark emotion. Fear was a demon he'd conquered many a time, but as he lay immobile, it tormented him, dancing in his head. Training his mind, he focused, forcing thoughts of riding the waves as a spectacular California sunset shined down onto the Pacific.

"That's better. Smile, baby. I don't know what you're thinking about but keep it there. Keep it strong." As relaxation set in, and Seth registered the feminine nature of her voice, he wondered who she was.

Hazy memories of his attack played like a show on the television, static breaking up the channel. The gunshot blasted through him as he stepped into the line of fire. He lost balance, the pain searing through his arm. The hard shove sent him hurtling over the edge of the cliff. *Falling, falling, falling.* Bouncing off the rocks, his life had flashed before him, and he'd accepted his fate.

Who is this woman? His eyes darted again to the weapons. Sniper and automatic rifles. Submachine guns. Ammo belts. *Dangerous.*

By the light of the fire, his rescuer unzipped the tight neoprene. As the black wetsuit peeled away, it revealed her creamy skin. Tiny but fierce, she stripped it off. Bared to him, she turned to meet his gaze. Seth knew that what seemed like an eternity was mere seconds. As she broke eye contact, and tended to the blazing embers, he noted how her long blonde hair hung in a thick braid down her back.

A load roar sounded, and Seth clutched the sides of the metal cot. Unable to move, he groaned in pain.

"Shhh," she told him. He watched in fascination as she threw on a robe, and grabbed a rifle off a rack.

"You're going to be fine. I'm going to leave you for just a minute now. You can't walk so don't even try to come after me, understand?" she instructed.

Seth attempted to nod but his head pounded as he bent his neck. A chill rolled through him as she opened the door. As his warrior princess turned back to him, she gave a warm smile.

The sound of a gunshot blasting rocked through the cabin. Seth jolted in his bed, agony tearing through every cell of his body. Unable to speak or cry out for help, he lay helpless, the fire crackling to his right. Staring at the door, he counted through the searing pain. For whatever reason, fate saw fit that he'd survived a three-hundred-foot plunge over a cliff. Although these might be the last minutes of his life on Earth, Seth swore he wasn't going down without a fight.

Romance by Kym Grosso

The Immortals of New Orleans

Kade's Dark Embrace
(Immortals of New Orleans, Book 1)

Luca's Magic Embrace
(Immortals of New Orleans, Book 2)

Tristan's Lyceum Wolves
(Immortals of New Orleans, Book 3)

Logan's Acadian Wolves
(Immortals of New Orleans, Book 4)

Léopold's Wicked Embrace
(Immortals of New Orleans, Book 5)

Dimitri
(Immortals of New Orleans, Book 6)

Lost Embrace
(Immortals of New Orleans, Book 6.5)

Jax
(Immortals of New Orleans, Book 7)

Jake

(Immortals of New Orleans, Book 8) (Coming Soon)

Club Altura Romance

Solstice Burn

(A Club Altura Romance Novella, Prequel)

Carnal Risk

(A Club Altura Romance Novel, Book 1)

Wicked Rush

(A Club Altura Romance Novel, Book 2)

About the Author

Kym Grosso is the New York Times and USA Today bestselling author of the erotic paranormal series, *The Immortals of New Orleans*, and the contemporary erotic suspense series, *Club Altura*. In addition to romance novels, Kym has written and published several articles about autism, and is passionate about autism advocacy. She is also a contributing essay author in *Chicken Soup for the Soul: Raising Kids on the Spectrum*.

In 2012, Kym published her first novel and today, is a full time romance author. She lives in suburban Pennsylvania but has a not-so-secret desire to move to a beach in southern California where she can write while listening to the roar of the ocean.

• • • •

Social Media/Links:

Website: http://www.KymGrosso.com
Facebook: http://www.facebook.com/KymGrossoBooks
Twitter: https://twitter.com/KymGrosso
Instagram: https://www.instagram.com/kymgrosso/
Pinterest: http://www.pinterest.com/kymgrosso/

Sign up for Kym's Newsletter to get Updates and Information about New Releases:
http://www.kymgrosso.com/members-only

Made in the USA
Middletown, DE
27 May 2019